The G

the BA

the BUS

BOOKS BY SUZETTE D. HARRISON

This Time Always
Basketball & Ballet
The Birthday Bid
The Art of Love
My Tired Telephone
My Joy
Taffy
When Perfect Ain't Possible
Living on the Edge of Respectability

The GIRL at the BACK of the BUS

SUZETTE D. HARRISON

bookouture

Published by Bookouture in 2021

An imprint of Storyfire Ltd.
Carmelite House
50 Victoria Embankment
London EC4Y 0DZ

www.bookouture.com

ISBN: 978-1-80019-174-7
eBook ISBN: 978-1-80019-173-0

To LaVada A. Kelley & Barbara J. Harrison,
My mother and mother-in-law respectively:
Thank you for living, loving, and overcoming
obstacles I will never see.
Your sacrifices have gifted us, your beloveds, with wings.

CHAPTER ONE

Mattie Banks

December 1, 1955
Montgomery, Alabama

"Gal, get those coins in that slot or you ain't going nowhere."

The driver on that first bus I'd incorrectly hopped on in my flustered state had fussed that at me. Now, here I was again. Fumbling. Hoping the driver on this right bus didn't flare up with the same kinds of indignities.

Head held low, I tried putting those coins in, hoping other riders couldn't see my face. Unlike the coins I kept fumbling with, my tears were pooled in place, unfallen as of yet. We had an agreement. Tears could flow all they wanted once I was safely situated back in the Colored section. Not until then. And definitely not in front of some impatient individual responsible for driving me to freedom.

Mattie Banks, get yourself together!

Plopping my suitcase at my feet, I had the good sense to wipe my sweaty fingers on my skirt first. Scooping up fallen coins, I managed to get the first nickel in. But that second one felt the need to make a fool of me. I couldn't do nothing except watch it slip from my shaky grip and roll backwards down the steps into the evening, as if escaping this uncertain journey.

That set the driver off.

He was fussing, close to cussing and calling me everything except a child of God and a nasty kitchen sink when the passenger waiting to board behind me intervened.

"Ma'am…"

Not that I knew every Colored person in Montgomery, but he was an older, unfamiliar gentleman. He hadn't been at the bus stop a moment ago when I was praying for another way to handle this predicament. Maybe he was the heaven-sent angel I needed?

Watching him mount the bus steps, I had enough sense not to correct Mister Angel Man about my not being a "ma'am." I was sixteen, but from the back he wouldn't have known that. I'd had what Mama called "womanish hips" since turning thirteen. Courtesy of my situation, they'd soon be on their way to further spreading.

Thanking him and standing aside, I watched Mister Angel Man deposit my rebellious nickel and his own fare before tipping his hat and descending the front steps. Grabbing my suitcase, I followed him to the rear, hoping the annoyed driver wouldn't take off just to prove a point, like some did, taking my precious ten cents with him.

I hate this double-entrance dance.

Drop your fare up front.

Hop off the bus.

Hightail it to the rear and board at the back like a less-than citizen.

It was a belittling ballet played to the melody of racism.

My great-granny's days of slavery were finished, but that didn't keep these White folks around here from using every opportunity to make themselves feel first-and-foremost. As if the rest of God's creation was insignificant, or an absent-minded afterthought. But right then, I couldn't spend time on White folks' foolery. Not with my own world laying heavy on me.

A true gentleman, my angel mister let me board that Cleveland Avenue-bound bus ahead of him. Good thing he did, seeing as how the Colored section was crowded with laborers and day workers who, unlike Mama and me, weren't live-ins. I didn't feel like talking, but I was raised better than to not say hello to those I knew. Last thing I needed was Mama hearing about me acting grown when I already had enough grown trouble of my own.

Trying to look normal and unsuspicious, I offered quick greetings to folks I recognized before claiming the last available window seat and breathing a sigh of relief that my nickel-fumbling hadn't earned me too much attention. No one stopped me, asked what I was doing on the bus that time of evening, or where I was going. That had me feeling like I'd won something. But my sense of winning disappeared the moment I sat and plopped that small suitcase on my lap.

Ain't easy feeling victorious when you're running from the first sin to the second.

I would have preferred being at the hand-me-down desk in the room Mama and I shared, listening to our tiny transistor radio and tussling with math problems, or getting gloriously lost in English Lit. Or aiding Mama with the evening meal for the Stantons. Setting dishes. Laying out linens. Taste-testing her mashed potatoes and gravy—the potatoes were always creamy, smooth perfection. Helping her serve then heading over to Sadie's. Instead, I was shrinking in that seat clutching a suitcase as if it was my lifeline to a better time.

Truth was, I was lost. Desperate.

Womanish hips didn't make me more than a scared sixteen-year-old Colored girl without options.

Sadie said it won't take but a few minutes.

Good sense should've had me running in the opposite direction, but I was in no position to ignore help and decided to credit Sadie with knowing something I didn't. Sadie James and I had been thick as thieves since my moving to Montgomery when I was three. Like sisters, we fell out regularly but couldn't stay mad at each other on account of I was Mama's only child, and Sadie was her parents' youngest, and only daughter. We needed each other. What I didn't need was Sadie's occasional superiority. That high-yellow girl with pretty hazel eyes acted as if having four big brothers, a librarian for a mother, and a dentist for a father helped her *know* things, made her an authority on life despite being sixteen right along with me. Nine times out of ten, Sadie's "knowing" was as reliable as a milk pail with no bottom. But like I said, I was desperate.

Lord, please let me live to regret it.

I'd rather live with a broken heart than bleed to death out there on the edge of town after Miss Celestine finished between my legs.

"I'll come with you, Mattie, if you want me to."

Lord knows I'd wanted to take Sadie up on that offer. Instead, I faked being braver than I was, telling her to stay at her house— where I should've been, working on a school project—in case Mama called.

"I'm not nobody's actress, Mattie! What if Miss Dorothy does?"

"Answer the damn phone like normal, Sadie, and tell Mama I'm in the bathroom! Or *something*. Just make it sound legitimate."

I knew better than fibbing or saying "damn" like some foul-mouthed man, but I was terrified.

Lord, please don't add dishonesty and profanity to my growing list of sins.

Staring out the bus window, I suddenly wished I was Catholic, not Baptist. Wished I had one of those long pretty rosaries. Some tangible comfort to occupy myself with while praying to the gracious mother of our savior, begging her atonement for the iniquity I was about to commit, and those I'd already transacted. She'd understand. The virgin was a woman and knew something about limitations and predicaments.

Having no such pretty beads, I fiddled with the handle of the suitcase Miz Stanton no longer needed. Mama's employer had given it to me despite the fact that she didn't pay my mother wanderlust money. The best we could come up with was heading to Louisiana each summer visiting relatives while the Stantons vacationed all over God's glorious earth—bringing home marvelous memories and trinkets for Mama and me to relish, envy.

Watching the streets of Montgomery pass by I wondered what privilege felt like. Privilege might've given me another way, an opportunity.

Dear Lord, I promise Sadie and I tried all kinds of scenarios. This is the only one that makes sense, and the best we could come up with. I repent for not knowing something different.

The tail end of that prayer wasn't for God but for me, or rather what I was hiding behind that second-hand suitcase pressed against my midsection. That suitcase was small enough to fit underneath the seat, but I needed it right then more than it needed me.

"Little Miss…"

I knew the voice without looking. It was the guardian angel of my runaway nickel. I'd been so busy staring out the window wishing up another way, that I didn't notice him taking the seat beside me. I had to blink away tears just to see him clearly.

His voice was quiet. Calm. He had a kind face with a fascinating birthmark, sort of like a pollywog swimming near his left ear. "Here. Use this."

I wanted to decline the spotless handkerchief his wife must've pressed. But it was either that or wipe my sleeve across my face like a little kid. Lord knew I wasn't that. "Thank you."

His response was a gentle smile that made me wish my daddy wasn't dead.

Vacating his seat as the bus eased to the curb, he faced forward, as if I deserved to cry with dignity, without anyone looking.

Guess the little boy across the aisle didn't see it that way. He was so busy staring, I figured I'd smeared snot across my face.

Turning the hankie over, I made good use of it, catching a hint of lavender water similar to what Mama used when ironing. Tidying myself, I realized Mister Angel Man hadn't solely left to grant me privacy, but because the Colored section was at capacity.

He wasn't the only man standing. Others had joined him in the aisle allowing the ladies now boarding in the back to sit in their places. A woman, smelling delicious, like fresh fried chicken, and wearing a domestic uniform plopped her weary-looking self beside me—a stained apron draped over her purse, and ugly-sensible shoes on her feet. Obviously, she did the same kind of work Mama did, but without being a live-in.

Giving her a polite semi-smile, I resumed window-gazing as if answers to my problems lived outside. Suddenly, that window was a barrier keeping solutions at a foggy distance. Or perhaps that was my warm breath distorting the glass with hazy illusions. Had me feeling that if I could break that window and reach creation my answers could get free.

I don't know.

I was tired. Scared. My thinking wasn't clear. I hadn't eaten since breakfast and what little I'd managed to swallow came back up into the commode. Being seated next to someone smelling of fried food suddenly wasn't working out too well, had me afraid I'd upchuck emptiness and fear. I thought to excuse myself and stand with the men, wiggle myself near the back door so I could get fresh air whenever it opened. But my seat partner's sudden hissing interrupted that plan.

"Jesus, what now? I'm just tryna get home."

Her words were weighted with something besides fatigue. I looked away from the window to see her weary expression had slid into a mishmash of exasperation and heightened caution. That had me following her tight gaze towards the front of the bus where the driver was raising sand. So caught up in private misery, I'd been unmindful of external happenings and the fact that we were idling curbside. Might've been there a minute or a long moment; only now was I refocused, noticing how the Reserved section at the front of the bus was as packed as the back.

"Reserved" was Montgomery's sugar-coated way of saying "Whites Only."

Water fountains. Restrooms. Diners. Libraries. The first-floor seats at the movies. If it was meant for public gatherings or consumption, race markers were posted reminding us of who was and wasn't welcome.

Neighborhoods didn't need signs. It wasn't just near about impossible to live on *their* side; we knew better than to try. You'd wind up with a fiery cross in your yard or a firebomb in your front room. Forget living. Some parts of town you'd better not show your brown face after sundown. Not if you wanted to see sunrise.

As for worship, I wasn't sure if we loved the same God, but clearly even heaven thought it best for Negroes and Whites to have their own sanctuaries come Sundays. Maybe it was because us Baptists and Pentecostals required more time and space for shouting and demonstrating? Then again, our African Methodist Episcopalians and Black Presbyterians, like Sadie's family, were dignified, restrained, used hymnals, and got out of church long before we did. Still, the Lord didn't open those White-church doors in welcome to even them. Truth be told? Didn't bother me that He didn't. I liked a White-free world two hours every Sabbath.

Even when *reserved* and *only* signs weren't posted or present, we knew. We only had to see or smell the shabby, unkempt condition of whatever it was to know it was meant for us, not them. It made me wonder if the first lessons a Negro child learned were A-B-C, 1-2-3, and separate and *un*equal living. The times one of us dared to eat or drink from a place not designated *Colored*? You best know there were repercussions. A ticket. White backlash. A handcuffed trip to the courthouse. A sentence of a fine or jail time. Or, depending on the severity of the offense and how "Christian" White folks and the law were or weren't feeling, we could wind up peculiar fruit swinging lifeless from trees like Miss Billie sang. Bottom line: we knew where not to be. Including up front in the Reserved section.

Case in point right then: riders were being ordered to make it light on themselves and give up needed seats. From what I could see, none of us were past that privilege line. So why was the agitated driver, giving those four riders the "what for" and acting indignant?

"Lord, these crackers. Don't make no sense all four of them gotta give up their seats 'cause *one* White man's standing." My riding partner sucked her teeth, punctuating her whispered sentiment with disgust.

That disgust didn't interrupt my focus. I was fixed on the folks up front.

Three of those riders were taking their time moving, yet complying. Their added bodies made matters difficult, but Colored folks already filling the jam-packed aisle shifted, miraculously making room for them. All except that one woman. She still sat, not moving fast enough. Or rather, not at all.

I couldn't see her face, only the back of her head with its dainty hat, but the lady wasn't vacating her seat as the driver demanded. She stayed fixed like it was a good night for sitting. Or maybe rebellion?

She wasn't in the wrong, as far as I could see. Wasn't she in the Colored section, in an aisle seat directly *behind* the Reserved line? She should've been left alone—wasn't bothering nobody, or violating nothing. But we all knew how this thing worked. If White folks wanted it, we had to give it, even if the thing in question was ours and they had no right to it. What we didn't give got taken. Sometimes with, sometimes without our resistance. From my vantage point, it looked like that lady had decided a tussle was her preference. Funny thing was, she wasn't loud or *uncouth*, like Mama liked to say. That lady simply sat in her seat, letting her stillness do her warring.

"I ain't telling you again. You getting up like I said?" That driver was some kind of mad.

When she declined and he threatened her with arrest, that lady said something I couldn't hear, but wished I had.

I didn't know, didn't care what the White folks up front were feeling. Back where I was? There was a whole mess of tension. Like some humongous, slithering snake had wrapped us Colored folks in its coil. Multiple feelings were probably mixed up in it, but clearly there was concern. Unease. Some impatience. And a lot of masked anger floating like steam clouds off our men. All of that made me uncomfortable until, suddenly, I'd had enough of whatever was going on. No, I didn't think the lady should have to move but I wanted her to. Anything to stop that venomous concoction boiling in the back and get that driver in his seat and get me where I was going. But he didn't sit down. That red-faced man stomped off the bus into the evening going only God knew where and escalating this thing.

"*Miz Rosa, you ain't moving?*"

I don't know who hissed it, but somebody did. That lady turning her head sideways was the only indication she'd heard them.

Seeing her profile, she felt familiar. Kind of resembled that lady who'd stopped Mama in the store, handing her a flier for some Colored folks' meeting the other day. Whoever she was, she seemed calm, like a warrior who might've known the war was stacked against her but was devoted to the bitter end. And bitter it got when that driver returned madder than ten wet hens. Not long after, two officers of the law joined him—their appearance on that bus halting whatever whispering or worrying might've been in progress.

Watching those police approaching that woman I felt the kind of nervous fear that keeps you from moving. All I could do was squeeze my suitcase and pray nothing horrible happened.

Horrible happened. And fast.

When those officers confronted that lady, Miz Rosa, questioning whether or not the driver had asked her to move and she confirmed he had, I held my breath. Her telling those policemen to their faces how she didn't feel she should have to stand had my whole world suspended and just about flipped on its head.

That soft-spoken, gentle-looking lady was standing up for herself like *that*?

I couldn't say if she had crazy courage or was plain zany. Maybe the situation called for a little bit of both? Or could be she was simply fatigued at the end of a work day, or was tired of giving up things she deserved as if they'd never been hers? Whatever the case, face pressed to the window, I couldn't crane my neck enough to see what was going on after those officers escorted her from the bus. But I wanted to. Like my seeing could help keep her safe from something worse occurring. Or as if by keeping my eyes on her I could soak up some of whatever it was that let her say *enough is enough, I ain't moving today.*

What directly transpired after that I don't recall. Thoughts were too busy rolling through my mind like wrecking balls, hitting barriers, knocking down walls. Riding that bus as it pulled away, I wondered what life would feel like defying rules and making my own decisions. The mere idea had something turning inside of me, deep in my core. Deeper than my belly. Kinda like a flame on a matchstick, dying and breathing its last only for someone to blow and spark its life again. Not some blaze running amuck across a cane field. Just a gentle flame safely contained in the palm of your hand.

"This ain't nothing but those two other gals all over again."

Expecting my former seat partner, I was surprised to see a different, much older woman seated next to me speaking so softly I had to lean in to hear. Again, I'd been caught by my thoughts and hadn't noticed the changes at the back of the bus. Who'd gotten on. Who'd gotten off.

"You heard about what happened to those two, didn't you?" She named the two girls who'd, not long before, tried the same kind of resisting on Montgomery's bus line.

My whisper matched hers. "Yes, ma'am."

"Hmph! They was about your age, trying something sort of like what Rosa just pulled." She laughed a dry, husky laugh. "I'd expect y'all's generation to be up to some tomfoolery. But this?" Shaking her head, she laughed that dry-as-summertime laugh again, but with something sounding like pride mixed in. "Can't say I blame her. I credit her for doing what she did. We gets tired of being the ones always giving. Dying. Just August they took that little Emmett and did awful things to him like he didn't belong to nobody." She shivered at the cruelty inflicted on a boy from Chicago, younger than me, who was brutally murdered while visiting relatives down in Mississippi. We sat saying nothing, until she continued, voice brightening. "Lord, I'd love to be a fly on the wall when ol' Parks learns what his sweet wife done."

"Yes, ma'am." My thoughts were so hooked on what had just happened that my response sounded flat.

Colored folks' pushing back wasn't a new notion to me. We might've been subtle with it most days. That didn't mean we didn't find ways to thumb our noses at Jim Crow living. Now, Miz Rosa's actions? I couldn't put a finger on it, but something about what I'd witnessed felt drastic. Frighteningly heroic. Like maybe I'd been privy to change in the making.

Thinking on Miz Rosa, I forgot about myself and what I was running to or from. When I finally refocused, that bus was nearly empty and just about to head back the way we'd come.

"Oh, Lord…"

Thankfully, I signaled my need to get off in time enough for my stop. With a mess of anxiousness piling up in my throat, I just about tumbled outdoors into that December evening with nothing but my suitcase and uncertainty keeping me company.

Which way is it?

"Look for that split tree standing all by itself next to that sunflower field. That narrow road running alongside it takes you all the way to her place."

That was the best Sadie could do seeing as how Miss Celestine didn't have a proper address living way out here off of the back end of Hayneville Road in what my Louisiana family would've called "The Cut-Off" with all its shot houses, or speakeasies, and other less than suitable establishments. Besides questionable businesses, wasn't much else around here but fields. A creek. A grove of trees that, in the descending dark, seemed close to creepy.

I didn't scare easily. My acting, in Mama's words, *too bold* was partly to blame for my being out there alone looking for Miss Celestine's. Being bold at home was one thing. Walking a dirt road in the semi-dark made me wish I was somebody's innocent lap baby snuggled safely. But I wasn't an infant. And far from innocent.

I didn't mean to touch Edward… or let him touch me.

I hadn't meant to do half the things we'd done until I was good, grown, and married. But I did. He did. Now, we had things to fix. Rather, *I* was taking it upon myself to handle the fixing.

Edward doesn't need to know my business.

That's why I was out there surrounded by high grass and weeds, clutching a suitcase, and keeping an eye out for critters and snakes instead of studying at Sadie's. Not only was I too bold, I was too nosey. Thank God. Otherwise, last night, I might've missed overhearing Doctor and Miz Stanton discussing Edward's coming home from college for Christmas break this weekend. Three whole weeks early, because of a broken leg! I'd needed every one of those weeks to figure out what to do about my monthly flow disappearing.

"Dearest, he'll handle getting back and forth to class on crutches. If that proves tedious, the infirmary made a wheelchair available. Edward'll manage fine until Christmas vacation."

I couldn't have agreed more with Doc Stanton.

Leave it to Miz Stanton to object. True southern belle, she couldn't tolerate the idea of her precious boy experiencing the slightest discomfort. His sister Abigail was two years younger, making Edward the oldest chronologically, but he was definitely his mama's baby.

"Baby…"

For the first time, I allowed that word to slip across my lips, whispering as if afraid of its power, portent. I also knew it would be the last utterance when I saw the shadowy outline of a small house in the distance. The sight of it left me shivering.

Sadie said Miss Celestine won't hurt me.

Soothing my mind with that yet-to-be-proven fact, I paused in the middle of a weed-infested path to consider the split tree that looked like it should've fallen long ago but was somehow standing. It was wider, taller up close than it appeared from the roadway. Some folks said God meant to lightning-strike Miss Celestine for dancing naked in the rain but had mercy at the last second and struck that tree instead. Others said the tree broke down the middle and bled with the weight of too many Colored bodies lynched from its limbs. Whichever was true, that split and twisted-looking tree might as well have been one of the white-gloved ushers at church ordering me along as if I had no say and couldn't choose an alternate direction.

A small creek ran alongside the path like Sadie said. Should've been some comfort in seeing that child knew what she was talking about for once, but it wasn't. The farther up that path I went, the less human I felt.

"She's gentle. Efficient." Quoting Sadie James while crossing a rickety footbridge, I knew I was desperate to be following my best friend's advice when she'd barely even kissed a boy. What did she know about *this* kind of business?

According to Sadie, she'd not only overhead her brothers discussing such things, but her cousin Brenda Lee had a friend who knew a girl who'd needed Miss Celestine.

"Brenda Lee told me her friend told her that girl said Miss Celestine burns sage and lights candles and calls on the ancestors before doing her business. She packs your lady parts with healing herbs afterwards, and lets you rest a while. Then you leave. Like nothing happened."

No hospital stay. No doctors asking Mama for more money than she made. No snooty "better thans" snubbing Mama and me because I was messed over and unmarried.

Approaching Miss Celestine's, I was feet away from rectifying my mistakes. But the notion of deliverance didn't keep sourness from burning the back of my throat, or sadness from swimming in my belly.

Pushing open a worn, weathered gate, I stepped into a tidy yard that seemed misplaced out there surrounded by overgrowth and wildness. Against the backdrop of Miss Celestine's spooky-looking house that yard was last week's spelling word: an anomaly. Meticulously kept. Cared for.

What I'd done was out of order. Anomalous. Now, I had something inside of me that didn't belong to a sixteen-year-old girl sharing a room with her mama in the Bible Belt, far from rich and too close to poverty. The deeper I stepped into that yard the more I wondered though if I *could* care for, love, and keep the living matter within me.

Prettying up the mess I'd made wasn't a choice for somebody in my position. Daddy was dead. Mama was a domestic and no matter if Doc and Miz Stanton treated us *almost* like family, that didn't mean they wanted us to be—literally.

I'm so sorry.

Miss Celestine was the only salvation my world was offering. If I didn't take it, shame on me.

Wiping the tears bathing my face, I headed for the wrap-around porch.

I hadn't mounted but one step when some huge, slobbering dog came barreling at me from the side of that raised porch—its motions swift, but oddly awkward. I knew better than to run, but that barking and snarling had me stumbling. Next thing I knew I was falling backwards, unable to catch the porch railing, suitcase sprawling in the grass and popping open. Landing on my back, curling into a ball and protecting my middle was my only thought. Lying on the ground, that dog coming for me, I wrapped my arms about myself, deciding I'd let that creature chomp on me before ever letting him taste my belly.

That simple, curled up protectiveness caused an internal shift. Something creaked open within me. Possibility?

"Cato!" A woman's voice shot out, unleashing a stream of words in a language I couldn't interpret.

Clearly, Cato could. That dog paused his pursuit and walked around me, growling low in his chest—head at an odd angle—sniffing viciously.

Daring to peek at him, I saw one eye was sewn shut; the other socket was empty. That explained his awkwardness. My attacker was blind while I had the benefit of sight. Still, he had a predator's advantage, and didn't fully back away until called again.

One arm about my middle, I sat up, trembling and praying nothing was injured while staring at the woman atop the steps, Cato standing beside her, protectively. Not sure what I expected after only hearing stories, but this Miss Celestine wasn't it. She wasn't old and hag-looking, like she boiled bats' wings, collected toad mucus, stared into crystal balls, or chopped up infants. A little older than Mama, with skin the color of browned butter, she was pretty.

"I knew you were coming." That was her greeting.

"Yes, ma'am." That was politeness speaking. I hadn't notified her so she couldn't have been aware of anything.

"That White boy knows?"

Reaching for my fallen suitcase, that stopped me cold. I sat back on my heels staring at her like maybe she *was* crazy. "Ma'am?"

"Binding your belly yet?"

She had me off-balance, jumping from topic to topic. Shaking my head, I responded. "No, ma'am."

"Just your breasts."

I nodded, wondering if she saw through my thick sweater to the strips of cloth I'd snuck from Miz Stanton's notions basket and wound about myself, trying to deal with achiness and swelling.

"You don't have much time before your waistline vanishes. So make up your mind about it." She looked off into the encroaching night with a sigh. "Guess you wouldn't be out here 'cept you already decided." She refocused on me, eyes shining as if seeing my most hidden things. "Everything you lay down here gets given back to God. I don't keep nothing 'cept the pay. Can't take coins, only paper money. You got enough?"

"I believe so."

"Fine. Come on up."

Looking at her beast of a hound, I hesitated.

"Cato don't want you, gal. Stop sitting in the dirt and get on up here."

Just like that I was back on the bus. Back in the overcrowded rows, holding my breath, watching Miz Rosa sit when she'd been told to stand.

Her "no" was enough.

What if she wasn't just speaking for herself, but for the Colored citizens of Montgomery? For folks tired of feeling like life mirrored the conditions on that bus, demanding we pay full fare while being crushed, crammed, and secondary? What if she spoke for *me*?

I wasn't trying to prove I was a woman, because I wasn't. I wasn't some nice, decent-looking Christian lady others could praise or admire for her bravery. Yet, what if I could do likewise and defy tradition and propriety?

"No…"

I shared a room. I made do with hand-me-downs. Didn't I deserve my own something? That two-letter word had been enough for Miz Rosa. It had to be enough for me, and what *I* was carrying.

"You letting that purple-eyed White boy do you that way and still keep this baby?"

Her words had me quivering. Did she know Edward, with his jewel-toned eyes like Hollywood's Elizabeth Taylor's? Was she a seer?

"He didn't take nothing." My voice was quiet, shaky, but I meant every word. I *gave* Edward what I wanted him to have, but the look on Miss Celestine's face told me she either didn't see it that way or thought I was fibbing.

Suddenly, her opinion didn't weigh as much as that matchstick from the bus reigniting itself back up somewhere near my heart. Its warmth didn't mean I wasn't scared. I was. So much so that I could barely push my fallen belongings back in my suitcase with my unsteady fingers.

"You didn't need luggage just to head nowhere. You never even wanted to be out here." Looking up, I found her staring hard at me. "It'll be dark in a second. Best get yourself home. Cato…"

When she turned to scratch behind his ears before heading indoors, I saw it. I swear! A pollywog birthmark swimming towards her left ear.

It was visible in the twilight only because it was larger than the man's on the bus and shades darker than her skin.

Before I could climb those stairs to confirm what I thought I saw, Miss Celestine was inside with the door closed. Between that pollywog and a hoot owl suddenly hooting too early in the evening, I took off running before leaving something precious out there that I suddenly needed.

CHAPTER TWO

Ashlee Turner

Current Day
Atlanta, Georgia

Denied. Denied. Denied.

Like a faulty neon sign in some rundown roach-infested dive, that message painfully flashed across my mind as I sat in Jeb Duncan's sumptuously appointed office, too proud to cry.

"Ashlee, our decision isn't a personal indictment. Without question, you've proven yourself invaluable to Duncan, Vachon, and Mallory. *Repeatedly.* However… as external competition increases, it's imperative that we maintain our leading edge by strategically positioning ourselves in order to continue a stellar, upward progression while satisfying our clients' expectations and needs."

Jeb's artfully arranged gobbledygook was politically correct manure from a horse's back end, a soft way of cushioning my failed advancement.

As if there was room for defense or argument, I wasted breath reminding our firm's founding partner of my laudable contributions and case wins despite Jeb being fully versed in them.

"The partners and I value your focus and dedication and feel you're on target to be considered for the next opportunity, but there are a few matters we can highlight to help sharpen your wins as well as that possibility."

I struggled to focus on his "suggestions for proper positioning" as hard truth settled in, scraping the fringes of my soul with unkind talons.

Been here, done this.

Despite an impressive case record with my previous employer, I'd been sidelined more than once while less productive lawyers advanced. When questioning the powers that be, my "lack of experience" was cited. Since securing a position with Duncan, Vachon, and Mallory—arguably Georgia's most prestigious corporate law firm—I'd dedicated myself to different outcomes, religiously following their rule book and playing the game their way. I dotted "i's" and crossed every "t." Did the schmoozing and networking. Accepted difficult cases that increased my visibility. Gave one hundred and twenty percent and surpassed my personal bests. Even mentored a newly hired junior associate per Jeb's request. I was a beast, a boss working my behind off. All in the name of upward mobility and securing this position only to, essentially, be informed that my efforts were insufficient.

This doesn't fit with my vision.

Never random, I always had definitive plans.

Per the Book of Ashlee, I'd be promoted to senior associate this year. Brad would put an engagement ring on my finger the next. We'd conceive our first child two years after that.

Now what? Like a savvy but suffering entrepreneur, rebuild and rebrand?

Fighting off a sense of futility, I reassured myself I'd vigilantly checked the boxes guaranteeing the upward mobility of a young, single, southern-bred African-American woman.

Debutante. Soror. Perfect diction and elocution. First-class education. Active member of a lawyers' association. I networked and attended conferences. Dressed the role in my badass designer suits and four-inch stilettos. My makeup was flawlessly applied, my flat-ironed hair subduing my curls and crinkles that could make colleagues mistake natural pride for militancy. Carefully, I navigated race-sensitive waters to avoid being dubbed an "aggressive" Black female while tactfully, shrewdly challenging the status quo when voicing my objections or opinions. But I couldn't—wouldn't—kowtow. My family had fought for civil rights; equality and justice were an inherent part of my legacy. As was dignity. My father was a chemical engineer; my mother an award-winning pediatrician. I came from greatness. Graduated law school in the top ten percent of my class. Co-owned a condo in Bankhead, and the luxury car parked on my side of the garage. Had a relationship that I still hoped would lead to marriage. I was a quintessential new millennial with all my self-empowering Black Girl Magic. I did the right things, made the right moves. Yet, there I was, feeling the limitations someone else imposed on me.

"… Ross has an impressive tort memory—"

The mention of my ungrateful, misogynistic mentee reclaimed my whole attention. "Pardon? Are you referring to Ross *Humphries?*"

Jeb needlessly straightened his perfectly placed silk tie. There was only one "Ross" at the firm; and Humphries was he. "Ashlee, again, this decision is based on what works best for the firm as a whole. Ross possesses the bandwidth to achieve our greater goals, his skill set thoroughly aligns with ours as well as our clients' needs in a senior attorney."

Jeb's nostrils flared as if bothered by the stench of his own B.S.

Staring incredulously, I remained silent, thinking Ross Humphries' passing the bar the first time and his impressive tort memory were the beginning and end of his finer attributes and qualities. A clumsy litigator who made deals on the golf course that he considered wins, what he lacked in legal finesse Ross made up for in ways that mattered to the elite. A beneficiary of the country club and caviar set and a member of one of the wealthiest families in the state, Ross came to the firm with a silver-spoon pedigree. Not to mention that Jeb and Ross's father were fishing buddies and brothers of the same fraternity. I was privy to such information only because Ross loved dropping unsolicited, position-affirming tidbits into our conversations by way of reminding me that my outranking him at the firm was inconsequential. At birth he'd already surpassed me.

Now, this junior associate whom I'd mentored at Jeb's request had been promoted instead of me?

Smoothing my hands over the skirt hugging my hips, I sat forward wanting to object, to reveal knowledge I'd gained when working late one evening, walking past the conference room and overhearing Tim Vachon's loud pronouncement during a partners' meeting that Ross had "the legal adroitness of a one-eyed mule." While that was reason enough to question their decision, what good would it do? I'd be painted as petty, desperate. Besides, Tim had evidently overcome his objections.

The Good Ol' Boys Club had spoken.

That harsh truth left me posing pertinent, perhaps expected, questions in an effort to understand Jeb and the founding partners' rationale. Framing my inquiries under the guise of how to better position myself for the future, the truth I really wanted Jeb to confirm was that ethnicity had been the deciding determinant.

Perhaps afraid I'd eventually hit that uncomfortable skin-tone target, Jeb provided long-winded responses before sauntering over to the brass coat rack in the corner of his office. Citing a narrow window until his next meeting, he slipped on a tailored suit jacket expensive enough to pay my half of the monthly mortgage. His concluding, "Keep your head clear, continue plugging away, make great strides, and you'll find your advancement to be virtually in the bag," missed its conciliatory mark. Had he patted me on the head, it wouldn't have felt more condescending.

Choosing not to reduce myself or grovel, I calmly stood in my four-inch stilettos, whose comfort clock was about to expire, thanked Jeb for his time, and exited. Bypassing my office, I headed for the ladies' room, thankful that it was empty and I could cry to my heart's content. Unfortunately, someone entered seconds behind me.

Dammit!

By nature, I wasn't a crier, but when I did I tended to get loud and animated. Sequestered in a stall, cradling my head, I engaged in deep-breathing exercises to avoid granting anyone the pleasure of labeling me an "unhinged, bitter Black woman."

Like you don't have a right to feel what you feel!

I absolutely did.

I was pissed. Disillusioned. But I was raised not to publicly disgrace myself and chose to act like I was my mother's daughter and had good sense. Savannah Turner, a member of The Links and Jack & Jill, was a pinky-lifting, sweet-tea-sipping Black soror of a southern belle who didn't raise her voice, and rarely broke a sweat. The only indication that any irritant may have crawled beneath Mama's café-au-lait skin were the lights snapping in her grayish-lavender eyes. Mama never granted anyone the pleasure of publicly seeing her cutting the fool and acting indignant. Unless of course, you wronged her family. That's when she morphed into Tiger Woman. But even then, Mama could cut you ten ways to Sunday with her genteel southern tongue before you knew you'd been nicked. If I gave into the temptation to come out my face and Savannah caught wind of it? She'd have my debutante ass on a platter until Thanksgiving.

I need to breathe.

Literally. My emotions were choked, and my head pounded as if some sharp-toe-shoe-wearing yard gnome was tap dancing inside my skull to a ditty Jeb unwittingly penned to the classic tune of "The Farmer in the Dell."

> *The bandwidth to achieve,*
> *The bandwidth to achieve,*
> *High ho the dairy oh,*
> *He aligns with our needs.*

Cancel the crazy, Ashlee.

Throat-choking that nasty gnome, I expedited my business, intending to hurry to my office and exchange high heels for the sneakers kept in my credenza. Walking the streets of downtown Atlanta would do me good, granting me much-needed fresh air and a different atmosphere.

Leaving the restroom, unfortunately, I saw none other than Ross Humphries. Thankfully, he was stationed at the opposite end of the corridor chatting with a colleague. Telling myself that being escorted off the property for assault and battery was not a good look, I declined the fantasy of knocking the smug satisfaction from his artificially tanned face with a solid right hook.

"Ashlee…"

God, really?

Seeing Ross excuse himself from our colleague, I pretended not to hear him calling me as I hung a left and headed for my office. With my bruised feelings, I wasn't magnanimous. Maybe after processing everything I could offer congratulations. Right then, I had zero need for conversation.

Successful in my great escape, I asked my paralegal to hold any non-urgent calls, closed my office door and hustled to my desk. Dropping onto my chair, I eased off my shoes and turned to the credenza for my sneakers only to be arrested by the smiling faces of my beloved.

My workspace wasn't decorated like some secondary, substitute home away from home. There were no cute-ugly, color-confused drawings from kids. Or positive affirmations on a myriad of Post-its. No plants. No candy jar for pillaging coworkers. The great-granddaughter of a domestic, I hated clutter. My decor was intentionally minimalistic. The nods to my existence consisted of my framed degrees, awards garnered during my career, a desk plaque Nana Mattie gifted me engraved with her favorite scripture, Jeremiah 29:11, and beautifully framed pictures. Me with my brother and parents. Me, Nana, and PopPop. My nephews and niece. My four-year-old goddaughter, Torrie. And Brad and me on our Cozumel vacation. On a white-sand beach with a turquoise ocean behind us, Brad and I were a picture-perfect swirl. With my Black Girl Magic and his dirty-blond, blue-eyed Chris Hemsworth kind of looks, we were worthy of the cover of an interracial romance novel. Relaxed. Vibrant. Sexy and in love. Qualities we seemed to lately lack.

Fingering the silver frames, I was hit by a forlorn sensation. *All the life I've missed...*

I'd relocated back to Georgia years ago to be near family after Nana's initial sickness, yet I'd forsaken much-needed precious time with them this past year. Ten months of, as Nana would say, hoeing the row and towing the line chasing a promotion had come to nothing. Other than overwhelming disappointment, what had I gained? A gross personal-professional imbalance that I was ashamed to admit. I couldn't count the sacrifices made or joys forfeited in my quest to be crowned Duncan, Vachon, and Mallory's newest senior associate. The late evenings, worked weekends. Church absenteeism. Missed date nights and family dinners, postponed trips, and forsaken time with girlfriends. Chance was the nature of the beast, still I felt like a five-inch fool for chasing a corporate-colored unicorn while depriving my heart, my spirit of essential needs.

Slipping on my sneakers, unable to recall the last time I'd taken a power walk or visited the gym, I stared at those photos only to be pressed back in my seat by a sudden, paralyzing wave of regret that far exceeded disappointment.

Was it worth it?

Regret ballooning like a tumultuous ocean wave, my adrenaline crashed and waned. After nearly a year of nonstop grinding, hustling, the plummet was so great that I felt physically sick. Nauseous.

Peppermints are the stomach's best friend.

Pulling my oversized tote bag from my bottom desk drawer, I scrounged through the zipper compartment until I found the cellophane-wrapped red-and-white hard candies with, per Nana, medicinal properties. Popping one in my mouth, I sat back with my eyes closed, waiting for its benefits to take effect.

I'm exhausted. Physically. Emotionally.

So much so that the mere idea of bending to lace my sneakers or walking to the elevator and waiting for it to descend twenty-five floors suddenly required more energy than I was willing to expend. Opting out of a walk, I turned to my desktop computer and launched the case file demanding the bulk of my attention.

I'd always been driven, but this past year of being swallowed up in work had provided a double shot of espresso kind of punch. Work was escapism, rewarding me with a sense of achievement and accomplishment that my personal cosmos recently lacked. But two hours later, I was still waiting for that high to kick in. When it failed to, I circled back to the truth: I was depleted.

Lying was futile. I desperately needed to regroup, refuel, and refocus. It was more than being bypassed for the senior associate position. I'd abandoned myself somewhere in the mix and needed to spend time reclaiming me.

Before I could talk myself out of a sudden, unshakable notion bouncing about my head, I hurried from my office and headed for Jeb's. Cautioning me about my unlaced sneakers, his executive administrator showed me in. Knowing better than to burn bridges or behave in a way that could end my tenure here, I respectfully presented my request. Based on his facial expression, he was clearly taken off guard. Maybe it was our ensuing conversation and my clear, reassuring plan of action; perhaps it was his relief that I wasn't there to plead my case and ask him to reconsider the partners' decision accompanied by emotional displays. Whatever his reason, *sans* protest, Jeb Duncan granted my request. After advising that his administrator would contact HR, I left with Jeb's blessing.

"Lara, do you have a moment?"

I paused at my paralegal's desk long enough for her to confirm she did. Stepping into my office, I held the door open, inviting her to take one of the cushy chairs reserved for guests while I perched on the edge of my desk to inform her of my newest development.

"*What? Why?*" Lara Philips was a paralegal dream. Sharp. Intuitive. Incredibly organized with excellent research and writing skills and an ability to multitask while remaining calm under pressure. Colleagues had tried and failed to weasel her away from me but over the past five years we'd developed wonderful synergy and I considered Lara's outburst heart-warming evidence of her genuine care for my well-being. "I apologize for screeching."

"It's unexpected news, Lara, so no apologies necessary."

Quietly we discussed the conceivable impact my decision would have on her before reviewing priority matters and strategizing the remainder of the work week. By the time we'd finished, Lara had stopped gripping the arms of her chair and folded her hands on her lap—her customarily calm self again.

"For what it's worth, the office won't be the same without you." In her mid-forties, a decade or so older than me, Lara's admission felt sweet, almost motherly.

"I appreciate that, but for you I'm always within reach."

"Thank you, Ashlee." With a soft, semi-sad smile, she headed for the door. Pausing before opening it, Lara playfully propped a hand on one hip. "Does this mean I have to get my own pastry on Fridays?"

We laughed, knowing that was my thing: stopping by the café downstairs and treating us to a breakfast of caramel macchiatos and stuffed croissants every Friday. Chocolate for Lara. Apple-almond for me. "I might be able to pull some strings."

Departing, she closed the door as if intuiting my need for privacy.

In the ensuing silence, I sat precisely where I'd been. On the edge of my desk. Not moving except to tilt my head back, close my eyes, and audibly exhale.

"Am I really doing this?"

I hadn't worked my behind off as an undergrad and fought my way through law school to walk away from my accomplishments or career path. Not in this vicious lawyers-eat-lawyers game where the slightest misstep could create irreversible damage for me, a thirty-two-year-old Black female practicing corporate law at a firm that others dreamed about and prayed for an interview with. At Duncan, Vachon, and Mallory, I'd been exposed to some of the finest legal minds in the nation. I worked long hard hours with a salary that provided worthwhile compensation, not to mention perks that could make a moralistic conservative opposed to corporate excess sick. In the estimation of some, I was a hot commodity capable of writing her own ticket. Why sabotage that?

That was the part of Lara's question I'd intentionally left unanswered. Not that I wasn't clear, but because the "why" was private.

Swiveling to enjoy the panoramic view of the Black Mecca, aka Atlanta, from my twenty-fifth floor window, I knew my actions were risky, and could be interpreted as my failure to thrive or pull my weight as a contributing and vital cog in a high-functioning, dynamic team. I risked being pronounced as weak, or incapable of readily rebounding from disappointment and excelling.

"It's only temporary. A two-week leave of absence."

While that may have seemed miniscule in the grand scheme of things, in a lawyer's world two weeks might as well have been two months. I was uncertain about the possible outcomes, but equally important were the reasons fueling my decision.

It's an act of self-preservation.

It was Wednesday. That gave me two days to finesse my most pressing cases to a place where they could be easily managed by a fellow associate. I didn't want to leave anyone in the lurch, or unfairly add to their load. Clearly my loyalty and commitment to the firm was far greater than theirs towards me.

"Unh-unh, not today. You're the granddaughter of Mattie Ilene. You don't do pity parties."

Dabbing at a tear forming in the corner of an eye, I reached across my desk, grabbed my cell from the top drawer and fired off a text to my masseuse. My weekly standing appointments had become inconsistent, another casualty of sacrificing myself on an altar of professional advancement. Appointment confirmed, I sat atop my desk gently swinging my still unlaced sneakers, staring out the window and reminding myself I'd be back tomorrow and Friday. After that? I had two weeks to decide my next steps.

*

"Girl, you should've told those trolls to kiss the crack of your natural, naked Black ass. Wait. Scratch that. With their latent Jungle Fever fetishes, they would've loved licking your booty à la Beyoncé."

Dorinda had me laughing as I pulled into my driveway. Comically outspoken and the mother of my adorable goddaughter Torrie, Dorinda and I had been besties since freshman year in college. Our winding up in the ATL together five years ago wasn't orchestrated, but utterly welcomed. I'd phoned her on the way home, needing to vent. Having cried, cussed, and fussed up a storm, I was emotionally spent. "Doe, stop it."

"Seriously, Ash, they're assholes and idiots."

"Duly noted."

"They are and you know it. Your track record, case wins, and performance reviews are excellent. You have commendations and compliments, not complaints, from clients. Your billable hours are through the roof. You've taken ten for the team. And let's not forget it was *you* who was enlisted to help that little meat-headed Ross when he first got there and came up struggling and looking ignorant. Why request that of you versus another associate?"

Exiting my car, I ensured the garage door descended fully before entering my condo and disarming the security system long enough to enter and arm it again. When Brad was away, I was extra cautious. "Because my caseload was lighter than my colleagues'?"

"*Ehhh!*" Dorinda made a sound like a game show buzzer. "Don't peddle that okey doke. Their *complexions* were lighter than yours. We know how this country club game is played. And all that 'bandwidth, alignment' mess is coded crap for their satisfying the White gaze. We're asked to help train or equip a struggling someone when we're supposedly inferior or inept. Why? The legacy of slavery."

I frowned while dumping my belongings and the bag of groceries I'd stopped for onto the kitchen counter. "The correlation between aiding a colleague and slavery, please?"

"Different situation. Same exploitation. We're convenient pawns for their advantage. That slave-owning society deemed our ancestors subhuman. Livestock. Animal property and husbandry. Still, what did massa and missus do when the missus birthed babies? Put 'em on a Black titty."

"Dorinda, *really*?" I kicked off my shoes, laughing loudly. "You're always extra."

"But am I lying? We—the alleged animals—played nursemaid? I mean, come on. Would you let your baby suckle a pig? A hyena? A pit bull? Hell, naw! And don't get me started on the hyper-sexualization of the enslaved. Again, that was for *their* benefit. Rape justification. If I'm an animal, and you're raping me for centuries, what's that make you? A perverse, bestiality-loving motherfu—"

"Stay on topic."

"Fine. You were assigned to Ross—'cause, after all, we're Mammy's descendants and love helping Mister Charlie's chilluns—and what happens? They promote up and leave us in their dust."

"Thankfully, I don't plan on suckling anyone."

"Honey, you already have. Ross Humphries got that good mother milk. Now, he's a massa." Dorinda had always been colorfully, boldly expressive. Sometimes she went on rabbit-trail diatribes, but after sifting through her fodder there were, typically, truthful nuggets.

Unfortunately, I couldn't counter-argue her statement. Conceding I'd been used by the establishment, I unpacked my groceries instead. "Where's Torrie? I need to speak to someone intelligent."

Bestie laughed her wildly carefree laugh that I loved. "Kenny took her to the park. I adore my baby, but I needed a quiet moment to finish this project without *'Mommy!'* every five-point-six seconds."

Groceries stored, I quickly sorted the mail, tossing junk circulars in the recycling bin. "Doe, you should've told me you were busy." A public relations specialist, she'd launched her own business after Torrie was born. Struggling and juggling work, marriage, and motherhood, she'd left her job for entrepreneurship. Now, she worked from home and loved it.

"Girl, I was on pins and needles waiting to hear if you got the job. Now? I'm finding one of Torrie's dolls and putting those pins to good use conjuring up a little law firm voodoo."

We shared a laugh.

"Seriously, Ash. The situation's disappointing, but I'm proud of you for electing self-care. Let this vacation from the plantation be all about you. Meditate. Exercise. Draw or do something you haven't enjoyed in a while. Eat healthy. Indulge periodically. And give Gomer Pyle some of that brown sugar booty *nightly*."

I'd made the mistake of pouring wine and taking a sip. Dorinda's quip had me spitting, splattering red wine drops onto my cream-colored silk blouse. Brad's southern drawl was hardly as thick or pronounced, yet Dorinda had nicknamed him Gomer Pyle. More alike than different, my lover and bestie fussed like siblings. "I hate you."

"Yeah, yeah. When's Gomer getting home, and what did he say about his Nubian princess getting played?"

"Saturday night. And, I haven't told him yet." Brad's being out of town at a conference worked to my advantage, allowing me to sleep on my decision versus being talked out of it.

"Hmm... well... I respect him and would be interested in his pale-male perspective. Ooo, wait, Kenny's texting that they're on their way home. Let me get off of here so I can enjoy five minutes of silence."

"I'll pick Torrie up Saturday at eleven." Feeling like a negligent godmother, I'd planned a fun day at the children's museum followed by all the pizza and ice cream we could eat. If time allowed, we'd hang at my place and whip up one of her favorite treats: Nana's teacakes.

"She'll be ecstatic. Ash, do me a favor..."

"What?"

"Contact the good reverend, Al Sharpton."

We disconnected, chuckling, knowing she was jesting. I also knew Dorinda's prescription for my healing was enticing, simplistic, and perhaps, what I needed.

Between oversleeping lately and work fatigue, my whole exercise routine was off. I could go from eating everything in sight, to experiencing an upset stomach that prevented me from enjoying anything. I hadn't picked up a sketch pad in forever. And as for sexing Gomer nightly? Brad and I had been unnecessarily at odds lately. Our sex life had become irregular. We were inexplicably out of sync.

"I'm hungry."

I chose to focus on satisfying a basic need versus worrying.

Scouring the fridge, I realized I hadn't eaten much since my conversation with Jeb that morning. Even so, nothing I saw tempted my taste buds except the salted caramel macchiato gelato I'd just purchased. Grabbing a spoon, I paused to dump my barely touched wine down the sink. Could've been me and my mood, but the overpriced cabernet had possessed an unpleasant, metallic aftertaste.

"Glad Babe can't see me."

My significant other of the past four years was a wineaholic. Not as in, ready for the twelve-step progam. Rather, he was a connoisseur of fine wines and would've busted a gut if aware of my waste.

Frozen confection and spoon in hand, I headed for the bedroom while dialing my parents, intent on a quick shower and mindless television.

When no one answered, my heart skipped a beat, my thoughts flew from A to Z.

Lord, I pray Nana's okay.

Diagnosed seven years ago with ovarian cancer, treatment had proven successful and my grandmother was in remission. Still, I experienced inexplicable moments of panic over her welfare. Particularly if too much time lapsed in communicating with my family. I needed to hear a voice from home to know that all was well.

Disconnecting, I dialed my mother's cell only for it to go unanswered also.

"Hey, Mama, just checking in. Call when you get this message. Love you."

With my parents residing on the same ten-acre property as my grandparents, I consoled myself with the thought that I would've been notified if something was amiss. Still, I texted my brother Avery who lived in D.C. but seemed to know more about what went on in our family's lives than I did.

Have u talked 2 Mama lately? Is everything ok?

Tossing my phone and gelato on the bed, I took that quick shower, moisturized my skin, and slipped into a thigh-length, cartoon-character pajama top before settling in. I was deep into my guilty pleasure of ratchet reality TV when Brad's ringtone chimed. I answered, genuinely glad that he was checking in despite our recent dry rut. "Hey, baby. Finished for the day?"

His sigh felt weighty. "Hey, yourself. Conference? Yes. The night? No."

"You sound tired."

"I am. Just returned to the hotel with a whole five minutes to respond to student emails before heading to the mixer and dinner. What's new in your world?"

That was Brad. An adjunct law professor and partner at his firm, he had little time for excess and preferred directness. His five minutes of freedom would not be wasted on chit-chat.

"I took a two-week leave of absence."

"I'm sorry. You… *what?*"

I confirmed the fact.

"*Why?*"

I kneaded the bridge of my nose, feeling as if we were about to wade into an ugliness neither of us wanted. "I value my sanity, and time off might preserve that for me."

"Ashlee."

"I left because I'm tired of nonsense."

"Be more specific."

Hearing him typing on his laptop sent some irritable imp skipping along the base of my neck. "For that right there. Because I'm tired of being ignored by White men."

"You want attention from a whole segment of the population?"

"You're typing while I'm talking, Bradley. And don't be facetious."

This time his sigh was directed at me. "I apologize. The laptop's closed. I'm listening."

I paused, hearing a chime. "Hold on."

Talked 2 Mama yesterday. Everything's everything.

I sighed with relief, seeing my brother's reply to my text. "Ross Humphries got the position."

"*Not even!*" Brad's subsequent, angry expletive reflected my feelings. "Wait… wasn't Jeb announcing the firm's decision next week?" As my significant other, Brad had dutifully attended his fair share of my office soirees, Christmas parties, and annual barbecues. With his legal acumen and golden boy charm, he'd practically been inducted as a member of the firm's family, even sharing time on the golf course with Jeb and the other partners. *Sans* me.

"Officially, yes, but candidates were informed today." I spooned too much dessert into my mouth as if in need of frozen fortification against weeping. I was suddenly tired. Hormonal. Teary-eyed and weary. "Baby, we're talking about my clumsy colleague, the one who never hesitates to ask me backdoor questions rather than coming through the front and admitting his ignorance or uncertainties before our superiors. The same man who wanted me to grab him coffee and Xerox his documents when he first arrived and didn't know I was a peer." The same tight ass who'd questioned which Historically Black College I'd graduated from and if I'd attended law school on a race-based scholarship, not knowing I'd completed my undergrad at Columbia and my parents sent me to Yale Law. "And let's not mention the jerk asking you what it's like *being* with a Black woman." Or that I'd denied his ignorant request to touch my hair. "Him! He's leveled up to senior associate."

We shared silent disbelief until Brad's, "Damn, Babe… I hate hearing this… but you can't take a leave because of disappointment. You'd be sabotaging your career. The partners could view you as intractable—"

"Meaning difficult. Angry. Hostile. Infantile? Code words too frequently employed against the P.O.C. community." I hopped off the bed to return my gelato to the freezer. My appetite had disappeared.

"Baby, we're discussing you, not an overarching people of color anything. And, yes, I know you're part of that community," he quickly inserted, knowing too well that I'd already opened my mouth to remind him of my ethnicity, unnecessarily. "You've more than paid your dues at that firm. The overtime all in the name of the team and particularly this promotion. No, it didn't happen. That's not to say advancement won't come. Don't narrow your chances or commit career suicide by doing something stupid."

Tossing my dessert in the freezer and the spoon in the sink, I poured another glass of wine before waltzing into the den, turning on the stereo, and plopping onto my favorite oversized chair. "So, now I'm ignorant."

"Don't twist what I'm saying."

"Twisting might be a by-product of having my head whacked one too many times against the glass ceiling. I've reached my threshold. I'm sick of ish."

All of it. Not just a colleague's promotion that proved the proverbial straw to break the camel's back. But the "drill down deeper, Ashlee," the being asked if I'd double and triple-checked my work regularly. The scrutiny that left me feeling as if I lived in a fishbowl, or that I merely fulfilled the firm's diversity quota. The daily microaggressions and cultural isolation that emanated within an industry not dominated by my gender and lacking persons who looked like me. The boating. Fishing. Golfing. Skiing. Hiking. Camping. Wine tastings. Timeshare getaways. All experiences the partners shared with other associates, and for which invites were extended at the last minute or not at all because it was assumed I'd be disinterested. As if minorities lacked the cultural capacity to appreciate such luxuries and living.

After hours indulgences aside, there were the "you don't look like a lawyer" comments. Or the day I'd overslept and had been running too late to work flat-iron magic and walked in with my hair pulled back in its natural, coiled and curly state, prompting uncomfortable questions, discomfort, and mild confusion. My being queried as if I were the spokeswoman and educator whenever atrocities against Black lives were publicized. As my lover and confidant, Brad was privy to it all. I felt zero need to relaunch a litany of micro injustices and indignities.

"I'm going to bed."

"So the conversation's finished?"

"Best to not waste your remaining two minutes on something 'stupid.'"

"Ash, come on—"

"Enjoy dinner. See you this weekend." I disconnected, feeling petty. Resentful. Hating the idea that I'd be pegged as paranoid for labeling such insidious exclusions and acts as racist. "As if there's an Olympics of Racism and only burning crosses or hate crimes qualify. Race hate did *not* die a rightful, undignified death with the Emancipation Proclamation or *any* subsequent legislation. It's still alive." As I lifted the wineglass to my lips, the mere smell made my stomach clench. Unable to drink it, I ignored Brad's calling again as well as my falling tears.

I thought I'd be all cried out after venting with Dorinda earlier that evening but I wasn't. Obviously this work issue and more was happening. Maybe Nana *was* sick and I was picking up on her spirit in addition to my psyche and soul being flat out exhausted.

Go home, Ashlee.

I needed real rest, the kind found only in the bosom of my family.

CHAPTER THREE

Mattie

What to do after leaving Miss Celestine's?

Clearly, that was one thing I hadn't given enough thought to. How to go home and look half normal so Mama wouldn't know what I'd been up to? Or maybe I needed a little time and space to fix myself, my face, to buy some magic that could eradicate all traces of the new mess I'd almost committed. For once money wasn't the issue. I still had what I would've paid Miss Celestine for what she didn't do in a sock pinned to my brassiere. It wasn't much, just earnings saved selling pop bottles and what Mama managed to squirrel away for me as rewards for my getting good grades. Although I'd never imagined myself needing to spend my precious loot on this kind of predicament, it gave me something to work with, enough for whatever was next.

That's where my problems kept coming in. I had no secondary plan. All I could do was pray and paste on a brave face walking that dark road, clutching the handle of my suitcase wondering where to go, how to escape.

You gotta leave Montgomery, Mattie.

I'd never been away from home. Not alone. And certainly no real distance from my mama. Just sleepovers. Mainly at Sadie's. I'd have to get farther than that to deal with what I was facing, and the only worthwhile options popping about my head like corn in a hot skillet were family.

Some of Mama's people were in Louisiana, and many of Daddy's were in Georgia. Most didn't have much, but that wouldn't stop them from helping me if I showed up. I was blood. I could appear on their doorsteps unannounced and family would invite me in, feed me, and find a way to help solve the mess I'd made. The problem? They'd notify Mama. Running might've been a coward's remedy, but I loved my mother and didn't want her hurt any more than she had been. With Daddy's death, her heart had been broken enough for eternity. She'd miss me but I could write her a letter once I got wherever I was going. It was painful to consider, but my leaving could spare her the pain and humiliation of seeing me in my condition.

Spoiled.

Ruint.

Messed over by that whipping stick between some White boy's legs.

Fair or not, those kinds of words were never fired at men. I'd overheard such whisperings directed towards girls "fool enough" to get themselves caught. As if their swelling bellies were solely their making. Now, there I was about to have disdainful labels draped about my neck like some smelly, moth-eaten scarf abandoned at the bottom of an unloved spinster's mildewed hope chest.

How would I react?

Forged in my father's fire, I often caught trouble from Mama for being outspoken and "too much." Yes, I was ashamed of being with Edward and doing what we'd done. But if pushed too long and tagged too hard with words like glass shards, I was liable to flare up. That could have consequences as terrifying as my not knowing what to do next. Ostracism. Abandonment. Invisibility rendering me unheard and without meaning. Just another "Colored whore" good for nothing but to be used and unseen.

"The Lord is my shepherd, I shall not want…"

Trying to calm myself out there in the dark, I quickened my pace while reciting the twenty-third Psalm. My Sunday school teacher, Sister Duncan, told us it was the best thing to do in times of crisis. Clearly, Sister Duncan knew her Bible business. I started feeling a whole inch better as those verses rolled over my tongue. By the time I hit "Thy rod and thy staff, they comfort me" my voice had picked up strength. I was less shaky, and my heart was calming. Even had the nerve to think I might figure out this thing until a car rolled up entirely too close.

"Hey, gal, ain't it a little early for spooks to be haunting the evening?"

That voice and those words undid every ounce of peace King David's psalm had fed me. Heart pounding, I looked straight ahead, not needing to look at the living contents of that car to know no-good was on its way to happening. Funny thing? My feet slowed instead of quickening. As if my body knew there was nothing I could do to outrun deviltry.

"You heard what I said, spook? Niggers ain't got no business coming out their caves early without a White man's permission. Especially no Black wench with some nice-looking nigger hips. You a virgin?"

Hugging my suitcase against my chest, I kept walking with unsteady steps, defenseless, shielded only by my silence.

"Spook, you hear me talking to you?"

When that car skidded to a stop nearly perpendicular in front of me, I froze while frantically considering my surroundings. Miss Celestine's was too far behind. Haynesville Road was too far ahead. Out there on that dirt lane wasn't nothing except me and trouble. Yet again, I was faced with limited options. Only this time those limits could cost me much more than I'd already given.

An imbalanced tradition required my eyes to study the ground as the car door opened and that White boy who'd been hollering from his window emerged. But something contrary flared up brighter than the fear clutching my bones, and I dared to glance at him, needing to see precisely what brand of evil threat was coming for me.

He's a boy tryna be a man.

Smelling like he'd gotten lost in his daddy's liquor, he looked to be around Edward's age. Maybe younger. Maybe that's what gave me courage to steady my gaze as he headed in my direction. I'd never seen him before, yet he felt familiar. Perhaps it was his intent marking him as something seen centuries before either of us got here. Such vile, age-old familiarity wasn't comforting.

"You one of them new kinda coons, huh? Not answering when spoken to."

"No sir." I hated the smallness of my voice and that custom forced me to address him as if he were grown.

"Well, why you out here? And I asked, are you a virgin?"

My body started shaking with horror. And indignity. This stranger had no business talking up under my clothing. My stubbornness set in, refusing him the pleasure of my answering.

"I betcha you are. Bet you ain't never had this good kinda lovin'."

"J.T., come on 'fore you make us late." The driver hollering out his window did nothing to divert this J.T. from whatever his intent.

"Seth, come here. I need your expert opinion." Even in the dark I felt J.T.'s stare raking my being. "Is this gal untouched, or she been romping in corn fields?"

The driver's door opening, the one who was obviously Seth exited, only to stand there, his irritability showing. "We ain't got time for this, J.T. If we catch hell from Coach for being late, I swear I'm going upside your head."

Rather than return to that car where he belonged, J.T. touched my hair.

I jerked backwards.

"Don't act like that. I ain't gonna hurt you, but if I do you'll like it later," he cooed, toying with the belt securing his Levi's.

"J.T.—"

"Gotdammit, Seth! Hold your horses. This ain't gonna take but a minute. I'm a charitable Christian and this nigger deserves an early Christmas gift."

"Fool, you ain't got nothing to give."

"Hell, Seth, her first time getting it from a White man is the purest gift she can have."

"You're not a man." Throat tight, words trembling, I'd spoken without thinking.

"What did you say?"

My right mind knew my life and so much more depended on my silence, but clearly I wasn't finished being that girl from the back of the bus. The one touched by wondrous, mind-altering defiance. "You're not a man." I repeated myself, knowing whatever came next, I'd spoken a truth for the ancestors and the ages. "Real men don't hurt women. Only cowards—"

The blow against my lips prevented me from finishing. Pain sent me staggering backwards as my suitcase crashed to the ground, spewing its guts. Again. Next thing I knew, that boy was hollering in my face, spittle flying, enraged. All I could do was pray Mama would hold up when they found me after this J.T. finished doing everything he meant to do to me.

I was so caught between wishing I was home and wondering how far I could get if I slammed a knee in his privates and took off running that I didn't notice the car approaching behind me. I was busy shuddering, sweating, backing away, unaware of its riders stepping into the night until hearing,

"What's going on here?"

That deep, soothing baritone had me feeling as if I was hallucinating. Spinning around, I saw three men, *Colored men*, coming towards me. Two with baseball bats, one with a tire iron, all three at the ready.

"Miss, are you—?" The one with a bat stopped suddenly. "*Mattie?*"

With the beam of the headlights blinding me, my heart thudded hearing that familiar voice, while unable to see him clearly. "Ransome?" We'd grown up together, but I'd never paid Sadie's brother much mind. He was a typical older sibling, teasing when younger, all but ignoring us the older we got. But right then Ransome James felt divine.

"Why're you way out here?"

Unable to answer, I merely shook my head.

"How 'bout you damn niggers go'n somewhere and mind your business?"

Before I could blink, Ransome had stepped forward, positioning himself between me and J.T. He'd always been taller than most, but right then he felt gigantic. "This young lady is our business, so we'll decline that invitation. *Sir.*"

Ransome's friends were on either side of me; the night air was suddenly thick with maleness.

"J.T., com'n here. I ain't tryna have Coach screaming at us. Plus, we gotta stop and get something to hide that drink on your breath." Intentionally or not, the driver had supplied his passenger with a way to walk away and save face.

"Yeah... I'm coming." He stood a moment longer, eyeing our gathering, making a good show of bravery before hawking something from his throat and spitting on Ransome's shoe.

Ransome didn't flinch. Simply held up a blocking arm when the guy to my left jerked forward as if ready for a piece of J.T.'s head.

Laughing, my terrorizer headed for the car. Pausing, he gave an exaggerated bow. "Have a good, niggardly evening, *Miss* Mattie."

With that, my tormentor rolled off.

When there was nothing but the distant glow of taillights, Ransome whirled on me. "Mattie, why the hell're you out here by yourself at this time of night like you don't have good sense?"

Scolded and embarrassed, I knelt and started scooping belongings back into my suitcase without answering, hands shaking like leaves in a hurricane.

"Mattie!"

"Ransome, hollering at me ain't gonna get you nothing," I shouted up at him, wishing he'd walk away so I could let the tears crowding my eyeballs roll down my face.

"I'm not trying to upset you, Mattie, I just—"

"*Go away!*" I wouldn't hear the end of it if Sadie found out I was bawling in front of her brother like somebody's big diaper baby, but I was. Every tear I'd held onto since hugging Mama and walking out the door earlier that evening poured down my face, leaving me sniffing and snotting while stuffing my suitcase haphazardly. My inability to shut the lid escalated my crying.

"Let me." Ransome's voice was so soft and gentle as he squatted down, taking over the task my fumbling fingers couldn't complete. When he stood and handed my suitcase to the guy with the tire iron and pulled me to my feet, I didn't cry. I started wailing. Like someone I loved had died and I wouldn't see them until eternity.

I barely felt Ransome easing me against the safety of his hard chest. All I could think about was the fact that God had sent three angels to keep me from suffering the fate of my ignorance.

"Go'n and let it out, Mattie. Everything's gonna be okay."

"How do you know?" My tears finally running thin, I started hiccupping. My tone held a challenge. "You don't even know what my problem is."

"You're right. I don't. What I do know is I need to get you home. Can we do that?"

I wanted to tell him "yes," but a surge of something decided to erupt from my mouth as if I was that volcano in Italy we'd studied in Geography last week. Ripping myself from Ransome's comforting embrace, I made it to the edge of the dry grass bordering the road before violently upchucking.

"Take this." He was there at my side when I finished.

Wiping my mouth with the hem of my sweater, I almost smiled seeing the stick of Doublemint Ransome offered. Growing up with his incessant smacking on bubblegum, Sadie and I used to secretly call him Mister Chewy. "Thanks."

"You okay?"

Slipping that gum in my mouth, I took a calming breath and nodded.

"Good. Come on."

When he took my hand to lead me to the car, some strange kind of something flashed through my fingers, up my arm. I ignored it, wasn't even sure what to name it, or if it had significance.

Sliding into the backseat, I mumbled a barely discernible greeting to the two who turned out to be Ransome's teammates. I remembered both from the times Sadie and I had watched her brother out on the field practicing, proving why he'd been drafted into the Negro Leagues.

"I promise to get you home soon as I drop Short Stuff and Peabo off."

Wanting to disappear in my corner of the car, I didn't care about time. Or who went where. I just wanted to be left alone to wallow in the mess that was my existence.

*

I didn't realize how utterly empty my belly was until Ransome dropped Peabo and Short Stuff at their respective residences. His simple mention of a thick, juicy burger from Mama Bea's had my mouth watering, stomach rumbling. It was a Thursday evening. I should've been at Sadie's. And I had no business being alone in a car with a man, even if it was only Ransome. But I was already past prim and proper, and considered dinner from Mama Bea's a well-deserved diversion.

Born a slave, Beatrice Lymons was over a hundred, and one of Montgomery's oldest living citizens. Her mother had been the head cook on a plantation and had taught her daughter culinary skills before being sold to a family in West Virginia mere months before slavery ended. Only ten at the time, Mama Bea never found her mother and became a plantation orphan. Her way of keeping her mother alive was staying in that kitchen and parlaying what she'd learned and remembered into a fifty-year-old establishment. She'd started in her home, moved to her church's basement, then to a small structure behind Goldman's Grocery. Old Man Goldman and his wife were Jewish, had endured their share of problems for being "Christ killers," and acted fair and decent towards us. Owning the land where their store was situated, they'd allowed Mama Bea to convert an unused shed and run her business out of it. Too old to manage it anymore, her grands and great grands had taken over, keeping the establishment in the family and serving *the best* burgers in Montgomery.

"So… you wanna tell me what's really going on?"

Parked at Bea's, Ransome's question slowed my greedy eating. He wasn't but six years older. Still, his baritone felt paternal and had me shrugging like a child facing a parent after misbehaving.

"Come on now, Mattie. I'm out there taking the long way home from batting practice, and I roll up on something no Negro man ever wants to see, and you just gonna sit there mad and sad and saying nothing?"

Don't ask me why, but I got irritated watching Sadie's brother talking and chewing, fussing at me around a mouthful like he had no table manners.

"Sorry for troubling you, but you didn't have to stop. You could've drove on."

"But I didn't... and I wouldn't. So dial back the sass and answer my question, Mattie Banks. What were you doing out there?"

Dropping a half-eaten fry back into the grease-stained paper bag in which they'd been served, I gave Ransome my best evil eye.

"Fine. Don't answer that. Answer this instead. Where, outside of Montgomery, were you headed?"

"What makes you think I was going somewhere?"

"Hmm... let's see... maybe the suitcase sitting on my back seat."

"This is your parents' car so technically it's not *your* back seat." I crossed my arms over my chest when he laughed at my playing word games with him. Why I was acting so belligerent was a question I needed to answer, but couldn't. "I see nothing funny."

He sobered instantly. "Neither do I. Mattie, you're old enough to know you put yourself in a world of jeopardy this evening. What if we hadn't rolled up when we did? You realize—" He stopped, not needing to finish. We were both well versed in the varying degrees of danger we lived with. But for God and these three earth angels sent to my rescue, I'd most likely be on the side of some abandoned road, skirt hiked about my waist, underwear missing, blood running from the center of my being.

The very thought had me sitting back, eyes closed in a silence so thick I didn't want to break it. But I had to. Enough to express my appreciation. "Thank you for doing what you did, Ransome. Sorry for—"

"No worthwhile Colored man would've walked away from what I saw so don't apologize to me. Apologize to yourself. Apologize to Miss Dorothy. Speaking of, where does your mother think you are?"

I looked out the window again, escaping Ransome's searing gaze. "Your house... working on something with Sadie."

His voice was significantly quieter when asking, "Were you running away?"

That simple question had me unsuccessfully wrestling a whole new deluge of tears.

"Come here."

When Ransome extended a welcoming arm, I scooted towards him and leaned against his chest, allowing truth to spill out as I tried to make sense of what I was dealing with. "Yes... I guess. *No*. I don't know what I was doing or where I was going. I feel confused." And caught. And incapable of making the life decisions required of me.

Not true. You're keeping this baby.

It was the one definitive choice I'd made that evening.

"Whatever's going on you may wanna let Miss Dorothy in on it. See what she has to say. Let her help you. Okay?"

Pushing out of his embrace, I nodded and reclaimed my side of the front seat.

"I'll take you home when you're finished eating."

"Miz Stanton usually drives Mama over to pick me up if I'm out in the evenings. I need to call home and tell her not to."

Digging coins from the ashtray, he held them out to me. "Here. Use the payphone."

I took what coins I needed before studying Sadie's brother. "I appreciate you helping me the way you have."

"You and Sadie been working my nerves since y'all was little. But now, I'm a gentleman."

For the first time that night, I laughed. "That's a matter of opinion."

"It is. And my opinion's the only one that matters on the subject."

"So says you." I'd opened the door and stepped outside when I heard Ransome call me. I bent to look through the open window. "Yes?"

"Make sure you know what to tell Miss Dorothy about your lip before you get home."

Touching the cut at the corner of my mouth, I headed for the payphone, wishing I'd never been out there on that road alone.

I hid my hand-me-down suitcase in the backyard tool shed just as I had when first concocting tonight's plan. No one except Mister Gillis, the gardener and handyman, entered it and he wasn't due back until Monday. Seeing as how Mama refused to enter that shed after seeing a garter snake in it, and the Stantons didn't do manual labor, my suitcase could remain safely hidden until Mama and Miz Stanton left early tomorrow morning to get groceries for the upcoming week. When they did, I'd sneak it back into my room and unpack without Mama being the wiser.

Steeling my nerves, I headed for the side door leading to the small living quarters I shared with my mother off the back of the Stanton's kitchen. It wasn't much besides a bedroom and our own bathroom, but Mama did her best making it comfortable when we moved in after Daddy died. Cohabitating was easier when I was young and didn't take up much space and wanted little more than the comfort of my mother's presence. Now? Easing into the room and fully expecting to see Mama ironing her uniform for tomorrow while enjoying her evening programs on the radio, but glad that she wasn't, it felt constrictive.

"Matilda Ilene Banks, you best thank the good Lord for the roof over your head."

Mama shot that at me whenever I dared to complain about the room's tightness. Which seemed to be more frequently lately. I didn't mean to act the ingrate, but the older I got the more this living cramped in a corner of a sprawling two-story colonial irked me. Made me miss those vaguely remembered days when Daddy was living. Back then we had our own everything, and I was safe and warm, needing nothing. I recalled homemade teacakes, and the smell of Daddy's hair pomade. Smothered neck bones and fried cabbage; and night sounds coming through the adjoining bedroom wall I shared with my parents. I didn't understand their swirling, consuming noises then, but they somehow made me smile and drift deeper into sleep knowing whatever was occurring on the other side of the wall, my parents were pleased. I wasn't naive enough to paint the past with perfection, but my heart still held memories of being well-loved and at the center of my parents' affection.

Kicking off my shoes, I ran a hand along the desk Abigail had outgrown and no longer needed. Or, better stated, no longer wanted.

That girl changes her mind on a dime.

Two years back this French Provincial vanity table was all Abby whined about. Within three months of receiving it at Christmas it was suddenly *passé* and she was on to another whim. Unwilling to see it go to waste, Miz Stanton decided it was perfectly suited for me.

"Sweetheart, if Gillis detaches the mirror it can make a nice desk for Mattie's studying and doodling."

"Doodling" was how Miz Stanton referred to my short stories and poetry. Not that I'd ever confide in her, but the airy way she talked about it made me certain never to disclose to her my dreams of one day writing professionally.

"Why remove the mirror, dearest? Mattie's a year older than Abby." Smoking a cigar in his favorite armchair, Doc Stanton tossed his voice through the newspaper he was reading, like some ventriloquist trick, before lowering his periodical. "Isn't Mattie interested in makeup and whatever else young ladies do at vanity tables?"

Conveniently eavesdropping while running the sweeper over the hardwood floors in the dining room, I'd glanced at Miz Stanton laughing as if her husband had said something supremely funny.

"Now see what you made me do. I missed a cross stitch," she'd complained, holding up her embroidery hoop as proof. "Sweetheart, Colored girls are disinterested in such ablutions."

"Doesn't Dorothy wear lipstick to church on Sundays?"

Miz Stanton's whole demeanor changed and suddenly wasn't nothing funny. Her voice dripped honey laced with arsenic. "I wouldn't know what Dorothy wears, and I wonder why you do."

That sent Doc back behind his newspaper without another word.

"Besides, Dorothy's grown, Howard. Mattie isn't. And Mattie has better ways to spend her time. Like schoolwork. Or helping her mother around this house. She doesn't need a mirror to learn how to properly apply lipstick. She's not ready for dating and wouldn't even know what to do with male attention. Besides, Colored gals mature much too quickly as is. No need encouraging that."

The day after that living-room conversation Mister Gillis had that mirror detached and I had a "new" desk, complete with colorful streaks, courtesy of Abby's nail polishing. Mama had helped me remove them with a paste she made from vinegar and sodium bicarbonate. It worked too well, lifting some of the white paint. Mister Gillis offered to refinish the desk for me, but I declined. I'd grown past the point of trying to make second-hand things feel as if originally mine.

Pushing that memory away, I pulled off my hand-me-down sweater from Abby only to notice a gaping hole rendering it beyond repair.

"*Shoot.* I can't let Mama see this."

We didn't have much. Or the finest. Yet, Dorothy Banks was adamant about keeping what we had clean and neat.

Don't ever leave this house looking unloved.

For Mama, walking around wrinkled, with a hanging hem, or your slip showing was a cardinal sin. But one I hadn't committed. When I left earlier, that sweater had been in good condition. Obviously, I'd damaged it falling backwards down Miss Celestine's steps.

"Just another something to add to the dismal failure this night has been."

Our ringing phone stopped me from chasing that bitter conclusion.

I answered, thinking Doc Stanton's having the room specially wired for our own phone line was one of those nice things he did that often made me forget he was a White man.

"Dorothy Banks' residence—"

"Why'd Ransome say for me to call you? Are you okay? Did you do it?" Sadie's whispered words flew so fast and hard it felt like she was in the room with me.

"Hold on." I scrambled to the door that led to the hallway and opened it, making sure Mama wasn't approaching before quietly shutting it and hurrying back to the phone and answering Sadie. "No."

"'No' what, Mattie? You're not okay or you didn't do it?"

Grabbing a pair of pedal pushers and a plain, short-sleeved blouse, I slipped them on, glad that leaving a blouse untucked was fashionable, and okay around the house. Plopping onto my bed, I answered Sadie, knowing I was about to get an earful. "'No' to both."

"What happened?"

"I don't feel like going into it right now."

"Am I supposed to care about what you do or don't want to discuss? You had me sitting up here ready to lie to your mama. Not to mention I was worried. So, like it or not, tell me *something*."

"Listen, Sadie—"

Mama's opening the door halted my continuing. "Why're you and Sadie on the phone when you just left there? And when'd you get in?"

"A few minutes ago."

"You better not tell me you walked home in the dark."

"No, ma'am. Ransome dropped me off. Sadie rode with us." I added that lie so my mother wouldn't know I'd been in a car alone with a man. If she knew I'd been with Ransome, Peabo, *and* Short Stuff she'd flip her lid.

"Why's your lip busted?"

Taking Ransome's advice, I'd fabricated a lie. "Me and Sadie got carried away pillow-fighting and I fell off the bed."

"You were playing instead of working on your project?"

"No, ma'am... I mean, yes ma'am, but we finished it."

Mama eyeballed me like her truth detector smelled something, but before she could dig deeper Abby flounced into our room. I always thought it unfair how she, unlike her brother, had inherited her mother's mousy brown hair, watery green eyes, and nondescript looks. "Did you tell her already, Dorothy?"

"I didn't, but—"

"No, don't. I want to. Mattie, hang up the phone and come on." An indulged southern darling accustomed to commanding others, Abby took the phone from my hand and chirped into it. "Mattie'll have to call you back, whoever this is." Placing the handset in its cradle, she pulled me off the bed, demanding I close my eyes while positioning her hands over them.

Lord, I'm not interested in this girl's shenanigans. "Abby, what're you doing?"

"Just play along. And no peeking."

Abigail Stanton and I hadn't played anything in years. Not since she'd wholeheartedly embarked on her quest to be a true paragon of a well-raised young woman moving and flowing in the upper echelons of Montgomery.

Not that you're beneath me or nothing, Mattie. It's just not proper for us to carry on the way we could when we were dumb little kids.

Making up stories and sharing adventures, we'd grown up in the same household and had been each other's readily available playmate. We fought. We fussed. Loved and hugged. She was spoiled, overly sensitive, and temperamental. Still... honestly? Sometimes I missed Abby. But my mother had long ago "learned me" how our friendship would inevitably dissolve and change with age. It was society. Tradition.

"Abby, don't you run me into nothing." Those words were barely out of my mouth when my hip connected with the hallway table. "Ouch."

"Sorry. Here. Hold my hand, but keep your eyes closed."

"Just hurry up so I can get back to what I was doing."

"Dorothy, get her other hand."

"You asking or telling?" Having helped raise the Stanton kids, Mama never minced words with them.

"Please."

Together, they moved me into what I knew to be the dining room where Doc and Miz Stanton were eating dessert, chatting, and sounding extra pleased until Abby shushed their conversation.

"Okay, Mattie, are you peeking?"

"Abby, come on already."

"You never did like surprises. Fine. Open your eyes."

I did—only to wish I hadn't.

There at the dining-room table eating a huge helping of Mama's peach cobbler, sat Edward, his crutches propped against the wall.

My mouth fell open.

Mistaking my speechlessness for excitement, Abby chirped brightly, "I know, huh? Mama ain't been feeling the best lately, so Daddy arranged it to help cheer her up two whole days early."

"Hey, Mattie."

Struggling to breathe, I couldn't respond to that raven-haired, purple-eyed, good-looking White boy who'd fathered my child.

CHAPTER FOUR

Ashlee

Clearly, overindulging in fettuccine alfredo with red pepper flakes too late on a Friday night resulted in my mind doing strange things Saturday morning. I was dreaming. Of running water. Steam. The scent of sandalwood and masculinity. Strong hands. Warm lips. And deep, intense loving. Even in my sleep my senses expanded, my body tingled. Moved towards satisfaction.

Mouth parting, head pressing against my pillow, I startled awake feeling my pajama top being raised and something wet stroking my nipple. My mouth opened in a scream.

"Babe… it's me."

"Brad?" Pushing up onto my elbows, I squinted in the darkness as if that could help my vision. "What're you doing here?"

He stroked and licked my breast in between speaking. "It's kind of *our* residence."

"Your flight wasn't due until this evening."

"I changed it."

"Why?"

Pulling me down onto my back, he placed a hand between my legs. "For this."

Leave it to Mister Pragmatic to not beat around the bush.

Sleepily, I grinned at my unintended pun, considering his hand position. "I didn't hear you come in."

"You were asleep. I was quiet."

"What… did it cost… to change… your flight?" My words were breathy. Spaced apart. A natural response to his slow, controlled movements.

"Can we table the money talk?"

"Mmm-hmm," was all I could manage as his mouth resumed its titillating exploration of my breast. "Oh. God."

Delicious sensations rolled like waves through my flesh. Left me drifting. Panting. Made me wonder why it had been so long since we'd last made love. What had it been? Five, six weeks? Which, for us, was unheard of, even scary. I wasn't getting sexual satisfaction elsewhere. Was he?

"Enough thinking, baby."

Brad knew me and my stellar ability to overthink things. He also knew how to shut that down and command my attention.

"*Mmm, honey, yes.*"

Wrapping my hand about his neck, I felt his hair, damp from the shower he'd clearly just had, and that had crept into my subconscious. His skin was fragrant with the sandalwood soap I'd bought him. When he stopped tormenting my breasts long enough to kiss me, his lips tasted like toothpaste and sexiness.

Starved for his loving, I eased a hand between us, pulling a groan from him.

"*Damn.*"

My moan coinciding with Brad's single-syllable pleasure, I wrapped my thighs about his trim waist and gave in to the magic.

Our rhythm was right. Our heat and hunger were high. Captured by the raw, wild needs of our bodies we rode every wave until exploding together in a climax that was mind-shattering and wide.

*

"For my lazy lady of leisure."

Seated on our back patio, I laughed as my love served me the only breakfast he knew how to make. I raised a hand like an eager student. "Ooo, teacher, let me guess what it is."

His sanguine mood after all that *brown sugar* reflected on his face. "Go ahead."

"An egg-white omelet with chicken apple sausage, smoked gouda, mushrooms and green onions, right?"

"Wrong. We're out of gouda, so you get cheddar."

Hand at my chest, I flopped sideways in my chair, pantomiming shock. "Dear God, call the gouda squad."

"Ha. Ha."

Grinning at each other as he sat across from me, I felt the absence of our old familiar comforts. The date nights alone, or with other couples. Weekend getaways. Spontaneous outings. Cooking dinner together. Flowers delivered to my office just because. Pillow talk and me rubbing his forehead until he fell asleep. Him massaging my feet. Deep emotional intimacy and unquestionable connectivity.

I miss us.

Too often lately, we'd been at each other's throats. Arguing over incidental things amounting to nothing. Irritable. Impatient. Synergy completely off. Our enjoyment in each other's presence had seemingly been relegated to the past. I'd started going to bed without him, leaving Brad in front of the TV in the great room or at his laptop working. It was as if our love was under attack and we'd silently retreated to our respective corners rather than fight for it or each other. We'd become so unrecognizable that I'd started questioning if he was truly "the one."

Staring across the patio table, noting his bed head and that post-coital sparkle in his eyes, I glimpsed the boyish charm beneath the sexy appeal and remembered why I'd chosen to let myself fall in love with him. "This is good. Thanks, baby."

"I do my best cooking after sex."

"That's sad."

"What?"

I ran my foot up his inner thigh. "You missed an opportunity to man-brag about your best cooking occurring *during* the act."

His slow, crooked grin was confident. "That goes without saying."

"Whatever, Bradley Caldwell. So, why'd you come home early?"

"Let's see…" Dropping his fork on his plate, he lifted a finger with every grievance. "One: you left your job. Two: you hung up on me. Three: you subsequently refused my calls and texts. So, four: considering myself utterly ghosted—"

"I didn't ghost you."

"Come on, bae, own up to playing shady."

"'Playing shady,' B.C.?"

"I'm not trying to read you, I'm just saying."

I laughed at his colloquial vernacular. "I need you to stop talking like you know something."

"It's what happens when you dip it in chocolate." He made a sexualized gesture with his tongue that left me laughing. "Changes your whole vocabulary."

"To think you used to be so White," I teased, enjoying long-missed banter and cavorting.

"I still am."

"You know what I mean." When we first met at a legal networking soiree four years ago, I wasn't particularly attracted to him despite his undeniable sexiness. Three years my senior, I thought him stiff, long-winded and seemingly ensconced in a cloak of pale-male privilege. But as the evening progressed, I warmed up, we exchanged contact information, and he called the next day concerned I may have considered him overbearing. Confirming that fact, he'd apologized, admitting he'd been uncommonly, inordinately nervous. I'd questioned why.

I've never encountered your kind of beauty. You made a babbling idiot out of me.

I'd considered that a flattering lie, but when he invited me to meet up at a smoothie bar I accepted, wondering what new brand of nerd I was dealing with.

And he was that. Nerdy. Brilliant. Intense. Passionate about legal and social justice. Uptight with questionable dance skills and a penchant for being clueless. But as weeks passed he relaxed, allowing me to experience his intrinsic essence without fear counterfeiting as cockiness. He was gentle, compassionate, had a sexy flare for fashion, and treated me with respect and dignity. That didn't mean I wanted to be with him. Unlike Brad's forays into interracial dating, my relationships had been exclusively with African-American men. He'd challenged me to consider new possibilities; to not hide behind our nation's painful racial history but to define my own wants and needs.

He was enchanted. I was intrigued, yet leery.

"I'm absolutely disinterested in participating in some massa-tipping-to-the-slave-quarters sexual fantasies."

Such was my flagrant response when questioned about my ongoing hesitation to a potential relationship.

He'd been offended but it had opened opportunities for deep, painfully frank discussions.

Raised by activists who'd instilled a deep sense of pride in me, the burden of race relations had made it impossible for me to come to the relationship without four hundred years of oppressive history about my neck. It was pathetic that even in this day such things had to be contemplated. But I admired Brad, and loved myself too much to engage in some Kumbaya, fake love-is-blind brand of romance.

I spent three months testing the constructs and depth of our budding relationship, as well as resisting him, before surrendering to the crazy way Brad moved me, and falling into bed with him and satisfying my needs. He was one of the most thoroughly attentive lovers I'd ever experienced and I went in for seconds and thirds as if ensuring some rare fluke hadn't made it so powerful and damn explosive. Four years later, despite our unraveling simpatico, or the recent infrequency of lovemaking, our sex was still insane... when it happened. And Brad wasn't as white bread as I'd initially pegged him. The man was suave and had a little swag.

"Back to the ghosting. You're right." I ate some humble pie. "It was juvenile. I apologize."

He took a long swig of cranberry juice before propping his arms on the table and leaning towards me. "What's wrong with us? Why are we so disjointed lately?"

Spearing a final bite of omelet, I held my fork suspended in air while citing contributory factors. "Work stress. Miscommunication. Not carving out time for each other. The usual culprits."

Leaning back, he studied me before shaking his head. "Yes. But no. It's something else."

I ate that last bite, before suggesting, "Maybe we should consider counseling."

"Agreed. Are you still in love with me?"

I didn't answer immediately. Rather, I gave his question some thought, concluding that I was. "Yes." Yet, we were suffering an elusive disconnect.

"You sure? I mean, it took you long enough to answer." His voice was tight enough to break.

"Brad, let's not. You know me well enough to know I wouldn't be here if I didn't."

Nodding, he conceded the point. "Even so, people can get to a place where love isn't enough. Is that us?"

Leaning back, I massaged my scalp, closed my eyes, and sighed. "Possibly."

We sat in prolonged silence until he posed an impossible question. "What do you need that you're not getting?"

That was a trillion-dollar inquiry. Unfortunately, I only had a buck-fifty.

It's like when your finances are slim and you mentally compile lists of everything you want and would buy. *If.* Then when extra cash finds its way into your hands you can't recall a doggone wish from your list. That's how I felt lately.

I'd had private conversations with myself about the long-lived frustration that had seemingly taken up residence beneath the surface of my skin. I'd met my educational goals. My career was on track, at least until three days ago. But sitting across from Brad, my personal aspirations felt distant. Marriage. Children. The current state of our relationship left me disillusioned. "I appreciate that question, but right now I'm not sure I have all the answers."

"Fair enough. Let's tackle this a different way. Name five things you enjoy or that make you happy."

"Drawing. Music. Reading. Travel. My family." Citing that list had me realizing how long it had been since I'd indulged these needs. True, I listened to music while driving to and from work, but I couldn't remember the last concert we'd attended. I hadn't drawn or painted in forever, and talking with my family via phone wasn't the same as sharing time in person. A pang of regret ripped through my gut. My parents and grandparents lived less than four hours away and I hadn't seen them in too long because of chasing a promotion that hadn't happened.

Shameful, Ashlee.

Enmeshed in self-recrimination, I nearly missed the dark shadow clouding Brad's face.

"List one thing you would change if given the opportunity." His voice was tight, deep.

"Are you okay?"

"Just answer the question. Please."

I eyed him a moment, wondering what his problem was, before responding. "My career."

"You mean your job?"

"No…" I sat up, my posture straightening as I realized what I'd unleashed into the atmosphere. My evasive wish list was becoming clear. "I'm no longer satisfied with my career." That admission felt wonderfully frightening. "I need something other than what I have—"

"Including me."

"No. Wait… *what?*"

"You're aware I wasn't—this relationship wasn't—mentioned on your list of satisfying things?"

I made a Black Girl Magic move: rolled my eyes, and sucked my teeth. "Let's not do this."

"I asked a direct question. You provided an honest answer. You're dissatisfied with us."

"Ummm, hello? Were you not present five minutes ago when we both admitted being displeased with the current state of our relationship?"

"Is your displeasure based on matters that are conditional, temporary, and merely symptomatic? Or is what we have inherently flawed? As in, ingrained and incapable of change?"

"You are not my professor, and I'm not your student. You're not grading a paper, so stop dissecting and analyzing. You asked me to name things I enjoy and I did. Why're you reading into the fact that I didn't specifically mention you?"

"Is it unreasonable to expect the woman I love to want me?"

"Oh, God. What're we doing? You're bigger than this, Brad. Stop acting insecure."

His barked laughter was clipped. "I'm insecure? Like a little bitch?"

"You said it."

We mean-mugged each other until he pushed back his chair and tossed his napkin on the table. "I'm going to the gym."

I watched him walk away, his back rigid enough to break.

Unleashing post-battle energy, I showered, dressed, and cleaned the breakfast dishes before attacking dirt and evil dust bunnies, sanitizing countertops, and separating laundry. I ignored the "dry-clean only" pile, knowing my being off work the next two weeks eradicated that need.

Tasks complete, I checked my watch to see I had enough time to check in with my family before picking up Torrie. Dropping onto my favorite, oversized chair, phone in hand, I was ready to get answers from my mother. She'd finally returned my call yesterday, en route to some auxiliary meeting. The conversation had been rushed and brief. I'd disconnected feeling as if she were hiding something. Calling my daddy proved equally frustrating.

"Well, Ladybug, I'd rather us wait and talk when your mother's available."

Whatever they needed to disclose required a two-parent conference call? *Lord, please don't let them be getting a divorce.*

To my knowledge, my parents were still very much in love and weren't experiencing marital problems. But then again, I hadn't been home in nearly a year and, unbeknown to me, problems may have transpired. Plus, Savannah James Turner was one of those Black mothers who'd quickly tell me, "I'm not one of your little friends." That typically applied to putting an errant, sass-talking child back in line. In this case, it meant I was not her confidante privy to grown folks' business. That didn't deter me from praying, while calling, they'd fully disclose whatever needed disclosing.

"Hey, Ladybug." My father's deep voice flooded the phone, bringing a smile to my lips.

"Hi, Daddy. How're you?"

"Blessed to be in the land of the living. You?"

"I'm good."

"Brad?"

"Is that Ashlee?" My mother interrupting in the background relieved me of having to answer an innocuous but unwanted question.

"Yes."

"Tell her to hold on while I grab the other phone. Dial Avery in. And don't say anything else until I'm on the other extension."

My parents were the only people I knew still using landlines with multiple connections.

"Did you hear those instructions?"

"Yes, sir, I did."

"I guess we just violated them by talking. You think she'll be mad?"

"If we get in trouble I'm blaming you," I teased while dialing my brother.

"*Pshhh!* I'm not afraid of her. That's your mama, not mine."

"I hope you two realize I've picked up the other line and can hear you."

Daddy and I laughed.

"Hi, Mama. How're you feeling?"

"Oh… not the best." She sounded exhausted.

That had me sitting up straight, tensing. "What's going on?"

"'Ey, big head, what's up?" My brother's coming on the line interrupted Mama's response.

"Hey, Avery. Mama and Daddy are here as well." I waited as they exchanged greetings before returning to my earlier line of questioning. "Mama, I'm waiting."

"Avery, is Janelle home?"

"Janelle's in the kitchen with the kids."

"Good. Ashlee, where's Brad?"

Mama's asking about my sister-in-law and my lover's whereabouts sent alarming shivers up my spine. "Mama, you're scaring me."

"Is Brad home, baby?"

"No, ma'am. Why?"

"It would be best if he's there with you when…" My mother's voice dissolved as she began to sob.

"Children, I'm going to hang up and go see about your mom. Hold on."

When Daddy disconnected, Mama's sobs increased, scaring the hell out of me.

"Avery, do you know what's going on?"

"No, Sis. I don't." Avery was attentive, connected, as if our roles were reversed and he was the dutiful daughter while I was out in these streets consumed with becoming a success. His not being privy to what was happening added to my fears.

"Mama?"

She didn't respond.

Oh, God. Please don't let anything be wrong with my mother.

A hand over my mouth, an arm about my waist, I sat praying.

Sound was muffled on their end, but I clearly detected my father's soothing tones as he entered whatever room Mama was in. Within seconds, he picked up the connection. "Okay, I'm here."

"Daddy, I can't take this. Is something wrong with Mama?"

His sigh was weighty. "It's Nana Mattie—"

"What's wrong with Nana?" My big, six-foot-three brother sounded as panicked as I felt.

"The cancer has metastasized—"

"Wait. Wait. *Wait.* What cancer?" My voice was shrill, shaky.

"Ladybug, you're fully versed in the fact that your grandmother was diagnosed with ovarian cancer."

"That was years ago, and she's in full remission!"

"Ladybug. Son." Daddy exhaled long and hard. "I hate telling you this, but she isn't."

"*God.*" Avery's helpless moan broke my heart.

"Daddy, please put Mama on the phone," I demanded irrationally, as if a different parent could deliver more favorable data. "Mama?"

"Yes, baby. I'm here." Her voice was so shattered and lifeless that I suddenly preferred speaking with my father.

Tears flooding my face, I could barely whisper. "Mother, help us understand."

None of it made sense. Not the cancer returning. With a vengeance. Or its vicious assault upon other organs. Or the fact that my parents had adhered to my grandmother's wishes not to "disturb" my brother or me with any of it.

I was livid.

"No one thought we had a right to know?"

"Young lady, I understand you're upset but you'd better modify your tone and your volume or else."

"I'm not upset, Mama."

I was devastated.

Disgusted.

Ashamed of the fact that I'd let my Atlanta life and professional aspirations consume my focus and existence. It was the middle of October and I hadn't been home since last Christmas.

Taking a deep breath, I tried composing myself. Now was not the time for self-pity, or shoulda-woulda-coulda indulgences.

"What're our options? Are her oncologists recommending chemo? Radiation? Are there natural alternatives?" While I peppered my mother with relentless questions my brother had become stoically quiet.

My mother was quiet a moment before advising, "The treatments proved harsh and ineffective. Mama elected to forgo them three months ago."

"*Three months ago?* When did she find out the cancer was back?"

"Last Christmas."

The whole family was there. At home that holiday. And no one told Avery or me anything?

I should've known something was off.

Nana and I phoned each other regularly and exchanged texts almost daily. Mentally reviewing our most recent conversations, I realized her texts had been uncharacteristically brief, delayed or oddly phrased. I'd mentioned it to Mama only for her to cite arthritis and forgetfulness or fatigue as reasons for Nana's inconsistencies. Having noticed her weight loss and how her skin seemed slightly discolored on our video chats, I chided myself for overlooking what was in plain sight. Perhaps, out of fear, I'd soothed myself with rationalizations and the bliss of ignorance. Now, there was no reasoning away the truth. A terminal illness had returned. "So... where do we stand?"

My mother knew precisely what I was asking. Yet, I wasn't prepared for her response.

"Two, three months at best."

"No."

"Ladybug—"

"Mama, I can't do this!"

"Ashlee Dionne, hush and listen."

"I can't. That's my nana."

"That's *my* mother! You're not the only one hurting."

"You had her longer. I'm her only granddaughter."

"Sis, come on."

"Avery, don't dictate my response!"

"I'm not, but you're acting as if the impact on you is greater than on anyone else. Don't be so damn selfish."

"Selfish? I'm—"

"You two will cease this bickering instantly!" My mother's voice had regained its strength. Knowing not to push her, we fell silent. "I will not, *cannot* have this family disintegrating. Not now. Not ever. My father needs me." Mama stalled. "My mother needs me. So, act your age not your shoe size, because I will not be your referee. Get yourselves together. Your grandmother is still here. For however long. We'll be here with her when she's ready to leave. And when she does, our love will let her go."

"Oh no, ma'am! I won't let go."

"Ashlee Dionne, if you don't hush up that Grade-A foolishness—"

"No, Mama. No, ma'am! Nana. Can't. Go."

Over and again that mantra spiraled through my head, the words flying from my mouth in a rhythmic, searing cadence as I stubbornly held onto an idiotic right to keep my grandmother alive.

"*Nana. Can't. Go.*"

I wasn't even aware that I'd fallen to the floor, a supplicant before heaven on bended knees, wailing that lament, or that Brad had walked through the door and was holding, cradling me.

CHAPTER FIVE

Mattie

I put everything into avoiding that smoky-eyed Edward. His being on crutches and not fully mobile certainly helped; still, I knew only time stood between us. I didn't want a confrontation, and definitely wasn't interested in offering explanations as to why I was acting strange. In the past twenty-four hours, I'd made a life-changing decision and didn't want to be talked out of nothing. Besides, the only person I owed an explanation to was Dorothy Banks. No matter how hard I'd stayed awake tossing and turning last night, I couldn't figure out how to tell Mama I was in the family way.

The morning after Edward's advanced arrival, I did as I'd planned, hurrying to the shed as soon as Miz Stanton and Mama left for the market. Entering, I screamed, seeing a critter curled up on the floor. My screaming didn't faze it any. It kept right on doing what it was doing: sleeping.

Creeping near for a closer inspection, it turned out to be little more than a baby.

"Shouldn't you be hibernating?"

I scooped up that garter snake, conceding any confusion wasn't its fault. It was December and should've felt like winter. Instead, the past few days felt like Mother Nature was contemplating revisiting summer.

"You're kinda cute, but you'd better get out of here before Mama gets back and takes a garden hoe to your rear."

Releasing it safely beneath the shrubbery, I hurried back into the shed for my suitcase only to find it missing. It wasn't where I'd left it last night, tucked in a corner. Five minutes later, my frantic searching had produced nothing. That suitcase was long gone as if last night never happened.

Had I imagined it all? The bus ride? That walk to Miss Celestine's and everything that transpired afterward? Perhaps, it was a figment of my imagination, a hyperactive dream. And where precisely *had* I been going? Truth be told, when I boarded that bus yesterday—other than Miss Celestine's—I truly didn't know.

Afraid of being late for school, I ended my futile searching, shut the shed door, and hurried back to the kitchen for my book satchel. Grabbing it, I flew out the door and ran to the bus stop feeling as if running was all I'd been doing lately. Confusion and fear had me fleeing last night, trying to put distance between myself and an uncertain destiny. Now? Wasn't nothing easy ahead of me, but I was clear about one thing. I wanted my baby.

School was a blur. If you'd offered me a hundred dollars to tell you what I'd learned that day, I'd have had the same money I had yesterday. I couldn't concentrate. Mister Lightfoot even called me out for what he perceived as daydreaming. Wasn't nothing light or bright about the thoughts I was thinking.

How much does a baby cost?

I couldn't afford a child on what Mama awarded me for good grades and pop-bottle pocket change. I'd have to quit school and get a job. Only problem was, I'd never been employed, had no suitable skills. Not like Miz James, our librarian, or Mister Reed, Montgomery's Colored mortician. Or even like Mama Bea, the proprietor of her own burger stand. Other than helping my mother at the Stantons' I hadn't worked a day in my life, didn't know how to begin finding employment. The prospect was terrifying.

I can't leave school.

Sometimes Math felt like a foreign language, but I adored Literature, loved learning, and would be devastated if I couldn't continue my studies, and had to drop out before graduation. That very thing happened to Fancy Rae Pruitt last year. She'd been expelled when one of the teachers found her retching in the bathroom. Her parents were called to the principal's office. Fancy Rae confessed to being expectant. That was the last time she walked these hallowed halls where immorality could not exist.

You're next.

Staring out the classroom window, my heart hurt imagining Mama's chagrin at my being rushed from the building as if a scarlet letter dripped blood from my forehead.

"Miss Banks, please begin reading where I left off."

My standing, a battered copy of *Moby Dick* in hand, was an automatic response to my teacher's request. Staring at the pages of that second-hand book, I felt like a fool not knowing where to pick up. Even worse was the fact that Mister Lightfoot knew it.

"You will see me before leaving for lunch, Miss Banks. Have a seat."

I didn't dare glance across the aisle at Sadie. I felt her looking.

Shamefaced, I found the passage where I was supposed to be when another student who was called upon stood to read.

I hate this.

Being caught and having to endure a lecture for not paying attention while everyone else went to lunch was bad enough. But turning a page and being confronted by a blood-chilling drawing obscuring the words was fifty thousand times worse.

"Mister Lightfoot, may I be excused?"

I was out of my seat without even raising my hand and waiting for permission.

"Sit down, Miss Banks."

"Sir... I can't." Grabbing my book, I rushed it to his desk before running from the class, hoping I made it to the commode before that expertly illustrated depiction of a Colored man being lynched had me upchucking in the hallway.

Our school administration did their best to check the interior of the books we inherited after White high schools finished with them, finding and erasing or removing ugly insults directed at us, the new recipients. But sometimes ugliness slipped through the cracks. We'd wind up finding "nigger," "coon," or "sambo" scrawled on the pages we were supposed to learn from. But that drawing? Whoever drew it was a gifted artist. Their pencil sketch showcased with gross accuracy the naked body of a Negro man hanging from a tree, his genitalia brutally missing.

"Mattie?"

Having upchucked my guts, I was sitting on the floor of the one and only stall when Sadie walked in. I didn't respond, just sat there with my knees pulled to my chest, staring at nothing.

"Mister Lightfoot asked me to check on you. What happened?"

"I'm fine, Sadie. Go back to class."

"I will once you open this door and tell me what happened. Did those crazy White kids write something nasty in that book?"

"I wish."

"Well, what was it?"

Opening my mouth, I couldn't speak, overwhelmed by the brutal image. Instead, I started bawling.

"Mattie. Open the door."

I didn't. I just sat there letting hurt seep from my body into my tears. Next thing I knew, Sadie was on the ground, wiggling her way up under the stall door. "What're you doing?"

"Rescuing my best friend."

"I don't need rescuing. And there's not enough room in here for both of us," I fussed, trying to reposition myself as Sadie squeezed against the opposite wall. When she finished all her wiggling and contorting, our ankles were overlapping, knees bumping, like two overgrown peas in a tight pod. "Sadie James, you're ridiculous."

"I do my best." She smiled triumphantly. "Now, what got you going?"

Taking a deep breath, I told her what I'd seen. The horror on her face perfectly reflected mine.

I whispered my fear. "I can't bring a baby into this hateful world. What if it's a boy and something like that happens to him? Or what if she's a girl and…"

Thinking on that J.T. who'd accosted me on the side of the road last night and what might've happened—what *had* happened to too many other Colored bodies since slavery—I couldn't finish.

Sadie whispered in kind. "Does this mean you're going back to Miss Celestine?"

"No. I can't do that either. This child might not've got here the matrimonial way, but it deserves to live."

"So you're keeping it?"

That little sliver of confidence I'd gained outside the toolshed that morning was suddenly suspect. "I don't know… I guess… I don't have a clue how to be somebody's mama. What if I make a mess?"

Sadie was quiet before stating, "You know there're orphanages for Colored children."

That had me shivering, thinking on rumors I'd heard of such places feeding children once a day, or allowing baths only when expecting visits from prospective adoptive parents. I'd even heard that wards were chained to their beds at night to prevent stealing from the kitchen… which wouldn't happen if those children had been fed properly to begin with. Those orphanages were unfit, mirroring society with their paltry resources and unkempt or unfair conditions for innocent children. All because of their skin. "Oh God, Sadie. All the race ugliness in this world and half of that lives in this child."

"What?"

"Its daddy's White. That side might make it hate the other half of itself. It could grow up despising me, my mama, and everybody else not living in pale skin."

Sadie held my hand. "Guess you're gonna have to figure out how to teach the daddy's blood to think another way."

The rest of the school day was a bigger blur. Lunch was spent half-listening to our group of friends whispering about what happened on the bus yesterday. Most of it was misconstrued or imaginative. Some fanciful person dared to claim Miz Rosa had resisted arrest and hit one of those police officers in the head with her pocketbook. I'd been there and knew it was a fib but didn't bother correcting misinformation. I was quiet. My mind was occupied, dreading going home and having to interact with Edward.

Of course what you dread is what happens. I think that's in the Bible, the book of Job, or something. My returning home, slipping through the kitchen door, and slamming smackdab into Edward is precisely what occurred. Literally.

I crashed into him so hard I had to catch him on his crutches.

"Well, hello to you too, Mattie." He laughed, showing those perfectly set teeth framed by full, almost Negroid lips. Favoring Doc Stanton with that jet-black hair and those purplish eyes, Edward was a looker and knew it.

"Sorry."

"Don't be. I've missed you."

I stepped away, intending to escape into my room but his gripping my hand halted that.

"Wait, Mattie, don't leave."

I'd never been afraid of Edward. We'd tormented each other and played together as kids. But his standing there, leaning on crutches and still being over six feet made him suddenly seem too much like a man.

"Where's everybody?" I asked.

"Mother's at her bridge game. Miz Boynton down the street asked Dorothy to help her with some curtains 'cause her maid's out sick. And Abby's at some extra choir practice for Christmas." We both knew Doc Stanton was at his office and not due for two hours. "Guess that means it's just us. You look good, Mattie. Different somehow. But nice."

I didn't like his open smile, or how his eyes roamed over me. It wasn't the way that foul-breathed boy had eyed me last night, all leering and nasty. Still, it held something hungry. Like he wished we could revisit doing the thing that left me missing my monthly.

"I have homework."

"Mattie, it's Friday. You've all weekend to tackle it. Come on. Sit down. Let's chat. Don't be your normal stubborn self," he added, pulling a grin from me.

"Five minutes is all you get."

"It's enough. I was about to make a sandwich. Want one?"

"No, thanks," I declined, despite not eating much that day. I was still wary about what my belly could and couldn't tolerate. "Want me to make it for you?"

Hobbling towards the Frigidaire, he laughed. "Don't act like Mother, treating me like I'm an invalid. How's life? School?"

"Fine. You?"

"Other than this leg ending my football season, everything's copacetic."

"Does it hurt?"

"It hurt like the dickens when it happened, but it's tolerable now and I've become a pro on these crutches. I told Dad I was fine and could tough it out until the semester ended. Plus, I kinda liked the sympathy I was getting from the fairer sex."

"You shoulda defied your mother and stayed on campus," I snapped, acting jealous, and knowing once Miz Stanton got an idea in her head nothing and no one but God could steer her from it. "Why'd you come home early if everything was so peachy keen?"

He waited until he and his sandwich were seated at the table before answering. "Because I liked the idea of seeing you. How come you never wrote me back?"

I suddenly found my book satchel fascinating and worth my interest, and started toying with the strap. "I didn't feel like it."

"Because?"

"Because that whole letter was ignorant, which is why I burned it. What if someone else had checked the mail instead of me?"

"Getting the mail has been your chore since you were ten. I wasn't worried." He bit into his sandwich as if the world rotated as he willed. "I wanted you to know what we shared… the night of my going-away party, wasn't frivolous. It meant something to me."

"It meant something to me, too. It meant we shouldn't have been drinking."

He grunted in the back of his throat the same way Doc Stanton did when reading something fascinating in the newspaper. "Is that all it was, us drinking too much after everyone else left?"

Staring into those violet-colored eyes was like staring into a magic crystal capable of sending you backwards in time to relive an event. Just like that, I was back at Labor Day weekend helping Mama set up and serve at Edward's cook-out and going-away party—seemingly attended by half the White population of Montgomery.

The night had been a mess of live music, wall-to-wall White folks, and excessive food. I'd spent the whole week helping Mama prepping what could be prepped in advance. With both Doc and Miz Stanton coming from money, their home in Old Cloverdale sat on a near acre and the back lawn was huge. Unfortunately, that meant Mama and me running from pillar to post like waiters in some fancy restaurant. By the time the last guests left, it was after midnight. Thanking Mama for her hard work, Doc and Miz Stanton turned in, leaving us to handle the aftermath.

"Go to bed, Dorothy. Abby, Mattie, and me can handle the clean-up."

Plumb exhausted from that night and every effort she'd expended leading up to it, my mother accepted Edward's generosity and the "thank you" kiss he'd placed on her cheek before heading to bed.

Turning on a transistor radio, the three of us cleaned, with Edward and Abby chattering about how much fun the night had been.

Ten minutes in, Abby was finished. "My beauty rest calls. Y'all can handle this."

We did. In a companionable silence that lasted several minutes until Edward broke it.

"The night was great, huh, Mattie?"

"For you. Not me." I was like Mama in that I never bit my tongue with him or Abby.

"Sorry... I wasn't thinking. You should've invited Sadie or somebody."

"For what? To help serve and clean?"

He stood there beneath a string of lights draping the backyard, red-faced, and looking apologetic before walking over and taking the trash bag from my hands. "Come on."

Leading me to the makeshift bar that had been set up outdoors, he forced me onto a seat.

"What're you doing?"

"Miss Mattie Banks, after all you've done to make my going-away celebration a success, you deserve to relax. Name your poison." He went behind the bar and found two glasses.

I simply laughed. "I don't drink."

"I don't either… Well, I've sipped some of Dad's whiskey. But I'm eighteen and on my way to college come Monday, so that makes a man out of me."

"Well, I'm not a man."

His voice dropped, and his words came out slowly. "I know. And I'm glad." Correcting his tone, he lightened it again. "Here. Try this."

"What is it?" I eyeballed the festive-looking drink in my glass.

"Sangria. Just fruit and juice."

"I might be younger than you, but I wasn't born yesterday."

"Fine. It also contains rum and wine. Just try it. If it's horrible, I'll find something to your liking."

I enjoyed that first sip a little too much. One sip became two glasses. And another with more rum added. By the time we'd finished our fifth, with twice as much rum as fruit and juice, we were laughing, telling stories, and trying to finish each other's sentences until he brought up my foolishness.

"Why'd you kiss me last week?"

It had only been a peck on his cheek before I took off running. Something done so Sadie wouldn't have bragging rights. Well past tipsy, I answered truthfully. "Because Sadie dared me to. Well not to kiss *you*. But we had to kiss a boy before summer ended. Whoever did it first would win. You were the only one convenient."

"Well then, you didn't win 'cause that was some sorry kiss on the cheek. Not the lips."

"It was close enough so hush."

He laughed before asking, "There aren't any Colored boys you like that you could've kissed?"

"Who said anything about liking you, Edward Stanton?"

Reaching across the slim space between us, he stroked my cheek. "Do you?"

The liquor wouldn't let me lie. "I don't know. Maybe. Sometimes."

Lately, I'd experienced too many confusing feelings towards him. And if how frequently I'd caught Edward watching me was an indicator, he might've been caught up in his own unsettling musings. Maybe it was his getting ready to leave. Or my body constantly developing and hips spreading. Whatever the reason, to me we'd started to feel less like longtime residents of the same household, and more like members of the opposite gender.

"Have you managed to get a boyfriend since then, Mattie?"

"That's none of your business."

"Fair enough, but I don't have a girlfriend."

"Who cares?"

Laughing, he'd placed my glass atop the bar and pulled me from my seat. "Let's dance."

Our drunken dancing was probably more like wobbling and stumbling. Still, I'll never forget being serenaded by The Penguins' "Earth Angel" while in the circle of his embrace. Or how he tenderly kissed my forehead. My nose. Cheeks. Lips. Before moving to my neck, his gentle but insistent attentiveness unleashing wild sensations throughout my flesh. Or his whispering in my ear how sweet I tasted.

How we wound up behind that shed, atop one of the reclining lounge chairs meant for lazing about the in-ground pool that Miz Stanton commissioned only to ax the plans after hearing about a boy drowning over in Huntsville, was anyone's guess.

Undressing each other just enough, we lay atop that recliner kissing, touching. Discovering. Until I answered his whispered, "Can we?," by relaxing my legs in welcome. Biting hard on my lip to prevent a pain-filled scream when he pressed into me, I freely gave Edward my body, my virginity.

"It was more than us being drunk, Mattie. I've liked you a long time. I just didn't want to admit it." His statement pulled me back to the present, away from Sangria and sin.

Staring him in the eyes, I lowered my volume to match his. "Nothing good can come of those feelings, so you might as well forget 'em."

"What if I don't want to?"

"Then you're a purple-eyed fool."

His throwing his head back on a laugh coincided with Abby's chattering nearing the back door. She burst into the kitchen, arms loaded, talking a mile a minute.

"I told 'em Peggy Boynton sounded like a cat with its tail caught in a blender. Everybody knows I'm a pure soprano. That 'O, Holy Night' solo should've been mine. But nobody was interested in what I had to say on the subject."

I looked at her like she was crazy. "Who're you talking to?"

Glancing back at empty air, she giggled. "Your mama was behind me. She must've stopped to chat with the gal watering the front lawn across the street. Oh, Mattie, I found your suitcase in the shed this morning when I was looking for old jars for my art project. I didn't find one decent jar. I bet Gillis broke 'em."

My heart started beating rapidly. "Where'd you put my suitcase?"

She stared at me, lips poked out. "There's no need for shouting, Mattie. It's on your bed. And why're you all packed up in the first place? You running away or something?" She giggled as if she'd told a supremely funny joke.

Before I could race to my room and hide the evidence of my intent, Mama walked in the back door, arms as loaded as Abby's, looking mildly frustrated. "Hey, baby girl. How was school?"

"Dorothy, you didn't hear a thing I said about Peggy Boynton stealing my solo," Abby butted in before I could answer.

"We live in a real world that doesn't always give us what we want, Abigail. Trust that I know something about that," Mama stated, peering at Edward and me. "What're you two doing?"

"Mattie's being a good sport listening to my boring college escapades," Edward lied. "That looks heavy. Let me help."

"No, don't try anything extra, Eddie. You're on crutches. Mattie can manage," said Abby, clearly misunderstanding that her brother had been offering his help to Mama, and dumped her bundle on the table in front of me.

"What's this?" I fingered what looked and smelled like old, faded linens.

"A gift from Miz Boynton. Come and help me cart it to the room," Mama instructed.

"Yes, ma'am."

"Dorothy, I wasn't finished telling you what happened." I hated when Abby whined, which was daily, but right then I loved her for it.

"What, honey?"

Mama's stopping to hear her complaint gave me the opportunity to hurry ahead. The suitcase sat in the center of my bed just like Abby had indicated. Hurrying inside, I knew I wouldn't have time to unpack and hide it. Hearing Mama's footsteps approaching, I dumped that pile of old linens on top of it just before Mama entered.

Closing the door behind her, she dropped the handled shopping bag she carried and sank wearily onto her bed.

"Mama, what's wrong?"

Sadly, she shook her head. "Four hours, baby. All that time spent taking down Miz Boynton's old curtains, ironing, and hanging up the new, for nothing."

"She didn't pay you?"

"That old bat said the pay was five dollars, but what did I walk away with?" Mama kicked the shopping bag. "Some musty curtains I can't do nothing with. Talking about 'these have been in my family for years, so consider yourself honored to have them.'" Mama sucked her teeth. "Honey, don't nobody want some mess that's been hanging around since the Civil War ended. Wasted my time off…"

The Stantons had a tradition of dining out every Friday, so other than the groceries, Friday was Mama's light day, with Miz Stanton letting her off a few hours early. If money permitted, sometimes Mama spent that free time at a picture show, with or without one of her girlfriends. Other times she attended a reading class at the church or maybe sat in the Colored section of the park. Whatever Mama did, it didn't include spending her free moments helping a neighbor lady down the street for cast-off curtains.

"I swear. Sometimes these crackers make me wish I wasn't a Christian. What can I do with six panels of heavy, musty-dusty outdated curtains in this small, one-window room? I shoulda known that five-dollar dream was too good to be true."

Hugging my mama, I kissed her cheek. "I'm sorry that happened."

"Me too, baby." She sighed. "At least that old nasty husband of hers wasn't home. Let me see your lip. It looks better than it did last night, but you and Sadie need to quit all that pillow-fighting and mind your schooling."

"Yes, ma'am. Where do you want me to put these?" I indicated the shopping bag.

"The rubbish bin." Mama and I laughed. "Oh, wait. Before I forget, hand me my pocketbook."

Locating it at the bottom of the wardrobe where we hung our clothes, I handed it to her.

"Thanks. A lady slipped me this when we were making groceries this morning. Explain it for me."

Well versed in my mother's code language, I knew that whatever was on that folded sheet of paper was beyond her reading ability.

My mother came from a family of sharecroppers who moved wherever seasons and harvests sent them, so her childhood had been nomadic. That, and the fact that her family needed her help in the fields, meant her education had been inconsistent, resulting in her having a reading level of someone younger than me. I made sure she knew how proud I was of her taking reading classes at church. Still, sometimes—particularly when she was tired—she didn't like stumbling over her words while reading in front of me. Her "explain it for me" was her way of signaling that she'd already tried and failed to decipher the mimeographed notice in its entirety.

Sitting beside her and reading aloud at a pace she could follow, I was half-way through before gasping. "Mama, is this really happening?"

"You see it right there in writing, Mathilda Ilene. So, I suppose it is. Close your mouth and keep reading."

Forgetting about proceeding at a pace Mama could follow, I finished quickly then sat staring at her, saying nothing.

"Well, baby, guess we gotta find you a different way to and from school."

"We're boycotting?"

Mama nodded. "They're asking all Colored folks to stay off the buses Monday."

"Just Monday, or longer?"

"At least Monday, in honor of Miz Parks' going to trial that same day. If it takes longer than that?" Mama shrugged. "Oh, well."

"But what's a boycott gonna prove?"

"It's not about proving anything, Mattie. It's about standing in solidarity. Demanding change. It's called 'public transportation' for a reason. We're part of the public. We have a right to ride and to be treated right. Not hollered at and talked to like we're children. Not forced to stand 'cause the back of the bus is crowded even when the front Reserved section has a whole mess of empty seats. Or having to stand so White folks can sit. No more of this being left at the curb after we've put our money in. Or the driver passing us by and not stopping to begin with. And why we gotta put our money up front and enter at the rear like some bastardized citizens? They don't treat us right? They ain't getting our dimes. And money's the only language some White folks respect. Take that away, maybe they'll hear what we been saying. So whether or not it goes past Monday, at least they gonna reckon that one day. Understand?"

"Yes, ma'am."

"So, you stay off them city buses till I say otherwise. Lord, I wish I coulda been on that bus to see what transpired last night."

I was.

The urge to tell Mama I'd been there and witnessed everything was strong. But that would require my explaining why I was on there in the first place.

"Guess I'd best get up from here and do something with these curtains."

I nearly lunged for the pile concealing the suitcase atop my bed. "I can carry these. Wait, Mama. These old things can keep. Why don't you treat yourself to a bath?"

The clawfoot tub Miz Stanton no longer wanted and moved into our bathroom took up more than half the space and was a beautiful eyesore. Time rarely permitted for luxuriating in it, but I needed Mama out of the room so I could deal with my secret sitting beneath the curtains.

"Are you tryna get rid of me?"

I gave Mama my most innocent smile. "No, ma'am. You weren't treated fairly today, so you're treating yourself to a long bath."

Someone knocked on the door, entering before Mama could say, "Come in."

"Dorothy... oh good, Mattie's here as well. I've been so busy lately, it keeps slipping my mind to tell you we'll be hosting the end-of-the-season celebration."

Mama stood and faced Miz Stanton. "Ma'am?"

"I know, Dorothy. I know. The football team typically holds its award shindig at the lodge, but there was an unfortunate pipe leak the other day and there's no way everything'll be repaired and back together in time to host the dinner in two weeks. I figure we have all this room, so why not here? We can even set up on the back lawn if this unseemly Indian summer doesn't stop. Plus, it's customary for the prior year's scholarship recipient to pin the new awardee. So, it makes perfect sense to host the festivities." Having won last year's scholarship, that honor belonged to Edward. "Nonetheless, I know it's close to Christmas and all, but Mattie's here and I've already talked to Jolene Boynton and Ruth Lewis about having their gals help. Let me know if y'all feel y'all need more hands than that. But it shouldn't be too bad with a guest list between seventy-five and a hundred. Oh, and you won't have to cook since it's a catered affair. And the lodge'll send their help to set up tables and linens. We just need you to be in charge like always 'cause we can't trust nobody else to do what you do, Dorothy. Your overseeing all the serving and aftermath is sufficient."

"Yes, ma'am."

I almost flinched when Miz Stanton turned cool eyes on me. "Mattie, I think it's about time we get you fitted. Hopefully those hips won't spread too much more and you can use the same uniform in whoever's house you get hired in once your schooling's done. Dorothy, I need to make a phone call, but meet me at my writing desk in five minutes so we can iron out more details for this dinner."

"Yes, ma'am."

Miz Stanton breezed out the room as quickly as she'd entered.

Mama closed the door, looking fit to be tied. "Lord forgive me, but like hell you will wear some damn uniform, walking around like some starched monkey just so they feel bigger and better than the rest of creation!"

Sweet, mild-mannered, and soft-spoken, my mother wasn't a cussing woman. And never had I heard her speak of her means of earning a living in derogatory terms. To the contrary, she performed her role with dignity. Clearly, Miz Stanton's expecting me to continue a servile legacy was too much for Mama.

"If she thinks I'm sending you to school just so White folks have more servants to choose from, she done lost her damn mind. Mattie, baby, listen to me. Don't you let *nothing* stop you from graduating. Get your diploma, and then you go'n to college—"

"We can't afford college, Mama." I said it despite my fantasies of earning a four-year degree.

"Hush that up! Whatever we gotta do to find a way, we find it. You gonna get a degree like your daddy and I didn't."

"Just 'cause you and Daddy couldn't, that doesn't make you ignorant."

"Baby, I know that. You know that. But some folks only value book smarts. And you got plenty. So, keep it. Finish high school and find yourself a way not to be somebody's live-in. You hear me?"

"Yes, Mama."

"You think this is all I want you to have?" She swept a hand about the cramped confines of our room. "Living in a corner of somebody *else's* house? No, sir. No, ma'am. Your daddy and me had bigger dreams for you. So, if we gotta fight for it we gonna fight 'cause, baby girl, you're better than this. Now, let me go use the restroom and wash my face before I have to stand up there listening to Miz Stanton and her 'Dorothy Do List.'"

"Mama…"

When she paused, I went to her, throwing my arms about her and hugging her hard. "I appreciate everything you do for me. I don't ever want to disappoint you…"

I couldn't finish for the lump in my throat.

"Baby, you ain't never been nothing except my purest blessing." Kissing my forehead and closing the door, she left me alone in our room.

I waited several seconds before running to my bed, flinging aside those curtains and grabbing my suitcase. Frantically unpacking, I was nearly finished when another knock on the door sounded. Expecting Miz Stanton again, I closed that suitcase, thankful my task was virtually finished. "Yes?"

The door slowly opened to reveal Edward and his crutches. He hadn't been in our room since he was a little kid. I was shocked at his presence. "What do you want?"

"You left this on the table."

Suspiciously, I eyed the folded slip of paper in his hands. "That's not mine."

"It is."

When I crossed my arms over my chest and simply stared at him, he placed the paper on my desk, shut the door and left.

I ignored it long enough to finish my task and slip my suitcase beneath my narrow bed where it belonged.

"What game is this stupid boy playing now?" Snatching that paper, I plopped onto my desk chair, unfolded the note, and read words in his sloppy scrawl that I, afterwards, wished I never had.

I love you.

"No, you don't. And no you can't."

Balling up that paper I closed my eyes, head leaned back towards heaven on high, doing all I could not to cry.

CHAPTER SIX

Ashlee

Making the drive home was something I typically enjoyed. The long stretch of highway. Georgia's greenery and open fields. The wide expanse of land that felt as if it held untold secrets and wonderful, maybe frightening, mysteries. I found it relaxing. A perfect way to leave Atlanta behind and decompress before seeing family. Not today. Time was of the essence, and I was plagued by a sense of urgency which led to my booking the first available flight out of Atlanta for Valdosta.

That hour-long flight couldn't happen fast enough to still my nervous energy. The flight attendants had barely finished their safety spiel, served drinks, and pre-packaged snacks before it was time to land. Yet, it all felt too long. As if every second I spent outside of Nana's presence was a waste of breath and substance.

Being a commuter flight, thankfully there weren't very many passengers so that when we landed I didn't have to stand in the aisle playing a waiting game while ten thousand people disembarked ahead of me. I was off of that plane within ten minutes of landing. With just my carry-on and no checked luggage, I hurried through Valdosta Regional Airport easily finding my father parked in the waiting area.

"Hey, Ladybug!" His hug was like cornbread and collard greens: warm, delicious, fortifying. "How's my baby?"

He never should've asked. There in that parking lot on a humid October day, I broke down in my father's embrace. Not caring about possible bystanders, I wept for ignorantly allowing my professional quest to infringe upon time with beloveds, for failing to prioritize matters of importance, for Nana's being pillaged by sickness and disease. I cried my ugly cry like a five-year-old who'd lost its new puppy and skinned both knees. My daddy, my rock, held me until my sorrow was exhausted and I could compose myself again.

Taking an ever-present hankie from his back pocket, he wiped my face just like he had when I was a kid. "Come on. Let's get you in this car and get us both home."

Our conversation wasn't much. Just enough. Nearing that final mile, a familiar comfort started tingling in my soul, rising in sweet waves until my spirit was engulfed in peace. The closer we got, the more my whole self felt light and filled with ease. Despite the circumstances, the spirit of my family's land didn't fail to offer precious tranquility.

"Good God, did Mister Moonlight get bigger since the last time I was home?"

Daddy chuckled. "That's what trees do, Ladybug. They grow."

Tearing my gaze away from the enormous tree in the middle of a verdant field at the start of my family's property, I looked at my father. "I know but Moonlight was already gargantuan."

"Well, he's an old man now and I suspect he's about as big as he'll get."

I appreciated Daddy slowing the car for my benefit.

Rolling down the window, I ignored the sticky autumn air rushing into the confines of the cool interior and deeply inhaled. My nostrils flooded with a rich, lemony fragrance seemingly as sweet as candy. Which was odd, seeing as how Moonlight wasn't in bloom. Still, it made me want to jump out the car, race up the slight incline, and climb those centuries-old limbs like my brother, cousins, and I did when we were kids, picking at Mister Moonlight's magnolia blossoms and rubbing them against our skin, camouflaging the zestiness of our own outdoor scents. Gazing in awe at that gigantic keeper of precious memories, I smiled, envisioning my young self again.

My big brother and I had named the tree one day during childhood play.

"It's just a tree, Avery. Why do we need to name it?" I'd demanded, hands on my six-year-old, nonexistent as of yet, hips.

"'Cause Nana said we gotta respect nature. And if we're gonna keep climbing up and down him, we should know his name and ask his permission."

"Why's he a he and not a she? That's sexist." Proudly, I repeated a word I'd heard my parents use without clue of its definition. "What's sexist mean, anyhow?"

My eight-year-old brother had shrugged his shoulders, and admitted, "I think it has something to do with boys not liking girls who can run faster than them. Okay, because I'm fair we each get to choose a name. The tree'll tell us which one it likes best. You can go first 'cause I'm not sexist."

"I pick Miss Magnolias 'cause her flowers are big and pretty, and magnolias're what Nana said they are."

"That's silly. Those flowers only come out once a year. Why name a whole tree after 'em?"

"'Cause I can, and you won't make me change my choice, Avery Turner, so just get on with it." Even at six I was strong-willed and opinionated.

"Well, I like Mister Moonlight 'cause PopPop said when the full moon hits it just right the tree comes alive."

According to family lore, my grandparents bought our land just for that tree, because Nana's mother claimed her deceased husband's spirit was bound to it. Over the years, as finances and good fortune permitted, additional acreage had been purchased so that ten acres were now in my family's possession. Both my grandparents and parents had built homes here. It was our little corner in a vast world but without doubt, our safe haven.

My brother and I had spent half that long-ago afternoon fussing over the tree's name until diplomatically allowing nature to choose.

"Let's each draw a circle in the dirt. The first circle that gets a bug to crawl into it wins."

Of course, four ants decided Avery's circle was best.

Accusing him of drawing his circle too close to an ant hill, I tossed out those results and demanded a recount with the vigor of a defeated politician. Hip to my opponent's tricks, I wiped out Avery's with my sandal and drew my own circle close to the ant hill. Those traitorous insects marched themselves right around it and headed for Avery's as if he'd been crowned the King of Insects.

Like any sore-losing politician, I accused him of cheating. "You must be hiding some candy!"

Fishing through the pockets of his denim shorts, he'd produced a lint-infested, partially unwrapped piece of taffy.

"See! Those ants were after that sugar. Get rid of it and let's do this again."

Thankfully neither of us had ever had a cavity needing a filling because that taffy my brother shared with me was stale enough to lift enamel from teeth. And again, nature affirmed Mister Moonlight's name when five minutes into our insect vigil, a roly poly crawled from the grass and into Avery's triumphant circle. Our ancient tree had been Mister Moonlight ever since, a beloved sentinel who watched over us with loving vigilance.

Our protector really does look like an old, praying man.

Its gnarled, majestic limbs created a beautiful silhouette of an old man—who playfully donned a flower hat annually—kneeling in praise and prayer. With its proud crown lifted high and a series of lower branches sweeping down then outward on either side, a huge, knobby protrusion had formed on one side of its base—a protective, healing response to someone once running a car into its trunk. My mother had had a front fence erected after that. Mind you, with Savannah Turner behind it, that border was deceptively decorative. But trust me, the portion bordering Mister Moonlight was constructed out of steel and concrete to prevent any further harm occurring to this massive tree.

Lovely thoughts of Mister Moonlight and spending childhood hours climbing his limbs, using him as our safe base when playing hide-n-seek, or sitting there eating popsicles or other summertime treats, were with me as we neared my grandparents' modest home.

"I'll drop you off then take your bag on up to the house." With my parents' home being farther back on the property, I accepted my Dad's offer, exited the car, and inhaled deeply before making my way up my grandparents' long driveway.

You will act like God gave you good sense, Ashlee Dionne.

I'd already cautioned myself not to fall apart when seeing Nana. Now that I was about to, I had to remind myself I was here for Nana, not to assuage any guilt I had for failing to visit. My family didn't need my self-recrimination added to an already long list of heaviness.

"Mama?"

Opening the front door, I walked in, calling for my mother before pausing to inhale the comforting scents and view the sights of my grandparents' home. The walls and mantle lined with framed photos. The knick-knacks and bric-a-brac that my grandmother loved collecting, and that my mother complained were mere dust magnets. The subtle scent of my grandfather's outdated Old Spice cologne that he refused to relinquish because he'd been wearing it when he proposed to Nana. These invaluable constants wrapping me in a blanket of wellness and welcome, I headed for the kitchen when I heard my mother call me.

The sight of Mama pouring coffee into one of PopPop's favorite mugs warmed my heart.

I rushed into her arms.

For several minutes we clung to each other. There was no need to speak. Our embrace was its own language.

"Let me look at you." When Mama finally broke our embrace, she did that mother thing. Looking me over, her laser gaze missed nothing. Taking my hand, she made me do a slow spin before leaning against the counter, one eyebrow comically arched, saying nothing.

"Why're you looking at me like that, Mother Dearest?"

"Like what?"

"Like Nana. Like you're chewing your words before you spit them out. What is it?"

It was nice hearing my mother laugh. "I'm merely thinking you look good, but tired." She sipped her coffee before adding, "And those hips are doing something."

"What's wrong with my hips?" I looked down, checking and prodding myself as if I didn't daily encounter my figure in the mirror.

"You never heard me say anything was 'wrong.' I said they're up to something."

Frowning at my mother, I wanted to suck my teeth dismissively. But even at my age I knew better. Particularly while within arm's reach. "Well, these hips are not my doing." Playfully, I patted Mama's thighs. "I inherited them from you and your mother, so blame yourselves if they're high and wide."

We laughed, knowing I was right. I'd inherited Daddy's pecan-brown coloring, and PopPop's height. But I'd been blessed with the same modest breasts, small waist, and round and healthy behind, and hips my mother and grandmother were endowed with. The one thing I often wished I'd inherited but hadn't, were Mama's odd-colored eyes. She'd shared painful stories of being teased and sometimes ostracized as a child for their grayish hue, as well as her soft wavy hair, and café-au-lait-colored skin that made her "different." But to me her eyes were mysterious, gorgeous.

"Is Nana awake?"

My mother's smile dimmed. "She's in and out, Ladybug."

She'd already briefed me that Nana was, essentially, floating in and out of consciousness. Sometimes unaware of or confused by her surroundings. At other times, completely lucid.

"Go on back. I told her you were coming."

Part of me wanted to run through the house hollering that I was home like I always did. The other part of me was tempered, sobered, slightly afraid of what I'd see when entering my grandparents' bedroom.

"You'll be fine, baby. Daddy's back there and he's waiting on you, so get to moving."

I squeezed my mother again as if absorbing her strength before heading to the back of the house. Nearing my destination, my steps slowed as I reminded myself that I was young, resilient, and that my family needed my presence.

Approaching the doorway, I stopped at the lovely sight of my grandfather seated in a chair beside my grandmother's bed, reading the newspaper aloud for her benefit. Every few sentences he stopped and spoke to her as if soliciting her opinion or exchanging ideas and responses to what he'd read. At one point he even chuckled and fussed, "I know that, Mattie Ilene! You ain't always gotta be schooling me."

With their six-plus decades of marriage I saw nothing odd in my grandfather's behavior, at his conversing as if capable of hearing my grandmother's spirit responding. Rather, I felt bad for interrupting.

"Hi, PopPop."

A huge grin took over my grandfather's face, and he laid his paper aside, and patted his lap.

Reaching his chair, I hugged him tightly before kissing his nearly bald head. "No, sir, I'm not."

"Oh, yes ma'am, you is."

We grinned at each other, knowing the retired school teacher in Nana would pitch a fit over his intentionally bad grammar.

"I can't sit on your lap anymore, PopPop."

"Why not?"

"You're old."

"Well, you're ugly but you don't see me advertising it."

We both fell out laughing.

"Ugly or not, I'm not sitting on your lap. I'm too heavy, plus Mama says my hips are up to something."

"You're built just like your grandma, so those hips can't help themselves. Now, sit on up here, you pretty thing, before I go get myself a new granddaughter."

As a little girl, I'd thought my grandfather the tallest man God ever made. Being hoisted on his shoulders was like climbing up Mister Moonlight. I always felt above the world, high. He'd never been fat. Neither thin. Rather, muscular. Solid. He hadn't stooped much, or shriveled with age. Wrapping my arms about his neck, I gingerly positioned myself, trying to avoid aggravating the injury to his left knee sustained while playing in the Negro Leagues. Pressing my forehead against his—eyes closed, nose-to-nose—I surrendered to the pleasure of his presence and his abiding strength.

"If Mama comes in, you know we're both in trouble, right?"

"Savannah doesn't scare nobody but you and Avery."

My palms against his smooth, butterscotch-colored cheeks, I begged his forgiveness. "I've missed you so much. Chasing a corporate dream is no excuse for my negligence. Please forgive me for not being here like I—"

"Hush up! We're not doing regrets. You're here now, aren't you?"

"Yes, sir."

"And that's plenty good. Your nana's been waiting on you."

I'd managed avoiding all but a cursory glance at the bed while entering the room. A soft sigh escaping my lips, I carefully shifted on my grandfather's lap and fully focused on the woman who appeared to be deep in sleep.

As if I'd forgotten my family's arrangements, I'd actually expected an overwhelming network of hospital machines persistently beeping. Some metal, hydraulic hospital bed and the nauseating smells of sterile antiseptics. A caretaker. Countless bottles of medicines. And tubes running in and out of my grandmother's veins, her face a tormented mask reflecting her terminal state. Instead, there was only a syringe, morphine, a heart-rate monitor, and the one IV drip providing a solution to keep her hydrated as my grandmother lay peacefully in the center of her marriage bed against a mound of pillows, defying death and morbidity, and looking small but more rested than she had in years.

"That ol' girl looks good, doesn't she?"

Leaning back against my grandfather's chest, my head cradled against his neck, I nodded in agreement.

"That comes from all her years of living well and doing right by God and man."

"Nana was… *is* a wonderful woman."

"That's why I snatched her up like I had good sense. Did I ever tell you about the fight that broke out the day we were married?"

"*What?* Who was fighting?"

"Me and Mattie. She even had the dagblasted nerve to throw a soda bottle at me."

"PopPop, stop telling stories."

"Don't sit here acting like you ain't well versed in your granny's penchant for stubbornness. Well, she was acting mule-headed so I told her I was finished with her and marrying someone else. That's when she threw that bottle like she was Satchel Paige or somebody. I'm serious," my grandfather insisted as I laughed. "You think I'm fabricating? Ask her yourself. Go'n. I dare you."

Lifting off my grandfather's lap, I approached Nana's bed and simply stood there as if a stranger seeking permission to enter a sacred realm. "Hi, Nana. I'm home."

The heart-rate machine made an odd beep, causing me to look at my grandfather with concern.

"Ladybug, that's nothing but her heart's way of letting you know you just gave it some extra happy."

Smiling, I turned to my grandmother, touched the back of her hand and the soft brown skin interrupted by a series of fragile veins running beneath the surface.

"Can she hear me? Does she know I'm here?" I asked my grandfather, while focused on the woman he still called "bride" after sixty years.

"Look at her fingers. She talks with them."

I glanced back at my grandfather. "Sir?"

"Watch. Ask her again. She'll tap once for 'no.' Twice for the affirmative."

"Nana, it's Ashlee. Can you hear me?"

It was subtle, but I distinctly saw the double movement of her fingers lifting and lowering against the cool, clean sheets about her body. "Ohmigosh, PopPop."

"Told ya."

My grandfather and I exchanged a bright smile.

"Nana, did you hear what your husband said about you throwing a bottle at him? I'd like to believe my dignified, beautiful grandmother did no such thing. Is PopPop tall-telling?"

I waited a while before seeing a singular rise and fall of a finger.

Seeing it as well, my grandfather cracked up laughing. "There you have it. Truth straight from the fountain."

Smiling, I gently stroked my grandmother's arm, desperately wanting to climb onto the bed and fold myself in her embrace. To hear her heartbeat, and simply melt in the love disease could never defeat.

"Go'n and sit with her, Ladybug. She won't break," PopPop encouraged as if hearing my inner longing.

Fearing she might actually shatter, I was painfully slow in perching on the side of the bed, gradually easing over until I was beside my beloved. My back to the headboard, I draped an arm across the top of her pillows, as if to shield her from further harm. My fingers gently toyed with what was left of her hair. Nana was one of those Black women who'd boasted a thick head of healthy hair all her life. When chemo devoured it she'd refused to wear wigs.

I've lived too long for vanity. Y'all can take me as I am or leave me be.

Many times thereafter, I'd kissed, caressed, and moisturized her bald scalp as if it were God's most beautiful thing.

Nana's hair never reclaimed its thickness or length. Instead, it grew into a soft, small halo; its downy softness felt lovely beneath my fingertips.

Curling onto my side, I watched her, feeling protective and uncertain. Was I siphoning what little strength she had? Would I exhaust her simply by being there?

I'll rest when I'm dead.

I smiled, remembering her defiant response whenever we wanted her to stop doing some chore and sit somewhere and rest.

"Ladybug, how's life at the big house?"

Wanting to kiss my grandfather for helping me ease into natural conversation, I filled him in on my job and my two-week leave, intentionally facing Nana to ensure she was included.

"Frustrating as it might be, looks like your two weeks off was part of providence," PopPop commented. "Now we get to have all your happy light shining on us."

"Such as it is. Right now my light doesn't feel like much."

"But, it is. You're like your grandmother. You can't help but shine, and you've always been more than enough."

I spent two hours chatting with PopPop and watching Nana's chest rise and fall. The mere motion soothed me, left me thankful for every remaining breath she'd yet to breathe. Only a need to use the restroom prompted me to leave my comfortable place in her bed.

"PopPop, do you want anything to eat?"

My mother had popped in earlier with the same question. He'd declined then, but decided to the contrary when I asked.

"I think this ol' stomach could use something."

"I'll fix you some lunch after I use the bathroom. I should put this back in the fridge." Grabbing the protein-packed meal replacement shake on Nana's bedside stand, I kissed my grandfather's cheek before heading to the kitchen.

Expecting to see my mother there, I was surprised to find the room empty, its pristine cleanliness marred only by the partially empty coffee cup my mother had left in the sink.

"Nana would pitch a fit."

Dumping the cup's contents down the sink before placing it in the dishwasher, I smiled, remembering my grandmother's homespun homily that "cleanliness is next to godliness, and dirt is of the devil."

Closing the dishwasher door, I turned, leaned back against the counter and let my gaze span the room. I found a memory everywhere I looked. Nana teaching me how to make cornbread using just my hands to scoop ingredients, no measuring cups or spoons. Her demonstrating the magic of gumbo.

Baby, it's all in the roux.

Her famous teacakes, cobblers, and pies we'd baked. Her ironing her dresses and PopPop's shirts Saturday nights for church on Sundays. My walking in and catching her sitting, on the phone gossiping and her cautioning me to stay out of grown folks' business. The times Avery or I had fallen outside and come in crying, and Nana had cleaned and bound our wounds. Sitting on her lap while she helped me sound out words phonetically when learning to read. Those occasions I'd entered the back door unannounced to find my grandparents kissing and swaying to the radio's tunes. It was all there. This room, this domain more than any other in the house, resonated Nana's spirit.

My heart feeling as if it had been hugged, I left the kitchen and went in search of my mother.

I found her on the family-room sofa, curled on her side, napping from sheer exhaustion. Apparently, my mother had all but moved in after Nana had been released from the hospital, declining further treatment. A caretaker covered the night shift so my mother and grandfather could rest, but even then Mama was up every few hours checking in, ensuring Nana was sleeping well, and hadn't transitioned.

Peering down at my mother, I felt small, insignificant, knowing there was nothing I could do to ease her pain. As an only child, she was her parents' delight, their legacy, and jewel. What she was experiencing had to be excruciating. Yet, there she was, ministering hands-on love, entrusting her parent's care to no one except herself.

I should've been here.

Despising my negligence, I wished for the power to take her hurt, fear, the fatigue and hurl them into a wide, consuming sea. Possessing no such power, I pulled a throw Nana had knitted from the back of the sofa and draped it over my mother to keep her comfortable beneath the cool flow of the air conditioner.

I texted Brad while heading to the restroom, letting him know I'd landed safely. His supportiveness since learning of Nana's fate had been stellar. I appreciated his attentiveness and realized how much I missed our intimate, spirit connection. The efforts we put into building each other up. Functioning as a solidified team. Even our playful silliness.

We have to do better, or we won't make it.

We'd wind up in the boneyard of relationships.

Sitting on the commode, I texted Dorinda. Almost instantly, she responded, reminding me to call anytime for anything, no matter the need.

Grateful, I placed my phone on the bathroom counter and focused on nothing. Taking deep meditative breaths, I let my mind drift until I felt an uncomfortable sensation in my abdomen.

It's just your period.

"Took you long enough…" My eyes slowly widened as my voice trailed off. Snatching my phone, I launched my menstrual cycle tracker only to find no recent entries. "That doesn't make sense."

Had life and work and my upward quest been so stressful that I'd forgotten to input the data? For me that was implausible. Still, my last entry had been two months ago, and I was religious about contraception and keeping track of my flow.

"Oh, God."

Refusing to panic, I reminded myself of the high success rate of my current contraception. Granted, I'd changed it recently from one method to another due to side effects and a prior allergic reaction. But, surely, it had taken effect. Plus, Brad and I hadn't been intimate lately. Not with any consistent frequency.

It only takes once, Ashlee.

Very aware of that fact, I scrolled my tracker, finding my last cycle and trying my best to analyze my sex life since. I ignored the sad truth that I could actually count the few times my lover and I had made love since then. Instead, I focused on pinpointing our sexual activity closest to the last entry.

"Samantha's wedding."

We'd attended Brad's cousin's nuptials in Durham, North Carolina. It was a beautiful, elegant, and moving affair. Clearly, we'd gotten caught up in the romance of it, because Brad and I didn't even make it to our hotel room before the foreplay began. On the return drive, his hand was already under my dress, and mine in his pants. Barely making it to our hotel room, we didn't even bother undressing once we got the door open. Dropping his pants, Brad lifted me on top of the entryway table, pushed aside my thong, and thrust into me with a force that was shocking, yet deliciously thrilling. Moments later I climaxed so hard I literally couldn't breathe. And that's how we spent the remainder of the weekend: as if long-lost lovers making up for missed intimacy. By the time we checked out, I was raw, whipped, and possibly delirious.

"Dear Jesus, I cannot be pregnant."

It was a prayer and a petition.

My career was in crisis. My relationship with Brad wasn't sanguine. We had yet to get engaged, and I was increasingly questioning if he was my one, thanks to mounting, incessant friction. Personally, I had a brooding sense of discontent within myself. And, most pressing: my beloved was dying.

One life leaves to make room for the next.

I'd heard Nana say that many times. Seated on that toilet, I earnestly prayed it was only an old wives' tale.

CHAPTER SEVEN

Mattie

With every passing day, I thanked God for Miz Rosa. For the bus boycott. And the hubbub Montgomery experienced when Colored folks demanded rights that should've been ours. It was all folks talked about, the biggest and most important matter on the mind. It allowed me to hide myself and my baby in plain sight.

Everywhere we went, the bus boycott was *the* topic. Church. School. We couldn't even walk downtown or through a store without Mama stopping and talking to somebody, sharing updates, and whispering information. Mama even took to hanging laundry on the clothes line in the backyard despite Doc Stanton gifting his wife an electric dryer last Christmas. It was winter and subject to rain, but Miz Stanton bought Mama's fabrication about the dryer acting funny, and the winter air contributing wonderful things to those clothes as if endowing them with transferable protection against illness. My mother simply wanted to be outdoors, sneaking in covert conversations with other domestics. Suddenly, there was a whole lot of borrowing a cup of sugar here, a cup of flour there; beating rugs on the back veranda and dallying around mailboxes. Ruses to allow an exchange of information and simply to chat about life-changing events impacting our community. Despite the excitement, they managed to keep their interactions seemingly casual and nonchalant, sometimes code-talking, successfully preventing backlash or suspicion.

The night before the one-day boycott was scheduled to happen, Mama and I lay whispering in our beds about the meeting at Holt Street Baptist Church the next evening.

"I'm going, Mattie. I wanna hear if Miz Parks wins her court case. I wanna know if this boycott is continuing, or if it's just one day."

"What're you gonna tell the Stantons?"

"That I'm grown and heading to a prayer meeting."

That Monday in English, Mister Lightfoot had a time trying to get us to pay attention. We were too busy whispering; our minds were enchanted and drifting. Finally, he gave up, divided the class in two groups, labeling one side pro, the other con. We were tasked with the great feat of arguing the bus boycott from the perspective of whichever team we'd been placed on. It got heated every now and again, but in the end we all agreed that Colored folks staying off City Line buses was about human dignity.

Unable to ride the bus, Miz James had been kind enough to go out of her way to pick me up that morning, and drop me and Sadie off. After school, I walked home with Sadie. We did our homework, ate dinner, and listened to the radio while our parents attended the Monday night meeting. Afterwards, Mister and Miz James drove me and Mama home.

Thanking them, Mama and I cautiously entered our room by its side door, completely bypassing the kitchen. Cautioning me to remain quiet, Mama didn't even turn on the lamp sitting on the nightstand between our beds, leaving us in the cover of night to undress.

Once in bed, our whispered conversation earnestly began.

"What was it like, Mama?" I'd wanted to attend but—not knowing what all might happen, if White Montgomerians would show up in protest, unleashing ugliness—she'd decided my absence was best.

"Mattie, I ain't never seen nothing like it."

In awe, I lay in the dark listening to my mother recount an evening of prayer, hymns, preacher after preacher uplifting the people, and declaring our staying off the buses had made history. The church had been filled to capacity. Its basement, balcony. Countless others flowed outdoors into a sea of Colored folks up and down the street.

"Thank God we got there early or we woulda been outside with them. But I tell *you*! The Spirit was so high, and they amplified the speaking outdoors so didn't nobody miss nothing. It filled my heart seeing all those men and women sitting there unified and full of race pride. I'm telling you, baby girl, I've decided to get out this house and go somewhere as much as I can this week just so I can see the bus coming and *not* get on it. I'ma feel real good about being me."

We laughed quietly.

"Wait, the boycott isn't today only?"

"It was scheduled that way, but when those ministers stood up there and asked if we'd had enough that church erupted with a 'No!' that sounded like thunder. *We* decided. We ain't getting back on not one bus until this transportation company recognizes we have equal rights."

Filled with a mix of pride and a hint of fear, I asked my mother how she felt about that.

"Baby, you know I ain't never participated in nothing like this. I've always been quiet, kept to myself, and just did what I had to. Now, your daddy?" She'd laughed softly. "He was built from a whole other fabric. That man was fuel *and* fire. That's what got him killed."

I frowned in the dark. "What did Daddy's personality have to do with his dying in the war?"

My mother didn't respond, causing me to shift and turn towards her side of the room.

"Mama, didn't Daddy die in the war?"

"You know who reminds me of your daddy?" she blurted, skirting my question. "Ransome James. Sadie's brother was always getting in trouble when y'all were little for talking out of turn and challenging everything. It was good seeing him and his friends there tonight. Gives them a place to put all that young energy," Mama remarked as if she was an old woman past youthful shenanigans instead of in her early thirties. "Matthew would've liked Ransome. Or maybe since they're so similar they woulda been enemies?"

Matthew was my daddy. The man I was named for. The one whose picture was at the bottom of the wardrobe in a cigar box where I kept the things sweetest to me. Like my short stories and poetry. "Do you…" I hesitated, not wanting to put pain on top of her joy from the evening. "Still miss Daddy?"

She sighed gently. "Every day and night of my life. Name one of your fondest memories with him."

I smiled, remembering. "Him pushing me and Sadie on that tire swing."

"What tire swing?"

"The one down by the creek."

Mama was silent a moment before laughing. "Baby, that was back home in Valdosta, not here in Montgomery. And it wasn't Sadie. It was your cousins, Ruth and Naomi."

"No, ma'am, I remember running through the backyard, getting Sadie, and Daddy taking us down to the creek. In that blue Thunderbird he had," I brightly added, proving my memory's voracity.

"Mattie, that was your Uncle Marvin. He and your daddy look like twins, and you were so little that I can see how they got mixed up in your mind. Matthew was already dead when we moved here. In fact, your daddy's dying is why we came to Montgomery to begin with." I could practically taste her sorrow when she finished with, "I couldn't stay."

I lay there trying to rewind time and access clarity, Wasn't it Daddy, Sadie, and me, and that tire swing; my best friend and me running between our connected backyards before Daddy went missing? "But Mama, we had that house. By Sadie."

"That was Marvin's place." Like Daddy, all of his brother's names started with the letter "M." "We stayed there the first few weeks after we got to Montgomery until I could take care of business. When Marvin left for Texas we came here."

"Why?"

"Matthew always told me if something ever happened to him, or if other family couldn't take us in to find Doc Stanton."

I was listening but not listening as my thoughts rolled backwards trying to clear cobwebs and make sense of what I thought I'd lived. So busy pulling and pondering I nearly missed what Mama said. "Wait... ma'am, what letter?"

"Mattie, baby, you asking questions but not hearing?" She chuckled softly. "That brain of yours is always on to next. I said your father gave me a letter of introduction so Doc Stanton wouldn't think we were tryna scheme him out of nothing. Matthew had more schooling than me and had some pretty handwriting. I guess they had code words they'd understand, but Doc Stanton read that letter and the next thing you know we were moved in. Been here ever since."

"What was in the letter?"

"I can't say precisely but..." Mama took a deep breath, continuing. "Well, shoot, I guess you're old enough now to know all of it."

"All of what?"

"I couldn't tell you when you were younger. Wasn't nobody supposed to know except me and Doc Stanton. Plus, it woulda been too much for you back then, but that middle initial 'S' on your father's G.I. papers? It stands for Stanton."

Chills running over my skin, I slowly sat up in bed. "Ma'am?"

The weight of my mother's sigh spiraled through the darkness, wrapping smoky tendrils about me. Capturing. Paralyzing.

"The tree they come from is pretty twisted at the root, but Doc Stanton and your daddy are related. *Distant* kin. But still family."

Swinging my legs over the edge of my bed, I couldn't do a thing but wrap my arms about myself and sit there as my mother gingerly unpacked a basket of secrets as if they were delicate trinkets. She laid each out carefully, aligning them into a perfect row of unbelievable realities. Every truth should've been a lie, but something in my soul, my blood stood up to confirm, testify. Besides, my mother detested dishonesty; deceit was something she'd never serve me. Even so, her words were like multi-colored forest fairies: impossible to believe.

"So… there it is. That slave-owning Old Man Stanton had two lines of children. One by his wife. The other by his slave woman. Some of 'em grew up side by side. Some didn't. Especially after slavery finished and Colored folks could live where they wanted. Matt and Doc Stanton were two of 'em that somehow reconnected and acknowledged each other enough to be on amicable terms. In fact, Matt said they spent part of their childhood together before your grandparents moved to Valdosta. They were pen pals or something as kids. Anyhow… your daddy said Doc was an honorable man. That helped me feel okay about coming to work here. I didn't have to worry about being taken behind the woodshed… if you know what I mean. So, that's it, baby. Glad I can tell you some things now that you're older."

I wish you woulda told me before I laid down with Edward.

Wanting to hurl those words through the dark with the force of cannons, I couldn't. Wrapping my arms about my middle, I lay back on my bed and stared at the dark ceiling, tears running down my face, wondering what I'd conceived, and what kind of person I was to share my body with a boy who was distantly, but still, related.

Must've been something in my mother's night-whispered words that made this baby want to show up and announce itself. As if it was proud of its legacy, of reconnecting two lines of distant yet inner-twisted Stantons. Suddenly, those cloth strips I bound myself with weren't strong enough. My skirts wouldn't zip up completely and my aching breasts felt like they were trying to bust through my shirts. Thankfully, Mother Nature had made peace with December and decided it was alright to be winter. The descending temperatures allowed me to hide behind bulky sweaters and jackets. But I couldn't hide the fact that my face was getting full, or that I didn't feel well. Lethargic and feeling way less than myself, I was grateful the adults were too caught up in what was going on in Montgomery, thanks to the boycott, to truly notice me.

"Dorothy, I'm of the opinion you sew good enough to pull it off."

Helping Mama clean the dinner dishes, I wished Miz Stanton would leave and go do something. Instead, she was going on and on about my being in uniform and helping at that stupid football award dinner next week. Apparently, her seamstress was away visiting family and wouldn't be back in time for a fitting.

Mama laughed it off. "Miz Stanton, you have more faith in my sewing skills than I do. I couldn't hardly match the fine quality you're used to. Plus, I don't want to short-change this football ceremony. I know how you like excellence, so I'm focusing on that and making sure the help is in line and taste-testing those catered foods like you said. But, I guess I could squeeze Mattie's uniform in. That's if you don't mind me doing that instead of helping Abby get ready for the Christmas pageant. I know I can't make a uniform from scratch, but I sew a fine hem, and Abby's dress needs re-hemming. Her hair needs washing and styling, and if you prefer taking her shoe shopping—"

"No, Dorothy, I'll see if I can find another seamstress nearby. If not, Mattie'll be fine in a black skirt and apron."

"Yes, ma'am."

Mama waited until the click-clack of Miz Stanton's kitten heels faded in the distance before looking at me and quietly stating, "You been walking 'round here looking like you lost your best friend lately. Hope you don't think I haven't noticed. You gonna use that the night of this football ceremony. You gonna get sick. Conveniently. You hear me? You ain't serving nothing to nobody."

I'd helped Mama many times before with the Stantons' functions, even as recently as Edward's going-away party. It wasn't as if it was new territory. But my wearing a uniform rubbed her wrong and had her acting subversive.

"Mama, I don't mind helping you."

"It ain't about helping me, Mattie, it's about you staying free!" Realizing she was yelling, my mother took a deep breath before lowering her voice to a near whisper. "Once you put that outfit on, they ain't never gonna let you take it off. So, you ain't putting it on at all."

She walked away, leaving me to finish the dinner dishes.

Five minutes later, I walked into our room and found Mama changing out of her uniform and into her regular clothing. She barely glanced at me. "Miz James is picking me up for a meeting. I should be back by nine thirty."

"Yes, ma'am," I responded, heading for the telephone as it began to ring. "Banks' residence."

"Mattie, where's Dorothy?"

"She's right here, Miz James. Is everything okay?"

"Put her on the phone, please."

A whole lot of worry in Miz James' voice had me hurrying to do her bidding. Handing my mother the phone, I stood there knowing I was violating rules of being in adult business.

"Hi, Virginia... *What?*"

Seeing my mother sink onto her bed, listening and saying nothing, my heart started galloping.

"Lord, Jesus, today. Was anybody hurt? Thank God for that. Okay, I'll be ready."

Handing me the phone to replace on the stand, my mother shook her head, her face marred by disgust and sadness. "Mama Bea's closed up early on account of tonight's meeting at the church. Her son remembered something he left behind, went back, and found it on fire," she offered without my having to ask.

"That's horrible! What happened? Did one of her grandkids leave something cooking?"

"Would her grandkids tape a note to a rock calling those flames divine retribution for Colored folks being disloyal and causing problems for the transportation system?"

"No, ma'am."

"Damn right they wouldn't. Nothing but some hateful crackers behind it."

Sadie and I violated a no-phone-on-school-nights rule to keep each other company while our parents attended that meeting. Neither of us would admit it, but we were scared.

"Why Mama Bea's, Mattie? She's never done nothing to nobody."

"It's simple backlash. Plus, they can't stand us having anything. We're separate. We're segregated. And what do they do when we get a little something? They destroy it. Try to intimidate and maybe even *kill* us. Remember what they did to Black Wall Street in Tulsa? And Rosewood?"

"Yep. You know what I think? White folks want us back on the plantation. Bet you ten dollars they'd have us in chains tomorrow if they could."

"Sadie James, I believe you'd win that bet."

We shared a quiet, tremulous laugh only to fall silent.

Seconds ticked by before I dared to admit, "The more things happen and the more I think on it, I know I'm making the right decision not to tell this baby who its father is."

"Mattie, if that baby comes out with skin and hair looking like them, that'll be one secret you can't keep."

"White folks've been mixing their blood in ours since we got here." Lifting an arm, I considered the brownness of my complexion. My parents' skin tones were equally rich, deep. But we'd learned something in science recently about genetics and physical traits. Taking the phone with me, I stood in front of the mirror attached to the wardrobe door and studied myself. "If my baby's different, I'll tell her or him those differences are mutations; that they reached way back in the family tree and picked up something."

"Mattie, you're crazy."

"Maybe." Cradling the receiver beneath my chin and with the phone in one hand, I unbuttoned my blouse as best I could. I'd left my binding on too long and my breasts ached. "Sadie… can you tell yet?"

"Not really. Except your face is looking a little funny. And your behind's wide, but I guess that's normal, so no. Ooo, that ol' Nosey Nedra asked me the other day why you so quiet and funny-acting lately."

"Whatcha tell her?"

"To mind her nosey business, and that the next time she wanna know something about you to ask you directly 'cause I'm not your secretary."

It felt good to laugh. "Thanks, Sadie."

"I'm not your best friend for nothing. And don't forget when it's time to name the baby what we agreed on."

Sadie and I had decided we'd give our first born each other's initials so that no matter where life took us, we'd remain connected and remember one another. With her name being Sadie Ernestine, I had "S" and "E" names to work with. "I won't."

"You'd better not. That meeting's probably over and if our parents walk in and catch us talking on the phone we'll be in trouble, so I guess we'd better get off."

"Okay. I'll be out front when you get here tomorrow." I lived too far from our Colored high school on the other side of town to walk, so Sadie's family had been kind enough to pick me up every morning. Usually it was Miz James, but Ransome also transported us occasionally. After school, I walked with Sadie to their house in Mobile Heights, waiting there until Doc Stanton got off. If he couldn't pick me up, Miz Stanton and Mama did, with Miz Stanton letting me know she wasn't happy about it—chattering the entire ride home about the boycott being "a nuisance."

The disruption might've been aggravating for her, but for me it was a blessing. It meant my being out of the house until evening, and provided a perfect way to avoid Edward. Since he'd slipped that note to me, we hadn't been alone and for that I was grateful. At times I mirrored his feelings. At others, I considered us both juvenile and misguided. It was complex and problematic, and beyond resolving that night as Sadie and I exchanged our goodbyes.

Returning the phone to its proper place, I locked the door leading to the hallway. Resuming my position before the mirror, I removed my blouse and the safety pin I'd secured that cloth with. Unwinding and tossing the cloth onto the bed, I winced when my hand accidentally pressed against a sensitive breast before judging their increased heaviness.

Just wait. They ain't even filled with milk yet.

Sighing, I removed the skirt I could no longer fully zip. Dropping it at my feet and leaving on my half-slip, I splayed my fingers over my protruding belly.

It wasn't much. Just a slight puff. Still, that tiny bulge had me shivering, more afraid than I'd ever been.

"I don't know what to do with you."

That admission was like a balloon. It floated through the ceiling, exposing to the night sky my sense of inadequacy. But the lift of it also made me more determined. I would figure out a way to raise this baby. Even if it meant I wore a uniform for the rest of my life. My child deserved whatever my sacrifice.

"If I don't make but enough for you to eat and I have to go hungry, that's the way it'll be. You're my—"

The sound of Mama's key in the outside door petrified me. Hearing her calling out a "thank you," my eyes frantically stared in the mirror at my half-naked body. Unthawing, I scrambled for my skirt in time to get it half-way up my hips before she'd opened the door and stepped in. Only the cool rush of December air against my breasts reminded me of their nakedness. Unable to reach my blouse, I hurriedly covered myself with my arms instead. But it wasn't swift enough. Eyes at my chest, mouth open, my mother stood like a statue before slowly closing the door behind her.

Mere feet separating us, we were a frozen tableau of Mama's shock and my terror.

When my mother finally stepped forward, stopping directly before me and gently grabbing my wrists, removing my arms from shielding my breasts, my terror gave way to tears as her gaze searched my hips, my waist, before landing on my tender breasts again.

"I *knew* something was off." Her voice was low and strained, tight with a soul-deep kind of ache. "That's why you been so willing to help with the laundry lately. Talking about you already washed your monthly underwear so I wouldn't have to bother with them."

"Mama—"

"You haven't had monthly issues, have you, Mattie?"

Eyes lowered, ashamed, I slowly shook my head.

"When was your last flow?"

"August or September."

"Which was it? You're too smart not to know."

"August."

My mother covered her face with her hands and turned her back to me.

I didn't realize she was silently crying until her shoulders began shaking.

"Mama?"

Stepping towards the outside door, she leaned her head against it, letting it take her weight and her woes until exhausting her sorrow. When she turned towards me, her eyes were red, puffy. Her nose was dripping. Opening the pocketbook she hadn't put down when she came in, she found the handkerchief I'd embroidered in home economics and gifted her last Mother's Day, and cleaned her face.

Tossing her pocketbook on my bed, she looked at me while repeatedly muttering, "Not my baby, Lord. Not my Mattie."

Her heartbreak broke me. Crying, heaving, I barely uttered, "I'm so sorry."

When my mother opened her arms, I rushed into them, letting Mama crush me against her chest. Ignoring the pain flashing through my breasts, I clung to her as we shed collective tears.

"We'll find a way."

Her whispered assurance gave me strength. If Dorothy Banks said it, so it would be.

Filling myself with that peace, I buried my head against her shoulder and inhaled her soft, powdery scent.

Solaced, I knew everything would be alright until Mama quietly asked, "Who's responsible? Whose baby is this?"

CHAPTER EIGHT

Ashlee

"Have you peed yet?"

"No, Dorinda, and I won't with you asking every three-point-five seconds."

"How much water did you drink?"

"Enough to make a camel urinate."

"And still nothing?"

"*Nada*. Zip."

"Okay, think about oceans. Rivers. Lakes. Seas. Rain. Orgasming."

"Huh?"

"You know. Like when it's *real* good, and you leak a little on orgasm. Send your mind there. He does do that for you, right?"

"We are not discussing my sex life," I pontificated like a puritan, while on the commode waiting for my bladder to cooperate so I could complete the home pregnancy test I'd purchased yesterday when my mother asked me to pick up a few items from the store.

"Actually we are, seeing as how you might be knocked up."

"Oh God. Doe, what if I am?" Elbows propped on my thighs, I leaned forward and massaged my temples, wondering why I was in this predicament. An attorney who'd graduated at the top of her class, clearly I was intelligent. I earned a six-figure salary, drank wine three times older than me, and even spoke a little French. With professional parents and a ten-acre family stead I was, arguably, part of the Black bourgeoisie. Yet, there I was, unmarried and possibly pregnant as if I'd never heard of contraception. Proof that oops or accidents were fluid and not governed by socio-economics.

"If you are, you'll have decisions to make. Like whether or not you want a child right now."

"Doe, you already know abortion isn't an option for me."

"I know, Ash. So, that leaves you with having and raising your child. Or adoption. Which are you most inclined towards?"

"Let's just work with whether I'm gestating or not for now. Once that's determined, I can decide next steps."

"Fair enough. Have you told Brad?"

I was so accustomed to Dorinda calling him "Gomer" that his name seemed foreign coming from her. Her mere usage of Brad highlighted the severity and magnitude of my situation.

"No. Again, I prefer to know before alerting or alarming him."

It wasn't that Brad and I didn't want children. We did. *After* marriage. For all my "I Am Woman Hear Me Roar" sensibilities, in this regard I preferred tradition versus modern approaches to building a family. I saluted my sisters holding it down and raising children single-handedly, but I had no desire for single-parenting. I had zero guarantees or immunities against the dissolution of a marriage but bringing children into a solid, stable, loving relationship where our household shared a last name and we were committed to go the distance was my right, my choice, *my* preference.

"I agree. So… are you peeing?"

"Do you hear anything?" I had Dorinda in speakerphone mode.

"No. Turn the sink faucet on for inspiration."

"That's wasting water, and I'm a conservationist."

"You're a woman who couldn't keep her legs shut, so run it."
Our laughter was light.

"On another note, how's Nana Mattie?"

I leaned forward, looking at nothing. "She woke up enough yesterday to register my presence. She didn't speak or anything. Just kind of smiled and nodded a bit. That's about it."

"You have the CBD?"

"Yep. I had it shipped ahead so I wouldn't have to check my bag at the airport. She moans sometimes in her sleep, and we have morphine to control the pain when that happens. But I'll massage her limbs with the CBD oil after lunch."

While the Federal Drug Administration had yet to approve cannabis plant extract as a viable cancer treatment, I'd researched it enough to know CBD provided relief. PopPop and my mother hadn't objected to my use of it, neither had Nana's oncologist. I knew my grandmother's departure from this life was merely a matter of time, but I was determined to provide her whatever relief I could in the interim.

"I told you it worked wonders for my father-in-law before he passed with MS. Hopefully, Nana Mattie will experience a reprieve from pain as well."

"I second that. Listen, nothing's happening here so I'm getting off this toilet so I can feed my face and sit with Nana."

"Sounds like a good plan. Kiss your mom and dad, and tell PopPop he still owes me a dance."

That was my grandfather's thing: making us dance to old school tunes with him whenever we visited. An honorary family member, Dorinda hadn't been down in years, but the last time she'd been so busy in the kitchen with Nana learning her gumbo recipe that she hadn't had her dance.

"I will. Bye. I'll text you when."

"Ashlee, wait! Tell Nana I love her and I'm praying."

Hearing my best friend's voice choke up, I choked up too and could only nod.

Disconnecting, I sat a few seconds and simply breathed, remembering Nana's support of my career, her graciously excusing my recent absences from family functions.

Baby, take care of doing what you're doing. We'll be here when you finish accomplishing.

"Thank God for it."

Grace had been good to me. Nana was still here. That made me unquestionably blessed despite overwhelming regret.

Washing and drying my hands, I rubbed in a bit of lotion and inhaled the clean lemongrass and citrus scent while exiting the guest bathroom. Walking down the hall, I could hear PopPop reading the newspaper aloud in melodious tones, determined to keep my grandmother in the know.

That's my grandparents.

They'd taken turns putting each other through college while young in their marriage. The struggle had been real, but they'd managed, instilling strong determination and work ethics in my mother that she'd passed down to us. Education, awareness of the world, equality, and activism were imperative to them. Even here in Nana's waning days, PopPop made sure his bride remained cognizant of matters in the world around us.

"Never get disconnected from something bigger," PopPop often said, reminding us that no matter how seemingly insurmountable our issues, or how important or consuming our private affairs, the Creator and the cosmos had a greater purpose.

"Something bigger…" Walking down the hallway, those words slipped from my lips, causing me to hone in on my recent disconnects. My love. My career. The former was fixable and worth the fight. The latter? I suddenly wasn't so sure. An Ivy

League graduate with a nice savings account and good credit, for all intents and purposes I was successful. I took annual vacations. Could afford anything within reason. My career allowed that. Yet, surrounded by the humble comforts of home, I was able to voice what I'd been unable to before: that I was possessed by a pervasive, ongoing dissatisfaction. My something bigger wasn't in effect, and as I'd subconsciously admitted to Brad, I was suddenly ambivalent about my chosen profession.

The magnitude of that fluttered down on me like falling leaves yet its weight was heavy.

What do you need that you're not getting?

Entering the kitchen and gathering sandwich fixings, I reflected on my love's recent question that I'd been unable to answer. He'd asked in direct correlation to our relationship, but I was wise enough to admit my wants didn't start and end with Brad or romance. I was a woman with needs and dreams before I met him and I'd still be an autonomous and independent woman with aspirations if—God forbid—we decided we no longer worked well together.

"I'll deal with that later. Right now I need to focus on family."

Loading a tray with sandwiches and drinks, I made my way to the back veranda where my mother was sitting listening to nature, taking a well-deserved break from caretaking.

Hearing my approach, she looked my way, smiling warmly. "Hey, baby."

"Hey yourself, gorgeous lady. I'm not going to ask if you ate, because I know you didn't. So, sandwiches by Ashlee it is. The one with the toothpick is PopPop's."

"It must have red onions, sweet relish, and horseradish."

"But of course."

"My daddy and his 'I gotta have some sweet with my heat' eating self," Mama quipped, taking her sandwich-laden saucer from the tray I'd centered on the wicker-and-glass table where she sat. "Ooo, this looks good."

I plopped down in the chair closest to her. "Turkey, Havarti, honey mustard, and veggies on wholewheat the way you like, madame."

Saying grace, my mother bit into her sandwich, closed her eyes and sighed. "Ladybug, I didn't realize I was so hungry. This sandwich tastes like gold," she complimented, washing down the bite with sweet tea.

"I don't know what gold tastes like but I'll assume it's good."

When my mother laughed, tiny lights floated in her funny-colored eyes. "Absolutely. Thank you, sweetie."

"Anything for my mommy."

"Remember that the next time I ask for another grandbaby."

Playfully making a cross with two fingers, I was too afraid to tell my mother her wish might be a possibility.

"Speaking of grands, your brother's working on getting a flight by the end of the week, but Janelle and the kids won't come until..."

There was no need to finish. My father had set up his iPad in my grandparents' room so Avery and his family could connect via video chat, but with the kids in school and airfare such as it was, my sister-in-law had elected to postpone arriving with my nephews and niece until Nana was no longer with us and we'd scheduled her homegoing. Hearing my mother sniffle and seeing her tears pooling, I shifted my chair in order to place an arm about her.

"I've never lived a day without my mother. This world can't feel right without her. When she leaves there'll be a hole in my soul no one else can fill."

There was zero I could say to soften the truth and impact of that. I squeezed Mama's hand instead and leaned against her shoulder.

Silent minutes passed until Mama laughed.

"What's funny?"

"I'm sitting here looking at Ol' Moonlight and remembering something my Nana Dorothy told me."

Sitting up and following Mama's gaze to our giant tree in the distance, my mind flashed on pictures of the sweet-looking, pretty brown woman holding me at my first birthday party. My great-grandmother passed away shortly thereafter, but between the stories Nana and Mama told, I felt as if I intimately knew her.

"What did Great-Grandmother Dorothy tell you?"

Mama looked around before beckoning me with her finger as if I wasn't already seated directly beside her. "You better not repeat this," she whispered conspiratorially when I leaned in. "Nana Dorothy told me Mama was conceived beneath that tree."

"Honey, *hush*! She was not."

Mama lifted her hand like a Girl Scout. "I'm telling the gospel truth."

"*Ooo…*" I refocused on Mister Moonlight, feeling wicked for imagining my great-grandparents out there, engaged in grown folks' doings, as Nana would say.

"That's not all. She told me where I was conceived. Care to know?"

"Ewww, just thank you but no! I do not need imagery of PopPop and Nana getting busy."

Mama's laughter skipped merrily as I gagged theatrically.

"Don't be uptight, Ashlee Dionne. Your generation's not the first to stumble upon the pleasures of good sex. My grandparents had it. Obviously, my parents did too seeing as how I was conceived behind a tool shed—"

"Oh my God, Mama, I can't with you! Please stop."

"Why? Sex is good, little girl. And if you don't know that you and Brad need lessons. Now, your daddy and me? No lessons needed. We might be pushing our early sixties, but I'll have you know we stay busy. And we don't need a little blue pill. Yet."

"And that, ladies and gentlemen, is when and where I exit."

Grabbing me as I attempted to vacate my seat, Mama went in on the tickling. She had to holler to be heard over my wild giggling. "I know you'd like to think you and your brother got here by immaculate conception or artificial insemination. But you didn't. You got here the old-school way. Sizzling copulation."

"Mama, you're gonna make me wet myself. Stop."

Laughing, she sat back, finished with her torment, sitting prim and proper, her typical dignified self. "Yes, ma'am?" She innocently batted enviably long lashes at my wordless staring.

"All of you. From Great-Grandmother Dorothy to you and your husband. You're degenerates."

"Perhaps. But at least you know you do *not* come from a line of prudes, and have something to look forward to in your senior silver years. Guess what I'm doing? And it has nothing to do with s-e-x."

"Good. What?"

"Retiring."

"*Really?* Mama, you love being a pediatrician."

"I've spent the past thirty-plus years loving it. I see absolutely nothing wrong with moving on. I'm ready for next. And I don't mean sitting in an armchair knitting hats. I'd like to travel more. Rejoin my book club. Maybe dibble and dabble in some art forms that held my interest but took a backseat to my profession. I even resumed my Spanish lessons using an app... until Mama got sick. But I'll get back to it."

I studied my mother. She was a stunningly gorgeous woman who made me a believer in Black Don't Crack mythology. The thick, raven hair that had finally allowed silver strands to creep in. The unlined café-au-lait skin. The extra fifteen or so pounds that had slipped onto her frame recently were, in my father's opinion, nicely distributed. Meaning primarily on those hips he loved to grip. She did yoga, walked regularly, and was an advocate of her own good health. But it was her fearless, vibrant spirit that held my admiration, respect, and attention at that precise moment.

"Savannah Turner, you just earned my fangirl badge."

She played coy, striking a simpering pose and batting those lashes again. "I do my best."

"Seriously, Mama, we need to continue this line of discussion after I make sure PopPop eats. I need to talk about... some things."

"I'm here when you're ready, baby."

Kissing her cheek, I grabbed a bottled water, my sandwich, and a napkin from the tray and headed indoors only to find my grandfather dozing. My intent was to tiptoe back out of the room. I was halted by his drowsy protest instead.

"Where you sneaking off to?"

"I thought you were asleep and didn't want to disturb you."

"Well, I was and you did. Is that my sandwich?"

"No, sir. I left yours on the veranda with your out-of-order daughter."

"Out-of-order?"

I feigned offense. "She's trying to expose me to matters of a delicate nature for which I am simply not ready."

"You leave my baby girl alone." He chuckled quietly while standing, stretching. Even with the effects of age, my grandfather was still a tall and imposing man—a proverbial gentle giant.

"Your 'baby' is sixty-something-young and talking nasty."

"You ain't heard nothing till she, Mattie, and your Aunt Sadie get to going. It'll either make you wish for temporary deafness, or put hair on your chest. Take your pick."

"I pass."

Pinching my nose, my grandfather walked out, leaving me to slide into his seat and eat while watching my grandmother sleep. Despite the beep of the heart monitor, my eyes went to the gentle rise and fall of her chest, confirming for myself the evidence of her yet being with us.

Sipping bottled water, I wished I could freeze the moment in time, to defeat death and stop its progress. Or to simply and eternally have this memory, this moment. I suddenly wanted to grab a voice recorder, a notepad, and capture all the lessons Nana had ever taught me, and those she hadn't but might've wished she had. I wanted to rewind time and experience my life with Nana, repeatedly.

"I just want to hear your voice again before you go."

Unable to finish my sandwich, I placed it on the side table and, after washing my hands, I sat at the foot of the bed and lifted the covers. Removing the fuzzy socks covering her feet, I frowned at the swelling about Nana's ankles. Grabbing the CBD oil, I poured it onto my palm, and rubbed my hands together to warm it before massaging her gently as if she were my fragile treasure.

Something in the steady motion of my hands was soothing. Or perhaps it was the phenomenon of me being the one to minister to my grandmother, physically. She wasn't wiping my tears, kissing my booboos, or rocking me against her chest due to some perceived insult or childhood ailment. I had the privilege of touching her with hands filled with love, appreciation, and honor. From her feet to her ankles and legs, I firmly but tenderly massaged until I was lost in therapeutic motion and found myself humming some old, nameless song as if a natural action.

"That's. Nice."

Soft as feathers and wholly unexpected, her voice shocked me so badly that I nearly dropped the bottle of oil. "Nana?"

Her weak smile was the sweetest, most brilliant sight I'd ever seen.

Hurrying to the head of the bed, I sat gingerly, facing her and holding her hand. "Hi, my beauty. How're you feeling?"

Her words were spaced out and delicate. "Like. Heaven's. Waiting."

Her sudden coughing kept me from responding. Quickly grabbing the water glass on her nightstand, I eased her forward while positioning the drinking straw at her lips, encouraging her to take slow, gentle sips. When finished, I repositioned her against her mountain of pillows. "How's that?"

"Should. Bite. My. Tongue?"

"Yes, you should Miz Mattie," I playfully scolded, loving the sound of her voice even though it was soft, weak, and her words were slowly formed. "Are you hungry?"

She shook her head. "Want. To. Read."

Coming from a retired teacher with so many books that my grandfather's anniversary gift to her one year had been renovating the largest of the two spare bedrooms into a library with wall-to-wall built-in bookcases, her request wasn't surprising. "What would you like to read?"

"My. Stories."

"Which stories, my brown beauty queen?"

"Mine."

I had no idea which book she was referring to; still, I used it as a bargaining chip. "I'll read to you *if* you eat for me. Nothing major. Applesauce, or grits, or a protein shake. Can you manage that?"

Narrowing her eyes at me, she called me a name. "Lawyer."

"Yes, ma'am, I am." I laughed when she stuck out her tongue. "I'll be right back."

Both my grandfather and mother were clueless as to what book Nana wanted. Assuring them I'd find it, I refused their help, and made them continue their lunch versus aiding my search, or running in to check on our beloved, interrupting our coveted alone time.

"Okay, which book does she want?" In the center of Nana's private library, I eyed her plethora of literature.

Designed for her comfort and bearing traces of Nana's signature White Linen scent, the room was an enchanted haven with its armchairs, loveseat, and side tables, its Black art and statuettes. It was a place in which the mind could rest while indulging in fantastical, literary escapes.

Finding a book face down on one of the side tables, I scooped it up, slipping my finger between the pages so as not to lose Nana's spot. I smiled when she pointed at the book the moment I re-entered her room.

"A deal is a deal, Miss Butterfield," I joked. "I'll read, but first you eat."

Triumphantly feeding her a single-serving cup of applesauce, I frowned when half-way through she lay a hand on my wrist and said, "Wrong."

"My apologies. Did you want something to eat other than this?"

She shook her head. "Wrong. Book."

"Oh. What's the title of the one you want?"

"In. The. Closet."

While she preferred the works of Harlem Renaissance authors, my grandmother was well-read with a somewhat eclectic taste spanning many genres. One of her favorites was thriller-mysteries. *In the Closet* sounded as if it fit that category.

"I'll get it for you," I promised while helping her to a few sips of water. Seeing the applesauce container was nearly empty,

I praised her eating, probably much as she had mine when I was a baby.

Making sure she was comfortable, I kissed her cheek before returning to the library.

Ten minutes later I was still searching.

A consummate organizer, Nana's bookshelves were neatly alphabetized by authors' last names. Within each author's section the titles themselves were in alphabetical order, offering further organization to Nana's haven.

"I can't help myself," she always claimed whenever we teased her fastidiousness. "That neatness comes from my being the daughter of a domestic."

Smiling but not knowing the author's name, I pulled my phone from my pocket and searched the internet. I found nothing. Similar titles, but not the one precisely mentioned. Still, I used the names of authors with the closest matches to aid me in searching the built-in bookshelves. Producing nothing, I headed back to the bedroom.

"Nana, there's—" Stopping when I realized she'd fallen asleep, I looked around her bedroom but was unable to find anything remotely close to what she'd requested. "I give up."

Intending to sit and simply be in her company, a sudden urge to relieve myself had me running down the hall to the guest bathroom. Dancing in place, I managed not to wet myself while fumbling with that pregnancy test which, thank God, I successfully completed.

"I refuse to sit here waiting on you to hurry up and do something."

Knowing the device was safe where it was, I washed my hands and left the restroom.

What if…

There was no need to conjure scenarios when I'd have sheer facts in minutes. But even mere minutes felt suddenly too long. I had to occupy myself. I did so by returning to Nana's library determined to find that elusive book.

When you're looking for something don't think like yourself. Think like the thing that's missing, or the person who last had it.

Remembering my grandmother's tidbit of wisdom, I tried thinking as she did.

"In the Closet…"

That's when it hit me. It wasn't a title. Nana meant the closet. Literally.

When renovating the bedroom cum library, my grandfather had left the closet intact. Opening the door, I found it proved a precious vault, housing an old typewriter atop a portable writing table, and countless decorative hat boxes lining the top shelf.

"I remember this!"

The keys of the manual typewriter made familiar clunking sounds when I depressed them. It was not a toy and was reserved for "serious business." Nana never let us play on it. She had, however, allowed me to use that magical machine to two-finger type a letter to my parents when I'd decided to run away at the age of eight.

Unable to recall what had my eight-year-old self in a tizzy, I clearly remembered typing that missive my parents found so hilarious they framed and kept it.

"Alright, Nana, where're these stories?"

Hat box after hat box revealed frothy creations perfectly suited for a southern, self-respecting, church-going African-American woman of a certain age. Some were so elaborate they could easily hold their own at the Kentucky Derby. Modeling one myself, I found the stepstool Nana kept on hand in order to access her tallest bookshelves when PopPop wasn't around. Standing on it, I searched behind the front hat boxes only to discover I'd overlooked nothing.

"Where the heck are these stories?"

So focused on finding them, I stepped down from my perch without paying attention, my foot hitting the floor hard, and momentarily lost my balance.

I corrected myself easily while registering a dull thud beneath my feet.

"What the...?"

As I stared down at the carpeted closet floor, for some inexplicable reason my heart started pounding.

My mother often told Avery and me that if we went looking for trouble we'd find it.

Why that flashed through my mind, I wasn't sure. But it did little to temper my actions as I squatted down and prodded the carpet, discovering a weak place that sank beneath my fingertips. Rolling Nana's typing table out of the way, I noted a frayed section of carpet in a near corner and pulled on it only for the carpet to easily lift.

Old floorboards beneath revealed a slat that was slightly caved in, weak. Telling myself I was simply doing my grandmother's bidding, I removed it and placed it aside only to see a huge decorative box on the subflooring.

Three times the size as the hat boxes overhead, it took some finagling and the removal of additional boards before I managed to get it through the opening. Doing so, I sat back on my haunches and removed the lid.

I was greeted by a fragrance of history, of old, if not ancient, things. A photo album filled with yellowed, fragile newspaper clippings. A small gift box holding my great-grandfather's military dog tag. Nana Dorothy's embroidered apron wrapped in tissue paper. Several manuscript paper boxes. And dried flowers.

"Why're these here?"

Knowing how my grandmother fastidiously kept cherished mementos—like lineup rosters from PopPop's days in the Negro Leagues or her awards from teaching—in safe places, this depository beneath floorboards made something tingle inside me, as if I'd unearthed a mystery. Thrilled by the idea, I opened one of the manuscript paper boxes, finding a bevy of letters with envelopes addressed to *Mattie Banks* stapled to the front of each, the massive stack bound by a pink, satin ribbon.

True to Nana's meticulous self, the letters were in order according to the date, the earliest envelope being postmarked November 1956.

"That was five months after Mama was born."

Adrenaline pumping through me, I read the simple missive emblazoned across the first sheet.

For Savannah.

That was it. No signature. Nothing. Just a two-word message that proved as consistent as the envelopes postmarked Montgomery, Alabama with no return address, no name, initials only.

Carefully filtering through the pile, I saw that the missives and postmark never changed. Only the dates.

"Who's E.J.?"

Knee-deep in mystery, I set the mound of letters with their attached envelopes aside to find a sizable stack of typewritten pages neatly clipped together as if some forgotten Hemingway manuscript.

Like the letters, the top page revealed two words only.

My Stories.

Lifting the cover sheet, the words jumped out at me.

December 1, 1955.
Montgomery, Alabama.

I got on that bus not realizing how that ride would utterly change my sixteen-year-old life. I was a child expecting a baby. I was afraid, and had made a hard decision to do away with the innocent evidence of my fornication. But history happened instead. And when it did, it led me down an entirely different path from which there was no turning back.

Stopping suddenly, I thumbed through the pages only to see what appeared to be a complete manuscript. "Oh my God! Nana wrote a novel?"

My amazing grandmother was a multi-layered woman, but how in the world had I not known of *this* particular talent? And why had her work been packed away rather than allowed to see the light of day?

Enthralled, I sat on that closet floor, Nana's Sunday-go-Meeting hat on my head, reading, so absorbed that I forgot to run and check my pregnancy test.

CHAPTER NINE

Mattie

Mama became sullen. Silent. As quiet as the unspoken secret between us. That secret swirled and swayed like a living entity, taking up residence in our already cramped living space. No matter how she pleaded, cajoled, or threatened I couldn't bring myself to identify the father of my child. I'd never defied my mother in anything, but my inability and refusal to reveal Edward's identity was for her sake.

She loved the Stanton children, had helped raise them. Her disappointment in me was crushing, but for her to know that it was Edward who'd put me in the family way would be devastating to her emotions and her money.

The day before Mama discovered me half-naked and unable to hide the evidence that I'd done married folks' business, I'd overheard her talking to the woman who worked for Miz Boynton down the street. Apparently two of their fellow domestics had been let go by their employers for participating in the boycott. Blackballed when their employers spread the word on their "turncoat doings," those two women had been unable to find new positions. The fine White women of Montgomery knew how to unify themselves against Colored insurgents. I couldn't make my mother another victim.

Mama's being a live-in not dependent on public transportation didn't make her immune to retaliation, in my opinion. If Miz

Stanton even thought Mama was up to something subversive there'd be repercussions. I was terrified at the notion of what Miz Stanton might do if faced with the truth that her precious son had been "playing in the woodshed with dark meat" and made a baby. She'd do more than catch the vapors. She'd unleash her genteel southern fury on Mama in a way that would leave us broken and breathless. Rather than subject Mama to that decimating whirlwind, I was stubbornly quiet, unfairly allowing her to make up scenarios.

"Is it that Daniel Davidson? I've seen him watching you when he's supposed to be listening to the sermon."

Hating the distance my secret created between us, I silently allowed my mother to suspect every Colored boy I was acquainted with. From school to church, and back again. When she relentlessly pressed, forcing me to speak on it, I offered three words only: "Mama, I can't."

That response never changed. Sometimes it was accompanied by tears. At others, I was dry-eyed. But I never wavered or gave in; and the wall between my mother and me grew higher as I failed to find a way to appease her need for knowledge.

Now, as I watched her from the corner of my eye, Mama's movements were efficient, precise. She was like an army general issuing orders to the additional help hired to assist with tonight's football awards dinner. Here, she was immune to any upset caused by a rebellious, secret-keeping sixteen-year-old. Her control and authority were unquestionable; every command met with, "Yes, ma'am."

"You have the front parlor. You have the rear. You have the dining room. Mattie has the foyer and the sitting room. When I'm not here in the kitchen, I will be walking each room making sure everything is as it should be and assisting. Do not at any time allow your serving trays to go empty. Return and replenish when they're down to a quarter capacity. Do not speak unless spoken to. Smile politely. And most of all, do *not* drop, spill, or otherwise upset anything. Am I clear?"

We all but curtsied as Mama began inspecting our appearance.

She nodded when pleased. Issued instructions to "straighten this" or "fix that" when adjustments were necessary. By the time she reached me, she felt formidable. But she said nothing, merely looked at me, the slightest sliver of sorrow behind the stoic mask she wore.

Dismissed, I took a tray of hors d'oeuvres and headed for the sitting room to be present once guests began milling in.

I felt less and less visible the more guests arrived and the more crowded the house became. I was a thing that blended into the background, essential to the comforts of others but, otherwise, nonexistent. I was a magical, animated piece of furniture performing a series of tricks solely for pleasing the fully living and legitimate.

This is servitude.

I felt what my mother wanted to keep me from feeling: the sense of being there but not there. Seeing, but not seen. Still, I functioned without complaint. In fact, I welcomed the diversion.

Busy playing at being nothing, I didn't have to think about the state of my relationship with my mother. Or the fact that she'd been attending more and more "church meetings" where strategies were discussed for the ongoing boycott: the continued walking, carpooling, and Colored folks with cars forming taxi services. I could forget the whispered conversations Sadie and I had at lunch with our school friends about civil rights workers trickling into Montgomery under the guise of visiting relatives; or the new young minister coming to the church on Dexter Avenue who supposedly had a voice from heaven and a degree in theology. Serving cute little fancy foods, I forgot about Mama

Bea's being burned down, and my mother signing up to cook and serve food at future strategy meetings. In my black skirt, white blouse, and apron, I thought about nothing. I simply performed the duties Mama never wanted me to without pretending to be sick and maneuvering my way out of it as she'd originally planned. My condition had Mama wanting to divert attention *away from* not to it.

Needing to reload my tray, I carefully but quickly made my way through the sitting room only to falter when hearing a voice I preferred to purge from my memory. Knowing better than to search those faces about me the way I wanted, I moved forward, focusing on my duties.

As if expecting me, Mama had a new platter of hors d'oeuvres ready and waiting. Nodding when I thanked her, she turned away, hurling instructions at the kitchen staff, leaving me to return to where I'd been.

Reentering the sitting room, I glanced about surreptitiously, trying to find the body belonging to that voice I'd recognized, that caused chills to race up and down my spine. Either the person had moved on, or the room was simply too crowded for me to see. Either way, an unsettled feeling started bubbling in my belly. Pressing past it, I silently functioned as expected.

By the time dinner had been served and the dishes cleared, I'd relaxed, telling myself it was a figment of my imagination. Following Mama's instructions to set up dessert buffet-style at the back of the dining room as Miz Stanton wanted, I was busy unloading a tray of sliced cake, my mind on everything except the man who was speaking.

A makeshift dias had been positioned in the front entry rotunda, and first-floor doors had been opened, allowing the speaker's voice to easily carry room to room. Based on the laughter floating about me, whatever joke he'd just told had been well-received. That meant nothing to me. I still wasn't listening until hearing Edward's name and the round of applause that followed it.

Glancing behind me, I saw Edward coming from wherever he'd been seated, looking handsome in a suit and tie and managing his crutches.

"In keeping with tradition, as last year's scholarship winner, this fine young man has the honor of pinning this year's recipient. I'm pleased to announce, ladies and gentlemen, that recipient is…" The speaker who turned out to be the team's coach stalled for dramatic effect. "Jonathan Travis Wallinger!"

I might not have paid attention but for the bubbling in my belly, and a glimpse of the person mounting the dias and shaking hands with the coach, then Edward. Smiling proudly, he allowed his jacket lapel to be pinned before turning to the audience. When he did, I saw that Jonathan Travis was J.T., the same White boy who'd slapped my face and would've done more if Ransome hadn't arrived on that abandoned road the night I'd fled Miss Celestine's. Up there proud as could be, next to Edward he looked like what he was: poor White trash wishing he was something.

Dinner was finished. Dessert and coffee had been served, but guests still milled about happily socializing as if in no hurry to leave. Staff made good use of the time by packing up catering items and restoring order to the kitchen. I kept busy just to camouflage being hotter than a swarm of hornets.

"You okay?"

"Yes, ma'am." I wasn't, still I lied to my mother's face.

She lowered her voice. "We can handle this if you wanna go'n back to the room and rest."

Declining her offer, I advised I'd return two folding tables to the shed. Mister Gillis, the gardener, had been kind enough to carry them in so we'd have extra surface space to use that night in the kitchen.

I was just about out the door with them when Mama called me.

As I glanced back at her, she made a hand movement, indicating I should step out onto the back porch where she joined me.

"I didn't want to say anything until I knew for sure… but I found us a place on our side of town. I'll have to find a way to and from work, but at least you can walk to school until…" Pointedly, she glanced at my stomach. "It's not much. The whole place can probably fit in the Stantons' kitchen, but at least you'll have your own room. And the landlord said we can paint and pretty it up however we want." She smiled for the first time in days. "How's that sound?"

"Real nice, Mama." I managed a smile despite my internal burning and churning.

"The Lord's working on our behalf. Everything's gonna be alright. Those tables can stay out here on the porch until Mister Gillis gets in Monday."

"They're not heavy," I assured, needing the December night air to help cool me down.

Affectionately squeezing my shoulder, Mama returned to the kitchen, leaving me marching down the stone path and across the lawn, mad.

"Makes no sense whatsoever! Here I am studying hard and wishing I *could* go to college and that would-be violator gets free money and a full scholarship. Why? 'Cause he's a White boy who can catch a football."

Angry, I managed to get the shed open and simply tossed in the tables.

What we referred to as "the shed" was actually a rather large storage room, at least the size of a one-car garage. Mister Gillis referred to it as his "workshop," and had painstakingly arranged it with shelving and crates to house his implements. My tossing those tables and hearing them crash into something, and the subsequent sounds of items falling, stopped me from stomping away.

It would be rude of me to make a mess and leave it for Mister Gillis to clean.

"I'm not Abby."

Flipping on the light switch, I examined the damage. It wasn't bad. Nothing was broken, and I'd only knocked some things from a shelf, which I quickly righted before storing the folding tables properly like I should've done in the first place. Turning off the light, I stepped out and secured the door behind me before turning towards the house, intent on getting back indoors. Before I could reach the stone path, a figure stepped out of the shrubbery, directly blocking me.

I didn't need more than the moonlight and the nasty, nasally twang of his voice to know it was that slewfoot J.T.

"Well, now, if it ain't *Miss* Mattie."

Feeling naked without my suitcase to hide behind this time, I tried to slip past him.

Easily, he blocked my path. "Wait, now. No need hurrying off on my special evening. You do know this celebration is all about me, don't you?"

Saying nothing, I stared through him, willing him to disappear.

"Of course you do. That's why you kept switching your fine nigger ass back and forth tryna get my attention during dinner. That ass made it hard to focus, but I managed."

When he touched my left hip, I pushed his hand away and stepped back.

He merely laughed. "Come on, Miss Mattie. We're old friends. Wanna congratulate me?"

He touched my cheek.

Before I could move, his fingers clenched my jaw, painfully. "We got business to finish, you Black bitch."

"Let go of me!"

"Shut up."

My throat closed when he wrapped an arm about my neck, nearly cutting off my airways and ruthlessly turning my body, propelling me towards Mister Gillis' shed.

Barely able to breathe, I couldn't make a sound as I flailed, kicked, tried digging my feet into the grass. Nothing stopped my forward projection, or my being thrown into that shed as indifferently as those folding tables.

Pain roared through my abdomen with such force that I could only lay there, winded and mewling like a tortured kitten when I hit that floor hard, landing on my stomach. Instantly he was on top of me, pressing my face against that concrete floor, his other hand underneath my skirt, wrestling down my panties.

Hearing him fumbling with his belt and unzipping his pants, I gulped as much air as possible, and screamed the name I could call on in crisis. Please forgive me, but it wasn't Jesus. "*Mama!*"

That stopped nothing. Not his trying to hike my skirt about my hips, or my resistance. Feeling the utter futility of it, I took to pleading for the life that meant more than mine.

"Please, don't hurt my baby."

Like a cup of water on a wildfire, that didn't slow him down one bit.

"Well, now, Miss Mattie ain't a virgin? Good. You'll like this."

There was a noise near the shed's entrance, and I felt his weight lift.

"Get off of her!"

Glancing over my shoulder, I saw Edward, one crutch in his hand, the other pressed into J.T.'s chest, pinning him against the wall of the shed.

"What the hell's wrong with you, Stanton?"

"Mattie, fix yourself and get inside," he barked, ignoring J.T. altogether.

"I can't." With powerful waves of pain ripping through my belly, I was too afraid to move, paralyzed by nausea.

Eyes flashing angry purple lights in the dark, Edward leaned into J.T.'s face. "What did you do to her?"

"Does it matter?" the latter challenged, unsuccessfully trying to push Edward off of him.

Even with one leg in a cast, Edward had the weight and height advantage, and used every inch and ounce of it. "Don't make me ask you again."

"Why you up in arms, Stanton, over some little loose-tail house nigger?" As if he'd solved a mighty mystery, a slow sneer twisted J.T.'s evil lips. "Well wait now, just a minute. Am I intruding on your territory? Is little Miss Mattie *your* nigger bitch? I guess that would make you the father of that mongrel baby she claims to be carrying. Am I right, goody two-shoes, almighty Edward?"

Time seemingly stood still as Edward stared at me on that cement floor, protectively cradling the life we'd created.

Taking advantage of his distraction, J.T. let loose a right hook before I could even warn Edward, sending him flying backwards. Bowing his head like a bull, J.T. rammed his head into Edward's midsection so that they both crashed into one of Mister Gillis' shelves, bringing the unit tumbling down about them.

Scooting backwards away from the fray, I looked for a weapon. Grabbing a garden hoe, I lifted onto my knees and brought that handle down across J.T.'s back with every bit of angry strength within me.

It was enough to knock J.T. off, allowing Edward the opportunity to scramble on top of him, despite his broken leg, pinning him to the ground as if their preferred sport was wrestling.

They were punching, snarling, ripping at each other, clearly out for blood. Only the shed door flying open, the light being flipped on, and Mama and two men rushing in prevented true carnage.

"Get off me, nigger!" J.T. was livid when realizing the men who'd intervened were the butlers hired for the evening. "Don't you dare put your filthy Black hands on me." Wiping blood from his mouth, he spat on the floor. "Is this the way Stantons raised their niggers? To think they're equal to White men and can put their hands on them? You so busy screwing these wenches you can't seem to get—"

"Shut your ignorant mouth!"

"Make me."

One of the butlers prevented Edward from lunging.

J.T. started wildly laughing before sobering and leering at me. "That poontang must've been some kind of good for you to be protecting it like you protecting a White woman."

I heard Mama's gasp, but ignored it as, leaning on one crutch, Edward straightened to his full height.

He was suddenly calm, the icy superiority of his voice leaving no doubt that he was his mother's son. "Say another word and my father'll see to it that you lose every penny of that scholarship. And we both know you need it. You can't get to college or have half a shot at the pros without it. Me? I play for pure enjoyment." He shrugged. "I can give back the balance of my award tomorrow and my parents would simply write a check for my tuition like that." He emphasized that truth with a finger snap. "You?" He laughed. "You and your whole backwoods, cross-breeding clan needs that scholarship money to give you half a chance at doing something other than swigging rotgut like your jobless daddy until your beer belly's big as his. Without it you'll be working ten-hour shifts at a factory making rent on a rundown, rat-infested hovel where you sit in a second-hand armchair, scratching your ass and playing king before beating your greasy-haired wife then humping her hard and passing out before you can use both hands to count all your snotty-nosed kids."

Edward's raw soliloquy was met with dead silence.

The standoff he and J.T. engaged in seemed to last an hour when in fact it was less than a minute before the latter stormed out the shed, tossing, "Enjoy your half-nigger infant," over his back.

"Follow him. Make sure he leaves this property without causing further commotion."

As they'd been throughout the night, Mama's orders were met with, "Yes, ma'am."

Closing the door once we were the only persons left, she turned, her gaze swiveling back and forth between me and Edward. Her voice was hot as fire when she finally spoke. "Are you this baby's father?"

His cool composure completely gone, he was a child in the face of my mother's wrath.

"I don't know anything about a baby, Dorothy! Mattie, are you…?"

I felt myself swaying as they both whirled towards me. Something warm and wet sliding down my legs, I blacked out as my mother screamed.

Days were nights. Nights were days. Time was nothing. I floated in and out of a hazy consciousness courtesy of the medicine Doc Stanton fed me. I felt words, and heard touches; my mind was so mixed up and my senses were so keen.

As if a fly on the wall, I was there but not there, resting in my bed yet privy to Edward's hot-as-hell argument with his parents. The confrontation over the ruckus between him and J.T. The shock and appall when my mother stood in Doc Stanton's study, informing them I was having their son's baby. My mother being dismissed to see about me while the three Stantons argued viciously. Abby, in her ignorant bliss, coming to our room, whining about everyone being on edge when we should've been excited about her upcoming Christmas pageant and asking what was wrong with me. Why was I in bed, acting so incredibly sleepy?

My mother was a she-bear, protecting me, tossing out Doc's medicine after several days and spoon-feeding me a broth made with healing herbs, packing my privates with cloths soaked in poultices to prevent my body from discarding my child. She fed me. Sponge-bathed me. Prayed and hummed lullabies, braided my thick, shoulder-length hair and nurtured me. She made me lie flat, wouldn't let me sit up until a week had passed and it was clear I wouldn't miscarry.

Not fully myself, but much better than I had been since being carried unconscious from that shed, I stood beside Mama when we were summoned to Miz Stanton's sitting room that following weekend. She and Doc sat in silence, an odd energy darting between them before she addressed me.

"You're looking well, Mattie. I trust you're better?"

"Yes, ma'am."

"That's good, dear." She plunged right in without taking a breath. "Your mother has made my husband and I aware of… your condition." She cleared her throat delicately. "Is Dorothy correct in informing us that you're expecting?"

I nodded while studying the elaborate pattern of the Persian carpet beneath her dainty feet.

"I see. You've both been with us a long time. Since you were a little girl, in fact. One would think you would have gleaned something from our standard of living. Perhaps you did, but clearly not in this instance. It hurts my heart to say this, but we are a God-fearing family with a moral conscience and as such we cannot shelter iniquity and a young girl who is in the family way without a husband—"

"What my wife means to say is—"

"Dearest, I'm capable of conveying my own thoughts," she corrected her husband when he attempted to temper her statement. Returning her full attention to me, she looked me over thoroughly. "You may be too young to appreciate this, Mathilda, but as the parents of an impressionable young lady, we cannot have our Abigail unduly or negatively influenced by your deeds. I know things are different for Coloreds, but we cannot allow a double standard in our home. We are Christian people. The morals we expect of ourselves, we also expect of our help. In light of the fact that you have chosen immorality, we can no longer allow either of you to maintain functioning roles within this household."

My mother's sharp intake of breath indicated she expected some form of discipline, but not this. "Miz Stanton, ma'am—"

"Dorothy, I am not finished speaking. We have been fair employers, taking you in and treating you like family. We pay and feed you well, and only deduct the slightest bit from your wages for room and board. Abby generously gives her unneeded clothing and things to Mattie. Yet, this is how our Christian charity is repaid." She paused to place a hankie at her nose and sniff back tears before sitting ramrod straight. "Our benevolence aside, we will refuse anyone an opportunity to cast a blight upon our name or reputation. This leaves us no choice but to go our separate ways." Pushing an envelope across her writing table, she sat back, fixing the hem of her skirt, uncrossing and re-crossing her ankles. "Inside you will find two one-way bus tickets to Baton Rouge. That is where you're from, isn't it?"

My mother's voice was stronger than I expected. "Yes, ma'am, it is."

"That's what I told my husband. In addition to the bus tickets, we've included two hundred dollars. It's a month's salary along with an outrageously generous Christmas bonus. I'm certain it's more than you're accustomed to having at one time, so please spend it wisely."

"Actually, there's five hundred."

Miz Stanton snatched her head around to gape at her husband.

"It's a token of our appreciation for your many years here. And a little extra for your discretion."

"In other words, no one is to know we share a grandchild, Doc Stanton?"

Both he and his missus turned red at Mama's bluntness.

Miz Stanton recovered first. "My husband's largesse ought to comfortably keep you in a manner Coloreds are accustomed to for quite some time. We've also provided you a letter of reference for your next employer. I've signed it using my maiden name to prevent any connection to us as Doctor and Missus Stanton, because you are correct, Dorothy. No one anywhere on God's green earth is to ever know anything about your time here or any stories you've concocted that may or may not connect us to *your* grandchild."

"There's no 'may' to it, Miz Stanton. Edward is responsible, and he loves me. He even wrote it on a note. I can show you if you want."

She actually laughed at my desperate blurting. "Mattie, I understand you've been sick this past week and might possibly be a little lightheaded. So I will forgive your insinuating that my son would ever demote himself to such a despicable level. And it would further behoove you to wise up and realize when it comes to what's in—and forgive my French—a woman's panties, men will say anything."

"But, Miz—"

"Mattie, please don't imagine yourself unique in any way. Your kind has been seducing our men and leading them astray for centuries, but that stops here. We will *never* accept nor admit to any half-Colored Stanton bastard. And, Dorothy, I thank you in advance for silencing this child's impudence."

I fell quiet when Mama gripped my hand. "What does Edward have to say about this?"

"Watch your tone with me, Dorothy Banks, or the outcome of this conversation can swing a whole different way." Satisfied with my mother's brooding silence, she continued. "As for Edward? Our son's a child playing adult games, but that's not your concern. Whatever his indiscretions and dalliances, we'll deal with them. As his parents, we won't tolerate anything less than the laudatory plans outlined for him. Those plans don't include fairytale notions of some Colored gal so hot to trot that her legs fell open. Our son will graduate college cum laude, meet and marry a fine upstanding young southern woman, build a life, a home, and a noteworthy career. Then and only then will he give us grandchildren worthy of the Stanton name. That, my dears, is the only bloodline that matters or that we can ever recognize or will ever exist. This family does *not* race mix."

"Perhaps not yours, but my husband came from Old Man Stanton's line. I take it you know that."

Mama's boldness was met with Doc Stanton's embarrassment and his wife's haughty iciness.

"The past is the past. You should be thankful for that or else your punishment for speaking to me the way you have would be utterly dire and different. Now… will you be accepting this gift? Or should we rescind it?"

When Mama eventually reached for that envelope, Miz Stanton glanced at her gold wristwatch and stood. "Good. We have just enough time to get you packed and to the Greyhound station."

"Ma'am?"

"You have my husband to thank for allowing you this past week of grace, but surely you don't think you're staying another night in this house now that Mattie's fine?" She waved a hand towards the door. "I'll escort you to your room."

I glanced at Doc Stanton only to find him staring at the wall across the way, stoically frozen and saying nothing.

She stood in the doorway like some plantation overseer watching us pack what little we had, making sure nothing that belonged to "her household" went on that Greyhound bus with us—including Miz Boynton's curtains. She even reclaimed the second-hand suitcase she'd given me, supplying me with brown paper bags for my belongings.

"Leave the house keys, and your uniforms for the next live-in, Dorothy. I'd rather not waste good money on outfitting new help."

"Yes, ma'am."

"I suppose you can't take the city bus line thanks to all these uppity agitators, so you may use the telephone one final time to call someone to transport you to the station."

With that completed, we were walked outdoors and unceremoniously left at the curb like the weekly trash pick-up.

Mister Gillis arrived in ten minutes flat. While he loaded his trunk with our bags, I made the mistake of glancing back. My gaze floating to the second-story room that was Edward's, I saw a shadowy figure in the window. It moved away so quickly, it could have been my imagination. But it wasn't. And I knew it. Climbing into the backseat of Mister Gillis' car, I fingered the note in my pocket, hating it more than I suddenly hated Edward.

Why hate him for upholding tradition?

He couldn't love me. I couldn't love him. Centuries of twisted race relations had seen to that.

Accepting that fact, I sat angry at myself for being fool enough, drunk enough, to play fleshly games with fate; to give away something that had been taken from far too many generations of Colored women. Determined to never again be anybody's idiot, I quietly ripped Edward's note into irreparable little pieces, feeling betrayed and stupid. Clearly all that love he claimed to have for me was real as pixies and fairies. Just the same, Edward could've come out that house and said goodbye at the very least. I'd given him my private self. He'd given me nothing.

On the way to the station, there was no conversation. Just The Drifters and The Platters on the radio. Mister Gillis never said a word, never asked one question. But once at the station, after helping us load our bags in the luggage area beneath the bus, I watched him quietly conversing with Mama. Ending their conversation with a hug, he handed me a five-dollar bill, told me to take good care of my mother, and that he'd sincerely miss us, before watching us board the bus.

The moment he drove off, my mother grabbed my hand and rushed me off of that bus again.

"Mama, what's happening?"

"I worked for them White folks for damn near twelve years. Now she wanna kick me out, tell me where to go, and how to get there? Hell, no!" She snatched our meager belongings from the bowels of the bus, stuffing some of the bags in my arms. "Come on."

Carrying the rest herself, she took off, marching indoors. She wasn't fully literate, but knew enough to follow the "Coloreds Here" arrow.

"What're we doing?"

"Just come on, Mattie, and hush."

Falling silent, I stood aside, watching my mother wait for her turn.

"Sir, I have two tickets to Baton Rouge, but I'd like to change the destination to Valdosta, Georgia. How much would the difference be?"

The man behind the counter quoted an amount that could have easily been the full price of a ticket and not an exchange.

Mama looked at him a moment before turning her back and discretely removing the excessive amount from her brassiere and completing the transaction.

"You got about an hour to wait 'fore the Valdosta bus pulls in."

"Yes, sir. Thank you."

Following my mother to the Colored waiting section, I said nothing until we'd found a seat in a far corner. I didn't ask why she hadn't called Sadie's mother, Miz James, to drive us to the station. I understood that she was Mama's dear friend and Mama needed time to digest what was happening before bringing others into our situation. My heart hurt thinking that had she done so, at least I'd have had one last opportunity to be with Sadie before leaving my best friend and the only home I remembered. Trying not to cry, I asked about the change of destination to occupy my mind.

"Why Valdosta and the Banks clan, instead of your people in Baton Rouge?"

She looked at me without blinking. "We're going back to your daddy. I need him. You need him." She placed a hand on my stomach. "And this precious little one's surely gonna need him 'cause I don't have strength enough, not for the three of us to make it in this world living with the ways of White men and women."

CHAPTER TEN

Ashlee

Even with the typewriter's defective keys that made capital Js and Ss look like each other, I could've read Nana's manuscript in its entirety in one sitting. It was that riveting. Instead, I was forced to stop after the young protagonist's fleeing the very fascinating Miss Celestine thanks to a matter called *my* possible pregnancy filtering back into my concentration and derailing my reading.

"Oh, God…"

Dropping the manuscript back into its box, I raced down the hall to the guest bathroom, locking the door behind me while snatching up that little testing device that held my future.

Eyes closed, I said an after-the-fact prayer as if capable of manipulating outcomes.

"Okay… Dear Lord… Your perfect will be done."

Daring to peek at that stick and seeing a positive indicator, I accidentally dropped it on the floor, too shocked to take it all in.

"No… wait. Lemme retake it."

I'd purchased an additional kit. Just in case. Having downed two bottles of water with lunch, I had no problem producing for that second test. And, again? The results were positive.

"Oh, Jesus! Are you serious?"

I blindly sat on the edge of the tub, afraid to move.

"I'm pregnant?"

What to do?

Had my contraception failed? Or was it a matter of engaging sexually before my new prescription took full effect? Was I that horny, or simply careless?

"What the hell, Ashlee!"

I was too intelligent to be so ignorant.

For all my meticulous life-planning, my mind was blank of next steps.

Think, girl, think. What was your opinion, your position?

Shaking my head to clear the cobwebs, I recounted my personal stance on abortion, that it wasn't my choice. What about adoption? What if, considering our messed-up relationship, Brad didn't want a baby? Or what if he did and I didn't? A thinking, independent woman with decisions that I, ultimately, needed to make didn't mean I was heartless, dismissive. The child I was carrying was Brad's as much as mine. His opinion held weight.

But it's my body.

My thoughts flashed so fast, so furiously, that I had to harness them in order to consult myself.

What do you want, Ashlee?

I wanted to do the right thing. For myself. For Brad. But most importantly, for this innocent baby who didn't deserve crazy people or messed-up parenting. This child's father and I had been so dysfunctional lately that we argued over toothpaste and other senseless ish. Why bring an infant into that?

Faced with my myriad uncertainties, I felt like the young protagonist in Nana's story. My having education and economic power that she hadn't possessed didn't simplify my options. We both had decisions. Miss Celestine had been her only choice. I couldn't say the same. Yet, something in her proactiveness, her bravery, surpassed me, spoke to me, demanded introspection, was sobering. Her bravery compelled me to look myself in the face, literally.

Laying those test wands on the bathroom counter and removing my T-shirt, I stood before the mirror in my half-naked state. Examining. Seeking physical changes. Marveling as my fingers slowly slid back and forth across my stomach, until, as if feeling some magnetic connection—my spirit spoke for me.

I'm having my baby. I think...

My heart hammered. I felt uncertain, lightheaded. I'd never envisioned myself unmarried and pregnant, and had goals yet to accomplish. Still. Nervous as hell, I repeated those words aloud, allowing their portent and truth to sift through me, praying over their accuracy, needing their tangibility. "I think I'm having my baby."

Hands protectively splayed across my stomach, I stared at my mirrored self, too afraid to breathe.

"Honey, I'm fully booked today and have no openings for the next three weeks. Oh, wait! I see a scheduled meeting has been pushed back to a later start time. If you can get here by seven forty-five tomorrow morning, I can see you then. It's early—"

"I'll take it. Thank you so much, Doctor Laurance."

"Don't mention it, sweetie. See you then."

"Yes, ma'am. Oh, Doctor Laurance! About Mama."

She chuckled lightly. "Doctor-patient privilege, Ashlee. Savannah won't hear a thing from me."

Thanking her again, I disconnected, glad to have had Doctor Laurance as my gynecologist from the time I was sixteen until I went away to college. With Valdosta being too far from Atlanta to visit my current practitioner, I'd phoned Doctor Laurance—who was also a close family friend and colleague of my mother's—needing clinical confirmation and discussion versus relying solely on store-bought proof of pregnancy. I appreciated her discretion and reassurance of her adherence to doctor-patient confidentiality. Additionally, she was part of my health insurance network. Even if she wasn't, any out-of-pocket expense would've been worth it. That solved, I was left with getting through the day with a straight face and minimal nervousness.

Clearly starring in school plays and reciting poems at church on Easter Sundays did not a good actress make, though. More than once Mama asked me if I was feeling well, causing Daddy and PopPop to stop eating dinner and grant me their undesired attention. At one point, Mama even felt my forehead and told me I looked strange before asking, yet again, if I was okay. And Nana? When I tended to her, her penetrating eyes seemed to track me.

Don't be paranoid, Ashlee.

By the time I climbed into bed that night, I was exhausted from dodging my family's inquisitive looks and inquiries. However, sleep evaded me as I lay thinking about my imminent life changes.

"I'm physically fit. Youngish."

Thirty-two wasn't too old for first-time motherhood. Right?

Kicking off the covers, I tried allaying fears that if and only if there was considerable risk to myself or the baby, I'd have to consider termination. I suddenly needed that knowledge before informing Brad that we were pregnant. Lying in the dark, a symphony of crickets drifting through the open window, I gave voice to haunting considerations.

Is my baby healthy?

What's the due date?

Is it too early to determine the sex? If not, do I want to know in advance?

How much weight will I gain?

Can I deliver vaginally?

What about Lamaze classes?

What does this mean for my career, and do I care?

If Brad walks away, am I strong enough to do this without him?

I had no answers for my many questions. Except the last. I offered myself and my child a sound "yes" without false promises to either of us about how amazing a parent I'd be. I could love this child unconditionally only because of the parental units who loved and raised me.

Daddy. PopPop. Nana. Mama.

My mind fastened on my grandmother and mother because I was them. Black. A woman. Yet, I was outstripped by their excellence. Even with imperfections they were brilliant. Women who mothered with their whole selves. Nurturers by nature. Seemingly fearless. Loving. They were my sheroes and I was awed by them. Growing up, I'd kept them busy with T-ball, cheer squad, ballet, and a host of extracurricular activities. Without complaint, they supported my interests. Dried my tears at my first heartbreak. Always listened as if my words were jewels, instilled confidence in who I was, and what I had to say. They comforted but never coddled. Disciplined me without breaking my spirit. Taught me Nana's teacake recipe and how to provide for myself. They'd set the bar so high I didn't think I could reach it.

"Now, I really can't sleep."

Remembering the treasure retrieved from Nana's library closet, I turned on the lamp, hopped out of bed, and grabbed the manuscript box from atop the dresser. There was something so engrossing about Nana's novel, an inexplicable connectivity. Perhaps it was the commonality of our being young, unwed pregnant females that made me feel as if I'd stepped intimately into her heroine's story. Picking up where I'd paused I read until sleep won and I drifted off, dreaming I was Nana's protagonist seated on the floor of her school bathroom, contemplating pending parenthood.

*

Leaving Doctor Laurance's office the next morning, I headed for the clinic's pharmacy to pick up prescribed prenatal vitamins, feeling somewhere between giddy and a little loopy. My best guesstimate was off only a bit. I was six, not five, weeks pregnant. A definitive due date was forthcoming with additional tests, but according to Doctor Laurance, I should expect "a bouncing bundle" mid-July next year.

Right around Nana's birthday.

That bittersweet thought circling my head, I checked the pharmacy's digital marquee. Seeing *A. Turner* was already in the queue, I found an empty seat and took deep, cleansing breaths.

I'm pregnant and I'm doing this.

My time with Doctor Laurance had helped push uncertainty to the background, allowing joy to flicker. What had started as an ember was steadily growing so that I felt its tender warmth in my belly. Resting a hand on my abdomen, I launched my email app on my phone while waiting for my prescription to be filled just to give myself something to do versus sitting there looking crazy and smiling.

Deleting nonsense that should've landed in spam, I responded to a few messages and took advantage of a discount from one of my favorite Black-owned body butter companies before landing on a work email I wished I'd missed. I managed to keep my blood pressure from rising by reminding myself that I was in public, and pregnant.

> *Duncan, Vachon, and Mallory is pleased to announce the promotion of its newest senior associate.*

Ross Humphries' fat face smiled out from the pages, his round, fish-belly cheeks all self-congratulatory and privileged-looking.

The write-up heralding his worth included statements from the partners as well as Ross himself.

"This promotion is a significant step towards my wife and I establishing a family."

I hope you're sterile and kissed with E.D.

The idea of Ross suffering erectile dysfunction had me laughing loudly. I quieted when an older gentleman across the way raised an eyebrow at me.

Be sweet, Ladybug.

Hearing Nana's constant caution, I told myself I was bigger than bitterness and tethered my laughter.

Call you in five.

That incoming text sobered me completely.

My father called me bossy; my mother, nosey. There was truth in both of their perspectives. Bottom line, I wasn't a woman who liked being on the giving or receiving end of surprises. The lawyer in me liked my data controlled, neat. My love was pretty much the same: surprises were *not* his thing. Honoring that fact, I'd left Brad a voicemail message the moment I walked out of Doctor Laurance's office. Now, he'd responded.

Ideally, I'd have preferred to tell him face-to-face, yet I knew it would be impossible for me to hold something as monumental as being pregnant until returning home at the end of next week. Respecting him and our relationship, I made the decision to say nothing to anyone. Not even Dorinda, who kept blowing up my phone. Texting that I'd get back to her as soon as I could was my only response. The father of my child deserved to be the first to know.

"Here we go," I muttered in response to my cell phone suddenly singing Brad's ringtone. Inhaling deeply, I accepted the call. "Hi."

"Hey, baby. How're you? How's Miss Mattie?"

"Nana's… still here." I'd noticed a decrease in the swelling in her legs and feet after massages with the CBD oil, but chose not to say anything in the event that it was a fluke. Besides, while any relief was welcome, decreased swelling didn't eradicate cancer from her body. "Thanks for asking."

"Of course. Please tell everyone they're in my prayers. Now, how're you?"

"I'm—"

"Wait. Babe, hold on."

Background noise indicated someone else had demanded his attention and I was treated to a muffled conversation that seemed slightly tense if not urgent.

He returned after a minute. "Okay, I'm back."

"What was that?"

"I'm on campus. The student group I advise have planned an all-day sit-in tomorrow."

"Because?"

"Students are protesting what they deem the unjust and racially biased firing of a Latina professor. The protest will be campus-wide with demonstrations and the press. Apparently, this protest is garnering unwanted media attention. So the dean called me, requesting an emergency meeting."

"What does he want you to do?"

"Haven't met with him yet, but knowing him, he'll ask me to confer with my student group and somehow prevent this protest. As if I can."

"You'd better go then."

"No, the faculty here is woefully White, so I say power to the people. Let the sit-in begin. In fact, I think I'll cancel my class tomorrow and protest with the students." This was the person I'd fallen in love with, a man of ethics and action. "Back to you. How're you holding up?"

Ashlee Turner.

Not only did the pharmacy's marquee choose that moment to flash my name in bright green, but the P.A. system blared it as well.

"Who's calling your name that loudly, and what're you doing?"

"I'm at the pharmacy picking up something for Nana."

Lord, forgive me.

Suddenly nervous, I couldn't bring myself to divulge the truth in a public place, surrounded by strangers in varying degrees of health and wellness. I desired privacy. Just my love and me.

"Oh, okay. Hey, before I forget, I read *The Journal* this morning and saw Humphries' promotion announcement."

Issued weekly, *The Journal* was a newsletter dedicated to legal professionals in the state, providing information both relevant and up to date. Brad and I were subscribers, but I obviously hadn't viewed the current edition.

"Yeah, I just saw the company's email. Damn delightful."

"It's trash. Plain and simple."

Making my way to the pick-up window, I listened to Brad going in, ranting on my employers, calling them cowards and imbeciles too stuck in the good ol' days and archaic ways to recognize and reward deserving talent.

When his tirade dwindled, words slipped from my mouth before my brain fully registered them. "I shouldn't even return."

He met my whimsical wish with silence.

"Miss Turner?"

"Just one moment." Exchanging a polite smile with the pharmacy technician, I handed her my medical insurance card and I.D. before turning and speaking quietly to Brad. "I'll call you right back."

"Please do. We obviously need to talk."

Disconnecting, I gave the technician my attention only to be redirected to a pharmacist for a consultation when confirming this would constitute my first time taking prenatal vitamins. That resulted in an additional wait. Twenty minutes later, I headed for the parking lot.

Seated in Mama's car, I took a moment to admire the soft light of autumn. Red and golden leaves floated effortlessly from branches, dying a death that was necessary and natural. Soon, branches that were once heavy with green would be stripped naked. The earth would slumber, refreshing itself before blooming again.

"I'm really pregnant."

A cocktail of fear and excitement flitting through my stomach, I acknowledged my own season of change, honored that life had chosen me.

I can do this.

"*We* can do this." Correcting myself, I dialed Brad. There was no answer and my call rolled to voicemail. "Call when you can."

Message left, I drove off thinking about the innocent life growing inside of me and the ten thousand ways I'd possibly fail at parenting. Could I do the things expected of me? Could I live up to Nana's or my mother's examples, or do half of what they had? Being a pediatrician hadn't prevented Mama from excelling at motherhood. She was there whenever I was sick. Made sacrifices. Returned to Valdosta after becoming pregnant with me just so my older brother and I could grow up on our own land surrounded by a loving family.

"But Mama reached her goal." I hadn't. I wasn't a senior associate, nor did I have my own practice.

Do you honestly want that?

That unexpected question was explosive, filling me with so much doubt that I backpedaled to what I'd blurted out on the phone to Brad.

I shouldn't even return.

I'd considered it a gut reaction to that Ross Humphries bit. But was it?

Heading for a park not far from our homestead, I clutched the steering wheel as an avoided truth commanded center stage. "Oh... my... God. I *don't* want this..."

Thankfully, I was safely parked as that weighty revelation hit. I had to sit a minute trying to process it.

"If that's true, why'd I spend the last ten months of my life chasing that senior position?"

Because I was supposed to, I'm deeply competitive, and it made sense.

Being my normal, laser-focused self and diving all in had also been a perfect way to camouflage an inexplicable brooding discontent.

Senior attorney was the logical trajectory I'd set for myself long before finishing law school. Making partner or establishing my own practice was next on that professional To Do list. The aspiration was honorable. But faced with the futility of the chase, surrounded by life's changes, those I loved and what was truly important, I questioned my take-no-prisoners pursuit.

Like the riddle about which came first, the chicken or the egg, I couldn't decipher if my life's imbalances had preceded the quest, or if the quest had contributed to them. Certainly, relationships were a two-way street, but I owned my ish, admitting I'd been stalked by and behaved according to internal discontent spewing from a broken fountain. I'd even allowed the stress and pressure of insane pursuits to infiltrate my home, my haven. Seated in my mother's car, honesty flowed through me, washing me of the compulsion to desire futile things.

"Mama's retiring from a thirty-year career." Exiting the car, I reminded myself of that fact as if needing permission to veer from my carefully scripted path. "And what if Nana's stories had been published?"

I had no knowledge of why they weren't or if she had ever tried but, undoubtedly, my grandmother's life would have differed had they been. Growing to adulthood in a time before personal computers and technology simplified things, and staring down the face of legally enforced prejudices, perhaps she had tried her hand at publishing. Maybe Nana had fought only to decide—like Mama and her career—it was okay to walk away.

"It's okay for me to walk away."

And to admit I want and need something different.

I wouldn't deny the anger resulting from being overlooked, yet suddenly, not getting that promotion felt like relief. And being away from the office had proved freeing.

"No more autopilot. Or doing what I do just because it's expected of me."

That picturesque autumn day was almost lost on me as I meandered about a park abuzz with mothers chasing toddlers, and a group of young and seasoned citizens doing Tai Chi in the sweet cool of the morning. When the instructor beckoned me over with a smile and a wave, I politely declined and kept walking.

What kind of mother do you want to be?

There was a simple connection between my career path and mothering: honesty. Like my mother and grandmother, I wanted to parent and live with integrity. They'd made sacrifices and lived without some dreams, but they'd lived honestly. I couldn't be my best self without walking in truth, so when truth came barreling at me I welcomed it, admitting I was missing my purpose.

Knowing my profession differed from my artistic and altruistic purposes, I unearthed memories of growing up with parents and grandparents who advocated for social justice. I'd been regaled with stories of my grandparents protesting during the Civil Rights era of the fifties and sixties. A retired teacher, Nana had conducted story time at the local library until two years ago; and PopPop had used his construction skills to help build houses long before there was a Habitat for Humanity. I'd personally witnessed their volunteering at food banks and feeding the homeless. I'd followed my parents' lead and volunteered at local campaign offices for Barack Obama when he was running for president; as well as marched as a family with Black Lives Matter. These were the people who raised me to know my own worth and power, and to understand I rose because of the struggles of our ancestors. All of my life I'd been told I was destined for greatness. Rising higher, going farther wasn't an option; it was my gift to the generations. Yet, it had been made painfully clear that my elevation wasn't simply for or about Ashlee. I had an obligation to better the world, and the lives of others.

Use every one of your gifts down here so that when you leave this earth your tank is empty, but the legacy you leave is overflowing.

Sometimes those words were spoken with loving encouragement, others as if a scolding; but my brother and I had heard them often enough from Nana's lips to know she meant business.

"What's my gift?"

Drawing.

It had been a passion since childhood—I'd been notorious for drawing on anything within reach. As a child, my parents had gifted me a variety of paints and brushes, but my enjoyment of painting couldn't match or parallel my love of sketching.

Encouraged by a high school art teacher to consider a career as an illustrator, I'd been too endowed with a sense of duty to even consider it. Now?

"What if?"

Girl, you're having a baby. Don't get crazy.

But, what if I found a way to utilize my artistic gift in a manner that was liberating for me personally and professionally? What if I could synthesize my artistry with being an attorney and somehow benefit humanity by involving social equality or justice?

"Ash, that makes zero sense."

Finishing a final lap about the pond, I wanted to laugh at myself until seeing a young dad hoisting his fussy toddler onto his shoulders. Instantly, fussy tears turned into wide-mouthed giggles and grins.

"That part! That's what I want."

I paused, enjoying that little one's glee while acknowledging the advancement opportunities my parents, grandparents, and ancestors known and unknown had granted me. They'd hoisted, carried, lifted me. Sacrificed their strength and ability. Allowed me to rest on their shoulders not merely to achieve academically or professionally. But so that I could be and breathe and move in this world in ways denied them. So that I could laugh and twirl and live with a sense of freedom that caused my spirit such joy that it giggled and grinned. It wasn't just the work; joy and wonder were bundled within the legacy as well.

"And that's what I've been missing."

Making my way back to the car, I admitted that life's pressures had diminished my joy and, in some ways, muted my internal colors and vibrancy. One hand on my abdomen, I drove home, spirit glittering with new possibilities.

*

My mother was on an urgent business call when I walked in; my father was at his office. PopPop was in front of the family-room TV, dozing. Tipping into Nana's room I expected to find her napping as well, only to discover her semi-propped up in bed.

"Dear sweet Jesus! Look at my nana sitting up here looking better than a billion-dollar business."

Laughing quietly at my foolishness, she patted the bed.

I eagerly accepted her invitation, remembering snuggling between my grandparents as one of my favorite places.

Holding Nana's hand, I kissed it before gently settling it on my lap. "How I wish I'd been here—"

"Mmm-mmm." Her soft grunt was filled with admonition as she fiercely shook her head.

Duly chastised, I reclined on my side, facing my grandmother and sharing a pillow with her. "Avery gets in the day after next."

"Baby." Her voice was faint yet distinct.

"No, Janelle and the kids aren't coming. Just Avery."

"Baby." She repeated the word more forcefully.

"Ma'am?"

Releasing my hand she touched my stomach. "This baby."

Too shocked to speak, I simply stared at her as she lifted her eyebrows as if challenging me to deny what she'd—with her wise woman's insightfulness—perceived. Unable to, I nodded affirmatively.

Her fragile smile was radiant to me.

"Good. Blessing." That said, Nana surrendered to the soft comforts of her pillows and fell asleep.

CHAPTER ELEVEN

Mattie

Valdosta, Georgia
January 1956

I don't remember much of Christmas. I can't claim being too keen over New Year's, either. Cherished holidays melted and flowed into weeks until time was nothing for me after Mama and I left Montgomery. Days and nights became mere stepping stones to my baby. It wasn't exactly easy, but Mama insisted we avoid bitterness after our eviction.

"We're not losing any sleep hating nobody."

Instead, we focused on the gift of life I was growing.

One of the first things Mama did after getting us situated with family was take me to a midwife so I'd understand how far this child had progressed in my belly. Having delivered hundreds of infants and known for her discretion, that backwoods midwife examined me with expert fingers, claiming I was good and healthy and would have a baby in my arms come the end of June. July at the latest. Too scared to be excited, I prayed that there'd be nothing wrong with my baby.

Sometimes I wanted to draw a family tree to see how closely Edward and I were connected. But I couldn't. It scared me too much knowing Daddy and Doc Stanton were related, that Old Man Stanton's blood flowed through both of their veins. When I had nightmares of birthing a two-headed baby, Mama assured me that years of mixing with outside blood had lessened any chance of deformities my child might inherit on account of its parents being distant relatives.

With Daddy being from a family of five brothers and six sisters, my Banks relatives were abundant and what I hoped they'd be: warm, welcoming. Despite my not having visited in years, aunts and uncles hugged me fondly, claiming I looked more like Matthew Banks than he'd looked himself. My presence offered them a piece of him; they treated me as if a beloved treasure from the past.

Mama and I wound up staying with Daddy's sister, my Aunt Odelle. She was a widow like Mama, raising four daughters by herself. Her oldest were twins about my age. Rather than exclude me from their twin intimacy though, they let me in, so that life with Naomi and Ruth was like being sandwiched between living bookends. Famous for finishing each other's sentences, they were talkative, curious.

"Mattie, what was it like?"

I'd gone from simply sharing a room to sharing a bed. Sometimes we slept one facing the foot, two at the head, or vice versa. That night, we were three in a row, insulating ourselves with each other's warmth against winter's cold.

"What was 'what' like, Naomi?"

"You know, getting yourself in a family way?" she whispered.

"She means doing it. Sex." True to her nature, Ruth was far more direct.

I'd developed a comfortable bond with my cousins but, other than with Sadie, I hadn't discussed the details of that night and what I'd done with Edward. Revisiting it felt strange. "It was okay. I guess."

"Was it or wasn't it?" Ruth challenged.

"Well… I was kind of drunk—"

"*Drunk*? Ooo, Mattie, you were doing all kinds of sinning! Drinking. Fornicating. You need to get outta this bed before I catch some loose woman's disease and lose my chance at heaven."

We couldn't help laughing at Naomi's comical theatrics.

"Fine. I'll leave."

Ruth grabbed my arm, preventing me. "Forget Naomi and tell me."

"I liked the kissing."

"Was he a good kisser?"

"Yes. I guess."

"Enough with the guessing, Mattie." Ruth had had her fill of any indecisiveness. "Stop hemming and hawing. Either he was or he wasn't. Which is it?"

"I'm no expert, Ruth. He was the first boy I'd ever kissed. I liked it. So I guess that means it was good. Maybe that's 'cause he didn't have White-boy lips."

You could've heard a mouse pissing on cotton, it got that kind of quiet. Even Ruth was so tongue-tied she said nothing as both twins shot upright in bed staring down at me in the dark.

It took a near minute for Naomi to find her voice. "Mattie, you're carrying a White boy's baby?"

I hadn't been present when it happened, but I knew by the sometimes sad way they looked at me that my mother had informed my adult relatives that I was carrying a mixed child. My cousins, however, hadn't been privy.

"Yes, Naomi."

Her sharp inhalation sliced through the night. "Did he... *force you?*"

The fear in her voice prompted me to reach for her hand. "No, cousin. He didn't. I did it 'cause I wanted to. 'Cause that liquor loosened me and had me thinking maybe I loved him, too."

"Do you?"

"Not anymore." Images of Edward turning away from his bedroom window as his mother evicted us flashed across my mind. He wasn't a full man yet and was still subject to his parents. Even so, he hadn't done a thing to defend me to Doc or Miz Stanton. And he certainly hadn't stood up for this baby. I couldn't forgive him that, or Miz Stanton for the evil things she'd said. Treating me like some vile whore who belonged in the streets, or some Jezebel trying to wrap her precious son in my web.

Over the shock, Ruth lay down and turned towards me. "I love this baby 'cause it's half yours, Mattie, but you couldn't pay me to let a peckerwood put his thing in me. Mama makes us carry protection whenever we go somewhere without her in case one of 'em gets a hold of us and tries something. 'Cause you know that happens."

Thanking God yet again, I pushed aside ugly thoughts of that J.T. "What kind of protection?"

"A switchblade. Razor blade. One of the girls at our school told me her grandmother made some kinda pouch for her to push up inside her *pocketbook*. You know… her privates. Anyhow, it's got thick cotton all around the outside, and a string attached so she can pull it out. But guess what's in that pouch?"

"What?" Naomi and I asked in tandem.

"Cayenne pepper and crushed glass."

"Stop lying!"

"Mattie, God's my witness. That's what she told me."

"Who?"

"Lettie."

Naomi sucked her teeth dismissively. "Ruthie, you know like I do Lettie Giles ain't got the good sense God gave a watermelon."

"Maybe not, but won't no peckerwoods be pecking in her pocketbook without slicing up his pecker and treating it to some red hot pepper."

Ruth's silliness had us laughing so uproariously that Aunt Odelle hollered down the hall from the room she and Mama shared for us to "hush up all that giggling!"

We took to whispering.

"Did it hurt, Mattie? You know, when he stuck it in?"

"Yes, Ruth, it did."

"A lot or a little?"

"At first, a *whole* lot. But it was a bit different by the end."

"Was it nice then?"

"Almost, but not really. Probably because it was my first time and I didn't know what I was doing. It actually felt kinda weird."

"Would you do it again?" Naomi questioned, tentatively.

"Not until I'm married. I don't want to be by myself with all kinds of babies."

"Well, Lettie says a girl won't get pregnant if you get the boy to pull out of your pocketbook before he bursts."

"Ruthie, why you all of a sudden listening to Lettie? Are you thinking about doing something?"

Ruth was quiet, not answering her twin directly, and causing Naomi to sit up in bed again.

"Are you?"

"Curtis asked me if I wanted to."

"We promised to tell each other if we ever thought about doing it." Naomi was indignant.

"Consider this your notice."

"We're fifteen and that's too young to be even thinking about boys pushing in your pocketbook. Plus, we gotta stay focused and finish school."

Something sad shot through me at the thought that I'd have to leave school soon, when binding my belly became ineffective and I could no longer hide my condition.

"Me? I'm waiting till I have a real husband with a real job and some real money."

"Naomi, lay yourself down and quit talking all loud before Mama hears. I only said Curtis asked. I ain't said nothing about agreeing to it. I simply thought about it."

"And?"

Ruth sucked her teeth. "I'm not doing nothing with that big-headed Curtis or nobody. No offense, Mattie—and not that this is you yet—but I'm too cute to be walking around feet swollen, fingers fat, nose taking up half my face, looking like I'm miserable enough to pop. I'ma keep my fine figure intact. And if Curtis can't wait, I'll send him over to Lettie. Let him help himself to some peppered-up, glassy loving."

Giggling naughtily, we settled down and fell asleep, snuggled up like a pod of three brown peas.

My tribe of cousins were a true godsend. That didn't keep me from missing Sadie.

"You can call her when we go into town Saturday."

Most of the Banks clan lived within walking distance of each other. If we had a dire need to phone anyone we could easily go to the house of a relative who had a connection. But being a domestic raising four children on her own, Aunt Odelle wasn't one of them.

Going "into town" in Valdosta wasn't the same as downtown Montgomery, but Mama's promise gave me something to look forward to throughout the week. Compared to Montgomery, Valdosta felt small. Country. But like in Montgomery, Jim Crow was very much alive, keeping those separated and segregated lines. Coloreds on one side. Whites on the other. The high school Mama enrolled me in was no different.

My cousins told me the state of Georgia desegregated schools last year, officially. Guess the schools in Valdosta were taking their sweet time with the implementation process. While I believed we deserved equal treatment and better conditions, I couldn't say I was in a hurry to go to school with White kids. I was a little afraid of how that might change things. For now, I enjoyed living close enough to walk to and from school with my cousins.

Our move to Valdosta coinciding with Christmas vacation, I'd started school there the first week of January. I was settling into school and at the end of the first week when, dismissed for the weekend, my English teacher, Miss Divine, stopped me while I was gathering up my belongings.

"Mattie Banks, may I see you a moment?"

Miss Divine's smile was like her name, lovely and light.

That did nothing to settle a sudden tightness in my chest. I was instantly on guard, nervous.

Is my belly sticking out?

I'd been blessed in not having to run to the commode every morning vomiting. And Mama said I was carrying similar to when she carried me, meaning my belly was barely bloated, while my hips and behind seemed to be bubbling up by the minute. Being new to town, folks weren't the wiser as to whether I was expecting versus being naturally big-boned and plentiful. Plus, wearing bulky clothing in winter helped my camouflaging. Calming myself with those facts, I approached Miss Divine's desk.

"Yes, ma'am?"

"Have you seen this?"

Accepting the flier she handed me, I shook my head as I read an announcement for a writing competition for the high schools in our district.

"I'd like for you to enter it."

My head snapped up. "Ma'am?"

"I'm well aware that you've only been a student here a week, but that's proven more than enough time for me to glimpse your extraordinary writing ability."

"Thank you, ma'am, but I've never entered this kind of competition. I don't think I'd be any good at it."

Saying nothing, my teacher got up and closed the classroom door before returning to her seat. "Remember the in-class responsive essay that was assigned Monday?"

I nodded.

"I shared yours with a colleague because it was so good. She, however, considered it brilliant. Seeing as how she's been teaching longer than I've been on this earth, I trust her judgment."

"But this is a creative writing competition," I insisted, holding the announcement up as if she was unfamiliar with it. "That's different."

"True. And the class, your own peers, voted your short story as the best on Wednesday, and your poetry yesterday."

Shaking my head, I softened my refusal with a smile. "Miss Divine, I really appreciate your kindness, but I can't see myself doing anything like this."

"Mattie Banks, you're gifted. Do you think the good Lord blessed you with such wonderful writing abilities for you to do nothing with them?"

When I remained silent, she took the flier, redirecting my attention to the bottom of the announcement.

A $50 cash prize will be awarded to the district's four finalists.

My eyes grew wide reading that those four would advance to a statewide competition next month, the grand prize being $500.

Hoping to save enough for our own house, my mother had been meagerly "pinching off of" that final pay received from the Stantons while looking for a job. Some wild thing in my mind shot free, daring to imagine myself entering this writing contest and actually winning. I'd gladly give those winnings to Mama to help secure her dream of owning something.

Clearly, that fantasy played on my face. It had Miss Divine smiling and nodding.

"It's not as far-fetched as you think, Mattie. No, you keep it." She declined my returning the advertisement. "Take it home. Discuss it with your parents, but the entry deadline is the twentieth."

"*The twentieth?* That only gives me two weeks to come up with something. What happens after that?" I listened as she explained the judging process and that semi-finalists would be notified by mail. Clearly, my expression conveyed I wasn't convinced.

She took my hand and smiled encouragingly. "Mattie, I believe in you. You can do this."

So stunned I barely thanked her, I hurried outdoors where the twins were waiting.

"Mattie, it's cold out here. What took you so long?"

I couldn't answer Naomi before Ruth piped in.

"And why're you looking all goofy like you sucked some funny gas or something?"

"Maybe she was in there kissing somebody."

Naomi's nonsense had all three of us giggling.

"I was talking to Miss Divine."

"What about?" they questioned, pinching each other to stave off jinxes for their simultaneously speaking.

"Ouch, Ruth, that hurt!"

"You pinched me first, Naomi."

"Unlike you, I didn't try to rip your skin off."

"Best be glad you didn't, or I'd be going home twinless."

"If you two don't quit." Linking arms with my cousins, we headed home with them fussing and me feeling something I hadn't felt since realizing I was having a baby: hope. And possibility.

"Mama thought I should write about that day I was on the bus." While traveling from Montgomery to Valdosta, I'd confessed to my mother about riding the City Line to Miss Celestine's and what had transpired. She'd been highly upset, but was careful to give the good Lord praise that I hadn't succeeded in my attempts to end my baby's existence. "But she told me to leave my name out of the story."

"Of course. You gonna do it?"

As I sat in the phone booth in the Colored drug store that Saturday, Sadie's voice sounded far away and grainy on the other end. But it was so good talking to my best friend that I didn't care. "No, that felt too new, like it might be too much for folks to digest." I would've loved penning a beautiful tribute to Miz Rosa, a thank you for her boldness inspiring me to think differently about my situation and find the courage to keep my baby. But like I said, this world didn't feel ready to honor her heroism yet. "I decided on a fantasy, instead. You know, with magic and supernatural crystals and a kingdom about to crumble because of a vicious battle of good versus evil."

"Oh, that sounds good! When do you have to turn it in?"

"In two weeks."

"You already started?"

"Yep. Last night. It can't be more than twenty pages. I already have six."

"That's 'cause you're gifted. Call and read it to me when you finish. Wait, Mattie. Your handwriting's atrocious. How's anyone gonna be able to read it?"

Sadie wasn't fibbing. My penmanship was about as pretty as a drunk, one-eyed, mangy mule in a sequin cocktail dress.

"Mama made me walk down to Aunt Lady's and Uncle Melvin's last night to call Miss Divine and tell her I accepted. My teacher was so excited she came by just to loan me her typewriter."

"God bless that woman."

We both laughed.

"Ruth's had two typing classes to my one, and she's really good. When I get tired, I lay down and tell the story out loud and she types it."

We chatted some more with Sadie updating me on the newest in the bus boycott back home until, seated in the phone booth, I saw Mama crossing the street near the corner diner coming to collect me. She had a look on her face I couldn't rightly interpret, but I knew something had happened.

Listening to Sadie, my attention was on my mother. The closer she got, the more she dropped whatever mask she was wearing so that by the time she reached the phone booth, she was smiling brightly.

I opened the door to her.

"You and Sadie aren't finished yet?"

"No, ma'am."

"Well, wrap it up."

"Hi, Miz Dorothy!" Sadie yelled as if Mama could hear her.

Obviously, she did. Laughing, Mama returned the greeting. "Tell Virginia I'll call her next weekend."

"Yes, ma'am."

"Sadie, Mama's finished window-shopping, so I'd better go. I miss you."

"I miss you, too, Mattie. I'll send you those newspaper clippings." She'd promised to send me updates on the boycott and what was happening with the fight for our rights in Montgomery. "Write me. We have to keep our pen pal relationship going."

"I will."

Saying our goodbyes, I hung up and exited the booth.

"Let's go get you a few new skirts and sweaters. Your clothes are getting snug." A size larger than me, Mama had been giving me clothes from her wardrobe to fit my growing body.

"Thank you, but we can't afford that."

"Oh, yes we can. I just got a job."

"*What? Where?*"

Mama pointed across the street. "I'm the newest cook at that diner."

Excitedly, I hugged my mother, knowing the one aspect of her domestic duties that she never minded was cooking. She loved it, actually, and prepared food with deft skill and excellence. Doc Stanton had often playfully blamed her cooking for sabotaging his fitness.

"That's wonderful! Congratulations."

"Thank you, baby. It's a nice-looking place, but you know we can't eat there." Like other establishments in the south, Mama could only enter and exit the diner through the back exit. She could cook for them but wasn't allowed to dine there, and all Colored patrons were served through a rear window and prohibited from the premises.

"We pay the same money without the same benefits or courtesies."

"That's Jim Crow living, Mattie. But that's enough of that before you sour my victory. Let's go get you some new things. Wanna come back here for some hot cocoa when we finish?"

"Isn't that a lot of spending?"

"I'm the mama. Let me worry about that. You focus on your sixteen-year-old things."

Doing as my mother suggested, my focus was firmly fixed on school, my growing baby, and that story competition. When I submitted my finished story to Miss Divine she hugged me, she was so thrilled. Together, we completed the entry form that required her signature. She took the required photo of me with a camera borrowed from the yearbook staff, sealed everything in a manila envelope, and promised to handle the rest. Telling myself not to get my hopes up, I went on about my business, but was careful to get on my knees that night before bed and pray heaven would favor my efforts before thanking the Almighty for what Miss Divine considered a gift and I'd only viewed as an ability. You could've blown me backwards with a feather when I received a letter telling me that my story had passed the preliminary round.

You, your advisor, and two family members are formally invited to an intimate awards reception for all finalists on Tuesday January 31st at six o'clock that evening. You will be photographed for publication in our local newspaper. Please dress accordingly. Your fifty-dollar prize will be awarded then.

The letter provided the date, time, location, and other pertinent details that barely registered; I was too busy screaming victoriously with the twins.

Mama was so happy she baked my favorite German chocolate cake, typically reserved for my birthday. That night we ate cake and danced around the radio, celebrating. When the twins and

I went to bed, I paused to kneel and offer up a thanksgiving prayer, feeling blessed and believing in miracles, as well as myself.

The evening of the reception Naomi and Ruth helped me bind my belly extra tight.

"Are we hurting you, Mattie?"

"Not much. I'll be alright," I lied. That binding routine was starting to be painful, leaving my midsection achy at the end of each day. Clearly, I couldn't do it much longer, but I didn't want to hurt Naomi's feelings. With Mama attending the reception with me, there'd only been one space for an additional family member. Trying to be fair, I'd suggested a coin toss. Ruth won. Naomi lost. She was acting a good sport about it, but I knew she was disappointed and made sure to give her an extra-long hug before climbing into the back seat of Miss Divine's car and driving off.

Our foursome chatted happily the entire ride, but as soon as we entered the parking lot I grew quiet.

"Relax, Mattie. This reception is partially in your honor," Miss Divine whispered as we neared the building where the event was being held.

Inhaling deeply after offering her a tight smile, I walked through the door Ruth held open.

Inside, two of the other three finalists and their guests had arrived. They were mingling, chatting and laughing, already serving themselves from a table nicely arranged with finger foods, a punch bowl, and platters bearing dainty cookies so perfectly formed and iced that they clearly came from a bakery. Music was playing from a source unknown, but even that seemed to hush when the gathering turned, silently staring at us.

A woman wearing heavy makeup, a bright-red beehive bouffant atop her head, and cloyingly sweet perfume that reached us before she did, thawed enough to move in our direction. She was wearing a badge that read "*Hello my Name is: Mrs. Adams*" on her dress. "May I help you?"

"Yes, ma'am. We're here for the award reception," my English teacher informed Miz Adams. "This is Mathilda Banks, one of the four finalists."

Busy smiling brightly at me, Miss Divine missed the other woman's flashing multiple shades of crimson. Looking at me wide-eyed and surprised, Miz Adams' horror and distress were painfully clear.

"*What're these Nigras doing here?*" A whispered hiss made it to our ears.

I felt Mama and Ruthie stiffen beside me, and reached for their hands. Unsure whether I was lending strength or drawing from it, I squeezed their hands before releasing them.

"I believe there's been some mistake." To Miz Adams' credit she was polite when asking us to wait there while she quickly retreated.

Ignoring the whispers and stares, Mama moved closer to Miss Divine, quietly questioning what precisely was happening.

"I'm not sure. Maybe we're at the wrong place. Or the right place on the wrong day—"

Before Miss Divine could finish, Miz Adams returned with a tall, white-haired distinguished-looking gentleman.

"How can I help y'all folks this evening?" His tone was even, but his expression was confused.

My English teacher quietly and calmly supplied the man with the same information as she had the red-haired woman.

"I see. Will you come this way with me please?"

Ruthie and I exchanged a look that said we both knew full well we hadn't made a mistake on the date or location before following Mama and Miss Divine down a hallway that led to a small office. Once there, the man closed the door before sitting behind a desk that seemed far too large for the space.

Clearing his throat, he focused on my teacher. "I hate that y'all wasted a trip this evening, but we're unable to include you in tonight's festivities."

"I don't understand, sir. Would you please be so kind as to explain why not?" Miss Divine wasn't disrespectful, but direct enough to cause the man's brows to lift.

Clearing his throat, he glanced at me. "You say this young lady is Mathilda Banks?"

"Yes, sir."

"Well, we apologize but there's obviously been a misunderstanding. Invitations to this competition weren't extended to Colored schools in the district. Her getting ahold of one was an error and mistake."

It might've been January, but my whole body suddenly felt hotter than an August day.

"Mathilda, do you have your acceptance letter?"

I immediately pulled it from my coat pocket when Miss Divine turned to me.

Unfolding it, she placed the notice on that oversized desk, turning it so that it faced him. "Sir, this is the letter my student received. If you would please review it you'll see that she was named a finalist and that—"

"Yes, I can see it came from our district office, but it shouldn't have. As I've already said, Colored schools weren't included in this competition."

"May I ask why not?"

A knock on the door prevented his response. "Yes?"

The beehive-haired Miz Adams scurried in, avoiding eye contact with us. "Here it is, Mister Lambert."

"Thank you." Accepting a file folder from her, he waited until she'd exited before opening it and lifting what I recognized as my entry application. Beneath that was my story, which Mister Lambert set aside as if looking for something. "Where is the student photograph that was to accompany the entry form?"

"We included it, sir."

With great care he searched the folder, riffling through every page of my story as if the photo might've slipped in between. Nearing the end of the stack, a piece of yellow notepaper fluttered loose, falling to the ground.

Picking it up, Miss Divine returned it to the desk as Mister Lambert concentrated on his search and grunted his thanks. "Unfortunately, Miss—"

"Divine."

"Yes, yes, I see your name listed here as Mathilda's advisor. The necessary photograph that was to accompany each student's entry isn't present. That alone constitutes an incomplete application. I take it you and Miss Banks thoroughly read the contest guidelines?"

"Yes, sir, we did and we strictly adhered to them."

"Then you're well aware that per those guidelines incomplete applications would not be accepted for consideration. This submission never should have been reviewed by our judges."

"But, Mister Lambert, sir, it *was* reviewed. And that review garnered Miss Banks a place as a finalist. I vow on my father's grave that a photograph was submitted. I personally took it and included it in the packet."

"I'll take your word that you did, Miss Divine. However, it is absent." He pushed the folder towards the edge of the desk. "You're more than welcome to search for yourself."

Miss Divine's shoulders slumped. "No, sir. Your search was sufficient."

He nodded, satisfied at her acknowledgment, before turning to me. "Sorry for your inconvenience, young lady, but I hope you'll have a good evening."

Understanding I'd been dismissed I turned towards the door ready to run to Miss Divine's car and let loose the tears of disappointment I was holding onto. But my teacher hadn't finished advocating for me.

"Sir, you have the entry form there. Our school name was clearly listed. That alone should've been an indicator of Mathilda's race."

Grabbing the form, he quickly consulted it. Something I could only call a triumphant smile flickered on his lips. "Actually, Miss Divine, it isn't."

"Pardon?"

He turned the form for her viewing. "Again, another piece of required information that's missing."

My teacher and I both stepped forward seeing the typewritten application.

My eyes grew big. "That isn't—"

Miss Divine made a cautionary, silencing sound before I could finish. "We apologize for that oversight, but may I ask, was the photo inclusion a means of ensuring entries by Negro students didn't accidentally slip through the cracks?"

Whatever tension had previously existed suddenly accelerated thanks to Miss Divine's bluntness.

Mister Lambert's ears turned slightly red but otherwise he was in control of himself and the situation. His eyes narrowed and he sat back in his chair as if he had reached his limit patronizing an office full of Colored women.

"Not that I owe any explanation, but that request allows us to include the winners' photos in write-ups with the local press."

"No, sir, photos are being taken tonight for that purpose."

Folding his hands on his midsection, he continued as if she hadn't spoken. "Plus, it prevents charlatans showing up claiming a prize when it isn't their work. For example, without a photograph of Miss Banks, how do we ascertain she is who she says she is? Or that there's no plagiarism?"

Unsure what possessed me, I recited the opening lines of my story that I knew in its entirety.

Possibly enthralled, Mister Lambert listened saying nothing until remembering his power didn't require him to indulge me.

"That was very nice, young lady. But, again, your entry is incomplete and we cannot in good conscience move you forward. Since you asked, I'll be direct. Yes, Colored schools being excluded is intentional. This preliminary contest is local, but the finalists advance to the statewide competition which is extremely vigorous so we never anticipate entries from the other side of the district. We don't believe in wasting opportunities, and want only our brightest students representing Lowndes County. Now, if you'll excuse me."

He stood, indicating the conversation was complete. Still, Miss Divine responded with something I didn't understand.

"Exceptional prose and structure."

Those four words had Mister Lambert's ears turning almost as red as Miz Adams' bouffant.

"Thank you for your time," she quietly stated, accepting my folder when he extended it to her.

Exiting and seeing the other two contestants enjoying the celebration, the emotions I'd kept at bay suddenly burst.

I took off running.

"Mattie!"

"I'll get her, Aunt Dorothy."

Slightly disoriented, I ran in the wrong direction and ended up near the restroom I knew better than to go into. There was no "Whites Only" sign, but this building, just like this contest, belonged to them. I was excluded. My only recourse was huddling in the corner of the alcove, crying.

"It's gonna be okay, Mattie."

I sobbed into my cousin's shoulder when she wrapped her arms around me. "Why's everything always gotta be this way? Why can't we have *anything*? I won that spot fair and square. Photo or no photo, that's my story. I wrote it!"

"I know you did, Mattie. I was right there with you. I even helped you type some of it. I can go back there and tell that man that if you want."

I straightened my stance and angrily wiped my tears. "It's not gonna matter any. He doesn't care about that." My voice rose with every word, and I felt myself shaking. "He only cares that the school district steps up on that statewide stage lily-white as always."

"Calm down, Mattie. If you get hysterical you might hurt the baby."

I opened my mouth to reply but the restroom door suddenly opened, causing me to fall silent. Out stepped what must have been one of the final contestants—a girl about my age with blonde hair cut in a bob. I couldn't tell if her green eyes were naturally that round or if the sight of us huddled in the corner caught her off guard. Saying nothing, she quickly looked us over before heading for the festivities.

"Come on. Fix your face. Aunt Dorothy and Miss Divine're waiting."

Making our way to them, I was grateful Mama didn't hug me. That would've had me blubbering all over again. Instead, she looped her arm about mine as all four of us exited the building, eyes straight ahead, heads high. Once in the car we shared a thick silence until Miss Divine hit the dashboard. Hard.

"Mattie, you shouldn't have had to go through any of this. That win was yours."

"It sure was," Mama cosigned, her soft voice wavering with emotions. "They robbed my baby. Is there somebody else we can talk to? Maybe the head of the school district?"

"You just met him. Joshua Lambert's the district superintendent."

That information had us all quiet.

A few minutes passed before something flickered in my memory. "Miss Divine, what did that 'exceptional prose and structure' mean? You said that before we left Mister Lambert's office."

"Yeah, and he turned mighty red," Ruth added.

"Remember that piece of yellow notepaper that fell to the ground? I read it when I picked it up. I didn't want Mister Lambert to see me so I only skimmed it, but what I did catch said, 'Mathilda's writing demonstrates exceptional prose and structure. It is easily a top contender for the entire competition.' We're getting to the bottom of this."

"What bottom is there to get?" my mother quietly demanded. "They assumed Mattie was a White girl. They found out she isn't and now she's paying the race tax because of the color of her skin."

"I know, Miz Dorothy, but something else isn't right here. I put that photo in the envelope."

"Plus, we didn't type my application," I added. "I handwrote it."

Seated in the backseat beside me, Ruth gasped. "Somebody changed it?"

"Yes."

"If you ladies don't mind coming with me, there's someone I need to pay a visit to," Miss Divine requested.

"If it has to do with helping my daughter, we don't mind at all," was Mama's response.

Ten minutes later I found myself seated in the home of Miss Divine's mentor declining the hot tea and pound cake she offered.

Not because I didn't want it, but because I was upset and nervous, and uneasy being served by a white-haired White woman.

"Mattie, do you recall me saying I shared your writing with a colleague?"

Hands fidgeting in my lap, I told my teacher I did.

"Miz Wheatley is the person I was referring to. In actuality, she's much more than a colleague. She's been my mentor since I was in high school."

I listened attentively to my teacher as she divulged that her parents were itinerant farmers needing her help in the fields, but that the woman seated across from me had persuaded them to allow her to finish school.

"Because of Miz Wheatley, I was the first in my family to earn a high school diploma."

"Penelope, when will you ever stop telling that story?"

"Never. I owe you an unpayable debt, Miz Wheatley."

"The only repayment I ask is your helping other young girls like I helped you. Which is where Miss Mattie here comes in." She directed a kind smile towards me. "I just about swooned when Penelope shared your responsive essay with me. That composition was the kind of genius educators crave from students but rarely see during the whole course of their careers. That's why I didn't hesitate to give Penelope that flier for the competition. I've taught for the past four decades, so I know brilliance when observing it. And you, my dear, have it."

"Thank you, ma'am."

"Thank your mother. Thank your father. But don't thank me for speaking the truth as I see it. Your work deserves light and recognition. So pardon me for fudging a bit."

"Ma'am?"

"Mathilda, you write like an old soul, but your printing's about as good as a seven-year-old's."

I cut Ruth a look when she giggled. "Sometimes I can't keep up with my brain so my writing gets rushed."

"Yes, with a fast-producing mind like yours that's plausible. Thank heavens you had the foresight to type your story. You didn't, however, take the same pains with your application... which is why I did."

Miss Divine and I both inhaled sharply.

"*You* changed my application?"

She nodded, looking rather pleased with herself. "Penelope was kind enough to bring me your submission packet when I asked for it. I wanted to make sure every 't' was crossed and 'i' dotted and told her I'd personally submit it. Which I did." Miz Wheatley smiled like a naughty child. "But I changed nothing. I simply typed it for legibility. We couldn't have you disqualified for poor penmanship before you could even get in the running, now could we?"

"But my teacher was supposed to sign it."

"Which is why I put Penelope's name on it."

"Miz Wheatley, you forged my signature?"

She waved a hand at Miss Divine's outburst. "No, darling. I traced it."

My mother laughed. "Lord, Jesus."

Scooting forward to the edge of her chair, my teacher stared narrow-eyed at the woman who'd been so instrumental to her success. "What happened to Mattie's picture?"

Vacating her seat, the older woman opened a curio cabinet on the other side of the room only to return with the photo in question. She handed it to me with a smile. "Looks like I conveniently forgot to include that, as well as indicate your school name which would have been recognizable as one in the Colored section. I didn't bother mailing your packet. I personally walked it in and spent so much time gushing over its wondrousness that those missing details were obviously overlooked."

I was amazed by her subterfuge. "But why'd you trouble yourself with all of this?"

"Because, Mattie, your lovely story would've wound up in the trash bin if that photo and your school name had been included. I can't imagine that's what you wanted."

"No, ma'am, it wasn't. I wanted my story to stand on its own merit and be fairly judged like everyone else's."

"Which is exactly what occurred until your race was discovered. So, dear Mattie, how shall we fight this?"

"You enjoyed doing all of this, didn't you Miz Wheatley?" Miss Divine interrupted before I could respond.

Her mentor's smile was luminous. "Yes, dear, I did."

"Mister Lambert won't appreciate you outsmarting those judges. What if he levies some form of disciplinary action against you?"

"Such as what? Termination?" Miz Wheatley's laughter was robust. "I'm retiring at the end of the school year, darling. Firing me would simply be an early vacation." Her attention once again fell on me. "That's not my concern. What is my concern is challenging educators so steeped in narrow-mindedness that they fail to give students the access and opportunities their efforts deserve. So, I ask again, Mattie, how would you like to fight this?"

I was suddenly back on that Montgomery bus witnessing how one woman's refusal to stand created an economic war against injustice. I didn't dare imagine my situation prompting anything as spectacular as that. I wasn't sure I even wanted to take on the school district and Mister Lambert. I wasn't heroic, and unlike a city full of Colored passengers being treated poorly, my case affected only me. There was no greater good to be gained.

"Thank you for taking an interest in me, Miz Wheatley, but I don't think I'm up to fighting anything."

Ruth's caution had scared me in that hallway. If my acting wild the way I had was something that could hurt my baby, I wasn't about to put my child in jeopardy with a bunch of protesting.

Mama must've picked up on my worries.

"Ma'am, are you suggesting my daughter be the face of some new revolt or something?"

"Not a revolt precisely, but what happened to Mattie perfectly exemplifies the need for the fair and equal educational opportunities that I've been harping about for years. As a young teacher, I was transferred from district to district because my colleagues complained my views were too 'upsetting.' The older I got, the more they simply ignored me as some doddering old woman."

"How come they never fired you?"

Smiling, she didn't take Ruth's question as rude. "My students always excelled and they and their parents loved me. But I was also a tutor, which is how I met Penelope. A long time ago I tutored a former mayor's son who was struggling miserably. My tutoring helped that young man graduate with honors and endeared that mayor to me. That mayor became governor. I suppose I became untouchable because I had his favor and the district knew it." She sipped her tea and ate a bit of pound cake before continuing. "I'm sure some would say I've taken advantage of that fact, but if so it was never for myself, but for my students."

Seeing my mother buttoning her coat and clutching her pocketbook, I knew we were through.

"Miz Wheatley, you're the kind of teacher schools need. As my daughter said, thank you for taking an interest in her writing, but we don't need this kind of aggravation. We appreciate your hospitality."

When Mama stood, Ruthie and I did, too.

Miz Wheatley was silent a moment before rising as well. "It was never my intention to cause Mathilda any distress. Forgive me if I have."

Mama simply nodded before heading for the door. We followed suit, leaving my teacher bringing up the rear, quietly conversing with her mentor.

Unlike the drive to the celebration, our mood on the way home was somber. When we pulled up in front of Aunt Odelle's, my teacher reached over into the back seat and squeezed my hand, telling me not to give up, that Miz Wheatley would do everything she could to get justice on my behalf.

I exited the car too tired to imagine that a different outcome was even possible.

"Mattie…" Mama stopped me when we got to the front door. "You can go on in, Ruthie."

"Yes, ma'am." My cousin gave me a hug before disappearing inside of the house.

Alone on the porch with Mama, I realized how much I missed our room at the Stantons'. It was cramped and didn't offer much, but we were together and her presence was the comforting blanket I needed. Her plaintive sighs in the night when she thought I was asleep. The sounds of her deep breathing. The powdery scent of her perfume. Standing there on that cold winter night, I suddenly missed the comforts offered in those close confines. When she opened her arms to me, I didn't miss a beat stepping into her embrace.

"I'm extremely proud of you, Mattie, and nothing that happened tonight decreases that. I don't agree with that Miz Wheatley or particularly care for her methods, but she has a good heart. And it's nice she's sticking up for you."

"Mama, why'd she do all of this? If she hadn't gone out of her way my entry would've wound up in the garbage like she said. She also helped Miss Divine finish school. Why would Miz Wheatley trouble herself for our kind?"

Mama leaned back with a laugh. "That's because she *is* our kind."

"Ma'am?"

"Mattie, Miz Wheatley ain't nobody's White woman. She's as Colored as us."

"*She's passing?*"

"Honey, yes. That woman's a trickster and has clearly done a good job of it."

CHAPTER TWELVE

Ashlee

CBD oil became my new best friend. I wasn't foolish enough to think it was a cure-all capable of fully restoring my grandmother. Only heaven could do that, and I wasn't sure earthly restoration was part of heaven's plan for my Nana Mattie. But every benefit those massages delivered proved a blessing that I humbly and gladly received.

The knowledge that our roles had reversed was abundant. I was honored to be the one ministering to Nana's physical needs rather than being on the receiving end of her loving touches. Morning, noon, and night, I oiled her limbs, massaged and gently manipulated them. Not merely to prevent muscular atrophy, but to aid her circulation. Amazingly, she exhibited signs of less discomfort and decreased swelling. Nana's pain reduction meant she didn't need morphine as much or as often, which resulted in improved alertness. Her waking moments increased, as did her awareness of her surroundings. We tried our best not to exhaust her, but Nana's improved lucidity, her staying awake for longer periods, had us wanting to simply be in her presence, so much so that one of us was always in her room.

"Is that too loud for you, PopPop?" Adjusting the volume of my phone atop the bedside table, I glanced at my grandfather.

"No, Ladybug, it's just enough."

From old standards to gospel and tracks featuring natural water sounds for their soothing ambience, I'd created a playlist for my grandparents' enjoyment. My grandfather humming along was proof of that.

"I need a dance partner."

I hopped off Nana's bed. "I'm at your service."

"I don't wanna dance with you, little girl. I'm dancing with my daughter," he announced as my mother entered the room, a plate of freshly baked teacakes in one hand, napkins in the other.

"Good Lord, Mama, you have the house smelling all kinds of delicious."

"Seeing as how it's your grandmother's recipe, that aroma is inevitable."

Unlike traditional teacake recipes, Nana's included orange zest and juice, and "two pinches" of cinnamon. She'd been making them since she was a teen, and even told stories of selling them back then to earn what she called "pocket money." Nana's teacakes were so good that they were demanded at practically every church social she attended. When Mama offered me the plate, I helped myself to three without hesitation.

"Are you hungry, Ashlee,?" my mother teased. "Or just greedy?"

"I plead the Fifth." *And I'm pregnant.*

Thanks to my inability to reconnect with Brad yesterday, I was still holding on to that sweet little secret.

Clearly, the universe was enjoying being mischievous, leaving the father of my child and me with a series of missed calls, voicemail messages, and texts. His on-campus meeting with the dean had lasted longer than expected. Its late conclusion had left him speeding back to his office for a client consultation followed by a late business lunch, several meetings, and a deposition. He'd finished those obligations only to be waylaid by a local reporter wanting the scoop on the student protest. The demands of his day were seemingly endless, so much so that it was well after nine last night before he called while on his way home. Unfortunately, I was so wiped out after that day's medical appointment, helping around the house, and tending to Nana that I was knocked out and hadn't heard the phone ring. Today? We were back to being engaged in a wicked game of phone tag.

"Baby girl, you wanna dance with me?" said PopPop to my mother.

Mama thrust the cookie plate in my hands. "Of course! I love dancing with my daddy." She stuck her tongue out at me, gloating and teasing.

"You two go ahead with your little father-daughter dance. You're not hurting my feelings. Watch me sit here and eat all these cookies without caring."

My grandfather laughed so heartily I barely heard, "I'll. Have. One."

We all three swiveled our attention to the frail woman in the bed.

"Hey, my brown beauty queen, you're awake. How're you feeling?" Placing the plate on the bed, I stroked Nana's hands.

"Like. I'm. Breathing."

"We thank the Almighty for that." The loving look accompanying my grandfather's words was enough to make me want to cry. "Ladybug, give my bride a cookie like she requested."

Holding a napkin beneath her chin, I make quick work of serving my grandmother. It wasn't exactly a nutritious meal, but it was the first time I'd heard her actually ask for anything since I'd returned home and I would gladly bring her all the teacakes in the world if it meant giving her pleasure and keeping her here. "How's that?"

Smiling, she gave my mother's execution of her recipe a thumbs-up before eyeing her husband and only child. "Keep. Dancing."

"You heard the queen. Get those feet moving."

"Hush up, bossy."

Laughing at my mother's playful reprimand, I placed a straw at Nana's lips so she could sip from her water glass. "Do you want more of your cookie, or are you finished?"

"Finished."

She'd eaten only two bites, but her showing an interest was more than good enough for me. I followed her gaze, saw the happy light in her eyes as she watched my mother and grandfather arm in arm, dancing.

"Savannah. Eve."

"Ma'am?"

Nana had our complete attention as she pointed back and forth between the two.

"*Your.* Daddy."

I couldn't precisely interpret the look that passed over Mama's face or her emphatic, "Always." But it left me with the impression that there was something between the other occupants in the room of which I had no knowledge.

Shaking off the disquieting feeling, I immersed myself in the pleasure of the moment, of seeing my mother looking up at her father with all the pure admiration of a child.

"Daddy, remember how when I was little you'd let me stand on your feet while you danced around the room?"

"That's probably why I have fallen arches and arthritis."

They both laughed before my grandfather kissed the top of Mama's head.

"Those are some of my sweet memories, angel girl."

"Oooh! So is this," Mama suddenly exclaimed as the opening notes of a song drifted from my phone. "This was your and Mama's song."

"Good ol' Johnny Mathis helped me get plenty of your mother's kisses," PopPop reminisced as the singer's old school ballad "Chances Are" had me feeling as if I'd been hurled back to the 1950s. "Angel girl, Ladybug, you think you can help me dance with my bride… one last time?"

We looked to Nana who lay there staring at her husband, smiling.

"We absolutely can," I supplied, seeing my mother too overcome with emotion to respond.

Jumping up, I stood there analyzing, trying to determine how to fulfill my grandfather's request. Grabbing the chair he religiously sat in, keeping vigil, I repositioned it as close to the bed as possible. "PopPop, sit here."

When he complied, I ran around to the opposite side of the bed.

"Mama, you get Nana from that side—"

"Ashlee Dionne, what're you doing?"

"Watch. Come on." Following my instructions, the three of us gently eased Nana into a sitting position on the side of the bed where PopPop was seated. Propping pillows behind and sitting on either side of her, carefully supporting her weight, my mother and I were her human bookends.

"Mattie Banks, may I have this dance?"

Hearing Nana's maiden name, I felt like an interloper on their romance while smiling at her giggled response. "Mama, hit the replay button."

My mother obeyed my instructions and Johnny Matthis started all over again. My grandfather—seated in that bedside chair—held my grandmother protectively in his arms and gently swayed side to side with her until the song ended.

By then, both my mother and I were silently crying. But when Nana placed a hand against PopPop's face and whispered, "Love. Always," and he, in turn, kissed the palm of her hand, I had to bite down hard on my lip to keep from losing it. Resituating Nana in bed, my mother and I left her parents to their private moment, knowing we'd been graced to witness the power of a six-decades-long love that death could never destroy.

"So… to make sure I'm understanding clearly and not adding anything to what's been said, you're actually allowing some undeserving prick's being promoted over you to cause you to walk away from a career that you've poured blood, sweat, and tears into?"

Seated on the enclosed back veranda, I massaged the irritation lines I imagined to be present on my forehead. "Brad, you're not getting it."

"What did I get wrong, Ashlee? The fact that you're leaving your job? Or the fact that Humphries' promotion is a key factor in that decision?"

"First of all, while my parents have done remarkably well in their respective careers, unlike yourself, I don't come from old money. I have no trust fund to fall back on. As a single Black female, I *always* have to be in a position to provide for myself. I don't have the luxury of simply quitting—"

"And because my parents are wealthy, I can?"

"If you chose to, yes."

His laugh was dry, mirthless. "What would I look like, a fully functional, grown-ass thirty-five-year-old man living off of his parents?"

"Comfortable. Relaxed." I knew Brad better than that. He staunchly shied away from capitalizing off of his family name and was fiercely independent. But we'd been on the phone for a while and I'd tired of our circular conversation and trying to help him understand my decision.

"So, just another White male sitting back enjoying undeserved privileges."

Knowing I'd been unfair, I sighed forcefully. "I apologize. That's not who you are or what you'd intentionally do." We'd never played race games in our relationship. There was none of this 'I don't see color, you can't help who you fall in love with' B.S. Our love had always existed alongside a conscious choice to see each other. I saw him. And I never wanted Brad to not see and recognize my brown skin and all it represented. Yes, we had our struggles, but he'd never used Whiteness as a weapon. And while he'd benefited from being who and what he was, I'd never known him to willingly misuse or abuse his status. If anything, he was quick to utilize it to the advantage of others. "Back to your point. He was the catalyst the universe chose to use, but this isn't about me running because of Ross Humphries."

"But you are running, Ash, and have been for a while. You're chasing something elusive."

"Actually, I'm chasing me. I want to live more holistically, to exercise all of my power, and utilize my gifts in ways that make a difference."

"You want to do something bohemian?"

"That right there is a perfect example, Brad. You're dismissive."

"That's not my intention. Maybe you're being sensitive."

"You know what—"

"Fine, Ashlee! Not bohemian. Altruistic?"

I was ticked but continued the conversation while I could. "Yes. I choose to figure out how to give of myself in a manner that's not merely rewarding to me, but positively impacts others. How can I make life better?"

His sigh was as heavy as mine had been. "Ash, baby, you're being idealistic. You spent years in college to practice law. Did you at any point of that educational journey stop to consider art and drawing as a means to make a living?"

I answered honestly. "I did not."

"Why then after school, after having passed the bar, securing employment, and establishing your career, are you just now considering such notions?"

I did something he hated and answered his question with a question. "Are you saying people and desires can't change?"

"No. I'm saying, that in my humble opinion, this is a knee-jerk reaction."

"Ashlee?"

Looking up and seeing my parents exiting the kitchen, I asked him to hold on while I answered my mother. "Yes, ma'am?"

"Clarissa's here so your daddy and I are headed to the house."

Clarissa was Nana's night nurse.

"Sounds good. You look exhausted."

"I am."

"Get some rest."

"I will. Tell Brad we said hello."

"What makes you think I'm talking to him?"

"'Cause you look like a woman fighting with her best friend."

"And we know it's not Dorinda or we would've heard her loudness the moment we stepped out of the house," Daddy added.

"My parents said hi," I told Brad with a dry laugh. I gave them his best as requested, exchanging kisses and "good nights" with my parents. I waited for them to leave before resuming our conversation. "Back to our debate."

"It's not a debate, Ashlee. It's a discussion."

"Honestly? It feels like the former. Like I've been tasked with the duty of enlightening you and proving my right to re-examine my life and make changes as I deem fit. Last week you asked what I need that I'm not getting and I'm telling you what that is. Fulfillment."

He was silent for a long moment. "Thank you for sharing that. Have you considered another firm, perhaps?"

"Dismissive. *Again.*" I wanted to reach through the phone, slap him upside the head and choke him for his stubborn insistence. Instead, I answered his dumbass question. "And, yes I have."

"And?"

"There'd be different partner names, but the same crap."

"Sounds pessimistic, but okay. Baby, listen, I don't have the blessing of being artistic—"

"But you have other interests," I interrupted.

"True. However, I don't allow them to impede upon or mitigate my success."

Stretching my legs in front of me, I tried and maybe failed to make my tone less edgy. "If my having the courage to consider something other than what I have or know constitutes failure then maybe our ideals of success don't match."

He sighed. "I think you have false notions of success. A rewarding career doesn't mean being pleased with its daily intricacies one hundred percent. There are highs. And lows. Moments of satisfaction, and sometimes contempt for whatever the obstacles it presents. Still, you had a clearly defined plan and were pursuing it. Why derail yourself and walk away from what you've worked hard to achieve simply because something doesn't work out the way you imagined?"

"Shouldn't alternative options be considered when something fails to work out as imagined? I consider that prudent... even if the failed thing is a partnership."

We fell silent.

I wanted to pull away from deeper truths blanketed within that statement, but couldn't. "You don't have to agree with me, Bradley. And maybe it's unfair to expect you to fully grasp it all when I haven't worked out the intricate minutiae. But I won't fault myself for wanting you to be supportive."

"I'm trying."

"I disagree, but we'll call that a matter of opinion. What isn't opinion is the fact that I've always had your back. When you were approached by the college and invited to apply for an adjunct professor position and you were interested but expressed reservation in juggling that alongside your responsibilities at your firm, what was my response?"

"Ash, come on."

"What was it, Brad? I remember, if you don't."

His heavy exhalation had me imagining him closing his eyes and chewing the inside of his mouth, as he tended to do when frustrated. "You said, 'Juggle the hell out of it, boo. I'll help you pick up whatever drops.' Baby, honestly, I'm not attempting to be unsupportive… I simply think you're underselling yourself and making a mistake you may later regret."

"Yeah, well, it'll be my mistake to make."

"Ashlee…"

I waited for him to say whatever it was he'd planned to. When he didn't, I stood and stretched. "I need to go. I'm exhausted."

"I understand. We can resume this after we've both rested."

"Actually, we can't. My exhaustion isn't physical. It's emotional, and mental. It's us."

"Meaning?"

The edge of fear in his tone didn't prevent me from speaking honestly. "I'm tired of fighting, of the distance, and disconnect.

I'm through with our only remaining strength being sex. I'm disappointed in you trying to push perfection onto me—"

"Babe, I'm not."

"You are. You just don't see it. I'm not a project that you need to course correct. I'm my own woman. I may want your support, but I don't need your approval. If I've veered off script, so be it. I love you to life and beyond, but I no longer choose to do this."

"What're you saying?"

"I said what I said, Brad, and you're too brilliant a man not to get it. So clear talk? I'm finished."

When he said nothing, I wiped the tears spilling down my face, said good night, and disconnected, not ignorant of the fact that we'd been too busy disagreeing over my choices for me to even tell him we were pregnant.

After a hot shower and a cup of chamomile-and-lavender tea, I helped Clarissa massage Nana's limbs, read the twenty-third Psalm to my grandparents, and made sure they were settled for the night before heading to the guest bedroom.

Moments later, I found myself lying in the dark staring at the ceiling, wondering if I'd overreacted to Brad. I wasn't ignorant enough to pretend I didn't love him. I absolutely did. Nor was I so insecure as to believe he owed me some unswerving archaic fealty. He had a right to question me. But our relationship seemed to have become one long episode of relentlessly challenging one another. Perhaps it was a casualty of our profession, but I'd tired of ongoing rebuttals and debates taking the place of what used to be open-hearted communication. And... part of me was afraid that his inability to handle a change in my career made him incapable of managing something as life-shaking as my being pregnant. Maybe my pushing the conversation to the point of "I'm finished" had been my way of preempting possible rejection. In a nutshell, I was scared.

Hearing the chime of an incoming text, I reached for my phone and read it.

Don't make me drive 2 Valdosta & put U in a headlock.

I smiled sadly at Dorinda's threat, prompted by the fact that I'd left her in the dark on my pregnancy status. What Brad did with the knowledge was his decision, but I still believed he had a right to be the first to know and fibbed, texting her that the at-home pregnancy test proved faulty, providing inconclusive results.

Fine. But if U R, U'll have ten-point-three minutes 2 tell Gomer & then your family. At ten-point-four I'm wrecking something.

I texted a promise that she'd be the next to know before trying to relax and get some much-needed sleep. But slumber proved elusive.

Ten minutes later, tired of rehearsing and rehashing Brad's and my relationship, and feeling slightly guilty for ending it the way I had, I resisted the urge to text him. Instead, I lay gently rubbing my stomach, wishing I had something to occupy my mind. Like a good book.

Nana's manuscript.

I turned on the lamp and got out of bed to open that beautiful but humongous box I'd placed atop the dresser. Instead, my eyes were drawn to the mound of two-word missives.

For Savannah.

"What was for my mother?" Staring at that 1956 Montgomery, Alabama postmark on an envelope and willing it to divulge its secrets, I felt an odd shiver run down my spine while peering at the upper left corner where there should have been a return address. There was none. "Who sent these?"

I went through the stack, careful to keep them in chronological order the way Nana had kept them. I'd gone through at least twenty and—seeing they were all the same—was about to give up and resume reading my grandmother's manuscript when the next in the pile caught my attention. It was faint, faded with the years, but there was a name. Barely visible, it looked as if, perhaps, it had been written then erased, or marred by time or maybe handling.

Perched on the edge of the bed, I angled the envelope in various positions beneath the lamp, hoping to improve legibility. When that failed, I pulled an old-school trick, located a pencil in the nightstand drawer and gently scribbled over the writing.

"Girl, quit being silly. You are nobody's detective…" My words trailed off as characters appeared within the pencil shading.

Staring at them, I felt something similar to the odd sensation I experienced when my mother and grandfather had danced for my grandmother and Nana reminded Mama of PopPop's parentage as if she'd ever be prone to forget. It had been a sensation of mysteries and withheld secrets. Once again, that feeling sat with me as I stared at that envelope, piecing those characters together and wondering who in the world was E. Stanton.

CHAPTER THIRTEEN

Mattie

February came in with a vengeance, bringing wet weather and strong winds with it. I welcomed them. Again, rainy days granted me a perfect way to hide my condition with all that bulky sweater and coat wearing. Come spring when the weather warmed up, it would be another story. I'd have to leave school and wasn't ready for that. Until then, I gave my whole self to learning, going to school with pleasure as if every day I attended was my last. Mama even made ginger drops to settle my stomach and minimize morning sickness so I wouldn't miss out on going to class.

It wasn't but two days since that competition reception, and my heart was still sore over my disqualification. Thinking about it caused angry tears to well in my eyes, but after Mama told me the baby felt what I felt I tried hard not to dwell on negatives. Determined to focus on positives, I told myself that big fat red A- on my writing assignment was still an A.

Skimming Miss Divine's written responses in the margins, I wished she was there to answer the questions her comments generated. Instead, our science teacher sat as a substitute at my English teacher's desk making me wonder, precisely, where my favorite teacher was. Hoping she wasn't sick, I followed our substitute's instructions to open our grammar books to page fifty-seven. Busy pulling my book from my desk, I was only mildly aware of the light rap on the classroom door.

"Yes?"

I barely glanced at a student entering with a folded note, my focus on finding the page we had been instructed to, until hearing my name.

"Mattie Banks."

I looked up to find other students turning, staring at me. Ignoring them, I responded automatically. "Yes, sir?"

"Collect your belongings and approach the desk, please."

Remembering how Nosey Nedra was pulled from class last year in Montgomery and sent to the principal's office when her father passed, my heart started pounding thinking on my mother, hoping there'd been no accidents at the diner.

Lord, please don't let there be nothing wrong with Mama.

Silently repeating that prayer, I took the folded note excusing me from class and hurried to the principal's office. When his secretary opened the inner door to escort me in, I stopped on the threshold at sight of the room's occupants.

"Please, Mathilda, come in."

Stunned at the presence of Joshua Lambert, I stepped into an office that felt even smaller with the two men present.

Our principal waited for his secretary to exit and for me to sit before turning towards me, face masked with an indecipherable expression. "Mathilda, I understand that you met our district superintendent, Mister Lambert, the night before last?"

Feeling the latter's eyes on me, I nodded.

"Your initial introduction pertained to your placement in the district's writing competition, an occurrence of which I had no knowledge. Is that correct?"

"Yes, sir. It is."

"I see. Is it also correct that you plagiarized the story you entered?"

"No, sir, it isn't!" I looked at Mister Lambert. "I didn't take anything from anyone. That was my own creation."

"Pressing business prevented me from handling this yesterday, but on the night of the reception I was informed that you didn't write that story in its entirety, but that you received assistance while typing it."

"I did, Mister Lambert, but only because I tire easily since—" Catching myself before blurting my condition, I stared at the white-haired man beside me, not liking the intentionally blank look on his face.

"Yes, you were saying?"

"I just... When my fingers cramped my cousin, Ruth, helped with the typing. But she only typed what I told her to."

"In other words, you dictated to her?" asked my principal.

"Yes, sir." I quickly confirmed his observation while wondering who had provided Mister Lambert with wrong information. "The story was completely mine, and Miss Divine was kind enough—"

"Penelope Divine will not factor into this conversation as she is no longer employed at this fine institution."

His words rendered me speechless. Miss Divine was gone? Had she quit?

Some unsavory sensation in the room had me believing she hadn't left of her own volition.

"Thank you for clarifying that you received typing assistance, but that really isn't pivotal to this discussion." My principal cleared his throat. "What is pertinent, however, is the more disturbing news also provided to our district superintendent by the same individual who alerted him to your possible plagiarism." Our principal was a dark-complexioned man, still he seemed to blush uncomfortably when continuing. "Mathilda, I must say that I'm distressed at Mister Lambert bringing this to my attention. I took pains to reassure him that this isn't behavior our school upholds or condones, and that appropriate action will be taken should these allegations prove accurate."

Overriding my principal's attempt at delicacy, Mister Lambert took control of the conversation. "Mathilda, I was informed you're expecting a child. Would you care to refute this?"

Other than the chills suddenly rushing through my body, my entire world grew still. I could barely breathe as cold waves rolled through me, knowing that unlike the false accusations of my being a thief and stealing my story, this part was true.

That's when I understood.

That blonde girl!

I'd been huddled in the hallway outside of the restroom with my cousin, crying my eyes out the night of the award reception, when she'd exited. While in the restroom she must have overheard Ruth's mentioning her typing assistance. Even worse, she'd clearly heard Ruth cautioning me to calm down so as not to hurt my baby. Her tattling wasn't even necessary. I had no chance of advancing in the competition. Still, she'd carried business that wasn't hers to carry just to make sure she never had to share the limelight with someone of my complexion.

"Miss Banks, do you have a response?"

There in that small office feeling overshadowed and consumed by the judgment of men, I chose to say nothing. I stared straight ahead, remaining as mute as any mute in the bible that Jesus didn't heal.

"I see…" My principal sighed at my silence.

"Have her parents been contacted?"

"Yes, sir, Mister Lambert. Miz Banks will be here directly."

"Very good. Mathilda, we regret to inform you that it is against the moral code of Lowndes County School District to accommodate female students in your predicament. As of this moment you are expelled and no longer enrolled here. Nor may you enroll in any other school within the district. I trust you have all of your belongings?"

Again, I stared ahead saying nothing.

Mister Lambert's voice was slightly softer when continuing, as if perhaps he felt sorry for me. "While we cannot honor your writing in the competition, we think it only fair to extend a token of recognition for your efforts."

I accepted the envelope he handed me, stuffed it in my coat pocket without looking at it, mumbling a "thank you" that barely passed for English.

"Very well, then." Mister Lambert stood and took his leave so that I was left with my principal, who launched into a lecture against deception, touting the importance of virtue for young Colored women as if I had no morals and making babies by myself was just what I did.

"I must say, Mathilda, that after how highly your teachers speak of you, I'm truly taken aback and disappointed by your actions. You've tarnished what was a promising future for yourself, not to mention the reputation of this establishment."

Asked to wait in the hall, I don't know what all Mama said to the principal when Daddy's brother, Uncle Melvin, brought her to pick me up. What I do know is the principal was slack-mouthed, wide-eyed, and adjusting his necktie when she marched out.

"Let's go, Mattie."

I followed, barely able to keep up as we exited the building. Mama must've felt my pace slowing at the thought of turning for one last glimpse.

"Don't you dare look back."

Wondering if, like Lot's wife, I'd become a pillar of salt, I overrode the temptation, climbed into the back of Uncle Melvin's sedan and rode off.

Mama and Uncle Melvin discussed the situation the entire ride, but their words didn't quite register with me. My head was too full of what felt like ceaseless misery as my mind latched onto my life of late. My thoughts were dark, disheartening. Touching and being touched by Edward, and all that it had led to. That evil J.T. trying to force himself on me. Being put out of the home I'd grown up in. The writing contest. And now expulsion. The humiliation. Degradation. Being treated like something less than. It all rose up inside of me with the force of a whirlwind.

"*It's not fair!*" My shrill scream brought the conversation up front to an end. "*Nothing's fair.* I'm glad they kicked me outta school 'cause I'm never writing another thing ever, *ever* again!"

Steadily hitting the back of the seat in front of me, I denounced life's injustices, only vaguely hearing Mama tell Uncle Melvin to pull over. Next thing I knew, Mama was beside me, trying to still my hands from pounding that seat like a crazy lady. Unable to, she let me vent my fury until, exhausted, I lay in her arms sobbing.

"Melvin, take us by the tree."

We were almost at Aunt Odelle's. All I wanted was to run inside, crawl in the bed, and hide beneath the quilt, enjoying privacy until Ruth and Naomi got home. Once they did I'd be subjected to their two-thousand-and-ten questions. I wasn't up to that and wished a corner room with Mama could suddenly materialize out of thin air. What I wasn't interested in was a trip to some doggone tree that couldn't do a thing for me.

"I need to go home!"

Mama softly spoke to sentiments I didn't even realize were buried between the layers of my heated expression. "I want a home of our own, too, Mattie. Be patient with me. Melvin, there it is."

Her tone was a mixture of excitement and dread. Still, I didn't care. I only wanted what I wanted, which was to disappear. Instead, I found myself in some unfamiliar patch of country as my uncle pulled to the side of the road.

Mama's taking a deep breath before exiting the car wasn't lost in the fray of my heightened emotions. "Come with me."

I simply stared at her when she held out her hand.

"Mathilda Ilene."

Distraught or not, I knew better than to disobey whenever my mother called my first and middle names. Accepting her hand, I exited the car and stood beside her.

"Dorothy, this may not be the best time for all this."

"Is there ever a good time for death and hard lessons, Melvin?"

My uncle faced the front, saying nothing else except, "I'll be here."

Mama closed the back door. "Let's go."

"Mama, please, can we just go home? I don't feel good."

"Neither do I, but we're doing this. Come on."

I had no choice but to follow my mother over slick grass and navigate ground that was muddy in some places thanks to recent rains. As we headed up a slight incline, I was suddenly cold and hungry and increasingly angry. I'd just been kicked out of somewhere I wanted to be, where I excelled, and had friends, and could almost pretend I was no different from any of the girls around me. Now, what would I have? Nothing. No teachers praising my work. No learning. No reading. Just helping Aunt Odelle with her two youngest girls. Without my education there was nothing ahead of me except laundry. Cooking. Cleaning. My life was about to become one massive invisibility.

I suddenly wanted to throw my head back and let loose an ear-shattering wail into the wind.

"Go 'head and scream," Mama encouraged as if she'd been inside my head. "Ain't nothing or no one out here can hear you except me and your daddy."

Mama's words sent pinpricks over my skin, and proved distracting. "Ma'am?"

She merely glanced at me and kept walking until stopping abruptly near the base of a towering tree recognizable as a magnolia despite not being in bloom.

"Where is it?"

Watching my mother walking around that tree, mumbling to herself while her fingers stroked its bark as if in search of something had me thinking maybe my breaking down had made *her* crazy.

"Mama, please, can we just leave?"

She spoke as if to an unseen presence. "She sure *is* gonna keep writing."

"No, ma'am, I already said I'm not writing anything ever in my life again."

Mama ignored me, kept talking to whomever else it was that had her attention until she found what she was looking for. "Here it is! Mattie, come here."

Hesitating before rounding that tree, I found my mother lovingly outlining a carving. When she beckoned me forward, I stepped closer and saw a large heart in the center of which was boldly detailed *M+D, 1940.*

"You see this?"

"Yes, ma'am."

"Good 'cause I need you to not only see but to hear, and hear me clearly. You wanna talk about unfair? Unfair is the fact that Matthew S. Banks is buried *right* here. Beneath your feet."

Startled, I looked down, seeking evidence of my father's presence.

"Unfair is your daddy fighting overseas in a war for a country that never recognized him as a man and treated him as less than human. Unfair is his being home on leave, arriving at the bus depot wearing that military uniform he had a right to wear, and being told by some ol' crackers to take it off. And what happened when he refused? They murdered my man."

"Mama, Daddy died in Europe, fighting in the war." My whole body was shivering with shock, my words were a desperate plea, grasping at the truth I'd lived with.

"*Your daddy's last fight was the one for his life!*" My mother was trembling violently. Fists balled up, she hit her thighs, growled through gritted teeth. "Right here in Valdosta! Against home-grown enemies. He was unarmed and lost his final combat right here in this town, Mattie!"

Too shocked to speak, I could only watch my mother's anguish, her panting, and rhythmic exhaling until she was semi-collected.

"Unfair is having to pack you up and leave the man I loved behind 'cause after what happened to him I was losing my damn mind and wanted to kill every cracker I could. Unfair is having to work for and live with the Stantons after all of that. They might've been a kinder brand of cracker, but in the end they proved no different."

"Well, other than Daddy's telling you to, why *did* you go work for them?"

My mother's laugh was a brittle rendition of itself. "Whatchu think I had, Mattie? Options? You think there was some agency full of employers happy to have me? I had the same options generations of Colored women before me did. Limited! You think our ancestors had some day-off plan letting 'em relax in bed after Massa crept in their cabin the night before inflicting sexual acts on 'em? Was there some advocate to report all that to? Honey, my granny got up the next morning and worked those fields!" She breathed easier, as if soothed by the knowledge that suffering was jointly shared and could be overcome. "My husband was dead. My education unfinished. You were barely four and I did what I could to keep us together."

We were quiet a while until I touched her arm. "Mama, you could've told me about Daddy."

Head bowed, her voice came out vaporous as fog. "I was wrong for feeding you stories, but it was easier than saying my husband was brutalized by hateful folks in his homeland. I didn't want to have to answer those kinds of questions from you, so I gave him a soldier's honorable death. But like I said, the truth of the matter is, Matthew died right here."

"What happened?"

Wrapping her arms about herself, my mother shook her head and pressed her back against that tree. "Baby girl, I'll never scar your soul with the details. All I'll say is when they brought your daddy's body to me wasn't nothing recognizable. Not that beautiful brown skin you inherited from him. Or that smile that used to give me butterflies. Nothing. Except that pollywog birthmark by his left ear."

Images of that kind man aboard the bus who'd loaned me a handkerchief smelling like Mama's lavender water had my whole soul shivering as I recalled the pollywog-like birthmark he bore, wondering if I'd been visited when I needed him most by my daddy's spirit.

"They killed his body, but they couldn't kill this love." Reaching for my hand, she placed it on the carving and cited its meaning aloud. "Matthew and Dorothy, 1940."

"That's my birth year."

"It is. It's also the year your daddy and me got married. We'd planned to wait till I finished nursing school but you happened."

"*Nursing school?* Mama, you never told me you wanted to be a nurse."

"I'm telling you now."

Fascinated, I listened to Mama's account of leaving Baton Rouge to attend a newly opened school for Colored young women aspiring to be nurses.

"That school was a dream come true. I'll never forget my family and church raising the money to get me there."

"But your reading?"

"I struggled. Did my best. And you know I have a memory like an elephant and can retain anything once I hear it. Plus, I made a good friend who'd read aloud to me. Took me longer to finish, but I never failed an exam. Anyhow, the first few months were wonderful. Then three months in, my classmates and I showed up one morning, and the building was locked. Took a while to put all the pieces together, but the school administrators were long gone. Honey, they took off with our tuition money and left us with nothing."

Too ashamed to return to Baton Rouge empty-handed, Mama stayed in Valdosta.

"I was already carrying you, so my staying here made the most sense."

"I'm sorry that happened to you. I hope those school administrators wound up paying hell on earth."

My mother smiled. "I don't dwell on that, Mattie. I focus on the fact that nursing school is how I met your father. He was a delivery driver. If not for that and this tree, you wouldn't be here."

"Why this tree?"

Blushing like a bride, Mama confided how she and my father used to sit underneath this tree while courting—on one of my grandmother's quilts, talking, picnicking, and sharing acts of love that brought me into existence.

"This was *our* place. Where I could be a woman. And your daddy could be a man. This place was priceless. That's why I buried him here. So yes, baby girl, I know something about life being unfair. That nursing school debacle was enough, but after what happened to Matthew, I swore I'd never set foot in Valdosta again. But sometimes you have to do the hard thing. What the Stantons did to us wasn't right, but it happened. And, I did this for you. I brought you back here 'cause you and this baby gonna need to be connected to some bigger strength, your bigger purpose. I sacrificed. Your daddy sacrificed." Stepping away from the tree, Mama cupped my face. "And you gonna do some things for this baby that you might not want to. You gonna keep writing, and you sure gonna get your learning."

"But how? I'm expelled."

"That's God's business to figure out. Now, let's get out of here before it starts raining again."

Arm in arm, we carefully made our way down that incline, leaving my parents' tree behind us.

It wasn't until later that night that I remembered the envelope Mister Lambert gave me in the principal's office. Retrieving my coat from the wardrobe I shared with the twins, I extracted its contents to see what turned out to be sheets of S&H Green Stamps.

"What kind of tomfoolery is this? Those White kids got cash money and all I get is some trading stamps?"

Naomi grabbed the sheet from me when I started tearing it. "Mattie, what's wrong with you? That's fifty dollars' worth of stamps. You know how much good you could do with that?"

"I don't want it." I flounced across the room and dropped onto our shared bed.

"You better get rid of that pride and keep *this*. It may not be actual cash, but it works pretty much the same," Ruth reminded me, detailing how I'd be able to walk into participating stores and trade in those stamps for merchandise as if it were truly money. "If you don't want it for yourself, fine. But think about all the pretty things you can get for the baby."

Sacrifice.

I thought about my father surviving fighting in Europe on the front lines only to come home and be killed. How my mother's dreams of being a nurse were ripped from her, and how she did what she had to, not necessarily what she wanted to, in order to take care of me. Surely, I couldn't be too proud to take these S&H Green Stamps down to the store and shop for my baby's needs?

I went to bed that night thankful for my parents, feeling closer to Daddy as if that visit to his and my mother's tree deepened our spirit connection, and praying for a way to help my mother while providing for myself and my child.

Two days later an answer to that prayer manifested on my doorstep.

Aunt Odelle was at her job working for a family on the other side of town. The kids were at school, and Mama was napping before starting the dinner shift at the diner. I was alone with my thoughts and a library book. I was so lost in *Little Women* and the house was so quiet, I jumped when someone knocked on the front door. Opening it and seeing the women standing there, I hurled myself into my English teacher's arms.

"Miss Divine! Were you fired because of me?"

"It's nice seeing you, too, Mattie."

We laughed at my outburst. "I'm sorry."

"Don't be."

"Hello, Mattie."

Staring at Miz Wheatley standing there, for all intents and purposes a White woman, I was less effusive. Not because of a complexion that allowed her to pass for what she wasn't, but because I felt used by her, and was distrustful.

"May we come in?"

Moving out of the doorway, I invited them inside, offering to fix hot tea which they both declined.

"I owe you an apology." Miz Wheatley didn't waste time with preambles and niceties. "My intentions were good, but my methods were questionable, and resulted in you being besmirched, and your integrity questioned. That is unacceptable. I am passionate about Colored women's success, but that gave me no right to take liberties as I did. I ask your forgiveness."

Moved by the sincerity in her expression and tone, I granted it.

"Good. Glad that's settled. Now, on to your continued schooling. Penelope and I will teach you."

"Wait. Miss Divine, are you teaching somewhere else?"

I listened as my favorite instructor revealed that after being terminated for no clear reason, she'd been blessed to secure a secretarial position with her uncle. "Uncle Theo has been hounding me for years to come help him at his one-man insurance agency. Now, I can."

"Good for Uncle Theo, but the reason you were fired is real clear: you openly challenged Lambert over this child's right to be in that competition," her mentor insisted. "But God works in mysterious ways and all's well that ends well is what I say. I retire at the end of the term so right now we're both working and it may feel like a little much until then, but Mattie Banks, if we have anything to do with it, you're taking that competency test next year and leaving with your high school diploma in hand."

I glanced back and forth between them. "You're tutoring me?"

"Yes, my dear, we are. We'll work out the fine details, but you will not sit in this house doing nothing except growing big. Yes, we know about the baby," she added when I looked away. "Mattie, look at me. Don't you dare walk around in shame. I don't care how that child got here, it's here and we'll treat him or her like we do you. With dignity and respect."

"But the father's—"

"It makes me no nevermind if the father of this child is green with purple polka dots. This child's half yours, right?"

"Yes, ma'am."

"Then that's enough. Now, when shall these private lessons begin?"

CHAPTER FOURTEEN

Ashlee

My mother dubbed me "nosey" for good reason. Since a child, I'd been driven by curiosity and questions, and rarely accepted less than a fully reasonable answer. Finding the name E. Stanton in the return address section of that envelope had me going back and scrutinizing all of the other envelopes and letters as well. It was clearly an isolated fluke; they were bare. All that did was heighten my nosiness. Unable to bypass a good mystery, I wound up online searching Montgomery directories for E. Stanton listings.

"Mama, didn't Nana live in Montgomery when she was little?"

"Mmm-hmm. Why?" Seated on the back veranda beside me, my mother was focused on the magazine she was reading—or not reading. Responsive to every little noise that came from inside the house, she was skimming pages and looking at pictures, essentially. But at least I'd gotten her to take a break as my grandparents napped.

Every day I'd been here Nana seemed to rally and regain strength. She stayed awake for longer periods, engaged in conversation, and even expressed an appetite. She typically only ate half of whatever she requested, but it was enough to keep us satisfied. Still, despite such positive signs, I'd read the hospice literature we'd acquired and knew that such "improvements"—like the calm before a storm—were temporary and not long-lived. As if heaven in its graciousness was smiling on us, granting us final opportunities to enjoy my grandmother's vibrant, beautiful spirit. Without false hopes of a deathbed miracle, I accepted heaven's gift.

"Just asking," I off-handedly replied to my mother's question, wondering what I was digging into, or if my mother would appreciate my doing so. After all, every one of those letters concerned her, but for whatever reason, Nana had elected to keep them hidden in a hat box beneath her reading-room floor. What if I was tampering with things better left buried?

You had permission.

Nana had asked me to find her stories. And I had.

Stories, Ashlee, not anything else.

She hadn't given me license to snoop through a lifetime's worth of sixty-year-old letters. Too late for moral reprimands, my curiosity cat was already out of the bag. Now, all I needed to know was, who was E. Stanton and what was her or his significance?

Mentally, I ran through a list of relatives.

There was a distant cousin, Essie, on PopPop's side, and an Elmer on Nana's; but, I couldn't recall if either of their last names was Stanton. And what would they have sent my mother on such a regular basis over a large span of years?

Money was my best guess. Though I couldn't even begin to imagine why.

Feeling as if I was closer to solving a riddle, something inside of me brightened.

Perhaps E. Stanton is the benefactor who put Mama through college.

My grandparents were never rich by some standards, yet with PopPop owning a successful construction company they could afford to put Mama through college. However, in her final year of high school an anonymous source granted my mother a scholarship, paying her undergrad and medical school costs in full so that she graduated without student loans.

This must be that person.

"Wait. No. That doesn't make sense." Those envelopes were postmarked when my mother was a child, not a young, college-bound adult.

"What doesn't make sense?"

Closing my laptop, I set it aside, wanting to ask Mama questions so the pieces of this puzzle could fall into place. Instead, my thoughts jumped track, leading me back to a conversation we hadn't finished. "Miz Savannah Eve, you told me the other day that you're retiring."

"I certainly did."

"When?"

"Next March. That'll make a full thirty-five years of service. I think that's significant, don't you?"

"I do. It's *remarkable*. I'm so proud of you. Not just for being the world's greatest pediatrician—"

"In your opinion."

"Which is the one that matters. I'm proud of you for having the guts to leave a profession you've loved to allow time for other interests."

"Well, that's your nana's doing. Mama always encouraged me to think different, be different, and to never abandon a dream. Not that I haven't enjoyed the life I've lived, but I'm honoring her wisdom and choosing to make the rest of my days some of the best of my days."

"Amen." Gazing into the far distance at Mister Moonlight, that huge magnolia tree Avery and I had named, I inhaled courage and serenity. "Mama, can I tell you something?"

"Is this an 'I need your opinion' conversation or a 'shut up, sit back, Savannah, and just listen'?"

"A bit of both."

"I'm multi-talented enough for that."

We shared a laugh.

"I'm listening, Ladybug."

"I'm not sure I want to practice law anymore. At least not the way that I have. And I'm not sure I want to spend decades figuring it all out before following another path."

Mama didn't miss a beat. "What other professions or forms of legal advocacy are you considering?"

"Wow. Why're you so calm about this?"

"Per your nana, the only constant thing in life is what?"

"Change," we finished in unison.

Mama played with curly strands escaping the ponytail piled atop my head. "Besides, darling, we've sensed your dissatisfaction for some time, so I figured we'd get to this conversation when you were ready for it."

Stunned, I stared at my mother. "Who is 'we'? And why didn't 'we' say anything?"

"Mama and me. It hasn't been easy watching you work the way you have this year, trying to override your misgivings and make sense of your career. Honey, your heart shifted. We knew it. But we had to let you walk into your own revelation without interference." Mama angled towards me. "You're my stubborn baby. You try to make things work just so they make sense. Our saying something would've had you digging in your heels, and maybe looking at us with resentment."

"Not true, Mama. I always do my best to respect yours and Nana's wisdom."

"Yes, but we're talking about a career you've dedicated yourself to. It wasn't about you respecting, but accepting. You had to walk that walk and do for you." She stopped suddenly when something in the distance caught her peripheral vision. "Who's that?"

My mind swimming with what she'd said, I barely paid attention. My beloveds respected my autonomy, trusted my judgment and decision-making enough to allow my wrestling with my future without interfering? Something in that was confidence-building. "Maybe Avery caught an early flight."

The CEO of his own software development company, my brother had experienced a level-ten emergency that required his presence, delaying his arrival by a couple of days.

"He must've communicated with your father…" Mama was so busy squinting and leaning forward trying to make out who it was that her words trailed off.

"And you call me nosey."

"You are." Walking to the edge of the veranda, she shielded her eyes with her hands. "I can't make out who that is, but it looks like some blond person."

Following her gaze to the road that ran through our property, I squinted at what seemed to be a black car rounding the curve near Mister Moonlight. "Maybe it's a delivery. Did you order anything?"

"Not that I recall." She leaned against the porch rail, steadily watching the car approach. "Oooweee! That's a Mercedes Cabriolet. If delivery persons are getting paid like this, I may have to make it my after-retirement gig."

Mama's laugh was lost on me at the mention of Mercedes. Stomach tingling, I abandoned my seat and was beside her as the car moved into clear view. What seemed black at a distance was actually metallic blue.

"Ladybug, that looks like…"

Brad?

A horn honked loudly.

"Did he get a new car?"

Unable to answer my mother except by nodding, I was speechless seeing the man I loved but couldn't seem to gel with and thought I'd said 'goodbye' to pulling up. "Wow, God."

The sight of him exiting his luxury coupe looking like good sex on a summer day had me wanting to run down those steps, the hair I hadn't flat-ironed since being on leave bouncing, not flowing, as if I was somebody's romance novel heroine.

I am not running to this man. I'm a dignified Black woman.

That didn't keep me from descending those steps though. Slowly. Pensively. Heart suddenly aching with all the things we used to be but hadn't recently been. True, I felt he'd been unsupportive lately, but to his core Bradley Caldwell was a damn good man. My whole soul knew that.

Gravel crunched beneath my feet as I moved up the driveway. The closer I got, the more I wanted to forget the foolishness we'd inflicted on our relationship and simply be in his arms, centered in love.

You will not melt for this man.

Forcing myself to a halt, my nostrils flared with the deliciousness of his cologne drifting on the tail of a warm autumn breeze. Watching his swagger, my traitorous mind skipped down a path of recollection I'd rather it didn't. A path lush with his taste. His touch. That gladiator physique. And the smooth way he moved during lovemaking. The way he held me beyond the bed. Looked at me. Treated me as if I was precious, invaluable. His queen.

Lord, I don't need these memories.

Straightening my spine, I reminded myself I was a warrior who knew how not to succumb to sentiment. "What're you doing here?" My voice sounded off. Evidence of how utterly affected I was by him. Despite being the one who'd said she was finished.

Saying nothing, he continued approaching, broad shoulders squared, face wearing that look that I always equated with unshakable determination.

By the time he reached me, towering over and simply looking down at me, my heart was pounding. Praying I looked braver than I felt, I returned his stare until the silence had me feeling too close to crazy. "Brad? *What?* Why're you here? What do you want?"

"Us." Snaking his hands in my upswept hair, he held me captive while lowering his lips, and kissing me with multiple levels of pent-up heat. Hope. Even hurt.

Whatever plans I had of walking away unaffected utterly failed. I was suddenly just me. Not a woman at odds with love or life. Not a heart broken by the fact that a beloved was dying. Or a professional whose career was in flux. Surrendering to the freedom in that kiss, I gave myself permission to simply breathe. To be. Without internal or external expectations or wrestling.

"We're not doing this." Breaking our kiss, he spoke those words against my lips.

"Doing what?" My voice was low, breathless.

"We're not doing stubborn, ignorant, or hot-headed. We're not doing the incessant arguments and not hearing or validating one another. If we need counseling, let's get it. Yes, I've been a jerk. Caught up in the increasing demands of balancing teaching with my career. Instead of being your rock I've let you down. I own that and ask forgiveness. But at the end of the day I only want you to have the best. And I'll be damned if we walk away without fighting for this. I love you with my everything, and that's not changing. Losing each other?" He shook his head, blue fire in his eyes. "Not happening."

I was weak when he kissed me again, pouring the power of his pronouncement into it. My whole soul rejoiced and rippled within—reaffirming in that moment that he was mine. I was his.

Wrapping my arms about his neck, embracing that truth and my man, a heavy weight seemed to break and lift. A smile in my heart, I ended the kiss and eased back a bit. "I need your forgiveness as well. I've been scattered. Distant. Caught up in my own hard-headed pursuits and allowing our love to suffer in the name of progress." I stroked the unshaven stubble on his chin. "That's unacceptable, and I want us."

"Same."

"I want to reclaim the things we used to do. Read to each other. Work out together. Fall asleep in front of the TV watching bad movies. Laugh at stupid jokes no one else gets. Crack open a deck of cards so I can whip you in spades. Go to ball games. Talk about nothing."

"And slow dance in the dark."

I frowned up at him. "We never did that."

"We will when you get back." He kissed me again with a slow deep intensity that sent electric vibes throughout my whole being. We had work to do to clean up the mess we'd made. I knew this, but it was hard to focus on that fact with our kiss getting hot and heavy real quickly. His hands had roamed to my behind, holding me tightly against him, treating me to his responsive thickening in his lower region.

I pushed him slightly away. "Babe, stop. My mom."

"I wouldn't disrespect Miz Savannah like that. She's gone."

Glancing over my shoulder, I found the porch was absent of Mama and her magazine. She'd returned indoors, allowing us privacy. "That woman's a class act."

"I agree." He stuffed his hands in his pockets, forcing them into compliance. "I won't lie and say I understand every intricacy of what it is you want to do—"

"My point exactly! Neither do I. This new venture isn't fully mapped out in my mind. I simply know the universe needs me to be open."

He nodded. "Understood, but it's a lot to grasp."

"Noted. Especially for a man who uses tags to perfectly organize his wine collection."

"You've got jokes."

"Am I lying?"

"Not necessarily." He grinned that lovable, lopsided grin of his before becoming straight-faced. "In all seriousness, baby, we can't keep acting like opposing counsel from different teams."

"Agreed."

"And I won't approach your need for change in fear, as if that includes me."

I experienced tender compassion towards his uncertainty. "Sweetie, I acknowledge that all of this seemingly came out of nowhere. If it's frightening for me, it's frightening for you and I could've been sensitive to that fact. But trust me when I say my needing something different doesn't include Bradley Keith Caldwell."

"The whole name, babe?"

"The whole name." I cupped his jaw, stroked his face. "I'm not running around on whims and leaving you behind. I want you with me when I get wherever it is I'm going. Can we stay Team Ashlee-Brad?"

"How about Bradley-Ash?"

I smiled as he wrapped me in his embrace, loving the feel of his heartbeat. "That works, too. I love you, but I won't be silenced or bullied."

"I know, and I'm listening. Now. Through whatever. And for always. I'm marrying you."

I laughed. "That's the most pitiful proposal ever."

"It's not a proposal. Yet. But trust, I've already spoken to and received the blessing from your dad."

I leaned back to get a better look at him. "Why would you tell me that?"

"Because you don't like surprises."

"A marriage proposal is the one time in life I'd like to be surprised. Are you rocking a ring in your back pocket?"

"Maybe."

"Brad, stop playing."

"What makes you think I am?"

"Because I don't feel anything," I countered, sliding my hands in the back pockets of his jeans.

"Keep digging around like that and you're gonna feel something." He pressed against me, moving his lower body in a subtle way that left me wanting.

"Fine." I ceased my search. "But if you *are* proposing you should do it sooner versus later."

"Because?"

"Because my being hormonal has contributed to our friction." Inhaling deeply, I shared our truth. "And I'm hormonal because we're pregnant."

"That's fine, we can…" Words trailing away, that man's eyes got so big I imagined I could see the world in them. Next thing I knew, his face was turning red. "Hold up! Did I hear you correctly? You said we're *pregnant?*"

"Yes, counselor, I did. Do you object?"

Raking his hands over his face, he turned and walked away. "Oh my God!" Rubbing his hands through his hair, he started pacing. "Okay. I can handle this." Clearly, he couldn't. Hunkering down on his haunches, his back to me, his shoulders heaved as if he was struggling to breathe.

Approaching quietly, I was afraid to touch him. "Bradley?"

He glanced up at me. "I'm fine, Ashlee. Hell. No, I'm not. We're having a *real* baby baby?"

I bit my lip to keep from laughing. "Yes, a *baby* baby."

"Not a maybe."

Taking his hand, I placed it on my stomach as my heart started hammering. "We didn't plan it this way, and if you're not prepared for this—"

He was on his feet, embracing me tightly before I could finish. The kiss he granted shimmered with an entirely different kind of passion. And reverence. Ending that kiss to cradle my face, he offered two of the sweetest words. "I'm ready."

After a day including a visit from her pastor and first lady, and Brad, Nana was exhausted. I'd given her a sponge bath, read from her bible, and fed her a bowl of oatmeal. Now, she was fast asleep, my grandfather on the rollaway bed we'd positioned in the room so he could be with her. Kissing my grandparents, I let the night nurse know I was turning in. Shower complete, I did so with a pint of strawberry cheesecake ice cream and Nana's manuscript to keep me company when what I really wanted was my man.

He'd fully intended to return to the city that night. But thanks to my bombshell announcement, he'd wound up staying, functioning in a daze—his expression vacillating between stunned amazement and that lovable, goofy grin. Several times during dinner, my mother had asked if he was feeling well. He'd assured her he was while squeezing my thigh beneath the table. By the time dinner was finished it was late and my mother insisted he stay.

"You're not getting on that road tonight after eating all this rich food. I will not have you catching the itis and falling asleep behind the wheel."

"Yes, ma'am."

Bent on propriety, my parents had offered Brad their guest-room. As if I'd ever disrespect my grandparents' home by being intimate with my lover in it.

As if we don't already cohabit and I'm not pregnant.

They weren't privy to our news yet. Wanting to allow Brad the night to continue processing that, we'd elected to tell them the next day at breakfast. Instead of being here with me, he'd been hustled up to my parents' house and talked into a game of chess with my dad.

I hope they still like each other when they're finished.

"They'll figure it out." Savoring my cold confection, I resumed Nana's manuscript where I'd left off.

Enjoying the night breeze blowing through the open window I was easily caught up by her protagonist's heartbreak involving a "raven-haired, purple-eyed, good-looking White boy" named E.J. Again, the sense that I was reading more than a manuscript pressed in on me. Marveling at our similarities, I absent-mindedly muttered, "Both Nana's heroine and I are having biracial babies."

As the breeze ruffled the window sheers, my mother's face flashed across my mind for some unknown reason. Lowering the pages onto my lap, I sat there feeling as if the universe wanted to tell me something. When the message remained unclear, I continued reading, grateful that, unlike Nana's young lady, my relationship with my child's father had been rerouted onto a right path.

My heart broke as her lover stood by allowing her to be cast out into a cold winter night. "Dang, E.J., man up already. Wait… *E.J.*?"

Something grabbed my mind, had me rereading that passage and speaking the name aloud. That merely evoked a feeling that I was on the precipice of knowledge I didn't know I needed. Flipping to the beginning of the manuscript, I confirmed when and where the story took place. "Montgomery, 1955."

Nana had lived in Montgomery when she was young, and 1955 was the year before Mama was born….

My thoughts were just starting to lose some of their elusiveness when my bedroom window slid upward. I almost screamed until seeing Brad's head poke through the sheers, a shushing finger at his lips.

"*Brad, what's wrong with you?*"

"Can I get some help here?"

My grandparents' home was a one-story built on a raised foundation to prevent flooding in an area that was prone to it, thanks to a nearby creek and river. Brad was six three, but without leverage, he was struggling.

"Use those muscles and manage it, Mister Always-at-the-Gym."

"*Ashlee.*"

"Shhh, before you have the night nurse in here."

"Stop playing and help me."

Abandoning my dessert, I assisted him through the window, wobbling backwards, and nearly knocking over the bedside lamp in the process. I righted it while Brad grabbed me.

"Whoa. You okay?"

"Yes, Mister Overprotective."

"I wasn't worried about you. My concern was for my unborn child."

I punched his rock-solid arm.

He quietly chuckled. "We're really pregnant?"

Having confirmed that for him multiple times that day, I smiled as he caressed my hips, my stomach. "Oui, oui, monsieur."

"The sudden use of French makes it definite."

Laughing, I placed Nana's manuscript safely on the bedside table before returning to bed. "Babe, our condo isn't kid-friendly."

He leaned against the wall, ankles and arms crossed. "Let's rent it out and buy a house."

"Okay. Are we breastfeeding?"

"*We* aren't. Ashlee is?"

"Absolutely. Disposable or cloth diapers? Time-outs or other discipline? Judeo-Christian upbringing? I'm Baptist and you're Episcopalian. What about childcare? I already know I'll be that mom using nanny cams. Oh my God, boo, if something happens to our child while we're working—"

"Ash, breathe please."

"I can't. I have six thousand more questions."

"None of which needs to be answered tonight. Right?"

"Wrong."

Chuckling, he crossed the room, knelt in front of me.

"You better not be proposing!"

"I prefer to do that when you don't look a hot mess. Your hair, which I love natural like this, is everywhere over your head. You have on zero makeup. And that pajama top is suspect."

"Oh, hush." Grabbing my ice cream, I stuffed a spoonful in his mouth, only to shiver when he lifted my suspect PJ top, pressing cold lips against my stomach.

"Regardless, my child's mother is beyond beautiful." His words kissed my spirit.

"Remember that when I gain sixty pounds carrying *your* precious angel."

"I promise to do my best."

I spooned more dessert for myself and him. When he kissed the inside of my thigh, I shivered again.

"We might be onto something with these cool ice-cream lips on warm skin." His voice was smooth, tantalizing. "Shall we add it to the repertoire?" Pushing up my top, he eased me onto my back.

"Maybe."

"I vote yes." Helping himself to more ice cream, he kissed between my legs.

Even with PJ bottoms on, the sensation was so delicious that my hips lifted off the bed causing me to nearly forget that this brand of intimacy was off limits in this house. That was all the encouragement he needed.

"We both have questions about parenting." He spoke softly while pulling off my bottoms. "We have uncertainties. But we'll work it out." He kissed a path up my legs. "Trust me?"

Loving his lips on my skin, I simply nodded as he continued his ascension. He'd reached the center of my thigh when a knock at the door interrupted his journey.

"Ladybug, can I come in?"

My grandfather's voice made me panic. "One moment, please." Yanking my bottoms on, I stood, snatching Brad onto his feet, hoping to stuff him out of the window as noiselessly as possible. Instead, I accidentally smashed his head against the windowsill and had to cover his mouth when he nearly yelled. "Ohmigawd, baby, I'm sorry."

"Ashlee."

PopPop's using my legal name was a rarity that caused me to hurry. Pulling Brad with me, I shoved him behind the door and opened it, carefully. "Yes, sir?"

A stern look on his face, my six-foot-four grandfather easily looked over my head. Scanning the room and finding nothing, his laser focus honed in on me. "Will your young man be exiting through this door or climbing out that window the same way he climbed in?"

My reply was guilty silence.

Clearing his throat, Brad stepped from his hiding place, red in the face. "Good evening again, Mister James."

Saying nothing, my grandfather pointed towards the hallway.

Watching the father of my child striding away, trying to hold his head up in dignity, I would have fallen out laughing if it weren't for PopPop's unflinching gaze.

"I'll tell you like I told your mother when she tried this same foolishness at seventeen: as long as I'm living it better not ever happen again."

"Yes, sir. We apologize."

My grandfather stared at me a moment before turning and heading for his room.

Closing my door, I fell onto the bed, propping a pillow over my face to muffle my embarrassed laughter. I was still grinning when Brad texted five minutes later.

That was insane.

My response was a gif of a woman eating ice cream and looking utterly content.

I went to bed that night feeling more peaceful than I had in a long while. My sleep was so restful and deep that my eyes flying open four hours later literally startled me.

Sometimes capital J looks like an S and vice versa.

Turning on the lamp, I sat up and grabbed Nana's manuscript, thumbing through the pages, finding every mention of the purple-eyed, raven-haired young man who had, at one time, been the protagonist's love interest.

"That's not E.J., it's E.S."

Like puzzle pieces falling into place, my thoughts caught and shifted. Nana's living in Montgomery. The postmark dates on those envelopes. The elusive E. Stanton. This manuscript I'd read as if a fictional tale of times gone by. All of these were intricately and intimately connected to the two most important women in my life.

I resumed voraciously reading until fatigue got the best of me, and I could see the pink rays of the rising sun in the distance. Even then, as I turned off the lamp and lay down, my mind was racing.

Names were changed, but this is a memoir, not fiction.

If that was true then Nana was her own protagonist and her reference to "My Stories" made perfect sense.

Closing my eyes and remembering her '*Your* daddy' edict that day of dancing, my heart fluttered, convinced that my mother knew something about E. Stanton.

CHAPTER FIFTEEN

Mattie

The months passed so rapidly sometimes they felt like days and weeks. The rains stopped. The seasons changed. So did my body. No longer attending school, I stopped binding myself and that little baby of mine took advantage. Blooming. Stretching. It was only early March and sometimes I felt big enough to burst. How I was going to survive another three or four more months of growing was a mystery. But that baby expanding inside of me was everything sweet and I loved her or him with my whole being.

It wasn't but a week after Miss Divine and Miz Wheatley showed up unannounced on the doorstep that I was in the kitchen helping Mama and Aunt Odelle string snap beans when I first felt a strange and sudden movement. It scared me so badly, I knocked the bowl of beans off my lap.

"Baby girl, what's the matter?"

Mama wasn't scheduled at the diner that day and sat at the table looking at me like she was ready to run and grab the Colored doctor who lived three blocks over.

"Mama, something's wrong." It wasn't the first time I'd felt something. A week or so after moving to Valdosta, I ran to my mother scared when something fluttered inside of me, like I'd swallowed a mess of butterflies or bees. She'd laughed and hugged me, explaining that was simply the baby making my acquaintance. But this was way different from that and all the sweet little butterfly kisses I'd felt ever since.

"Wrong how?" Aunt Odelle demanded.

"My body's punching me."

"Demonstrate." My mother held a palm up. I tapped it with similar force.

When she asked where the punch occurred, I put her hands on my swelling abdomen, held my breath and waited. I yelped when, a minute later, it happened again. "See!"

Mama looked at Aunt Odelle and they both fell out laughing. I simply sat there rubbing my sore belly.

"Mattie, honey, that's nothing but your baby kicking."

"Will it keep happening?" I felt foolish for overreacting, but I'd grown so accustomed to the butterfly kisses and couldn't say I was too keen on this kicking, punching business.

"You better pray to God it does," Aunt Odelle insisted.

Mama's response was more gentle. "It might be uncomfortable, but you want your child kicking and letting you know it's alright. It's like you two communicating, sharing language on the inside. Wish we had a book to tell you more about it."

"What she need a book for? You're her best teacher, Dorothy."

"I know that." It wasn't that Mama had never talked to me about babies or man-woman things; however, it was a delicate subject and she'd told me just enough. Removing her apron, Mama pushed back her chair. "But it don't hurt to have some extra learning. Mattie, come with me."

Next thing I knew, Mama and I were headed to Valdosta's one and only library.

"Have a seat on that bench and let me deal with this."

I knew we would have to wait at the library's rear window while a librarian searched for a book, and that I would only be able to take it out on loan for one week—versus the three-week loan period afforded Valdosta's White residents. Why Mama thought that would offend me more than any of the other inequities faced in our daily living was odd to me. But my feet were aching after the walk and could use some rest, so I did as Mama said. Five minutes later she returned empty-handed.

"They didn't have anything?"

"Not a lick. I wanted you to have medical knowledge, but nothing wrong with mother wit. Guess I'll be teaching you myself."

Trusting my mother's intelligence unquestionably, that was fine by me. "Why'd you ask me to sit and wait?"

"I'ma let you go ask for a book about babies so nosey folks can be in your business? No, ma'am. Let me do the asking. I have a wedding ring." Flashing the thin gold band on her left hand, Mama kept walking.

We hadn't been in Valdosta long enough for folks to know our ins and outs, but it was a small town and small towns put quick feet on news and stories. Not that our social circle would ever include the White women employed at Valdosta's main library, still, my mother was clearly trying to spare me the gossip and disdain that came with being a young, unmarried girl who was expecting.

"Since you love writing, when we get home you're gonna start yourself a list of facts about babies... and *other* things. You might've done what it takes to make a child, but you still need some understanding."

That's how baby behaviors and *other* things wound up on my curriculum.

Miss Divine blushed at Mama's request, but Miz Wheatley —a widow who'd enjoyed having a *special friend* the past seven years—was perfectly fine discussing everything from A to Z and in between. Birthing a baby. Child rearing. Marriage intimacy.

She was so descriptive with the latter that sometimes my unmarried English teacher found herself fanning.

"Despite popular opinions, as women we need never simply lay there letting a man satisfy himself. We, too, have a right to completion."

Face frowned up, I had the nerve to ask, "What's that, Miz Wheatley?"

"Oh, it's that pleasure place." She placed a hand on my belly. "It's okay if you didn't experience it this time. But going forward? Honey, don't let him stop until you reach completion."

I jotted that in my list of life facts for the future. Right then I didn't want a boyfriend or a husband. My focus was on me, my baby, and studying every lesson my tutors assigned so I could finish my education. But by the time March flowed into April and April into May, I was sick of schooling at home. Sick of waiting on a baby.

Day in and out it was the same ole thing. Wake up. Bathe. Dress. Eat. Do chores. Sit at the kitchen table or out in the yard studying, reading, sometimes writing until Miss Divine picked me up each evening for lessons at Miz Wheatley's. During the day, I was bored and lonely, counting the hours until Ruth and Naomi got home so I could laugh at their "what happened today" stories. That eased the loneliness, but I still felt left out of things I could've been enjoying. Like school dances. Dates. Sipping malts at the Colored-owned drug store and gossiping. I was grateful for the vicarious experiences provided, but it was different from being included.

It was the same with Sadie.

My best friend and I made efforts to stay in touch, but sometimes her life was so full with school and extracurricular activities that she didn't have much time for me.

"Don't worry, Mattie, I'll be there after the baby comes."

We were excited about her visiting this summer, and looked forward to seeing each other.

Personally, I looked forward to being able to sleep on my stomach again. No more feet swelling, and waddling to the restroom every five minutes. No more wanting crazy things like cinnamon candy stuffed in dill pickles dipped in lemonade. And no more backaches. The more time passed and the bigger this baby got, the more I wanted my body back. I needed space. Rooming with the twins I felt pressed both on the outside, and within. So, when Mama came home early from the diner one night and told me she had a surprise, I never imagined what it turned out to be.

"What do you think?" Standing in the empty living room of a small, two-bedroom cottage four houses down from Uncle Melvin, my mother was beaming.

"It's pretty."

"Would you like the first bedroom?"

Heading towards the kitchen, I stopped abruptly. "Ma'am?"

"It's smaller than the one at the back, but I figure I deserve that seeing as how I'm the one paying for this."

My eyes grew big. "Mama, are we renting here?"

"No, indeed! I'm buying it from Mister Freeland."

The owner of the diner where Mama worked was a rough-n-gruff ex-Army officer who barked at his staff and rarely had a smile for anyone and, on appearances alone, was the epitome of a racist redneck baked in a southern sun. But, according to Mama, Mister Freeland was *the best* employer she'd ever worked for. Beneath that grizzled exterior was a person of fairness and justice. And this simply proved that.

Pulling folded papers from her purse, she handed them to me. "I have enough left from the last time the Stantons paid me for a down payment. Might have to take on a couple of extra shifts to manage the mortgage, but it'll be worth it. I haven't signed anything or paid a penny yet, but that's our agreement. I looked it over some but I'ma need you to read it to me," Mama stated, feeling self-conscious about her abilities despite her progressing nicely since—not having reading classes at church like we did in Montgomery—I'd started helping her with her reading. Quickly, I skimmed the papers. Thankfully, there wasn't a mess of legal terms. "I think you should have Miz Wheatley look these over."

"Okay, but for now tell me your gut reaction."

"It's clear and honest."

"Shall we do this?"

Mama squealed when I nodded. Next thing I knew, we were holding hands and dancing in a circle, rejoicing over a gift granted in Valdosta.

Miz Wheatley's lawyer read the agreement, calling it a bit unconventional, but fully legal. With Mister Freeland owning the property outright, Mama would deposit payments at his bank and receive receipts, receiving the title papers once paid in full. Still a bit gun-shy, Mama consulted our new pastor who prayed and asked heaven's blessings. Two weeks later we moved in.

I loved our little house. It wasn't grand like the Stantons', but it was ours. There were nice-sized yards in front and back with lemon and peach trees and a tiny berry patch. The outside paint needed love, and some of the floorboards creaked. But for the first time in a long time I had a space that was all mine and felt blessed.

That first Saturday in June, just days after we moved in, I woke up to the sound of loud arguing. Startled, I looked for Mama, but her side of the pallet we'd been sharing was empty. Hefting myself up, I didn't even pause for the restroom, but pulled on a robe and wobbled outside to find my uncles fussing and Mama looking humored by their nonsense.

"What's going on?"

"Morning, baby. Your uncles are being contentious."

"Ain't nobody contentious, Dorothy. I'm simply saying we paint the inside first and get that to drying so y'all can sleep tonight without choking on fumes," Uncle Melvin contended.

My Uncle Morris, however, felt they needed to tend to the roof.

"Why? You expecting rain in June?"

Mama and I were laughing at the two going back and forth when a honking caravan of two trucks and three cars pulled up, occupied by relatives and church folk either there to help or bearing house gifts. Nothing was fancy or brand new, but by the time evening rolled around our home had practically everything we needed, including beds so that Mama I no longer had to share a pallet.

Teary-eyed all day over their generosity, Mama expressed her gratitude by cooking up a mass of fried chicken, milk rolls, potato salad, and collard greens. In her element, she bustled about the kitchen, calling out instructions.

"Mattie, whip up some teacakes."

"No ma'am! Can't nobody make those as good as you."

"You been helping me make 'em since you were little. We need dessert so have at it."

I had to sit at the table for all the backache and kicking this child of mine was doing, but I managed, treating our benefactors to teacakes after dinner.

That night I lay awake in my "new," second-hand bed joyfully thanking the good Lord, dreaming up how to decorate my room with its soft yellow walls and small writing desk that left just enough space for the bassinet my tutors surprised me with the following week. With Ruth and Naomi's help, that room became my haven and something pretty. But waking up in the middle of the night two weeks later, I was terrified.

I'd been moving slowly the past few days, experiencing increased discomforts and aches, was tired and never seemed to find a comfortable sleeping position. I'd barely managed to drift off when a river of warm liquid gushing between my legs had me pushing myself into a sitting position.

Thanks to my life-lessons list, I knew what was happening and called down the hall to Mama only to remember she was at the diner on the late shift. That's when terror set in.

"Mattie Banks, don't you dare."

Knowing my baby needed me, I waited for a stabbing pain to pass before easing off the bed, peeling off my soaked gown and changing. I barely had my house shoes and robe on when another pain hit me so hard it left me leaning over my desk, moaning.

Hadn't the midwife said to expect my child late June? It was only the beginning of the month.

"It's. Too. Early."

Babies come when they want to.

That truth in mind, I somehow made it out the house and down the street to Uncle Melvin's. By the time he responded to my knocking, I was sprawled on the front porch rocker, pains so great I was crying. Between him and his wife, Aunt Lady, they got me inside before my uncle ran out, hollering, "Call the diner and tell Dorothy to be ready when I get there!"

I was left with Aunt Lady and fire ripping through my belly.

"Oh… dear… God."

I had no idea what pulled that from my aunt, but my eyes clenched tightly, I didn't need to see her face to know something was wrong. When I tried sitting up, she held me down and started humming. Distracting me from whatever she was seeing. When

Uncle Melvin returned with Mama and the midwife, my aunt was singing spirituals like we all needed Jesus.

"*Lord, this baby ain't in the right position.*" Mama's voice was shrill with panic.

"Dorothy, it's breeched sideways. I gotta turn it or neither one of 'em gonna make it." The midwife took control of the room Uncle Melvin carried me into, turning it into a hive of activity. "Lady, hold her on the left. Dorothy, on the right. Mattie, bite down hard on this. You hear me?"

Nodding as something rugged slipped between my lips, I did as instructed. That didn't keep me from screaming when the midwife laid hands on my belly and started moving, manipulating, trying to turn my baby like it should've been.

"Bite down, Mattie!"

Tears streaming, I did so for what felt like agonizing hours, but was only minutes.

"Alright, now we're bathing with water!"

The midwife's happy adage told me everything was okay. That didn't hold back fiery pain after pain, or my feeling like I was being ripped in two.

"Baby girl, look at me. Breathe with me."

I focused on my mother as Aunt Lady ran from the room, obeying the midwife's request for old sheets and boiled water.

"And bring some of that water in a cup," Mama called.

Five minutes later I was sipping something that tasted like hot garbage on a rainy day. Still, it helped ease my body so that when the midwife checked me down there and said I was ready sometime later, I didn't object to Aunt Lady and Mama bracing either side of me as I pushed until I couldn't push again and felt my baby's head coming out of me.

"One more, Mattie!"

Lord knew I didn't have anything else to give the midwife or myself.

"Push, Mattie, this baby ain't breathing!"

Fear slicing through me worse than any pain could, I stole strength from somewhere.

"There ya go! I got the shoulders. That's enough. Good job."

Panting, flat on my back, I ignored the women hustling and bustling around me. I was too busy praying desperate prayers until my baby's first cry filled my ears.

"You have yourself a girl."

My whole heart smiled, but when my baby was finally in my arms, her sweetness made me cry.

Awed, I could only whisper, "She's beautiful." Never in my life had I seen someone so precious, perfect. I was so enchanted I didn't even mind the midwife fiddling around down there handling what she called "act two." I contented myself with counting my baby's toes, kissing her tiny fingers, and cradling a head that was practically bald. I giggled. "Mama, she doesn't have any hair."

My mother smiled. "Bald babies usually make up for it later. What're we naming this princess?"

Remembering my pact with Sadie to use each other's initials with our firstborn, I proudly announced, "Savannah Eve."

"Savannah Eve," Mama repeated, stroking my daughter's tiny, alabaster feet. "That's pretty. Well, little Miss Savannah, I'm your grandmother, but call me Nana 'cause I'm too young for 'granny.' Mattie, that baby's looking for something."

My daughter was whining like a hungry kitten, her mouth near my chest, opening and closing.

"That baby's hungry," the midwife announced. "Let's clean you up so you can feed her."

Settled in a clean gown borrowed from Aunt Lady, I watched Mama holding Savannah as the midwife made me drink another foul-tasting tea while she massaged my breasts with warm compresses.

"This'll help your milk come in."

All that massaging hurt but not half as much as when Savannah got a hold of me.

Propping a pillow beneath my arm, Mama helped position her, but that little baby didn't need help finding her way to what she wanted. I yelped when her mouth clamped down with newborn vengeance. Hurting like the dickens, I told myself what Mama told me, that mother's milk was liquid gold for Savannah Eve. Rather than focus on the pain, I focused on her name, quietly repeating it over and again.

I stayed three days at Aunt Lady's and Uncle Melvin's until Mama felt it was okay for me to be up and about. My uncle offered to drive us home, but that felt ridiculous with us living only four doors down. Besides, after days convalescing I wanted to stretch my legs.

"Don't walk too fast, Mattie. Take your time."

We were probably a comical sight, with my aunt and uncle aiding me on either side, and Mama behind us carrying Savannah. Other than minor discomfort when climbing the front porch, I was fine. But it wasn't until my aunt and uncle left and it was just us that I felt something settle inside. Watching my mother gently lay my baby in her bassinet I realized that something was peace.

I'm blessed. Right here with our little family of three.

Thanks to attending summer school to make up for a failing grade, Sadie's visit was delayed and Savannah was a month old by the time she arrived. Still bald as a beetle, my precious baby had finally stopped looking fully White and was getting a little color in her skin. She was fat from all the nursing she liked to do all hours of the night and day. She had plump thighs that I loved kissing and the prettiest doll-like face. Mama claimed she looked like me, but every time I saw her funny-colored eyes, I thought of Edward.

He don't even know he has a daughter.

Sometimes I wanted to write and tell him all about Savannah and how exquisite she was, but the Stantons had made their position clear. For them, half-Colored Stanton bastards didn't exist. Edward's turning his back in the window that night we'd been evicted was the final punctuation, stamping his agreement with them.

"That's why your last name is Banks." Nursing my daughter, I smiled at her little hand clutching my breast like I'd better not go anywhere. "I'll never leave my angel."

Mothering was hard work. The bathing. Feeding. Dressing. Rocking and burping. The interrupted sleep. Washing and hanging diapers on the clothes line to dry. Soothing her when she was fussy. My world belonged to Savannah, but she was heaven's gift and worth any inconvenience. Still, the thought of having time with Sadie, being our silly carefree selves, had me so happy I'd gotten up early that morning to help Mama clean the house and even had teacake dough resting in the Frigidaire.

"Your Aunt Sadie's gonna love you."

"Mattie, they're here!"

Stuffing myself back in my brassiere, I buttoned my blouse and patted Savannah's back while rushing to the front of the house in time to see Sadie exiting a car that wasn't her parents'.

"*Mattie!*"

Handing Savannah to Mama, I ran down the steps to my best friend. We were squealing, hugging, and making such a ruckus that I didn't even notice the person exiting the driver's side.

"Mattie, look at you, you're beautiful!"

"Thanks, but I feel like a milk factory."

Hugging again, we were giggling when a deep voice stole my attention.

"Hey, Miss Dorothy."

"Ransome James, if you don't get up here and hug me!"

Releasing Sadie, I linked arms with her and turned towards the stairs, pausing when I saw that good-looking man hugging my mother.

"Mama's so into the bus boycott she wouldn't even let me take Greyhound. She and Daddy had some big meeting they couldn't miss, so Mister Chewy had to bring me. If you ask me he just wanted to show off his new car."

Recalling the nickname we'd given Ransome for his constant gum-chewing, I grinned at Sadie's statement while her brother hugged Mama before turning our way, his eyes meeting mine and causing something warm to flash through me. We'd grown up together. He'd come to my rescue that night after Miss Celestine's, and sometimes carted me and Sadie to school after the boycott started. But standing there staring up at him—with his butterscotch skin and hazel eyes same as Sadie's—taller, broader, more of a full-grown man than I remembered, he felt like a stranger.

"Hello, Mattie."

Feeling shy, I barely returned his greeting.

"Ooo, lemme see this baby!" Hurrying onto the porch, Sadie welcomed Mama's placing my angel in her arms. Thank God they were too busy cooing over Savannah to notice Ransome and me stuck in some weird staring game. Telling myself my recently having a baby was responsible for the strange sensations rolling through me, I ignored the feeling of my breasts swelling, leaking when his eyes slowly roamed my physique.

"Ransome, look at this living baby doll."

Wanting to kiss Sadie for breaking whatever that crazy spell was, I watched her brother observing my child, thankful for the cotton stuffing in my brassiere catching the milk that was suddenly dripping.

"She's a fine baby, Mattie." His compliment was genuine. "Sadie, I'll get your bags."

I moved aside when he descended the steps. That didn't keep me from catching a whiff of his scent. It was road dirt, travel, whatever cologne he'd put on in Montgomery, and utterly captivating.

Mattie, you been schooling at home and washing diapers so long you're starving.

Mounting the porch and showing Sadie to my room so she could finish burping my angel, starving for what, was the question.

Having feasted on Mama's catfish, fried green tomatoes, Hoppin' John, and hush puppies, we sat around too stuffed to move, catching up on life in Montgomery. With U.S. government and politics being two of the subjects Miz Wheatley taught me, I'd kept up with the boycott through lessons, the news, and newspaper clippings Sadie sent. But it was nice hearing it directly from someone still living there.

"Miss Dorothy, I don't think anyone anticipated this boycott lasting as long as it has, but I'm proud of us maintaining our fight for equal treatment and not giving in."

"Amen to that, Ransome. Nobody knows its outcome, but this boycott definitely won't be forgotten. How're you enjoying the Negro Leagues?"

He'd signed on with a different team right after we left Montgomery and I wanted to hear what he had to say, but I couldn't for Sadie chiming in on the latest with Nosey Nedra. Instead, I watched the movement of his full lips as if commanded to by some invisible force.

"Miss Dorothy, I hate to eat and run, but I'd better get going." He stood, leisurely stretching that tall frame that made me appreciate the way a man moved.

"I *know* you're not getting on the road and making that long drive back to Montgomery by yourself at this time of night." Mama looked content holding Savannah and rubbing her back.

"No, ma'am. One of my former teammates lives not far from here. I'm staying at his place, and he's heading to Montgomery with me in the morning."

"Oh good. I was ready to get you some blankets so you could bunk out on the sofa."

He laughed. "Thank you, but no need."

"Well, you and your teammate swing by here for breakfast before you leave tomorrow. We'll make sure you eat and fix you a little something to take on the road with you."

"Will that something include your world-famous teacakes? I probably ate a dozen tonight."

Mama waved off the compliment. "They're not world famous, and that was Mattie's baking, not mine."

"Mattie, you finally learned how to crack an egg?" His teasing left us laughing.

"Ransome James, I can handle more than an egg."

Unwrapping a stick of gum and sliding it in his mouth, his grin was warm and seemingly just for me. "So, I see."

"Mattie, wrap up some of those teacakes so this starving child can enjoy a few more tonight."

"Yes, ma'am." I hurried to the kitchen, glad to escape Sadie's brother grinning at me, making me feel butterflies in my belly worse than when I was expecting Savannah.

Tired from the day, my best friend and I lay in bed chatting in the dark later that night. I appreciated Mama rolling my baby's bassinet into her room to allow us time together. Missing Savannah, I told myself to enjoy the break: she'd be back at her next feeding.

"You did good with those S&H Green Stamps, Mattie."

I'd used them as the twins suggested, getting a few things for my room, but spending most on Savannah. "Thanks, Sadie. I didn't know babies were so expensive. I think I need a job. Not just to take care of Savannah Eve, but so I can help my mother." Mama was still working extra shifts. She never complained, but sometimes she came home so tired she fell asleep in the front room before taking her apron off.

"What could you do, and who would take care of our angel?"

"I guess one of my aunts. Mama doesn't want me working as a domestic, but I don't know what else I could do."

"You could sell those cookies."

"What cookies?"

"Your teacakes."

"Girl, anybody can make those."

"Yours are different. Better."

I'd modified Mama's recipe with orange zest and juice, and a hint of cinnamon.

"Just think about it, Mattie. It's something you can do while home with the baby and still earn a little money."

"It's a nice thought, but I don't know."

"You already have one customer."

"Who?"

"My brother." Even in the dark I could tell she was smiling when Sadie turned towards me. "I saw y'all."

"Doing what?"

"Don't play innocent. Every time I turned around, y'all were staring at each other."

"Clearly, all that turning made you dizzy."

She laughed good-naturedly. "You know what I mean. All evening. Both y'all. Just *looking*. I think he's interested in you."

"Again, I think you're dizzy." I pushed on to another subject, but that didn't mean her words hadn't affected me. They had. Ransome James had always been good-looking, but now he'd gone off and grown into a full man. Something in the way he looked at me, how his deep voice spoke to me, left me wondering if his interest was a possibility. Or just my wishful thinking.

CHAPTER SIXTEEN

Ashlee

My mother, with her baby-loving self, was ecstatic when Brad and I made our great reveal the next day. Not so much my menfolk. Granting me smiles and hugs while giving Brad their tight congratulations, PopPop, Avery, and Daddy looked at my child's father like he'd stolen something that they wanted back. Intuitive as always, my mother pulled me aside before I could get upset.

"Honey, don't let them fool you. They're as happy as Mama and I."

"Well, can they tell their faces that 'cause they look mad."

"Ashlee, you're unmarried. All that gruff stoicism stems from their being concerned and wanting to make sure Brad does right by you and that you're not left raising this child alone. Instead of being perturbed, be thankful you have protective men who love you."

Accepting Mama's wisdom, I stayed close as Brad made his round of goodbyes just in case Avery or Daddy felt the need to choke or lay hands on him, requiring Mama and me to intervene. Thankfully, nothing jumped off as he made his way to Nana.

Wanting fresh air, she'd asked to join us for brunch. Finding the wheelchair she'd needed when first diagnosed years ago, Avery and Daddy placed her onto it, allowing PopPop to wheel her onto the back porch. Now, watching Brad kneel before Nana and take her hands, my heart was full.

"Miz Mattie, you're a remarkable woman. Thank you for the unquestionable kindness you've always shown me." He paused, choking up, knowing this would be their final farewell. "I'm honored to love you."

I was already watery-eyed but when he raised her hands to his lips and kissed them, I had to hold onto my emotions.

Nana, still daily amazing us with her strength, caressed his head. "You're. The. Right. One."

I smiled through my tears, knowing it was a blessing and benediction, and that Brad would never let me hear the end of it. If I wrecked his nerves or questioned his judgment, he wouldn't hesitate pulling "Miz Mattie said I'm the right one" out of his arsenal.

Hugging her, he stood and kissed her forehead before wiping tears from his face and squaring his shoulders in order to walk away. I watched as he kissed my mother, exchanged handshakes with my father and brother. Reaching PopPop, Brad extended a hand. My grandfather refused it, hugging him instead.

Quiet, somber, we walked to his waiting Cabriolet.

"Drive safely. Call me when you get in."

"I will. I'm a day late and a dollar short, but I get it, Ash."

"Get what?"

"Life is precious. And entirely too brief to expend energy on what makes you miserable. Or living an obligatory life without satisfaction. Be bold and take your leap, baby."

"And if I fall?"

"You won't."

"But if I do?" I stubbornly insisted, wanting him to articulate his commitment so the universe could capture it.

He stroked my chin. "I'll pick you up and brush your wings off."

"See, that's why I like you. Are they looking?"

Sliding his sunglasses on, he glanced over my head. "Yep. Like I'd better not touch you if I want to live."

"Kiss her already. You have my permission!"

Chuckling at my mother's antics, he did. Slowly. Completely.

Waving as he drove away, I was relieved to see only Mama and Nana on the porch when I returned to the house.

Mama grinned at me. "You look relieved that the testosterone brigade's no longer here with countless when's-the-wedding kind of questions."

"Amen to that. Should I take her in?" I nodded at Nana who'd fallen asleep, a light blanket draped across her lap.

Mama's smile was half-mast. "No. Let her have all the fresh air she wants."

I sat beside my mother wondering how to plunge into the matter consuming my thoughts. Not only had I read until dawn, but I'd plunged back into Nana's writing the moment my eyes opened later this morning. I'd cried bitter tears over that writing competition only to weep with joy at her perseverance as her English teacher became her mentor and tutor. She'd fought and faced the limitations of her education, resources, Jim Crow, and racism. Seeing her adapt and shift to embrace the unexpected, I was inspired, empowered to face the decisions I had to make and welcome the newness I'd yet to encounter. Holding that manuscript against my chest, I was humbled by her strength. Now, I felt something akin to dread.

I'd read, deduced, added two plus two. If my summations were correct, my lineage was in question. "Mama?"

"Hmmm?"

Rubbing my hands over my jeans, I was more nervous than expected. "If I'm being insensitive or broaching a subject that I shouldn't, forgive me." I explained the contents of the treasure trove Nana had directed me to in her private library before asking, "Who's E. Stanton?"

For the longest time Mama stared at me, saying nothing until closing her eyes with a sigh. "Ask your brother to come take your grandmother inside while we walk to the house."

My parents had remodeled the interior of their house so that it offered all the features of a modern structure, but my childhood home still emanated precious memories of the past. Seated, waiting in the family room, I latched onto its peace as my mother walked towards me, a large plastic portfolio in her hands.

Gingerly, she perched on the edge of the sofa beside me while pulling an aged magazine from that portfolio and placed it in my hands. It was a medical periodical that she subscribed to; the publication date was twenty-plus years in the past. The edges were frayed and the colors faded, but its photo cover featuring a smiling man in surgical garb and the caption were intact.

The Healing Hands of Thoracic Surgeon, Dr. Edward Stanton.

I gasped.

His face was so like my mother's that I felt catapulted into a different reality. Her eyes, their color and slant. The shape of her jaw. That raven-black hair that curled into a mass of ringlets when wet, but never needed chemicals to straighten, only heat. It all made sense as I sat for the longest time staring between the two, comparing, astounded by their similarities. There was zero need to ask, still I did. "Is he…?"

She nodded. "My biological father? Yes."

Mama had to take the magazine from me, my hands started shaking so badly. Placing her hands over mine, she held on until their quaking slowly began to subside.

Opening my mouth, I struggled and failed to get words out. Tears flowed instead.

"I know, baby. It's a lot to take in." Easing back against the sofa cushions, she pulled me against her chest. "Breathe. I'm right here."

My tears were for Nana, for my mother. For the confirmation that my grandmother's manuscript sprang from the truths actually lived. The horrors of Jim Crow injustices. My mother being rejected by her paternal grandparents. The struggles of Great Nana Dorothy to give her family opportunity. And my beautiful Nana. She'd been prematurely thrust into adulthood with its countless cares and responsibilities. Yet, she'd maintained her zest for life. Faith and tenacity had carried her through heartache and impossibilities. Rather than bitterness or hatred, she modeled for me grit and graciousness. Pride soared through me at the thought that I was fruit from the indomitable spirits of transcendent women.

I sat up, catching my breath, wiping my face and exhaling soundly.

"Are you okay, Ladybug?"

"Yes, ma'am." I touched my mother's face before looking at that magazine again.

"I know. It's eerie." She smiled gently. "All my life I've been told I'm Mama's spitting image. Then there's this."

I struggled to speak the unfathomable. "Growing up... you didn't know PopPop wasn't...?"

She shook her head. "Never. I was tall with a fair complexion. So is Daddy. Yes, I'm lighter than him but not by much. Plus, you know our DNA. Black folks can pull up physical traits from generations ago."

I nodded, thinking how Avery looked exactly like a picture of Daddy's great-grandfather. "But your eye color…"

"Daddy's aren't that far off. Mine are just more gray. But I'm telling you, Ladybug, there was never a reason to think I wasn't my daddy's daughter. Not the way he's loved me. Yes, sometimes I was teased about my eyes and skin coloring, even by family. But…" She shrugged before laughing softly as if at a memory.

"What?"

"I just remembered the time Cousin C.J. and I were playing marbles in the yard and he accused me of cheating because I was winning. We got into it. He pushed me." Mama snickered. "I punched him in his stomach. That boy got so mad he was crying and screaming and told me to go back to my White family."

"You didn't think anything of it?"

She shook her head. "Being Aunt Ruth's child, Curtis Junior was as mouthy as his mama. We both got in trouble for fighting, but when I told my side of the story Aunt Ruth spanked C.J. for, what I thought at the time, was lying about me having a White family. Thinking on it now, that spanking probably resulted from him saying what he had no business saying."

"Which he wouldn't have been able to if he hadn't overheard grown folks talking."

"Exactly. Nana Dorothy used to say, 'Little pitchers have big ears and children will repeat what they hear.' Anyhow, if I needed my birth certificate for anything Mama always handled it. I had no reason to question that. Aunt Sadie, my paternal uncles, and grandparents never treated me as if I was another man's child, so…" She inclined her head against mine. "I didn't know."

We sat in silence until I quietly asked, "How'd you find out?"

She pointed to the magazine on her lap. "It was a Saturday. Your daddy and PopPop were fishing. You kids were outside playing and Mama brought the mail in. We were sitting in the kitchen sipping sweet tea and eating her teacakes that I'd just baked, talking. Laughing. I started going through the mail, got to this magazine and the next thing I knew Mama had dropped her glass."

My mother had started cleaning the shattered mess, thinking nothing of it until seeing my grandmother violently shaking.

"Ladybug, it scared me so badly I forgot all my medical training and started screaming for my daddy. Mama was the one having a physical episode and she wound up having to calm me."

Enthralled, I listened to my mother recounting their conversation, and how Nana chose not to water down her reaction, rather revealing the cover subject's identity and why it had shaken her so badly.

"While they didn't disclose it themselves, my parents had agreed that if the subject was ever broached or if they needed to for health reasons, they'd tell me about Edward Stanton. Well, there he was in my kitchen, so Mama and I dealt with him."

"How did PopPop respond?"

"He was more concerned about me than himself or our relationship. It was much to process, but I made sure he knew nothing between us had changed. As far as I'm concerned, Ransome James was, is, and will always be, not just my daddy, but my father."

I agreed. "May I?"

Mama handed me the periodical and sat patiently as I read the article in its entirety.

"Mama! You're a fourth-generation medical professional. Edward Stanton's father *and* grandfather were doctors."

"I know. Maybe something in my DNA predisposed me to wanting to be a health professional. I think that's what started my searching."

I listened attentively as she shared her forays into satisfying her curiosities.

"Mama was open and honest in answering my questions, and she and Daddy weren't opposed to my reaching out to my biological father. They understood I might need to discover those pieces of me. Truthfully? I was the one who vacillated." One moment she wanted to make the connection; at others she was hesitant until finally deciding to discover what she could remotely. That led to hours of searching the internet, following his social media accounts, and devouring articles and watching every recorded interview she could. She found Doctor Stanton to be fascinating, but sensed that there was little space in his universe for her. "Maybe I was wrong, but that's how I felt. Besides, by that time he was married with children and grandchildren. I didn't care about being disruptive as much as I was disinterested in being the speck in the buttermilk or the spook who came to dinner." The Stantons' deeply southern roots were more than she chose to tangle with. She softly sighed, concluding, "Besides, I had no daddy hunger that needed filling."

We sat quietly a moment before I spoke again. "Mama, it might be a stretch, but…" I shared how I'd unearthed those two-word letters with contents designated for her. "Do you think those envelopes contained money from Doctor Stanton, or that he could've been the secret benefactor who paid your college tuition?"

"They did. And he was."

According to Mama, Edward Stanton had contacted Aunt Sadie five months after Mama was born inquiring about her welfare. After giving him an earful for his traitorous ways, Aunt

Sadie had refused to reveal where Nana and my mother were living, but agreed to forward those monthly letters on his behalf.

"And she did. For years. I never knew about them but every month Mama treated me to something new and gave me an allowance. We're still clueless how he knew what high school I attended to send the scholarship notice to, but he did. After graduating med school I wanted to send a thank-you gift and graduation photo to my benefactor, but the university advised it was a private donor. However, they gave me a P.O. Box address of a foundation in Montgomery."

"Which was?"

Taking the magazine, Mama thumbed to the last page of Doctor Stanton's spread, at the bottom of which information for Kathryn T. Stanton Thoracic Foundation was listed.

"I never forgot the address because the last three digits coincided with my birthdate: 609. June ninth. He was CEO at the time. And Kathryn Stanton, who died of a thoracic aneurysm in his last year of med school, was his mother. So, there it is."

Kathryn Stanton.

She'd been Nana Dorothy's boss and nemesis. But my great-grandmother, and Nana as well, had overcome that woman's rejection and bitter pronouncements. Freed from Jeb's dismissiveness, I couldn't do anything less. "Does Avery know any of this?"

Mama laughed. "You two always have to be the first in the know."

"Well, does he?"

"No. If I was wrong for not telling you and your brother, I'm sorry. But whatever you do, don't allow any of this to interfere with your relationship with your grandparents. Particularly Daddy."

I needed to process the fact that my grandfather's blood didn't flow through my veins. I *hadn't* inherited my smile or height from him. Biology aside, I'd been loved, nurtured by PopPop, and possessed many of his ways. He was part of my heartbeat, and I was part of his. "Like you said, Ransome James was, is, and will always be my PopPop. Period."

"So Gomer's shooting real bullets not blanks?"

"Dorinda, you're stupid, but yes, I'm preggers."

My best friend's piercing squeals required a lowering of my phone volume to preserve my hearing as I stood at one end of the veranda keeping a close watch on Nana.

"Ohmigawd, I'm so excited! You're about to have a little biracial baby."

"Nut, are you crying?"

"Yes. And? You cried when finding out I was pregnant with Torrie."

"Those were tears of pity for my goddaughter having you as a mommy. And where is she?"

"At a cousins' play date with Kenny's niece. I'll let her call you when she gets home. I cannot believe you're pregnant! Ooo, girl, wait. Pregnant sex is some of *the best*. At least in the early trimesters before your baby bump interferes. Everything's *hyper*sensitive. It's like even your toenails orgasm."

"I'm starting to rethink your role as godmom."

"I'm just saying."

"I'm hanging up."

"Wait! What're you going to do about the three stooges swapping out your paralegal with bonehead's?"

I'd received a call from my paralegal, Lara, after talking to Mama. Nearly whispering, she'd informed me that Jeb had summoned her to his office with news that, as of next Monday, she would be reassigned to Duncan, Vachon, and Mallory's newest senior associate: Ross Humphries.

Jeb said you weren't informed and I didn't want you blindsided.

Thanking Lara and assuring her I wouldn't betray her confidence, I'd hung up feeling as if the writing was on the wall.

Prior to my coming home to Valdosta, such underhandedness would have left me livid. Defensive. Feeling as if I'd been sabotaged, professionally violated. But in a matter of days my life had experienced tremendous change. I'd gone from taking a leave of absence, flying home to a failing grandparent, to discovering I was pregnant and putting my relationship on the mend. I'd learned my grandfather wasn't biologically mine, was ushered into the treasure chest of Nana's early experiences, been inspired by and, hopefully, matured because of them. My life's changes had impacted my perspective, reminding me that my peace, spirit, and essence were invaluable and deserved to be protected. My plan of action for the future was undefined, but clearly my remaining time with Duncan, Vachon, and Mallory was limited. "Doe, they're going to do what they do. Me? I choose to be unbothered."

"You're not clapping back?"

"I'm well within my rights to make my displeasure known, but I have no intention of going full battle-mode over this. God has more for me, Dorinda. Plus, I prefer self-preservation *and* elevation, and this firm is not my end."

"Alright, queen! Come through. I see you, boo! When you go back, catwalk down the hall with a fur stole around your neck, a black leather halter top, and the ass of your pants cut out all Grace Jones-ish with attitude like, 'I ain't bothered, *bitches.*'"

That girl had us cracking up.

"Let me get back to Nana."

"Kiss her for me."

Promising I would, I disconnected and joined Nana where she'd taken up residence, her wheelchair angled so she could easily view Mister Moonlight in the distance.

Bury. Me. There.

My grandparents' directives in the event of incapacitation or death were long established. Even so, that morning, she'd reminded us of her desire to rest eternally with her parents, buried beneath Moonlight's majesty.

Sitting beside her wheelchair, I kissed her head. "That's from Dorinda. And that's from me." I kissed her again. "My beauty queen, you're sure you don't want to go inside?" Even with the ceiling fans of the indoor porch circulating, it was hot, humid.

She shook her head. "I. Like. Heat. Ask... Grandaddy."

"Ooo, Nana! Don't be nasty."

For me, her saucy smile was a hearty laugh.

"Drink some water for me, please." Holding a straw to her lips, I was satisfied with the several sips she managed.

Taking a swig of my water, I opened the manuscript box atop the table that held the typewritten pages I understood to be her life's story. "Nana, this is your memoir, not fiction, correct?"

She nodded.

"Why'd you hide it in the subflooring of the closet instead of keeping it in your file cabinet?"

"Because. You're. Nosey."

"I am not!"

Shoulders shaking as she softly laughed, she beckoned me close. "Wasn't. Your. Time yet." Cupping my face, she kissed my lips. "Had. To. Hide. Until. You. Were. Ready."

I smiled, understanding that the manuscript was a beacon, appointed for such a time as this, to help illuminate my steps. "I'm almost finished reading it. I want you to know your writing style and your story are stunningly gorgeous. Did you ever try to publish it?"

"Yes."

"What happened?"

My heart ached when she rubbed the back of her hand, indicating the color of her skin.

I couldn't afford to pretend ignorance of America's lengthy legacy of disenfranchisement. Still, sometimes I was stunned by the outright and overt ways restrictive practices or policies had impacted the generations before me. "I'm so sorry for their ignorance."

Her sharp shake of the head declined any pity. "You. Do. It."

"Ma'am?"

Her pantomiming a hand sketching on paper provided no room for confusion. Still, I dug through the manuscript box until finding the pencil I'd noticed and sketched a rough picture on a blank page as confirmation.

As I showed it to her, her smile was doubly bright this time.

"You want me to adapt your story into an illustrated book for children?"

She held up a finger.

"Yes? No? What? Young adult readers?"

Her holding a second finger had me guessing again.

"A novel?"

Waving three fingers in my face, she nodded triumphantly.

"*Really*, Nana? I've never written a book in my life and you want me to write, not one, but *three separate stories?*"

She tucked her lips in and gave me the evil eye. "Get. Help."

I didn't want to point out the absurdity of the idea. Just like I had zero desire to broach the subject of Edward Stanton. Rather than dredge up an unfortunate past, I chose to treat those parts of her life into which I'd been invited with respect, knowing her welcoming me into the intimate spaces of her existence was a gift.

"Get help," I repeated. "Okay… let me think about this."

"Do it." Her words were clear, unbroken, and not to be played with.

I offered the requisite, "yes, ma'am" despite her mandate and wish leaving me feeling uncertain, and perhaps inept.

"Preserve history. Help someone."

"Now, you want to guilt me with obligation?"

She closed her eyes and laughed.

"Alright, Nana, we'll continue that discussion. Guess what I want to know? Since this was a memoir and not fiction, does that mean you were on *the* same bus as Rosa Parks that night?"

She smiled.

"Are you serious! Rosa Parks, Civil Rights icon, 'mother' of the movement?"

Her stare dared me to challenge that fact.

I turned towards her, propping a leg beneath me and leaning in. "*Ohmigawd, Nana!*" I knew my grandparents had participated in sit-ins and freedom rides, but this was something my grandmother had experienced by herself as a young teen. "What was that like?"

Exquisite peace veiled her face. "Changed. My. Life."

CHAPTER SEVENTEEN

Mattie

The summer of 1956 was splendid. I had my beautiful angel. And the company of my best friend. Originally Sadie had planned to stay two weeks. Seeing how good it was for me having her there, Mama invited her to extend her stay. We were ecstatic when her parents agreed so that she wound up staying until it was time to return to Montgomery to start her final year in high school. We were sad about the fact that we wouldn't share that senior year together, but those summer months were magnificent.

Ruth and Naomi came by often. Thankfully, Ruth's big mouth didn't bother Sadie. In fact, they were both opinionated and we spent much time laughing over their foolishness. Mama was relieved that I had company while she was at the diner, and extra hands to help with the baby. Between those three, Savannah could barely make a peep before one of them took off running for her bassinet, scooping her up as if it were a sin to let her cry for more than a second.

"Y'all gonna spoil my baby rotten. If it weren't for the fact that I nurse her, she'd wind up thinking she has four mamas." I fussed, but it thrilled my heart seeing my precious daughter being the recipient of so much tenderness.

Savannah Eve was a good baby with a sweet temperament, and her smile made my heart dance every time I saw it. I felt sorry for Edward missing out on the joys of this perfect creation, but he'd made his choice and Savannah wasn't it. Not that a daddy didn't matter, he did. But my family loved that baby hard and fierce as if accounting for the fact that her father couldn't. And Mama? She was crazy about her granddaughter.

"Your daddy would love this baby!" Cuddling Savannah, she'd tell the baby stories of Matthew Banks even though she was too small to retain any of it. Mama shared her memories as if embedding them in my daughter's spirit. I loved hearing those stories and valued how supportive she was. She even arranged to work a few day shifts and stayed home with the baby, granting me summertime fun with my cousins and best friend. I always nursed Savannah real good before leaving so she'd sleep with a full tummy. Walking out the door with Sadie and the twins, I missed my daughter, but I never objected to those few hours granting me a taste of freedom.

Most times we walked to town for burgers at the Colored drug store food counter or went swimming in the creek. But there were a couple of days that we saw picture shows at the movies. Of course, we had to climb the outdoor rear staircase and sit in the Colored balcony, but that didn't prevent us from enjoying those films.

Most of those movies felt so trite and far from our realities. While White girls down on the main floor were sniffling over heroes sweeping heroines into their arms, we were up in the "buzzard roost" laughing as if watching a comedy. It was during one of those "comedies" that I met Bobby and discovered the misconceptions boys like him had of me.

I'd noticed Bobby and his crew on a prior visit. That particular day they were there again and asked if they could sit with us. Ruth was still sweet on Curtis, so having only three in their crew worked out, with Bobby and his friends sitting next to whoever struck their interest. Savannah was my life and I was disinterested in a boyfriend, but admittedly it was nice having a boy sitting there sharing his popcorn with me. That is until I felt his arm slide around my shoulder half-way through the film.

Initially, I tensed and turned to look at him. Bobby sat staring at the screen as if sliding his arm about me was involuntary. When nothing else occurred over the next few minutes, I relaxed. Apparently, too fast because the next thing I knew his hand was sliding over my shoulder, trying to grip my breast.

"Boy, what's wrong with you!"

My outburst had other movie-goers hissing for me to hush.

"Mattie, what happened?

"Sadie, this fool tried to grope me."

"Oh, no he *didn't*!" Ruth was ready to jump Bobby.

That boy had the nerve to look genuinely confused. "What's the big deal? Don't you have a baby already?"

That made me so hot, I jumped up, barely able to talk. "What I do or don't have is none of your nasty business. I'm not some loose girl you get to feel up. Don't *ever* touch me again."

"Yeah!" Sadie added, throwing a handful of his popcorn at his head.

"Ooo, that makes me so mad!" We'd exited and were marching down the street towards the drug store, arms linked like four soldiers ready for war. "Why would he think having a baby gives him the right to touch me?"

"Just plain ignorant!" Naomi lamented.

"I may have a baby, but this is my body."

"Amen to that," Sadie and Ruth said at the same time, which set off a round of pinching each other against jinxing. Their antics had us laughing and lightened the mood, but I learned a lesson that day about what certain boys thought of young ladies like me with babies. Sliding onto a chair at the drug store counter, I determined to never let a man treat me as if my virtue, worth, or integrity was something he had a right to define or diminish.

*

"I'm missing this angel already. Can I take her with me?"

It was Sadie's last night with us. Ransome and Miz James had arrived earlier that day. Mama was thrilled by a visit from her longtime friend, and Miz James had fallen in love with Savannah on sight, and hadn't treated me any differently, was kind and warm as always. But Ransome? Something had changed.

Sadie's observations from before proved accurate: every time I turned around he was watching me. Unlike that boy, Bobby, there wasn't anything indecent about Ransome's demeanor. Rather, it was as if I was a familiar puzzle that had been intentionally altered just to stump him, and he was trying to figure me out while clearly enjoying my differences. I masked my expression to keep him from knowing I, too, wanted to sit and study his ways.

Watching my best friend holding my baby and kissing Savannah's chubby fingers, I pushed aside thoughts of her brother and laughed at Sadie's request. "No, you may not take my child, but if it's any consolation she's gonna miss you, too." In the nearly eight weeks Sadie had been with us she'd help spoil Savannah so that my daughter acted as if our arms, laps, shoulders (and my breasts) had been exclusively created for her benefit. Mama was constantly fussing at Sadie and me for holding her so much.

"Y'all gonna spoil that baby rotten." As if she wasn't as guilty, coming in from work and Savannah's being the first face she wanted to see.

"Well, you're gonna need to get a camera so you can send me pictures of this pumpkin *every* month," Sadie insisted.

"I can't afford a camera with no job."

"Guess you'd better get one. Seriously, Mattie, sell your cookies." We'd baked Mama's teacakes so often that summer that it was amazing Sadie hadn't gained ten pounds and that the weight I'd put on carrying a baby had disappeared. "Bake some. Take 'em to church, or pass 'em out downtown. Get folks interested. Then start taking orders."

Sadie had it all worked out in her head.

My attention captured by the sound of a car pulling up front, I promised to think about it. "Who's that?"

"Probably Ransome."

"Why's he back so soon?" He'd spent the day with his teammate and wasn't expected until late evening.

"To see you."

Seated on the back porch taking advantage of the summer breeze, I cut her a look. "Sadie, I'm not studying you."

"Fine. But you'd better study those boobies if you don't want them bothering my brother."

It was so hot that after nursing Savannah I'd left my sundress unbuttoned to rub ice over my bosom. "Oh, Jesus!" Rushing, I managed to resituate myself just as Ransome rounded the side of the house.

"Y'all lazy bones were out here when I left. You're still…"

When his words trailed off, I followed his gaze and saw my being buttoned up wasn't enough. All that melted ice had left my skin slippery and my sundress clung to me, outlining my milk-heavy chest. I might as well have been naked. Mortified, I excused myself, took Savannah from Sadie, shielding myself with my baby's body, and scurried indoors to not only change into dry clothing, but put on the brassiere I should've never taken off.

Our house was small so it wasn't easy, but I tried avoiding Ransome for the rest of the evening and was successful until Miz James pulled Sadie indoors to finish packing, and Mama had to run down to Aunt Lady's and Uncle Melvin's for something.

Declining my offer of help, Miz James took Savannah with her, relegating me to the company of Ransome. A cooling breeze was blowing across the backyard, and he'd dozed off after devouring three helpings of my mother's red beans and rice, leaving me to enjoy tunes from the tiny transistor radio stationed between us.

"You like Valdosta?"

His voice startled me. "I thought you were asleep."

"Maybe I was. Maybe I was faking. You have an answer for me?"

"Valdosta's smaller than Montgomery so sometimes it's kinda boring, but that's okay, seeing as how having a baby keeps me from going anywhere or doing much of anything. So I guess it's fine for me, but I couldn't see someone like you being satisfied here when you're accustomed to bigger things. Especially with you playing ball, traveling, and seeing nice cities. And probably all kinds of pretty girls. Sadie said you did real good last season. Congratulations."

My words came out in such a babbling rush that when I finished I was startled by the quiet.

Chuckling softly, Ransome relinquished his lounging position and leaned towards me. "What're you nervous about, Mattie?"

"Nothing." *Lord, forgive the lying.* Having that man's attention had my insides tumbling. "You still like the Leagues?"

"I've loved it since I was a kid and remember attending packed-out games with my brothers and Dad. Since Jackie Robinson integrated the sport the bleachers aren't as full, so it won't be a way to make a living much longer. And Jackie's breaking the color barrier doesn't mean other teams are rushing for Colored players. So?" He shrugged wide shoulders, stretched his legs. "I'll enjoy the game while I can. But back to you, Queen Mattie. What makes you think I've been chasing pretty women?"

The fading sun cast enough light for me to see the mocking lift of his full lips.

"You're too handsome not to have a girlfriend in every city you've played in."

"What if I told you I'm interested in one particular young lady in a small town I visited?"

The bottom of my belly felt tight with something inexplicable, and my tone was unfriendly. "I'd say good for her and that's your business."

I disliked the way he threw his head back, laughing at my expense. "Mattie Banks, you're a jealous mess, but it's *our* business."

"Pardon?"

"Valdosta's the place, and you're that young lady. I'd like to call on you from time to time. If I may?"

I was so taken aback that it took me a moment to respond. "We don't have a phone."

He chuckled again. "I meant in person."

"Montgomery's not exactly around the corner from here. Why would you do that?"

"You're worth the distance."

My heart fluttered, still I resisted. "Driving back and forth is a waste of good gas."

"Lord, the stubbornness," he remarked, digging into his pant pockets and extracting a mess of coins that he placed in my hands. "That'll cover multiple trips to the phone booth. And my driving back and forth to see you is my choice."

I stared at him for the longest, wondering if—like Bobby with his popcorn—this man thought being nice would grant him certain rights. "I may have a baby, Ransome James, but that doesn't mean I'm something you can climb in bed and play with."

His jaw hardened, then relaxed. But his tone was steely as if offended. "Mattie Banks, if that's what I wanted—as you said—I have plenty of options." He stood and headed for the patio door, stopping abruptly. "When you realize I want something different use those coins and call me."

It took me two weeks after Sadie left to find the courage to walk to the drug store and dial the James' residence. God obviously loved me because Ransome answered instead of Sadie, as if he'd been waiting.

"Hello, Queen Mattie. I forgive you for questioning my intentions, but your atonement consists of mailing me teacakes every week."

I laughed softly. "Why don't I call you instead?"

That was how we started weekly calls that turned into courtship.

I did my best to keep the house spotless and on the days Mama worked I cooked so she wouldn't have to. Yet, wanting to eliminate her having to work extra shifts, I took Sadie's suggestion and started selling Mama's teacakes, placing them in mason jars decorated with a ribbon. Family and fellow parishioners were quick to purchase them but, going door-to-door, others proved less eager.

"That's 'cause you out here with a baby and no ring on your finger," Mama explained. Removing her slim, gold wedding band, she handed it to me. "Wear this and try again."

Must've been some truth in Mama's theory because I sold out the next time I pushed Savannah in her buggy, sharing space with my jars of cookies. Still, I didn't make but enough to buy a few grocery items until I had a wild idea to approach Mama's boss, Mister Freeland. Not only did that old rough-and-gruff ex-military officer make Mama bring leftovers home at the end of her shifts so we'd have extra in our kitchen, but he owned two diners in nearby towns.

When I served him my teacakes he practically growled, "Bring me two dozen tomorrow morning. If those sell out, I'll take two dozen Tuesdays, Thursdays, and Saturdays for all three locations. Bring 'em in a basket and don't waste jars on 'em."

Within two hours of delivering them, those teacakes disappeared.

Between Mister Freeland and my other regular customers, I earned enough to take care of Savannah and help Mama. It wasn't easy caring for my daughter, selling cookies, *and* studying but I was determined to pass that high school proficiency test and earn my diploma. Whenever I was tired enough to quit my mind would float back to that night on the bus, recalling a woman who'd tired of her rights being infringed upon. Her sitting gave me courage to stand. Sometimes I fell asleep, book in hand, cookie dough on the counter, and Savannah in my arms nursing but I never quit and by November my tutors felt I was ready for that test.

"Mattie, I suggest we register you for the midterm competency exam. June feels so far off and at the rate you're going another six months of this might prove too much," was Miz Wheatley's opinion. "However, we'll need to register you for the exam in a different school district." She was unwilling to jeopardize my chances by registering in my current district, risking Joshua Lambert recognizing my name and withholding his signature from my official graduation papers.

"Students have to reside within the district they take the exam in," Miss Divine posited.

"True… or they simply need a corresponding, verifiable residence." Eyes glinting mischievously, Miz Wheatley listed her home address on my registration. "I worked in Lambert's district, but I don't live in it." Mistaken for a White woman, she'd lived on the "other side of the tracks" for years. Once again, she used her presumed identity to someone else's benefit.

Studying hard for my exam, Mama delivered cookies for me and Aunt Lady sat with the baby. I'd earned enough to be responsible for a house phone so Sadie and Ransome consistently called with encouragement. But that night Sadie made me mad.

"Mattie, don't get angry, but Edward came by the house two days before Thanksgiving."

"*For what?*"

"He wanted to know your whereabouts. I didn't disclose nothing. I just agreed to forward something for him."

Three days later I received the first of many letters reading "For Savannah" with a twenty-dollar bill inserted. As the years progressed the amount increased, still I used it only for my baby. But that week before Christmas 1956, I bought a good-luck dress for her to wear during my competency exam even though she'd be home with Mama. Sitting in the hallway while my exam was graded and learning I'd passed with flying colors, I rushed home to Savannah, looking like a doll in that fluffy pink and yellow ensemble, her giggles delighting my heart as I spun in circles, bubbling with the goodness of God.

"I never doubted you'd do it. Queen Mattie, you're brilliant." Even through the phone, Ransome's voice felt like velvet that night when I informed him.

"Thank you, and when're you gonna stop calling me that? It sounds like some ol' Elizabethan woman."

"You prefer a different term of affection?"

"Yes."

"How about bride or missus?"

Mama was bathing the baby. I was washing dishes and nearly dropped a plate at his suggestion. "That's not funny, Ransome."

"Do I sound like I'm kidding? I love you, Mattie. Marry me."

I had to sit to keep from falling and was unable to form a single word for countless minutes.

"Mattie?"

"I'm thinking." And I was. About his monthly visits, and his always bringing me a bouquet and something sweet. His strong hugs and tender kisses that set something tingling in my nether region. The way Savannah—sweet-natured as she was—didn't take to men. Maybe because their voices were hard and heavy, and she was accustomed to women. Yet, she squealed and wiggled happily whenever she saw Ransome. How she liked falling asleep against his chest. How Mama practically worshiped him. How loving Savannah expanded my capacity, opening me to loving that man—flaws and all—like nobody's business. But I was seventeen and knew nothing about building love everlasting. "I don't know if I'm grown enough for this type of thing."

"I haven't spoken to Miz Dorothy yet. But if your mother gives us her blessing, will you consider it?"

"Yes."

His January visit resulted in Mama's tearful, ecstatic blessing, and our planning a wedding for October 1957 after the playing season finished. Instead, an on-field collision landed Ransome flat on his back. A shattered patella ended his career.

His physical pain and recovery was one thing. His trying not to sink beneath bitterness was another.

"The league is drying up, but being knocked out prematurely isn't how I wanted it to end."

"I know, honey, but in everything God has a plan and purpose." I couldn't identify that purpose, yet I did my best to be encouraging. "Maybe Maxwell?" Montgomery's air force base hired Colored men.

"That's about as close as I'll get to the military with this knee like this."

"What about going back to school?"

He'd dreamed of being an architect before joining the Leagues. "I can't. I'm about to get married. We have a daughter. When this knee heals, I have to grab the first job I'm offered to take care of my family."

It wasn't architecture, but Heaven's grace granted him a place in construction—not designing, but building, satisfying his love of creating.

With new houses going up all over Montgomery, White contractors didn't penalize our men for the fallout from the bus boycott or their inherent complexions. There was often trouble with fellow workers, but contractors? They needed able-bodied men. Dressed in a suit and tie, my love walked into the office of one site and exited with a job. It was a blessing, but it also meant missing out on our shared weekends.

"Baby, we wanna eat? I gotta work. Plain and simple. I'll get to Valdosta every chance I can. For now, save whatever I send so it's there when we get married. Minus, of course, anything for Savannah."

Living at his parents', he mailed every penny not required for his own personal needs for me to hold onto. I had a good man and thanked the Lord daily, but when Sadie called telling me about that other female slinking after Ransome and his handling that situation in a way I found unacceptable, I called off the wedding.

"Mattie, Nosey Nedra's always had a thing for Ransome! But swishing her high behind to that construction site and taking him lunches is plain underhanded. She knows you two are together."

Immaturity and jealousy getting the best of me, I told Ransome that evening that, had he given me a ring, I'd have tossed it in the toilet. "I wish you and Nedra an unhappy life!" Slamming the phone down, I cried myself to sleep that night.

Walking to Aunt Lady's two days later, I was so caught in my miserable fog that I barely heard a horn honk. Only his, "Mattie Banks, I know you hear me!" snagged my attention. Recovering from the shock of seeing Ransome's car pulling to the curb, I reversed my direction and hurried home, so outdone my hips were swishing.

He caught up to me on the porch, before I could get through the door. "Stop being so damn stubborn and talk to me, Mattie!"

I whirled when he gripped my arm. "Let go of me! Go get Nedra if you need some touching."

"What is all this ruckus?" Mama snatched the door open, frowning. "Come inside before you two tell the whole neighborhood your business."

Once inside, we both started talking fast, trying to tell our separate perspectives on the mess that used to be our relationship.

Mama threw up her hands. "I don't wanna hear it. You got problems with each other? *You* fix 'em. I'm taking my grandbaby out of here." Retrieving my napping daughter from the room, my mother marched past us and out the door going God knew where.

"You can leave as well." I held the door open.

"I'm not going anywhere."

"Fine. Stay and talk to yourself." Shutting the door, I stomped into the kitchen, ignoring him and attending to dinner.

Shame on him for following. "Mattie... baby, come on... Why're we doing this? What am I guilty of? Nedra coming to my work site?"

"You're guilty of unfaithful fraternizing."

"I have no control over someone coming by my job—"

Slamming corn meal onto the counter, I interrupted. "Did you eat her little nasty sandwiches?" When he said nothing, I resumed my task. "Mmm-hmm, that's what I thought."

His heavy sigh filled the kitchen. "Woman, I swear you're exasperating. Fine. I ate her food."

"And?"

"I thanked her and that was that."

"Must've thanked her awfully good 'cause she came back." Looking for baking powder and not finding any, remembering that I'd been walking to Aunt Lady's to borrow some, I navigated about Ransome as if he wasn't present. "Guess I gotta make hot water cornbread instead."

"So now I'm not here?"

Placing Mama's cast-iron skillet on the stove, I started humming as if he wasn't.

"Go 'head. Ignore me. You'll still hear what you would've heard had you let me finish speaking the other night before hanging up on me and refusing my subsequent calls. Clearly, I messed up by eating what another female served me. For that I'm sorry. But I haven't touched another woman since we've been together. I'm faithful, Mattie."

The truth of his words swirling like luscious nectar inside of me, I continued acting stubborn, checking on the sweet potatoes in the oven while ignoring him, knowing full well he was a good man.

"Would you please stop cooking so we can talk?"

I headed for the Frigidaire, mumbling about a jar of preserves like he hadn't spoken.

"Forget it. I'm finished." I'd obviously pushed his limits. "If I marry Nedra or anyone else, blame yourself."

When he turned to walk off, I grabbed my near-empty Cola bottle from the counter and threw it at his head. Thankfully, it missed, shattering loudly against the kitchen wall.

The storm on that man's face when he turned my way told me I'd gone too far. I found myself backing against the sink as he stalked in my direction.

"Woman, I swear—"

"Ransome, I'm nobody's woman! I'm a seventeen-year-old girl with responsibilities. You've had associations. I've never even had a boyfriend. What am I supposed to do with a grown man six years my senior? We haven't even… done it—"

"And we won't until we're married."

Lord knows, I hated whining but couldn't seem to stop. "What if you don't like me that way? I'm not all," I wiggled my body, "juicy and experienced like Nedra and your other women."

"Don't say it again."

"What? Your other—"

"*I don't have other women!*" I'd witnessed Ransome upset, but never furious. "All I've *done* since we've been together is try to do right by you. I work. I go home. I work some more. Come Fridays, I might get a beer. I send *you* my money. What little I keep for myself I'm *sure as hell* not spending on some woman."

"Why—?"

"Why what? Do what I do? 'Cause, Mattie, I'm training myself to be the man you'd want to marry!"

I couldn't say a thing for a long while. When speaking, my voice was soft, hesitant. "Do you still want to?"

"Want to… what?"

"Marry me."

Exasperated, he massaged the bridge of his nose before lowering to a knee. "Maybe the phone wasn't the best way to do this initially, so let's repeat." Removing a small box from his pocket, he opened it to display the prettiest gold band I'd ever seen. "Mathilda Ilene Banks, will you please stop throwing Cola bottles"—his voice grew serious—"and do me the honor of marrying me?"

I laughed while crying, nodding.

Slipping the ring on my finger, he stood and kissed me until I couldn't breathe.

"Ransome, I'm sorry, baby."

"You should be." Slowly, he granted me that smile that unleashed butterflies in my belly. "Got me afraid to accept a glass of water from any female except my mama."

Grinning, I cupped his face, stood on my tiptoes, and kissed him again. "Let's do it. Tonight. No, not *that*," I corrected when his eyes went wide. "I wanna get married before you leave."

"You're serious?"

"Yes." I wasn't about to give that big-breasted Nedra my man.

"We don't have a marriage license. And what about family in attendance?"

"We'll have a nice party next month. If the courthouse isn't too busy, I bet we could get a license today. And if Reverend Patterson is free…" I shrugged, not finishing my sentence. But it was enough. Next thing I knew, we were in motion.

Finding Mama at Aunt Lady's and Uncle Melvin's, we told her what we were doing. She went slack-mouthed before screaming happily and shooing us out the door in order to make it to the courthouse before it closed, but Savannah pitched such a fuss we wound up taking her with us, arriving with ten minutes to spare.

"May I help you?"

When the woman at the counter looked up and saw us she turned whiter than she was. Staring at me, she may have forgotten my name since that writing competition, but I'd never forget that fiery-red bouffant or Miz Adams.

Saying nothing as Ransome explained our need, I told myself her working there now versus the school district wasn't my business and simply handed Savannah to him as I completed my portion of the license application.

"I'll give you a receipt, but we're closing soon so you'll have to come back Monday for the official document."

"Ma'am, we apologize for the inconvenience but is there *any way* we can obtain it today?" Ransome requested.

She looked at Ransome holding Savannah, drawing her own conclusions before glancing at me, her cheeks housing the slightest tint of embarrassment as if remembering my being evicted from the awards ceremony. Perhaps memory of that injustice prompted her to act on our behalf. "Wait here."

She disappeared behind a closed door, returning ten minutes later with the completed document. Showing us where we were to sign, as well as our officiant, she advised we'd receive a copy after submitting it.

Thanking her profusely, she merely smiled and ushered us out so she could lock up and begin her weekend.

Mama's strategic abilities were in effect when we returned. She and Aunt Lady had laid out my best church dress, had a hot bath waiting, and had tasked Uncle Melvin with cutting roses from his yard for my bouquet. "Reverend Patterson's on his way."

With Savannah in her playpen, they fluttered about me with such precise efficiency that within forty minutes I was face-to-face with my groom before the living room's unlit fireplace.

From years of playing on the road, he'd developed a habit of keeping clean clothing in the trunk of his car. He might've preferred something fancier, but to me Ransome Anthony James couldn't have been more handsome in his simple tie and jacket as we exchanged vows before our witnesses—Mama, Savannah, Aunt Lady, and Uncle Melvin—Friday evening, April 19, 1957.

I'd barely exchanged that initial kiss with my husband before Mama rushed me to my bedroom in order to nurse Savannah.

"I already fed her real good, but you know she's not going to sleep without your milk in her tummy." Mama had arranged for them to stay at my aunt and uncle's, giving my husband and me *our* time.

"What if she wakes up during the night?"

"She rarely does. But if that happens, we'll be fine. You just focus on that man you married."

A round of congratulatory kisses and hugs later, Ransome and I were alone to enjoy the dinner Aunt Lady had placed on the kitchen table, the glow of a candle kept for whenever storms caused a loss of power as our sole illumination.

"You're beautiful, Missus Mattie James. You happy?"

"Ecstatic. And you, my handsome husband?"

"Unquestionably blessed." Dropping his fork on his plate, he pushed back his chair and came to my side of the table. "May I have this dance?"

Taking his hand, I laughed. "To what music?"

Turning on the transistor radio Mama kept on the kitchen counter, he took me in his arms, humming to what became our tune, "Chances Are," until the final notes wafted about us like an intoxicating fragrance. That's when he scooped me up and carried me to my room.

My space felt smaller with Ransome in it, my bed too narrow for his magnificence. Laying back as he placed me there, my heart pounded like a drum corps with nervousness. With each kiss, each gentle touch, he drew me away from fear and into an overwhelming ocean of sensation and want. But when he undressed himself and then me, I felt too tense to even breathe.

"I love you, baby." His lips against my neck, his soft whisper fluttered into my ear. "Relax."

Inhaling deeply, I touched his face, ran my hands over his chest. That was the extent of my boldness.

Smiling tenderly, he took my hand and guided my acquaintance with his body.

It was beautiful, with hard muscle and strength, and I found myself wanting to kiss, taste it. So, I did. With an appetite I never knew existed. But his hunger for me was all-consuming as he savored every soft place and curve of my creation with tongue, teeth, lips. When he pressed me onto my back and raised himself over me, we were both panting, needing. As he settled himself between my legs, I wholeheartedly widened myself in welcome, gasping at his initial entrance.

He stiffened immediately, questioning if I was okay.

I nodded and kissed him, wanting what waited past the pain.

With slow, measured movements he entered fully and simply rested, allowing me to adjust and settle about him. Feeling as if light were expanding inside of me, I sighed contentedly. That sigh inspired his moving. Slowly. Deepening that divine possession of me. His worshiping sensitive places designed for more than nursing felt delicious, intoxicating as our bodies and our breathing racing towards a cliff until I spiraled off of it. Joyously screaming. Breaking midair into countless pieces of brilliance that rendered me useless, incapable of anything except receiving the molten rush, and his roar, as my husband's pleasure exploded inside of me.

Entangled about each other, we lay in that satiated state until he carefully lifted himself and rolled onto his back. Instantly, I missed his weight, snuggled against him when he pulled me to his chest and exchanged "I love yous" decorated with kisses. Drifting towards euphoric sleep, I smiled, thinking Miz Wheatley would be pleased at my sublime completion.

CHAPTER EIGHTEEN

Ashlee

Everything within me wanted to extend my leave of absence indefinitely and stay, to be present at Nana's appointed time.

Beloved, the scriptures say "it's appointed unto men once to die." I've made my appointment with God. I'm not leaving a second sooner, and I'm not staying a second too long.

I remembered Nana stating that when first diagnosed with cancer. She'd faced the diagnosis with bravery and pragmatism that reflected the way she'd lived. Now, her "appointment" was near. I wanted to be at her side when it occurred. Yet, I couldn't avoid the fact that my grandmother expected me to go home and confront my challenges rather than use her condition as a means of escape. There was no need for me to haunt her bedside waging war against death or resisting its inevitability. Rather, I surrendered to the truth that my grandmother's assignment on earth was finished. She'd worked hard, lived a full, rich, and eventful life and was being promoted to rest. It wasn't my place, I didn't have the power nor could I be so selfish as to keep her here. Instead, I poured my love on her, did my best to remember and retain her essence for myself and others. She'd poured so much life and love into me, but those final days together I sensed that she'd shifted the mantle onto me and her power was mine.

The remaining days of my leave, I sketched every picture I could of and with my Nana Mattie. Again, her strength and determination were amazing as she dictated my drawing—praising when it was right, frowning when it wasn't, even plotting what parts of her story she wanted illustrated. By the time I was packed for Atlanta, we'd essentially crafted her children's book.

"Publish it."

Holding her close as we shared the chaise lounge Daddy had placed on the back porch, wishing I had the power to recapture every second we'd ever shared, I could only nod.

"I mean it, Ladybug." It was the fullest, strongest sentence she'd uttered during my stay and I knew better than to deny her.

"I will. I promise."

Satisfied, she smiled and closed her eyes.

"Nana, you don't have to talk. Just listen. This world doesn't possess the language to express how I utterly love you. You're a steady beat in my heart and I cannot appreciate you enough. Just know that I do. Thank you for being my beauty queen. For loving me. For teaching and correcting me. For being an illustrious example of Black womanhood and showing me I could do anything." With our roles reversed, I held and sheltered her in my arms. "I thank you for surviving every pain you ever experienced. I thank you for not merely surviving but thriving. I salute you for making magic out of the mess the world served you. I honor and admire you. I've never lived a day without my nana, and neither know how nor want to, but I promise you I won't quit until *my* end. I'll do my best to walk in wisdom, reflect your kindness. My children will know countless stories featuring Great Nana Mattie. I will never be perfect, but I won't disappoint your legacy."

Tears rolling down my face, I couldn't say more, simply closed my eyes and inhaled Nana's scent to store in my memory.

My eyes opened at the sound of her whispery humming. Recognizing the tune as one she sang for me and Avery when we were children, lyrics naturally flowed from my mouth on the final refrain.

"Yes, Jesus loves me. The Bible tells me so."

"Ladybug, we need to go. Your plane leaves in an hour."

I smiled at my daddy's sudden appearance. Turning to Nana, I tried to kiss every inch of her face, whispering my love each time I did. "Mattie Banks James, you are absolutely splendid but don't you get to heaven and start bossing the angels around."

Tears leaking, she grinned.

"I promise you I'll publish your stories." I confirmed my plan to honor her request and create a children's illustrated, young adult, and mainstream novel even if it meant contracting an author to write them. But my gift to her was that the proceeds would go to the Mattie Banks James Literacy Foundation I'd establish, which in turn, would help fund educational scholarships for underserved populations. "How's that sound?"

"Ladybug, that's divine."

Leaning near her ear, I whispered, "I finished reading it last night. Now I know why those Js and Ss never worked right. You and PopPop were simply scandalous."

I will forever remember her cupping my face as she leaned her head back and laughed.

My return to the office was uneventful. At least for me. The partners and certain colleagues, particularly bonehead, Ross Humphries? They treated me with kid gloves as if it were only a matter of time before I went off. True, before going home to Valdosta and knowing I was pregnant, I might have embarrassed my upbringing and told them where to kiss it. In professionally acceptable language, of course. I didn't. Instead, fueled by the grace of my grandmother's story, I refused to trap myself with others' idiocy. Nana had refashioned expulsion from school and that writing competition into homeschooling before homeschooling existed. Outsmarted the system and earned her diploma. Taken teacakes and baked her way into self-sufficiency all while raising a baby. Surely I could handle some workplace ish that didn't amount to life and didn't diminish my substance. Meeting with my new paralegal, I conveyed my expectations, talked strategy, and discovered his favorite croissant flavor for those Friday morning treats. Pleased, I kept it moving.

I didn't slouch on my job, but I knew only time stood between me and leaving. Whether from my profession or just that firm was unclear, but on that plane ride home I'd started researching logical alternative careers. Some were more appealing than others, but it was liberating knowing I had options.

Rightly or wrongly, I took advantage of whatever guilt the partners were feeling and arranged to telecommute on Fridays so that I could fly to Valdosta Thursday evenings and be with Nana as much as possible until she transitioned.

Heaven was gracious. I flew home that Thursday to find Nana even stronger than my prior visit and we enjoyed a wonderful weekend together. But the following Tuesday, when my phone rang at four o'clock in the morning, waking me from a dream in which I sat in a field of flowers surrounded by a cluster of ladybugs that suddenly took flight, I didn't even need to hear my mother's tearful voice to know. Nana had received her wings. She was gone.

We were splendid, dressed in white. Like a sea of angels gathered to honor the life of Mathilda Ilene Banks James. The sanctuary was packed beyond capacity with fellow parishioners, former students and colleagues, members from the community and the civil rights organization to which she belonged, and family. There were tears. There was laughter and hilarious stories. A resolution from the mayor's office for an extraordinary, award-winning educator who'd dedicated herself to a forty-year career. Songs. Remembrances. A eulogy that was inspiring and had folks on their feet, clapping, praising. Through it all what was unquestionably clear was Nana had made an impact, and she was well-loved.

Watching my brother Avery and the other pallbearers rolling the casket out of the church at the end of a beautiful tribute and service, I held onto Brad while clutching Dorinda's hand. Walking that church aisle felt like a mile, but our work that day had only begun. Honoring Nana's wishes to be buried beneath Mister Moonlight, only family and close friends would be attending the internment. We'd arranged a repast at the church for those desiring to attend, but immediate family were to assemble in the foyer to receive well-wishes from mourners.

"How're you holding up?"

Whisking tears from my face, I nodded at Brad as we took our place in the receiving line. His concern didn't only pertain to grief, but the fact that I'd been unable to eat that morning. Stationing himself beside me, he wrapped a steadying arm about my waist, allowing me to lean into him.

Faces became a blur with so many people extending kind condolences. Periodically, I looked to the top of the receiving line to check on my grandfather and mother. PopPop stood with the aid of the walking stick I'd gifted him from a trip to Ghana six years back, as if needing its added strength. Mama, with Daddy at her side, was grief-stricken yet somehow radiant, as if imbued with Nana's spirit. Avery, Janelle, and the kids. Aunt Sadie. PopPop's two remaining brothers. Aunt Naomi. Cousin Curtis. Extended family. We were all there, the tribe of Mattie.

Feet aching in heels and stomach starting to feel queasy, I was relieved to see the tail end of the procession in my peripheral vision. Shaking the hand of a woman wearing a huge hat Nana would've liked, I smiled. That smile faded as I saw the final well-wishers: a young woman pushing the wheelchair of a silver-haired man.

Shocked, I glanced at Mama who was occupied with the person speaking to her at that moment and returned my attention to the man in the wheelchair stopping before me.

"My condolences to you and your family." His voice was quiet yet strong, his hair was silver, but those eyes were still purple. "I knew Mattie when she lived in Montgomery. She was a wonderful young woman who inspired me to fight for the civil rights of others... like I didn't fight for hers. You're Ashlee." He pointed his chin in my brother's direction. "That's my... your brother, Avery."

"Yes, sir. As well as his wife and children."

"Your names are all here," he said as if soothing himself while rubbing a hand over the funeral program on his lap before looking up at me again. When he extended a hand, I took it. "You have a fine family."

"I agree."

Releasing my hand, he indicated to the person pushing his chair that he was ready to leave.

Watching him proceed, I wanted to station myself behind my mother in case she needed extra shoring up when coming face-to-face with her biological father. She didn't. Daddy on one side, PopPop on the other, she stood strong, gracious. Too far down the line to hear what Edward Stanton said to my grandfather, Mama told Avery and me later that he'd thanked Ransome James for being her father.

*

A catered banquet waited, as did Nana's orange zest and cinnamon-scented teacakes. My parents' living room had been turned into a vibrant, makeshift museum, decorated with photographs, her career awards, and framed newspaper clippings that showcased Nana's past—its struggles, its glory. But right then we stood beneath the cool arbor of a centuries-old tree, watching my grandmother's casket being lowered into Georgia's cool, red dirt as her pastor quoted the Twenty-third Psalm. As a family, we tossed white roses onto that casket as if fragrant teardrops. And when the final rose had been kissed then released by Ransome James, Nana's one love, a container of white butterflies was opened.

Watching that symphony of beauty floating on gossamer wings, I wiped my tears and blew a kiss to the sky knowing that letting go was part of love, part of life.

EPILOGUE

Mattie

My life was harder in some places than others, but I wouldn't erase one day for nothing. It was my living and I was never perfect, just better for it. I did my best to be a good person, to treat others with respect, but life also taught me to be good to me. To value who I was. To think well of myself and those I loved.

I was a good mother and a good wife, and couldn't have asked for a better husband. That Ransome James? Lord, that man worked from can to cain't, taking care of his family and giving us his best. All those years working construction, driving down to Valdosta on weekends until Mama said, "Baby girl, I'll be fine. Go be with your husband," and I packed us up and moved Savannah and me back to Montgomery. Sometimes I worried about running into Edward. Guess I have segregation to thank that that never happened. The color line kept our lives separate and we were fine there until Mama suffered a stroke a few years after. That's when my Ransome bought an acre of land out where Mister Moonlight is and built us a house that Mama and Aunt Odell shared until they both passed. By then he'd left his job and started his own construction company. Never did get those big contracts like the White outfits, but that man did so well that each year he bought another acre until we wound up with ten, built up Mama's house, and moved there after having grandkids. But before grandkids, when our lovely Savannah was still little, he put me through college and after I finished, he went. Earned his degree in business. My only regret with that man was conceiving his babies but having one stillborn and losing the other to miscarriage. After those heartbreaks, we decided not to test fate and focused on loving Savannah.

My sweet Savannah Eve. Oh, my precious angel. She was and is something. Brilliant. Tender-hearted. Devoted. Gorgeous enough to be an old Black Hollywood pin-up. Accomplished. She taught me all about selfless loving. Love got me out of bed in the middle of the night when she was teething, fussing. Love had me walking up to strangers selling teacakes in the name of providing. She was my joyful baby, a darling little girl, didn't give us much trouble as a teenager, and didn't just marry well, but did good for herself. The apple of our eyes, she's my truest gift. That precious little girl changed my entire existence, made me grow up and learn the wonders of myself.

Folks may not understand why I didn't tell my daughter and grandchildren that I was on the bus that historic night with Miz Rosa, but I had no need to brag, to add my rendition to those already told. My being on that bus was a matter of desperation. I'd been headed somewhere to rid my belly of a beautiful angel. The fact that I'd almost gotten rid of her out of fear was a secret I was too ashamed to tell. But for God and witnessing Miz Rosa's defiant heroism, I would've forfeited my precious gift. And without her, I wouldn't have my unmatchable grandchildren or great grands.

I'm proud of my Avery. I had to smack his backside only a couple of times when he was little for misbehaving, but like his daddy and his PopPop, he's a good man devoted to his wife and children.

As for Ladybug? I couldn't help loving her, looking so like her mama when she was born, with that bald head and pale skin. But by her first birthday, she was pecan brown with hair all over her head. Now that one there? She took after me and my daddy—has a temper, is fiery. Bossy. Nosey. Never wanted to break her spirit, but we had to work with her to see the world wasn't one huge debate or gladiator arena. That's probably why she's a lawyer. She likes arguing. And winning. But at her core, my remarkable granddaughter is pure softness. I charged her with publishing my stories not for my fame, but for her blessing. To teach children Black history, and so that when she steps away from all that corporate lawyering she has direction, a vital sense of purpose. Because she will leave that law firm after publishing my stories and winning all kinds of awards for her drawings. I'm just glad she has a fancy laptop and isn't reliant upon my old typewriter to make it happen.

I loved that typewriter the moment my Ransome gifted it to me on our first anniversary. I'd sit typing stories and poetry after he and Savannah were asleep. He'd tease me, saying that my typewriter got more attention than he did. At one point, I guess it did. Instead of getting mad, one night when I claimed I needed just a few more minutes to finish, he got out of bed, interrupting by moving me off my chair, taking my place, and sitting me on his lap.

"Ransome, what're you doing?"

"Keep typing since you wanna type so bad. And read it to me as you do."

Thinking him crazy, I indulged him just because I needed to finish so I could sleep without words swimming in my head.

Resuming my typing, I was doing just fine until his hands started moving. Touching me the way I liked being touched. Kissing my neck. Hiking up my nightgown. That loving got so good and fierce that at some point my precious typewriter hit the floor. After we floated back to earth, I teased my husband that his intentional sabotage failed. My typewriter had nominal damage—sometimes capital Js and Ss came out looking like each other—but it was otherwise fully functional.

That's life. Sometimes we have to make the best of what's imperfect. And we can. I learned that from strong, dynamic people. My mother. Miz Wheatley who passed away in her sleep at the age of seventy-six. Miss Divine who married and moved to Little Rock, had five children, and is still living at the age of one-hundred-and-three. Aunt Lady and Uncle Melvin who treated me like a daughter and helped raise Savannah Eve. I even learned from Kathryn Stanton how not to be—elitist, unyielding. But I do thank Miz Stanton for thrusting me into a place where I learned my own strength.

Now, I'm here in this peaceful space filled with rest. Surrounded by my great cloud of witnesses. Daddy. Mama. Ruth. Ransome's two brothers. My parents-in-law. A host of relatives and all manner of glorious beings who left before me. Our spirits live and breathe. But my earthly temple, this body sleeps beneath our towering magnolia tree where I was conceived. Where Daddy carved his and Mama's initials in a heart for themselves and posterity. Where Ransome carved our own heart in an overlapping, connected pattern. And where Ashlee and that fine young husband of hers will do the same, continuing a cycle that cannot end.

My earthly temple is here, where Ashlee and Avery installed lovely new benches with plaques bearing our names and dates so that my beloveds can visit with us whenever they want. Where my Ransome can come sit when he longs to be near me. These beloveds of mine and the generations after them, on this land my husband and I bought, are wise enough to know I'm gone, yet never far. I'm here, resting but ready should they ever need me. And, inevitably, they will.

AUTHOR LETTER

Dear Reader,

Thank you so much for choosing *The Girl at the Back of the Bus*. I hope you thoroughly enjoyed it! If you did and would like to keep up to date with all my latest releases, just sign up at the following link. Your email address will never be shared, and you can unsubscribe at any time.

www.bookouture.com/suzette-d-harrison

Also, if you enjoyed *The Girl at the Back of the Bus*, I'd be very grateful if you could write a review. I'd love to hear what you think, and it makes such a difference helping new readers to discover my work as well. If you're using a Kindle, the app lets you post a review when finishing the book. How cool and convenient is that? So, please take a minute to share your perspective. Your review can be as brief as a sentence, but it has tremendous impact. And by all means, please tell a friend!

I love hearing from my readers—see below for how you can get in touch with me.

Blessings until next time,
Suzette

sdhbooks page

SdhBooks

1998239.Suzette_D_Harrison

suzetteharrison2200/

ACKNOWLEDGMENTS

I could never be creative without the Creator. It is to the divine One that I give all praise and glory. Thank you for choosing me.

I thank my beloved husband and children for believing steadfastly in me. I cherish your support, and for your ability to ground me with humility.

I also acknowledge my extended family, dedicated readers, and fellow authors—particularly those women writers whom I affectionately call "Lit Sis." You help me hold it down and not give in. Special thanks to Tiffani Quarles Sanders, who helped me see through Mattie's eyes by treating me to a rich, virtual tour of her beloved Montgomery. Additionally, I thank my long-time, dear friend Felecia A. Weaver for graciously aiding me with Ashlee's legalese.

Thank you to the wonderful staff at Bookouture for inviting me into this incredible story.

And last, but never least, I'm honored to acknowledge my amazing editor, Emily Gowers. Who would have guessed that your reading of *Taffy* and one chance email would result in all of this? You saw something that led you to believe in me. Your reaching out resulted in a divine connection, in Ashlee, and our beloved Mattie. Thank you for imparting your expertise, but also for trusting me throughout our journey. You never suppressed my voice. You allowed me to sing.

Made in United States
North Haven, CT
10 July 2022

21145326R00173